After a time the rain relented. The sky's cloudy dark gray seemed a bit lighter.

No moon, no stars to tell him how close dawn was. But it felt close. It had to be close. It had been a long, long night.

He stood and swayed. It was surely a lighter gray overhead. He sang a hot song, he sang a song to the sun. He called for the sun, the great god of warmth and good cheer. He was tired and cold. But he wasn't so cold he would die. He would make it to dawn, he could feel it. This was his wander, this was how a shaman was born. He howled till his throat was raw.

"This is a grand tour of an intensely imagined interplanetary future of modified human beings, terraformed planets, experiments in economics and sociology and hundreds of other delights. All of it is in Robinson's eloquent, enthusiastic and inimitable prose."

—*Morning Star* (UK)

"An sf masterpiece."

—*Library Journal*

"*2312* paints an absolutely credible and astonishingly beautiful picture of the centuries to come, of the sort of schism and war, the art and love, the industry and ethics that might emerge from humanity going to space without conquering it and without solving all its problems."

—Boingboing.net

By Kim Stanley Robinson:

The Memory of Whiteness

Icehenge

Three Californias
The Wild Shore
The Gold Coast
Pacific Edge

The Planet on the Table

Remaking History

Escape from Kathmandu

A Short Sharp Shock

The Mars Trilogy
Red Mars
Green Mars
Blue Mars

The Martians

Antarctica

The Years of Rice and Salt

Science in the Capital
Forty Signs of Rain
Fifty Degrees Below
Sixty Days and Counting

Galileo's Dream

2312

Shaman

SHAMAN

KIM STANLEY ROBINSON

www.orbitbooks.net

Orbit
Hachette Book Group
237 Park Avenue, New York, NY 10017
www.OrbitBooks.net

Printed in the United States of America

RRD-C

First trade edition: June 2014

10   9   8   7   6   5   4   3   2   1

Orbit is an imprint of Hachette Book Group, Inc.
The Orbit name and logo are trademarks of Little, Brown Book Group Limited.

The Hachette Speakers Bureau provides a wide range of authors for speaking events. To find out more, go to www.hachettespeakersbureau.com or call (866) 376-6591.

The publisher is not responsible for websites (or their content) that are not owned by the publisher.

The Library of Congress has cataloged the hardcover edition as follows:
Robinson, Kim Stanley.
    Shaman / Kim Stanley Robinson. — First edition.
        pages cm
    ISBN 978-0-316-09807-6 (hardcover) — ISBN 978-0-316-23557-0 (ebook)
1. Prehistoric peoples—Fiction.   I. Title.
    PS3568.O2893S53 2013
    813'.54—dc23

                                                              2013004665

ISBN 978-0-316-09808-3 (pbk.)

To the memory of

Ralph Vicinanza

SHAMAN

LOON'S
WANDER

We had a bad shaman.

This is what Thorn would say whenever he was doing something bad himself. Object to whatever it was and he would pull up his long gray braids to show the mangled red nubbins surrounding his earholes. His shaman had stuck bone needles through the flesh of his boys' ears and then ripped them out sideways, to help them remember things. Thorn when he wanted the same result would flick Loon hard on the ear and then point at the side of his own head, with a tilted look that said, You think you have it bad?

Now he had Loon gripped by the arm and was hauling him along the ridge trail to Pika's Rock, on the overlook between Upper and Lower Valleys. Late afternoon, low clouds rolling overhead, brushing the higher ridges and the moor, making a gray roof to the world. Under it a little line of men on a ridge trail, following Thorn on shaman's business. It was time for Loon's wander.

—Why tonight? Loon protested. —A storm is coming, you can see it.

—We had a bad shaman.

And so here they were. The men all gave Loon a hug, grinning ruefully at him and shaking their heads. He was going to have a miserable night, their looks said. Thorn waited for them to finish, then croaked the start of the good-bye song:

This is how we always start
It's time to be reborn a man
Give yourself to Mother Earth
She will help you if you ask

—If you ask nicely enough, he added, slapping Loon on the shoulder. Then a lot of laughing, the men's eyes sardonic or encouraging as they divested him of his clothes and his belt and his shoes, everything passed over to Thorn, who glared at him as if on the verge of striking him. Indeed when Loon was entirely naked and without possessions Thorn did strike him, but it was just a quick backhand to the chest. —Go. Be off. See you at full moon.

If the sky were clear, there would have been the first sliver of a new moon hanging in the west. Thirteen days to wander, therefore, starting with nothing, just as a shaman's first wander always started. This time with a storm coming. And in the fourth month, with snow still on the ground.

Loon kept his face blank and stared at the western horizon. To beg for a month's delay would be undignified, and anyway useless. So Loon looked past Thorn with a stony gaze and began to consider his route down to the Lower Valley creekbed, where knots of trees lined the creek. Being barefoot made a difference, because the usual descent from Pika's Rock was very rocky, possibly so rocky he needed to take another way. First decision of many he had to get right. —Friend Raven there behind the sky, he chanted aloud, —lead me now without any tricks!

—Good luck getting Raven to help, Thorn said. But Loon was from the raven clan and Thorn wasn't, so Loon ignored that and stared down the slope, trying to see a way. Thorn slapped him again and led the other men back down the ridge. Loon stood alone, the wind cutting into him. Time to start his wander.

But it wasn't clear which way to get down. For a time it seemed like he might freeze there, might never start his life's journey.

So I came up in him and gave him a little lift from within.

I am the third wind.

He took off down the rocks. He looked back once to show his teeth to Thorn, but they were out of sight down the ridge. Off he plunged, flinging the thought of Thorn from him. Under his feet the broken gritstone was flecked with pock snow, which collected in dimples and against nobbles in a pattern that helped him see where to step. Go as agile as a cat, down rock to rock, hands ready to grab and help down little jumps. His toes chilled and he abandoned them to their cold fate, focused on keeping his hands warm. He would need his hands down in the trees. It began to snow, just a first little pricksnow. The slope had big snow patches that were easier on his feet than the rocks.

He tightened his ribs and pushed his heat out into his limbs and skin, grunting until he blazed a little, and the pricksnow melted when it touched him. Sometimes the only heat to be had is in hurry.

He clambered down and across the boulder-choked ravine seaming the floor of Lower Valley, across the little stream. On the other side he was able to run up the thin forest floor, which was all too squishy, as the ground was wet with rain and snowmelt. Here he avoided the patches of snow. First day of the fourth month: it was going to be trouble to make a fire. The night would be ever so much more comfortable if he could make a fire.

The upper end of Lower Valley was a steep womb canyon. A small cluster of spruce and alder surrounded the spring there, which started the valley's creek. There he would find shelter from the wind, and branches for clothing, and under the trees there wouldn't be much snow left. He hurried up to this grove, careful not to stub his senseless toes.

In the little copse around the spring he tore at live spruce branches and broke several off, cursing their wetness, but even damp their needles would hold some of his heat against him. He wove two spruce branches together and stuck his head through a middle gap in the weave, making it into a rough cloak.

Then he broke off a dead bit of brush pine root to serve as the base of his firestarter. Near the spring he found a good rock to use as a chopper, and with it cut a straight dead alder branch for his firestick. His fingers were just pliable enough to hold the rock. Otherwise he didn't feel particularly cold, except in his feet, which were pretending not to be there. The black mats of spruce needles under the trees were mostly free of snow. He crouched under one of the biggest trees and forced his toes into the mat of needles and wiggled them as hard as he could. When they began to burn a little he pulled them out and went looking for duff. Even the best fire kit needs some duff to burn.

He reached into the center of dead spruce logs, feeling for duff or punk. He found some punk that was only a little damp, then broke off handfuls of dead twigs tucked under the protection of larger branches. The twigs were damp on their outsides, but dry inside; they would burn. There were some larger dead branches he could break off too. The grove had enough dead wood to supply a fire once it got going. It was a question of duff or punk. Neither spruce nor alder rotted to a good punk, so he would have to be lucky, or maybe find some ant-eaten wood. He got on his knees and started grubbing around under the biggest downed trees, avoiding the snow, turning over bigger branches and shoving around in the dirt trying to find something. He got dirty to the elbows, but then again that would help keep him warm.

Which might matter, as he could not find any dry punk, or any duff at all. He squeezed water out of one very rotten mass of wood, but the brown goo that remained in his hand resembled dead moss or mullein, and was still damp. The firestick's rough tip would never light such shit.

—Please, he said to the grove. He begged its forgiveness for cursing as he had approached it. —Give me some punk, please goddess.

Nothing. It became too cold for him to keep kneeling on the wet ground digging in downed logs. To make some heat in him he got up and danced. With this effort he could warm his hands, and it was important they not go numb like his feet had. Oh, a fire would make the night so much more comfortable! Surely something could be found here that would burn under the heat of his firestick's tip!

Nothing. His belt contained in its fold many little gooseskin bags in which there were spark flints, dry moss, firestick, and base. Dressed and carrying all his things, he could have survived this night and the fortnight to follow in style. Which was why he had been sent out naked: the point of the wander was to prove you could start with nothing but yourself, and not just survive but prosper. He needed to come back into camp on the night of the full moon in good style.

But first he had to get through this night. He began to work hard in his dance, throwing his arms around, spinning his hands in big circles. He sang a hot song and wiggled all over. After doing this for a while, everything but his feet began to burn. But he was also getting tired. He tried to find a balance between the cold and his efforts, walking in a tight circle while also inspecting the forest floor for likely punk and duff shelters. Nothing!

In every grove some wood will burn.

This was one of the sayings that Heather often repeated, though seldom when talking about fire. Loon said it aloud, emphatically, beseechingly: —In every grove some wood will burn! But on this night he wasn't convinced. It only made him mad.

Dig!

He went at the underside of a log which had broken over another one in its fall, a long time ago. They were two crossing mounds of dirt, almost; not an impossible source. But at this moment, wet through and through. And cold.

When he saw how it was, he beat his fist on the soft wet logs. Then he had to start walking in circles again.

Later, more digging into another log gained him only a knot that was still hard, with two spurs extending away from it at an angle much like the angle needed to make a spear thrower. He replaced his first firestarter base with this flat knot, which was better. His alder firestick still looked good. All was ready, if only he had something dry enough to catch fire.

And if only it would stop raining so hard. For a while it pelted down, cold enough to be a little sleety, and all on a gusty wind. In the hard gusts it was like getting hit with cold sand. He simply had to take shelter, and so he crawled under a spruce with big branches right against the ground, where he could snuggle in tight around the trunk and feel only a few drips on him, a few tickles of wind. The spruce needles were scratchy and the ground was cold, but he flexed his shoulder up and down, and sang a hot song and swore vengeance against Thorn. Talk about bad shamans!

But all boys have to become men one way or another. Their wanders had to be trials of skill and endurance. Hunters' wanders were just as bad. And other packs' shamans insisted on even harder trials, it was said.

Loon banished Thorn again. He tested all the branches at the bottom of the spruce. If a dead one could be broken, a dead one well dried but still a little resiny, possibly he could pulverize a spot in it with a rock point and make a mash of splinters fine enough to catch fire under the spin of the firestick. Worth a try, and the effort itself would help keep him warm.

But it turned out there didn't seem to be a branch around the bottom of this tree that he could break.

When the rain let off, he squirmed back out and crawled around under the other spruces looking for such a branch. His hands were so cold he could scarcely grasp the branches to test them.

After a while he had broken off a few likely-looking branches. If he could get a fire started in one of them, the others would be good wood to feed to it.

He found an adequate hearth rock, and a better smasher rock. He took the best one of his dead dry spruce branches and placed it on the hearth, then hit it with the smasher. It resisted, and it was clear it would take a while to get it right, but it seemed promising. Smash smash smash. He had to be more careful than usual not to catch a finger, his hands were so clumsy. Once two years before he had smashed a fingertip, and it was still fat and a little numb at the end, its flat claw lined with grooves. He called that finger Fatty. So he hit his smasher on the side of the broken branch very carefully, once or twice hitting the hearth instead. A spark or two from those accidents made him long for his flint firestrikers. A few scattered sparks were not going to be enough to do it on a night like this. The wet wind whooshed its laughter at him, loud in the trees.

Eventually a spot on the side of his target branch was squashed into a splay of splinters, perfectly dry. He sat cross-legged with his body arched over the branch, and it seemed like the mash of splinters might burn. Breathing hard, warm except for his feet, he crawled under the best of the spruces in his grove and arranged his new kit around him. Smashed branch on the hearth rock, held there between his feet; firestick placed almost upright in the mash of splinters on the branch, held at its tilt between his palms. All set: spin the firestick back and forth.

Back and forth, back and forth between his hands, gently pushing the point of the stick down into the branch. Back and forth, back and forth. His palms ran down the stick with the force of his pushing down, and when they reached the lower end of the stick he had to grasp it with one hand, put the other against the top, and move up and catch it and begin over again, with as little a pause as he could manage. Meanwhile it kept raining outside the shelter of the spruce, and under it, even right against the trunk, drips were dripping. Really it began to look impossible, given the conditions. But he didn't want to admit that. It would get an awful lot colder the moment he admitted that.

After a long time, maybe a fist or more, he had to give up, at least on this branch. The mash of splinters was a bit too massy, and after a while, a little damp. He could get the spot just under the firestick so hot that it slightly burned his fingertip to touch it, and the splinters around that spot had even blackened a little, but they would not burst into flame.

Loon sat there. This was going to be a hard thing to tell Thorn about, assuming he survived to tell the tale. The old sorcerer would flick him on the ears for sure. You had to be able to start a fire, anytime, anywhere; the worse conditions were, the more important it got. Thorn, like most of the shamans at the corroboree, was exceptionally good with fire, and had spent a lot of time with Loon and the other kids, teaching them the tricks. He had put a firestick to their forearms and spun it, to teach them how hot the spinning got. Eventually Loon had learned how to make fire no matter how the old man complicated the task. But there had always been some dry duff, one way or another.

Now he crawled out from under the spruce and stood up, sobbing with frustration, and danced until the cold was held off him by a thin sheath of sweat. When the rain let up a little, he steamed. Already he was hungry, but there was nothing for it. Time to chew on a pebble and think about other things. Chew a pebble and dance in the rain. Cold or not, this was his wander. When daylight came at last he would find better shelter, find some dry duff, find an abri or some smaller overhang. Begin outfitting himself for his return at full moon. He would walk into camp fully clothed, belly full, spear in hand! Clothed in lion skins! Beartooth necklace draped around his neck! He saw it all inside his eyes. He shouted the story of it at the night.

After a while he sat again under the best spruce, his head on his knees, arms wrapped around his legs. Then he got back out and shuffled around in the grove, looking for a better tuck, finding one after another and testing them. If they were good, he added them to a growing little round of camps, each with its own strengths and weaknesses. He chanted for long stretches, cursed Thorn from time to time. May your pizzle fall off, may a lion eat you...Then also from time to time he would shout things out loud. —It's cold! Thorn would sometimes howl his thoughts that way, using old words from the shamans' language, words that sounded like the things themselves: Esh var kalt! Esh var k-k-k-kaaaal-TEE!

He stubbed a big toe and only felt it in the bone; the flesh was numb. More curses. May the ravens shit on you, may your babies die...Lie on the ground under one big spruce, only his kneecaps and toes and the palms of hands and his forehead touching the earth. Push himself up and down with his arms, staying rigid. If only he could fuck the earth to get warm, but it was too cold, he couldn't get his poor pizzle to antler, it was as numb as his toes, and would hurt like crazy when it next warmed up, prickle and burn till he cried. Maybe if he thought of that girl from the Lion pack, a raven like him, therefore forbidden to him, supposedly, but they had made eyes anyway, and it would warm him to think of plunging her. Or Sage, from his own pack.

That line of thought trapped some time: seeing it all inside his eyelids, seeing her spread her legs to him. Be there inside her kolby, forget this cold rain. Her kolby, her baginaren, her vixen. Start a little fire behind his belly button, get his prong to spurt. But it was too cold. He could only mash the poor flesh around and make it burn a little, warm it in the hope it would not get frostbit. That would be so bad.

After a time the rain relented. The sky's cloudy dark gray seemed a bit lighter. No moon, no stars to tell him how close dawn was. But it felt close. It had to be close. It had been a long, long night.

He stood and swayed. It was surely a lighter gray overhead. He sang a hot song, he sang a song to the sun. He called for the sun, the great god of warmth and good cheer. He was tired and cold. But he wasn't so cold he would die. He would make it to dawn, he could feel it. This was his wander, this was how a shaman was born. He howled till his throat was raw.

Finally dawn came, wet, gray, dull, cold. Under the storm the colors of things did not quite return, but he could see. Low clouds scudded in from the west, cutting off the ridgetops. The undersides of the clouds hung in fat dark tits. A sheet of rain fell on Lower Valley downstream from him, a black broom standing in the air between cloud and forest. With the big snow patches everywhere, the ground was lighter than the sky.

Then in just a few blinks everything got much lighter, and a white spot glowed in the clouds over the east ridge. The sun, wonderful god of warmth, over the ridge at last. Cloudy or not, the air would almost certainly get warmer. Only the worst storms had days colder than the previous night. And now the sky didn't look too bad to windward; the clouds tumbling over the gray hills had little breaks between them that were bright white. It was still windy, however, and the rain began to come down in little freshets.

Whether this day proved to be warmer than the night or not, he was going to have to keep moving to stay warm. There would be no relief from that until he got a fire lit. So he gathered his unsuccessful fire kit and held the two pieces of it in his left hand, and clasped a good throwing rock in his right hand, and took off downstream. He wanted a bigger copse of trees, with a good mix of spruce and pine and cedar and alder. The ridges and hillsides and valley slopes, and the upland behind and above them, were mostly bare rock dotted with grasses, and now covered by old snow; but in the valleys against the creeks, trees usually grew, making ragged dark green lines in the palm of any valley. Downstream a short walk, where Lower Valley's creek was met by a little trickle down its eastern flank, a flat spot held a bigger clump of trees, surrounding a little oval meadow and climbing the slopes to each side.

He made his way around the wet part of the little meadow and went to the thickest part of this grove. He slipped between the trees, grateful for their shelter. It was windier now, and there was more rain falling than he had thought when he left his night copse. In this larger grove things were very much better. He was well protected, and now that it was day he could see what he was doing. A broken cedar at the center of the grove had exposed a big curve of its inner bark, which he could pull free and use to make some rough clothes. A couple of snow-rimmed anthills spilling out of the end of a decomposed cedar log gave him sign of potential punk. There was a small hole at the end of the log; he bashed it in with his rock and tore the hole deeper, then reached in and up: on the underside of the still solid wall of the log was a section of punky duff, quite dry —Ah mother! he cried. —Thank you!

He pulled out a big handful and carried it quickly to the lee of a gnarled old pine. —In every grove OF SUFFICIENT SIZE some wood will burn, he said aloud, shouting his correction. He was going to tell that to Heather in no uncertain terms. She would laugh at him, he knew, but he was going to do it anyway. It was important to get things right, especially if you were going to make sayings out of them.

He left the dry duff well protected in a cleft at the base of a broken old pine tree, and quickly gathered a bunch of branches and broke off several more. He stashed these with the duff and then broke off ten or twenty smallish live branches and arranged them around and behind and over the broken pine tree he had chosen, making its wind protection even better. Bush pines like this old one had multiple trunks, and were thickly needled; this one was a great tuck to begin with, and with his branch walls added, hardly any wind or rain was making it through to his fire area.

After that he gathered the pile of firewood next to him, then sat down with his back against the trunk, curled in a crouch to make his body the last part of the windbreak. He crossed his legs and placed his unfeeling feet against the sides of his base.

He chopped at his firestick's tip until it was a little cleaner and sharper, then placed it in the dent on the knot base, very near his new duff. When all seemed right, he began to spin for dear life, back and forth, back and forth, feeling his hands sliding slowly down the stick, feeling also the pressure of the stick against the base as it spun, trying to hold the combination of speed and pressure that would make the most heat. There was a feel to that, and a dance with each return of the hands from the bottom of the stick to the top, a quick little move. When he had it going as well as he could, and had made several swift hand shifts from bottom to top, he toed some of the duff closer to the blackening cup spot, a little depression in the knot which was what had caused him to pick this base in the first place; it was just what you would have cut with a blade in a flat base.

He watched the duff blacken, holding his breath; then some of the newly black spots glowed yellow and white at their edges. He gently blew on these white points, contorting so his face was closer to them, breathing on them in just the way that would push the white away from the cup into the bigger mass of duff. He bent his backbone like Loop Meadow and blew as gently as seemed right, coaxing the white heat to grow, feeding it a little wind that would not blow it out, giving it just what it needed, emptying himself out to it, puff puff puff, pufffff, this he could do, this he knew how to do, puff puff puff, puff puff puff, pufffff

and the duff burst into flame. FIRE! Even this tiny flame lofted a little waft of heat into his face, and he sucked in a breath and blew even more ardently than before, still very gently but with a particular growing urgency, like blowing in a hole on the flute when you want to make a wolf's cry jump. As he did this he also shifted to his knees and elbows, using his face as the closest windbreak for this gorgeous little flame, and breathing on it in just the way that made it bigger, making love to it, oh how he wanted it to feel good, to be happy and grow! He gave it his breath, his spirit, his love, he wanted it to spurt, to leap up like the spurtmilk out of a prong, to burn in his face: and it did!

When he saw that the little spurt of flame was holding, he began placing the littlest and driest twigs over it, in a way that would catch as much of them alight as possible without harming the blaze below. It was a delicate balance, but one very well known to him; something he was good at, Thorn having forced him to practice it twentytwentytwentytwenty times. Oh yes, fire, fire, FIRE! Almost everyone was pretty good at fire, but Loon thought of himself as exceptionally good at it, which was part of what made the previous night's failure so galling. He was going to be embarrassed to tell the story of that first night. He would have to emphasize the terrible power of the storm, but then again, as his pack had spent the night just one valley over, they weren't going to believe much of an exaggeration. He would just have to admit he had had a bad night.

But now it was morning, and he had a fire started, and the first twigs were catching and adding their burn, so he could add more, including some bigger ones. Soon there were ten or twenty twigs alight in a fiery stack over the first burn, and their flames were a tangible yellow. Very soon the moment came when it was safe to put a pretty large handful of dry twigs gently atop the little blaze, and they would all catch almost immediately. He did that and said —Ha! Ha! and put on some larger branches. Finger sticks, then wrist branches. Happily he watched as the growing flames blackened the rounded sides of so many twigs and branches. A fire makes all right with the world.

Smoke now flew up, and the hiss and crackle from the wood showed how hot the fire was getting. The heat smacked his naked chest and belly and pizzle, which burned horribly as it warmed, in the usual agonizing tingle. He squeezed it in one hand to hold the pain in, and felt that it was a good pain, so good it was easy to feel it as a harsh form of pleasure; ah, the too-familiar burn of numbed flesh coming back to life, the itch deep under the skin, the painful tingle of being alive! Now he was going to be able to warm up even his feet! They would burn like mad as they came back to him. Ah fire, glorious fire, so friendly and warm, so beautiful!

—Such a blessing, such a friend! Such a blessing, such a friend! One of Heather's little fire songs.

Now things were really looking good. The previous night was put in its place as a mere problem, a dark prelude. With a fire lit, the storm still blowing overhead did not matter anything like as much. He could keep this fire going for the whole fortnight, if that seemed best, or he could take it with him a certain distance, if he wanted to move, and reestablish it elsewhere. He could focus his efforts on food, shelter, and clothing, and no matter how those went, he would always have the most important thing. And it was only the first day of his wander!

He sat on the windward side of the fire and stretched out his legs around it, held up his arms over it. Hands catching the heat from right in the smoke. Oh the tingle of life coming back: —OW! It was a very different howl than the ones of the night before. Like the wolves, like his namesake the loons, he had a whole vocabulary of howls. This was the happy one, the triumphant one: —OWWW!

When he was warmed right to his toes, and had several big logs burning on a broad bed of red-hearted gray embers, he walked the perimeter of his little grove, then spiraled in through it, inspecting it. There was that cracked cedar at the edge of the little meadow, and in the shallows of the creek he found a block of flint with one sharp end and a length of rough edge, so that it resembled a massive clumsy burin. It would make an adequate chopper. He took it back to the cracked cedar and began to hack at the split in the trunk, detaching the bark and then peeling off the inner layer in sections as big as he could make them. Some of the strips were longer than he was.

When he had stripped the tree of all the inner bark he could get off, he took it back to his tuck, added some branches to the fire, and then in its glorious warmth sat down to tear the inner bark into strips. This was slow and meticulous work, but very satisfying as the strips grew to a considerable pile.

By midday he had more than he thought he would need. After tending to the fire again, he arranged the strips on some snow-free ground near his tuck. He had four or five score of them. He laid six in a line on the ground and then wove six more across them, pleased at the simple but effective over-and-under pattern. He used longer strips for the ups, and shorter ones for the arounds, and he offset the starts of the arounds each from the next, so that the resulting tube would not have a weak line down it. Finally he reached under and pulled the weave up the middle, then wove more arounds around the back, bringing the ups that had been farthest apart together; and after that he had a tube. A legging.

He did that again, and had leggings. Then a triple-stranded length to serve as a belt to hang the tubes from; then hangers, and a simple crotch strap to cover his cold pizzle. He stepped into the leggings and tied them to his belt, and felt them catch his warmth immediately. —Ha!

After that a vest; then a hat; lastly, out of the remainders, a ragged short cloak. In rain these clothes would get wet and then tear easily, but meanwhile, in his shelter, they would give him some warmth, and when it stopped raining they would give him some protection too. What he needed for proper clothes was fur skins, of course, but that would take some getting. For now his bark suit was the best he could do, and far better than being bare, or so he hoped.

Now, being warm, he felt a real pinch of hunger. He had spotted some berry patches back in the meadow, so after putting three more big branches on the fire, he ventured out in his clothes to relocate them.

It was still windy, but the rain had stopped, and the clouds were breaking up. The verge of the meadow was furred by a bramble of duck's eye berries, and he reached in carefully and pulled some of last year's dead berries off the ground. These were black and flat, but they would give him something.

Then he went to the place where the creek left the meadow. As often happened, he saw trout in the water there, tucked under the last curve of the bank above the outlet. He was not far from his grove; through some trees he could see his fire blazing merrily away.

He walked downstream until he saw a shallow spot that would work. He heaved rocks from the bankside into the stream until he had made a little dam across it. The creek poured through the gaps in this dam so easily that the water didn't rise the slightest bit behind it; but a fish of any size could not get through. Then he hurried back upstream to the meadow.

There he took off his new clothes, stepped into the creek, and walked downstream. When he was upstream from the last meander, he pulled a big rock from the bank and threw it hard into midstream, at the same time jumping up and down and shouting. No fish flashed by headed upstream, so quickly he sloshed downstream, still shouting. He saw there were no fish under the bank at the last turn; presumably they had escaped downstream.

He waded downstream toward his dam, a rock in one hand, a stick in the other. He hit his rock against rocks in the water, yelling as he went.

Then he came to where he could see his dam. Ahead of him in the water, caught between him and the dam, were three trout. He dropped his rock in the stream and reached up onto the bank and as quickly as he could pulled rocks into the water and built another dam. As he finished he had to fend off a couple of upstream rushes by one of the fish, but even that one was too frightened to try to flash past him, and the other two didn't even try. With the second dam built up well above the level of the creek, he had them in a little fish pen. —Ah! he cried. —Thank you!

He sloshed upstream to give a quick look to his camp. His fire was still burning well. He got out of the creek and walked downstream and stepped into his fish pen. He stalked one fish, he thought the one that had rushed him, moving into a position where he could reach down with both hands, very slowly, until they were next to the fish, which was trying to hide by staying still. With a single scoop outward he splashed water and fish together up onto the bank, where the fish flopped till it died. He stifled his shout, to keep from scaring the other fish, and moved slowly to the next one, tucked under the bank. He stuck his hands down very slowly, scooped again, and the second fish flew up in its mass of water and thrashed out its life.

The last one darted about and evaded several of his scoops, but then he caught it, and it too died on the bank flopping this way and that. After that he had three nice trout, each well over a hand long.

He sang the fisherman's thanks, got out of the creek and put his clothes back on, then carried the fish to the fire.

Old alder sticks broken with a twist eventually yielded an edged point sufficient to cut the fish and gut them. Then he stuck them on longer pine branches and held them over the fire until they were cooked and sizzling at their edges. They tasted great, unseasoned but trouty. He would pluck sprigs of rosemary and mint to add to later meals. As he ate, it occurred to him that he should have opened the upper dam of his fish pen before leaving it.

But that would be something for tomorrow. With his stomach full and his body dressed, sitting there by the warm fire, he was suddenly sleepy.

In another short tour of his grove he gathered more spruce branches for bedding and blanket. He made the bed right next to the fire, and when the softly needled branches were piled to his satisfaction, he went to the creek's bank and gathered wads of moss and took them back to dry them by the fire. While they dried he gathered more firewood for the night, then laid the dried mosses on the branches of his bed. He lay down on the padded bed and pulled spruce branches thick with needles over him, still wearing his bark clothing. He would keep the fire high. It would be a very comfortable night. It was still twilight, but he lay there anyway next to his pile of firewood and watched the flames, feeling happy. Only his second night, and he was fed and clothed, and in a bed by a fire! Now that would be a story to tell.

He lay there, comfortable and warm. The moon was on its second night, nicely thicker than the curved line of a first night. A fortnight goes fast, as they said. Soon the crescent set, and the night went full dark, stars pricking the black above a few remaining clouds. The undersides of the trees above him flickered together in their firelight dance. Second day of the fourth month, a wet chill in the air outside the bubble of fire warmth. Sleep took him away.

Around midnight wolf cries from a distant ridge woke him, and he threw a few branches on the bed of embers, pulsing redly under fluttering white ash. Splash of sparks; watch a branch blacken, watch it catch fire, that sudden yellow pop into the world, that hypnotic transparent dance, and he was out again.

Later he dreamed of running up a crease under a ridge to catch a glimpse of three ibex, seen as they were topping the rise. He came on the animals right there before him, all three facing him foursquare and at ease, their neat curved horns poking the sky. Rockdancers; his mother's favorite animal; and suddenly she was there beside him, and his father too. They were looking at the rockdancers in the time of the caribou on the steppe, when the low rumble of caribou hooves sounded like distant thunder. His mother was raven clan and his father eagle, but they both clearly loved the ibex; this was what Loon remembered from that moment. He knew that being with his parents was unusual, and this knowledge woke him.

The stars had circled, it wasn't far from dawn. He tried to dive back into the dream, failed; tried then to grasp what memory of it he could, before he was exiled from it for good. All of it stood before him at once; then he tracked it from faintest moment to boldest moment; then from beginning to end. Some dreams want to be remembered, but others don't and have to be chased down. This was one of those.

So, his mother and father had visited. That had not happened for a while. He tried to see in his eye what they looked like, or understand how in the dream he knew so well who they were, even though they were just standing there beside him, not saying anything he could precisely recall. Sometimes he recalled dream conversations, other times not. This time he had known their feelings without them having to talk. They had been filled with benevolence and concern for him, and with love for the rockdancers. Loon whimpered at their absence from the living. What was it like to be in the spirit world only, how did they live there, why couldn't they cross back? Why had they died, why did things die? The mystery of it all swept through him, and he felt tiny, pierced by a vastness. If it weren't for the fire his desolation would have been complete. With the fire there beside him he could look at these matters, allow himself to feel the hurt in them, the vastness.

Right after dawn it clouded up again, but the cloud layer was thin and had no rain in it. The wind blew in fitful gusts, tearing away flakes of ash from his bed of embers. His tuck was mostly protected still, and although the side of him away from the fire was chilly, it was easy to turn and feel the radiance singe his cold skin. This was the second day of his wander; but now, despite his comfort, he felt sad and alone. He sighed. This was his initiation as a shaman, after all. He was walking into a new world, a new kind of existence; it was not meant to be merely time spent alone. This was what his parents had come to tell him: he had to face something, learn something, accomplish something. Change into something else: a sorcerer, a man in the world. Of course his parents were dead.

He went down and drank from the creek, foraged for more firewood, hefted and carried back a big chunk of old log that would help keep the fire going, becoming first its roof and then part of the ember bed.

Then it was time to find more food. He walked over to the meadow, looking for prints or scat or other sign, maybe a place for a snare. Snares were best when made of hide thongs. Bark ropes were not often strong enough. On the way past the meadow outlet, he removed the upper dam on the creek, checked and saw there were no fish in last meander to scare, so he continued across the meadow, avoiding the old snow. There were watering spots on the banksides there, with many animals' prints, but they tended to be open places, and a snare would be hard to hide. He needed a tight passage between bushes, so that an animal scared away from water would perhaps rush through the passage without looking. Eventually he found such a place. The material of the snare itself remained a problem. He went to an alder with his choprock and cut a number of switches, flexible and strong and long, and split their ends and braided them together in a triple weave. These tied low above the ground could serve as a snag that might trip a young deer or goat. It was the best he could do that morning, so he laboriously set up the snare between the two bushes. If it even tripped a small beast while he was watching, that would give him time to leap on it. He would have to lie in wait and be there when it happened, or whoever got caught in it would thrash its way free. He would return at sundown, then, and hope to scare a drinking deer into a dash.

When the snare was as good as he could make it, he walked back toward the fire looking for good throwing rocks. Even a snow hare or a grouse would be very welcome. When he had two good rocks, he foraged up the sunrise slope of the valley, looking for more of the previous year's berries on the ground. He saw some mistletoe up in a bare-branched tree and considered climbing to it and chewing its white berries; this would make a sticky stuff that could be stranded between branches to catch small birds sticking to it. But there were no small birds yet. He came on a blackberry bramble, and while eating some old dead berries also swallowed some little white mushrooms he knew to be safe. Then he hurried back to see how the fire was going.

The fire was fine, and he placed another log on it and went out again in the other direction. Downstream, Lower Valley deepened but did not get wider, and its east ridge gapped where Lower's Upper dropped into it. Lower's Upper was a higher canyon leading northeast. Where the east ridge rose again, beyond that gap, a tall rock called the Skelk's Antler overlooked a short broad cliff. Below the cliff a steep forested slope dropped to Lower Valley creek, still mostly snow-floored.

Loon headed down to the confluence of Lower Creek and Lower's Upper, where a little frozen flat above an alder brake might have something interesting on it. There would surely be tracks.

A crashing among the trees on the slope froze him in place, and he was perfectly still when a young doe burst out of the trees up there, pursued by two brown bears. The doe had a broken rear left shank, and three-pointed down the slope slower than usual. The lead bear on the other hand ran downhill with startling speed, and caught up to the doe and knocked her to the ground and went for the throat like a wolf. Loon had seen other bears bite down on the back of the neck, like a cat. But bears would do anything. They were almost like humans in that way, which made sense, given that they had been human in the old time. And they still looked human: big dangerous people in furs.

Loon stayed still, watched the first bear take a few bites of the deer's throat and lick up the blood. Loon's mouth was watering as he watched. The deer was still shuddering through its death; bears had no regard for propriety when it came to that.

Then the other bear attacked the first one from behind. Two young males, Loon saw, now fighting, mostly with ferocious snarls and swipes that did no damage. It looked like the continuation of some ongoing fight. They were totally oblivious to anything else, so Loon threw his two rocks at them, and hit both. They were startled by the sudden pain out of nowhere and ran off together into the trees without looking around. After that it sounded like they were fighting each other still.

Loon ran hard to the deer, completely intent and trying to see in all directions at once. He surely didn't have much time before the bears came back, or someone else came along. None of the rocks lying around had edges sharp enough to skin the deer, and the first bear had only gotten started on eating it. He pulled the body onto its belly with its legs splayed out, and with a Thank you began to hammer at the rear hips with one of his throwing rocks, soon enough breaking the hip, then separating the leg from spine, and cutting skin and ligaments, smashing the joint apart with the idea that he could carry away a leg if he had to flee. For sure the smell of blood was on the wind, which was blowing upcanyon.

He was still pounding away at the deer's hip, but it was not quite free, when a movement upslope caught his eye. It was worse than bad; three lion women were there in the trees, approaching in their easy padding way.

Loon leaped out of the little clearing and ran doubled over between trees, up the other side of the canyon and over some boulders, where he threw himself flat and tried to catch his breath without gasping.

The lions had stopped at the deer and were sniffing it as they looked around. They knew the deer had just been killed. Loon picked up two more rocks under him. If he could get back to his fire, he could probably hold these lions off, although if they saw he was alone it would be difficult, if they wanted him; they were very good at assessing their chances in any possible hunt, and would know they could kill him if they didn't care about first taking some punishment from thrown rocks. Lion women would run right into a rain of rocks if the notion took them. Hopefully the dead deer would take their attention, take the edge off their hunger.

He crawled for a while on the two held rocks and his toes, like a lizard. When he was far enough away to stay out of their sight when standing, he got up and ran as quickly and quietly as he could to his fire.

It was still burning well, banked down but ready to light any wood thrown on it. He threw on branches of all sizes to generate a quick burn, also to prepare some torches for a better defense.

That done, he hustled back toward the kill site, but on a traverse that took him above it. An open snowy stretch on this slope gave him a view down to the little flat and the lions.

The deer was now substantially eaten, but what remained would still be a feast to Loon, and the skin and bones very useful too. He had to be like a raven, if he could, and shit on them until they abandoned the remains, while not getting swatted out of the sky. So he slipped down the slope toward them, completely on point, skin tingling, the whole valley present to him, everything looking fine-edged and particular, as if he had become a hawk. Boulders glowed with light from within, and trees quivered and hummed on the breeze, which still flowed upcanyon.

The lions, each one as big as a small bear, now lolled by the remains of the deer, cleaning their bloody muzzles with their paws like any other cat. Lions with full bellies could be driven off a kill by a rain of rocks, but usually this was done by several men also holding spears. A single man was different. The lions might decide such a presumptuous fool would make a good dessert, when they wouldn't have bothered if they weren't being annoyed. So it was important to gauge their mood and the bulk of their bellies, now splayed beside them like pale tan water bags. Loon stopped behind a fallen tree and watched for a while. The lions were big and beautiful, glowing with the magical presence they always had—immense cats, the same in form as the little ones that hung around camp, except these biggest ones, as heavy as two or three men, ran in packs like wolves. That was an awesome combination, terrifying in what it meant for any other creature. Beautiful gods wandering the world, hunter gods who feared nothing.

A rock of the right size, thrown hard and striking the head, was a terrible blow, especially coming from well above. But it was more likely he would hit them in the body, if he hit them at all. Would they then slope off, hurt and affronted, or would they charge to kill the nuisance? This was not a question he could get wrong.

For a long time he waited and watched the lion women groom themselves. Certainly they were among the most beautiful of animals, one of the nine sacred creatures, and how could it be otherwise? What living creature could be more godlike, with their indolent grace and murderous power, their feline wolfishness? The way they looked around with their black tear streaks dripping away from their eyes like festival paint; the way their gaze would come to rest on you, and you would quail and shrink; no, there was nothing like it. They could kill anything they wanted to.

This time, one of them got up after a while and wandered down to the creek to drink, and the others followed. Thus they were now some distance away. Loon judged the distance sufficient, and dashed down and chopped free the sad remnant of the leg he had intended to take originally, also with a great two-handed blow he severed the chewed head, then he grabbed both up and ran back up the canyon all the way to his fire, fast enough to sweat and gasp most of the way. When he got to his camp his heart was pounding hard.

He built up his fire again, and through the rest of that day and well into the dusk, he chopped and pulled the skin and ligaments away from the deer's leg, roasting and eating scraps of meat as he worked. When the leg was completely broken down, he moved on to the head, and feasted on the remnant of the tongue, the brains, the fat pads behind the eyes, and the jaw meat. The leg skin and its bone and ligaments he took down to the stream and washed, working by the light of the bowl moon, third night of the month. He took it all back to the fire to dry, hoping these parts would not be attractive enough to bring in any nocturnal scavengers big enough to challenge him.

Again he built up the fire enough that it would last till midnight, and slipped under his branch blanket with the deer bits right next to him and the patch of leg skin as his pillow, its short hair soft against the side of his face. He rested then in his spruce bed and felt how full he was, how tired. It was the feeling of a good day; but he was uneasy, too, when he thought about falling asleep with no one else to keep watch over him. Those lions were out there somewhere, and they hunted at night. They would know what the fire was if they saw it or smelled it. But he was too tired to stay up all night. Sleep kept flickering out of the fire and washing over him. He could not resist it, but only gave a last order to his inner eye, to stay open and on guard. He slipped under with a rock in his hand.

That night in his dreams the lion women were hunting him, and he woke groaning several times, feeling the dread of that. When dawn finally grayed the sky he felt like he hadn't slept at all. He was sandy-eyed, and hungrier than ever.

There were new heavy clouds to the west, briefly pinked by sunrise, coming in on a new wind. Another storm, maybe. Third day of his wander, second storm. But he could stay by his fire through this one and work up the deerskin scraps into some clothes and kit.

So, back out into the cold. In the rocks bordering the creek he found a squarish block of flint that would serve as a source for blades and points and choppers. For a knapper he chose a big long chunk of chert. He carried these rocks back to the fire, and then went to the creek's meadow outlet. There were trout again under the bank at the curve, so he took off his leggings and splashed in and scared them downstream, then reconstructed the upper dam. He clambered over the dam into his little fish pen and patiently scooped four fish onto the bank, growling wolfishly as each one flew up in a sploosh of water to flop out its life. Cooked trout; and this time he was going to add some meadow onions he had seen sticking out of the melting snow at the upper end of the meadow. They would accompany every bite of trout. His mouth watered, his stomach pinched. He went to the patch of meadow onions and dug up some bulbs using the deer's leg bone, then returned to the fire and ate the four fish with the onions. He emptied the fish guts and cooked them on the embers and ate them too when they were black; they were a bit grainy, but good.

When he was done he took the rocks he had collected and found a flat bedrock to work on. Every strike of knapper against flint he performed with the utmost care; he couldn't afford to have a smashed finger this fortnight. With that extra caution the knapping didn't go particularly well, as he was striking small and mashing flakes off. But eventually he cleanly knapped some rough blades, and one was right enough to hold in his hand and slice the deerskin. Even uncured the skin would be strong and flexible. He wanted some of it to make a proper belt to hang his leggings and crotch strap from, because what he had for a belt and ties would soon break and the leggings fall down. Other than that the cedar bark weave was holding up pretty well. A good belt would have a fold in it too, which he could use to wrap and carry his kit in. Not that he had much of a kit.

Slowly he cut strips of skin. When he had made a good belt and replaced his cedar one with it, he tied two scrap strips together to make a necklace, then punched three holes through the strip with a sharp point of flint, so he could fit some of the deer's teeth through the holes. This was not a good design for a necklace meant to last, but it was something he could make now with what he had. If the chance came later to make a better necklace, he would, but at least he had this one, if that chance never came. He wanted to return to his pack looking as good as he could.

The next morning he woke before dawn and considered the possibility that the lions might track him by his scent, or by blood that had dripped from the deer parts. It was also true that his grove was running out of easy firewood. It would be safer to move. The storm seemed gone for now, the western sky only lightly clouded. So he slipped out of his tuck to see if anything was drinking in the meadow where he had set his snare.

There was; a young ibex was standing in the shallows. Loon crawled to the side of the meadow opposite the snare, then jumped to his feet and shouted. The ibex leaped at the sound and charged right up the passage between bushes, hit the snare and staggered, then burst through the ropes and bolted away, leaping right up the steep rock side of the valley. She didn't stop until she was high on the slope, pronging upward from rock to rock in leaps that only an ibex could perform. Far above she turned to look down at him, offended; shook her head, as if dismissing Loon's plan for her; hopped in another quick prong up, and disappeared over the ridge. Rockdancer indeed.

Loon found a stone resting in his hand. There hadn't been time to throw it. It was very hard to make a good snare without leather ropes. This one had always been a long throw.

You can only kill disappointment with a new try.

He went out to scout a new camp. He knew the area pretty well; they had crisscrossed it many times when out on the hunt. At the upper end of Lower's Upper, its creek passed through a draw and entered a high basin called Hill In the Middle, where the creek split and ran around both sides of a rounded hill that was as tall as the basin's ridges. The east ridge of this high canyon was an edge of the uplands, the west ridge dropped to a shallow valley rising farther west, up toward the ice caps. In terms of camping suitability, the creekbeds had the trees, but also the hunting animals. Possibly some kind of protected nook high on the valley walls would be better, or even a point on a ridge, overlooking a confluence. With a fire it would be impossible to hide, unless he were to find a perfect cave. The cliffs in the area were dotted with caves, but they were for the most part known, and used by both people and animals. Finding an unknown one did not seem too likely. And a big fire was his best defense, really. So, best perhaps to get a bit of height above a confluence; or head to the top of a drainage, the steeper the better, and camp in the highest copse of trees, as the place that would get the least passthrough.

He fed his fire with a big section of dry log, then took off at a fast pace, watching his footwork carefully. He was on the hunt, skin tingling, everything big and sharp in his eye, be it ever so far away. Up the frozen creek of Lower's Upper, staying clear of the bramble beds to both sides of a small icy waterfall, trying as he climbed to imitate the smooth flow of the ibex who had scorned him. Help me up, sister, make me a rockdancer. The creek lay back, and a small line of trees led to a copse under the headwall, thickest around a spring, with a flat spot overlooking the spring. Lots of downed wood, not too much snow or damp. Black spruce and bush pine for the most part, both good burners if the wood was seasoned. Quickly he searched the copse and assembled on a flat rock over the spring a pile of firewood and a mass of twigs. He even set a ring of stones and the first twig stack, with a hole for his arm to reach in to place the live ember on the flat stone in the center. All very welcoming.

Then he ran back to his old site, pacing himself to what Thorn called active rest, and gathered up into the flap of his new deerskin belt all the little things he wanted to take. He built up his fire one last time, ate some meadow onions, then coaxed a glowing pine branch, burnt through but otherwise whole and entire, out of the fire onto the ground next to it. With his choprock he broke off a piece of this ember branch about twice as long as it was wide, and pinching the yellow piece between two rocks, he placed it on a handful of fresh spruce needles, then wrapped this hissing mass into a ball and put it inside a hollowed burl he had found. Shells from the great salt sea were best for carrying embers, but those were rare, and always owned by women. Women were as good with fire as men were, and better at moving a fire from camp to camp. But his mass of needles in a burl was pretty good for a fix-up; he could hold it in one hand, keep a throwing rock in the other, and carry his fire kit and the remnants of the deer in his belt flap.

Off he ran to his new camp, pushing the pace hard this time. Every step had to be watched into its place. Overhead giant white clouds floated east on a mild breeze. It was cool in the sunlight, chill in the shade. A perfect day for moving camp.

So he was happy as he ascended Lower's Upper to his new nest. But as he approached the flat over the spring he saw that his prepared hearth had been swept clean of the wood he had left there.

The sight froze him instantly, and in his stillness came the jolt of fear, when the most likely explanation for the change struck him fully. He slipped to the ground behind a rock as smoothly as he could, feeling more afraid heartbeat by heartbeat. Everything in the little canyon quivered in his sight. It was quiet, no squirrels in the area chittering away. Gurgle of the spring's water sliding out of the spring. The air was flowing downcanyon, and he sniffed repeatedly, tried to sniff like a bear, tried to identify and locate by smell whatever was out there lying in wait for him. If there was anything. Actually, to have swept his fire rock clean of wood was a strange move.

Then a sniff gave him the answer he most feared, a waft of smoke and grease almost like his own smell, but different. Old ones. They smelled different than people. Thorn had forced this knowledge on him once when they had come upon a dead old one, lying in one of the shallow cliff caves downstream in the gorge. Thorn had grabbed the dead one's bearskin cape and held the collar of it to Loon's nose. Lunkheads always smell like this, Thorn had said, flicking him hard on the ear.

Now Loon was sweating from his face and palms. The day had suddenly become one of his nightmares: a silent still world, stuffed with dread, something unseen in it hoping to kill him. Stories about boys on their wanders being eaten by old ones had always seemed like just stories; all the men Loon knew had come back from their wanders. And if you ran into an old one, they always seemed about as harmless as any woodsman.

But woodsmen could be dangerous. And the old ones were burly people, as strong as bears or wolverines. One of Thorn's stories told how an old one had married a bear by mistake, and neither of them had noticed; their daughter told them about it years later, not at all pleased with them.

They definitely knew how to hunt. They didn't use spear throwers or javelins, and they only used stone for their points, never antler or bone or tusk; but their spears were stout, made for thrusting and short throws. They were experts at ambush, that was their way. When they were in pairs or trios, one would sneak around while the other watched from a blind. They hid better than any other animals, even humans.

So setting up his firewood stack had been a mistake. It would only have saved him a few moments anyway. Something to remember. If he survived.

He regarded the live ember there in his hand, still glowing in its needles and burl. It would be giving off its own smell, he realized. There's nothing like the smell of a fire! as the saying had it.

He put the ember on the ground, the open end of the burl down, so that it would perhaps suffocate the ember. Now it could be a decoy.

He crawled back downstream as smoothly and quietly as he could. It was like hide and seek when they were kids, now horribly suffused with nightmare dread.

Where there were trees and boulders big enough to hide among, he moved up the west slope of Lower's Upper. Lower's Upper fell into Lower over a short cliff; the waterfall there was called Old Piss. Probably the old ones would know about the cliff, but if they didn't, and tried to follow him directly down the creekbed, they would be briefly held up, and he might get away.

When he had traversed high enough that the trees were shorter than him even when he was crouching, he lay in a moss-filled hollow between two of the gnarled little pines and looked back down toward the copse with the spring.

There they were: three of them. Danger comes without warning. Big-headed, hairy, heavy under their fur capes. Spears at the ready, thick short things with perfect leaf blade tips of red chert: spears made to stick in mammoths. Loon shrank down as far as he could. The nightmare world had jumped into day. And just as it would have happened in his dreams, one of the three old ones suddenly pointed at Loon and skreeled like an angry hawk.

Loon leaped to his feet and dashed for the ridge above him. The three old ones croaked to each other like ravens as they clambered after him, somewhat slowed by their spears. Loon had a good jump on them, and was close enough to the ridge to reach it while they were well below. He ran south on the ridge to make them think he was going that way; if they angled to cut him off, they would hit the ridge where it was cliffed on the other side, the same cliff that made the Old Piss waterfall farther down.

But the old ones were much faster than he had thought they would be, and closed on him despite his panic speed. When they saw he had crested the ridge and would soon be out of sight, all three threw their spears, which lofted up toward him with awful quickness. People said they never threw their spears, and yet here they were! Two were going to hit below him, but one was flying right up at him, he had to jump off the other side of the ridge to dodge it, something he watched himself do, feeling amazed he was making such a leap, down the first little drop of the long cliff.

He landed and felt something twist in his left ankle, rolled to keep it from twisting worse, and at the end of the roll smacked that same ankle against a tree. The two pains merged to one, and together they made it hard to run, but he had to, so he ran down the slope into Lower Valley, each landing on the left leg a shocking burst of pain, despite which it was necessary to run on at full speed and in complete silence. He ran open-mouthed, sucking in and blowing out in a way that made no noise. It took a lot of air to run all out, and he had to set a pace he could hold for a time, but it also had to be faster than the old ones, no matter what, even if they burst a sprint. Old ones were supposed to be a slower than people, but now Loon didn't trust anything he knew about them. They were so strong, no doubt they could run uphill as fast as people. But now Loon was heading downhill in Lower Valley, limping hugely and hoping nothing was broken in his left leg. He had always felt fast before, but not now.

By the time the old ones topped the ridge he was almost down to his old site, where his fire was still burning. They had indeed hit the ridge too far down, and were looking down the cliff at him, so now they had to backtrack up the ridge. Loon saw that and came into his camp and looked around. They could easily have come upon him here and killed him before he knew they were nearby: it had been a bad way to camp when alone. He knocked at the fire with a stick, wanting to make more smoke to mask his scent, also to disturb their sense of what was happening. Possibly they would stop to ponder why he had done this, they were said to be slow thinkers, so he took a burning branch and threw it across the creek, then three or four more in different directions, then continued pegging downcanyon, past the confluence under Old Piss, along the creek trail, feeling his muscles burning almost as much as the hurt in his ankle. He was not bleeding, not leaving a blood trail, although his right big toe had been abraded and was beginning to bleed enough to leave drops. He bared his teeth in dismay when he saw that, and paused to sit on the ground and suck the first flow of blood out of the cut, run his tongue back and forth to start the stanching, then press some creekside sand into the broken skin, after which he hopped up and away. For speed and endurance both he should have these old ones beat. They would know that too, and hopefully give up. But he had to go on to make sure. It was time to shift modes, find his second wind, pace himself for a run down Lower Valley, then up one of its slopes to east or west. Climbs to the valley's ridges could not be made everywhere, in fact both sides of the canyon had long low cliffs right at the ridge, making it a hard valley to get out of. But he knew there was one break in the cliffs to the east, so he headed for that, hoping the old ones would continue downvalley. Once over the east ridge he would be on the high etched tableland overlooking the gorge and its canyons, and could find some kind of tuck that would keep him hidden.

He ran favoring his left leg, breathing hard, really sucking it in, needing the air. After a while, he felt the second wind catch him up: that was good. He looked back often; no sight of them. Hard to know if they would continue their pursuit for long. They had had to recover their spears. Why mammoth spears down in the canyons? Maybe it was true they had nothing else. And they hadn't used spear throwers. Almost-people, nightmare people, crossed over into the day world. Or he had crossed over into theirs.

The ramp he was climbing was clean. He could see the break in the cliffs that would get him to the ridge. The cliffs were the usual white rock, flecked with black lichen. He was bleeding a little again from his right toe, so he stopped as he climbed to shove dirt into it again to clot the blood. He was working so hard that his blood was shooting out of him, even though the scrape was not very deep.

The ramp cut through little cliffs, and the slope lay back and gave him a clean run to the ridge, well covered by head-high trees. He sped over the ridge, which was broad here. Surely now he was clear of the old ones. They would not come up to this particular spot just to look.

Still he kept on, impelled by the memory of that spear flying up at him. It had been spinning on its axis like a firestick. The long chert blade would have pierced him right through. Think what that would be like! He had seen it often with small animals, speared them himself and watched them writhe, heard them shriek before they died. Best to keep running. Run in the same way one would run on the hunt, just as hard and steady, just as long. Indeed given what was at stake it made sense to go much longer than when on the hunt. Run right through his second wind, run until the rare and elusive third wind filled him, then run some more.

Finally the long afternoon of running slanted to its close. The moment came when afternoon became evening, a matter of failing light in the still-blue sky. He kept on through the dusk that followed, and even when darkness began to fall. The moon was now a day less than half there, thus almost directly overhead. Still over half a fortnight to go before he could return to the pack! He could not imagine getting comfortable enough with his situation to start another fire, not with old ones somewhere nearby. And his ankle still hurt. He could not move his foot without pain.

But he was alive. And he could go a week without food if he had to. And a week without fire, too, at least if it did not storm again. Even if it did storm. Anyway the important point was that he was alive. This was his wander, it was not meant to be easy. He had escaped three old ones! If he had. Now he would really have a story to tell! If he could bring it home.

*   *   *

He gathered some dry leaves and branches and pulled them after him into a nook of boulders under a dense cluster of ground-hugging spruce. The trees had been splayed over the rocks by the force of the constant downslope wind. He ripped a tear in his bark vest getting into the nook, and his leggings were already in tatters. But he was able to make a rough bed, and he felt he was well hidden. Spruce gum daubed over his chest masked his own scent, although he ended up sticky, and felt pricked everywhere by spruce needles stuck to his skin. He was going to be cold, and his ankle throbbed with every heartbeat. He needed some artemisia tea to suck down, some mistletoe pollen to smoke. As it was, he could only clench his teeth. He named his hurts, as Thorn had always insisted he do; the cut in his toe was Spit, the hurt inside his ankle he called Crouch. Spit and Crouch sang their little duet, and he listened past them to the wind in the pines, nervous at any other sounds. There were some rustlings, and some of these made his heart pound; he wondered if he could leap out of his lair before the spears plunged through it and pinned him to the ground. Probably not. Loon had speared snow hares through just such cover. He knew just how it would go. Probably the rustlings were only hares or grouse, or even squirrels or mice. But the image from one time he had speared a snow hare through the neck was a hard one to fall asleep to.

He slept lightly, and when he stirred to huddle in a new position against the cold, cuddling chilled parts and thus inevitably exposing warm parts, he would listen, and sniff the air, and worry a little, before dipping back under. Sleep with one eye open. Thorn claimed you could do it. It meant he did not so much dream as think, but in a jumpy disconnected way. A moment came when he surfaced to full wakefulness, both feet cold, ears and pizzle cold, even though he had wrapped his arms around his head when he fell asleep. He began to shiver, and realized he would therefore not be able to fall back asleep, and indeed could not even continue to lie there; he was shivering too hard.

Fearfully he pulled himself out of his tuck and looked around. The near-half moon was about to set in the west, so the night was half done. Unhappily he began to bounce up and down in place, staying always on his right leg; also to bunch his fists, and twist side to side. At first it felt like he was too tired to be able to dance hard enough to warm up, but by the time he had gotten the shivering to stop, he was fully awake, less tired, and interested to see what he would not have seen in the tuck, which was the plateau in the last of the moonlight, shadows stretching across it broad and black. Nothing moved. The night was still. He rearranged his bark clothing as best he could, trying to tighten it around him, and after a time burrowed back into his nest. Any tuck is better than none. This was his wander, he told himself, he was becoming a shaman, it was supposed to be a trial. He had not only to survive, but survive in style. Now with Crouch, and the old ones wandering about, his task was made more difficult. But he was halfway through, almost. Eight days left at most, maybe nine. He was actually having trouble keeping count. But the moon would do it.

Whatever he managed in terms of style would have to come later, and be accomplished by day. At night, to avoid both the old ones, who might spot his fire, and night-hunting animals, who were only held off by fire, he was going to have to find a better refuge than this one, which was both cold and exposed to view. Some hollow, some cathole or marmot house where he could keep a little warm, and yet see anything approaching him. Under a boulder, perhaps, with some boughs dragged in for warmth. Live like a marmot for half a fortnight.

Crouch was barking and it was hard not to groan. The memory of his big bed of embers, radiating heat so intense he had had to keep a distance from it, now struck him as an incredible gift. Luxury is stupid: another of Heather's favorites. It goes too far, she would explain. Enough is as good as a feast. But tonight he didn't have enough.

He had been acting as if the womb canyons etching the border of the uplands would be empty, just because no packs made their camp in them. His own presence should have told him he was wrong. Old ones, woodsmen, travelers, lions, any could have wandered by and killed him by his fire. Starting in the storm had apparently frozen his wits. Wrong from the start. In the storm itself one could assume everyone would be hunkered down. After the storm, no. Strangers could always pass by. You have to beware. He had forgotten that, seduced by his fire. Fire was a giveaway, there was no denying it. Although perhaps a very little one, down in some hollow, lit at twilight, kept barely alive, fed just before dawn: surely it would be all right?

No. Not really. Just hop in place and sing a little back-and-forth song, right right left, right right left, on and on. No real weight on the left. All the while looking at the moon, trying to see it fatter than it was. He truly had lost count of how many days he had been out, but ran back through them in as much detail as he could recall, to recover the number. He kept track with his fingers, using them like one of Thorn's yearsticks. He had been out five days. Yes, five. He had gotten a fire started on the second day; watched the bears kill a deer on the third; made deerskin clothing on the fourth; tried to shift camps on the fifth. This was going to be the sixth day. He almost groaned aloud, but let Crouch do the talking. He was going to have to find a way to stay warm without a fire, and he was going to have to find something to eat. He could forage, but it would be best if he also found something to kill. Some animal with fur.

The moon set, ever so slowly. Best not to look, it went so slow. But he did look. The stars creeping down blinked out over the furred black horizon, one after the next. He danced from time to time, in a kind of waking, standing sleep. Let it all settle into one's breathing. Let Crouch do the talking.

At some point he opened his eyes and saw that the eastern sky just over the horizon was a pale gray. Just a fist or so to sunrise. Always coldest before dawn. But he could endure. He felt the life in him, barking like Crouch.

When it was light enough to see, he limped across the plateau, downslope to a trickle of a creek that ran to a drop into the gorge of their river. He braided some tallgrass and set a small snare near a grass bank marked with hoof and paw prints. After that he stood behind a downed tree that served as a blind, rock in hand, and waited.

The sun rose. A pale watery light filled the air over the plateau. Where sunlight struck his skin he could feel the warmth like the burn from a fire. Please prosper, oh radiant god. Come back to summer again.

For a long time he sat there, sleeping lightly in the sun. Then a crashing sound launched him to his feet and when he saw the deer in the snare he threw the rock in his hand as hard as he could, and hit the deer in the rear leg at the knee, a solid clunk that buckled the deer just long enough for Loon to throw himself across the log onto her. He grabbed her short antlers from behind and twisted as violently as he could, trying to break her neck or choke her. She rolled to keep her neck from breaking, and he rolled with her, snatching up the same rock he had thrown and swinging it hard onto her head between the antlers, trying for a clean hit. He missed the spot and hit again, over and over as fast as he could while the deer thrashed and rolled, but his were glancing blows, while he took a hard kick on the thigh, then missed outright with the rock, and then at last connected: a desperate swing crunched into the skull. The deer slumped, and he smashed her on the forehead several more times, just to be sure. The deer lay there quivering as she breathed her last breaths, bleeding from her eyes and a big gash on her forehead.

—Thank you sister! Loon cried, joy filling him like a drink of water. —Good deer!

Immediately he set to breaking her apart. A young doe. He would not be able to defend the whole body, indeed he needed to leave the scene as soon as possible, and without dripping blood as he went. He wanted the rear legs still linked at the spine, so he could carry them over his shoulders; then also the skin and the heart and kidneys. He ate as much of the brains as he could while he cut away with his clumsy choprock, frustrated at the lack of a good blade, which would have made this work ever so much easier. As it was he had to bash away. It was a ruination of the poor deer, and he apologized to her, explaining his need for speed. He smashed and pulled and cut as best he could with the tip of his bad chopper. He was going to take the hide with him, no matter what kind of scent it cast. He would find a good place and hide in this hide, and although uncured it would keep him warmer.

Even at speed the skinning and breaking up took a couple of fists, and when he was done he was sweaty, bloody, exhausted, but full of food. He had had to cut away the skin in two big parts. The doe's heart and kidneys he bundled in the two pieces of hide, which he could tie to each other and hang over his shoulder with the two legs. He was almost completely covered with blood. Under a dead pine he found a walking stick to help keep Crouch happier. In his other hand he held Chopper, large enough to crush but small enough to throw, a nice heft to feel in one's hand. A rain of thrown rocks could make even a solitary man dangerous. No animal is safe from a man with a good arm! He was floating a little with the joy of the kill.

He limped downstream with the deer's rear legs and her organs wrapped in her hide, all slung over his shoulders. Sometimes he walked in the little creek itself. His walking stick he named Prong. When he was far enough away, he stopped and washed the deer's hide in the creek, and the legs too, also himself.

He had taken the hide off in two sections, because given the bluntness of his chopper, he could not get the hide cleanly off the spine. But two pieces was fine. He would probably cut the leg skin off later to make patches. He chewed away at a bite of the deer's heart. Normally hearts were cooked, but this wasn't bad. Raw meat had to be chewed for a long time, and starting with small chunks was best. Loon liked the taste of heart, and enjoyed chewing for such a long time.

The creek was cold, and he sat on its bank and wiped his legs dry before working further on the hides. Uncured as they were, it was not so easy to cut them straight. Nevertheless, out of one half of the deerskin he cut parts for a rough vest and a skirt. The remaining half would serve as cape and blanket.

This day was almost done, it had flown by as if the sun were a bird headed west. He needed to find a place where the night hunters on the plateau couldn't reach him, and that was going to be hard. A cave with an entry he could block with a rock would be so nice; or a tree that only he could climb. These were both very unlikely things to find. But where the plateau began to break toward its drop into the canyons, it did ledge off in a way that provided low walls and wind-gnarled trees. If he could find a good refuge before night, this would have to be counted a great day; but now the sun was tilted hard west, the half moon palely visible in the afternoon sky, just east of overhead.

Under one little bluff dropping toward the river gorge, he found an overhang. There was no cave at its back, so it was exposed, but only to half the world, and that half was really on the opposite side of the gorge. A tiny abri, in effect. And in fact someone had painted a bison and horse on the flat back wall at the bottom of the over-hang. Loon was heartened to see this, and examined the paintings closely. The painter had smudged the animals' coats to a very hand-some blackened red or reddened black, the same color for both bison and horse. Thorn always kept the two colors separate. It was good to know that another human had been here.

Looking down toward the gorge, which was not visible except as a line between the foreground and the next stretch of plateau, he saw under him a broad squat bush pine that had broken off and then grown again, in a swirl around the break point, which had become a hollow of exposed heartwood all filled with leaves. That hollow would not be out of the reach of climbing cats, but he might be able to defend it from them; and nothing looking up at the tree from below would see him. He would have to try climbing it to see if he could, so he pronged down to its foot and looked up at it. Climbing was not an activity that Crouch was going to like.

Loon did his best to work around the hurt, using his left leg only to hold positions, never to lift him higher. That put a lot of strain on his good leg, but that one could take it. Eventually he grunted up into the high hollow and slumped there, pleased to find that it must have been cracked at its bottom, for it was dry. Indeed it would make a comfortable bed of leaves and duff. And good views in all directions. Awkwardly he moved around his nest, and with his choprock broke off a large dead branch to use for protection. Refuge! He thanked the Raven, and curled around like a cat until he had found the least bumpy position.

That night a wolf pack howled at the half moon, and Loon listened with his skin goose-pimpling, as silent as the rest of the animals out there listening. The old ones would not be out and about on this night, not with wolves nearby. And tucked in the wrap of his big piece of deer hide, he was warmer than he had been since being forced to give up his fire. That night he slept as well as he had during the entire wander.

What to do?

No answer is also an answer.

The next day he stayed in his nest, and either slept or chewed on the deer's legs. Same with the day after. Gibbous moon, oh yes. Nights mostly lit by the pale fuzzed light of the pregnant goddess. He supposed there would come a day when the deer's legs went too off to eat, too smelly to stay near. Until that happened, he had no reason to move. And getting down from the tree was going to be painful. He was content to rest, and hope for healing.

Thus four days passed, and the moon swelled fatter every night. Big pregnant belly, soon to give birth. Give birth to a new shaman.

On the fifth night in the tree, however, the rustling below resolved into a catlike shape, and he stood in his nest and shook his big branch at the black shape with its scarily wide-set, starry eyes. A big head on a big cat. Lion, or worse yet, a leopard. Dappled in the moonlight in a way that suggested leopard. Either way, disaster. Again his heart pounded so fast he burned. He had to seem bigger than he was, so he stood on the highest branch he could balance on, deerskin blanket over his shoulders. When he had a clear view he threw a few thick branches he had cached down at it, and saw it dodge some, even get hit by one. All the while he cursed the cat viciously, waved Prong overhead as he made all the bad sounds he knew, animal or human; not the fearful sounds, but the angry sounds, the hungry sounds. He cursed in a rage till his throat was raw.

When dawn finally came, the cat seemed to be gone. He waited until midday, but never saw it again. He climbed down the tree, letting his left leg hang mostly free. It seemed both that he had just arrived a short while before, and that he had been up in the tree for years. Either way, it was over. Crouch was quieter now, but still hanging around. It would be a long time before Crouch left, he could feel that.

As soon as he started walking he had to stop and shit, and after that effort he felt a little sick, but emptier, and then better, and ready to limp on through the day. Wash in the creek, find some berry patches in the sun, eat as many old berries as he could. Newly awakened bears would be doing the same, he knew. But better bears than cats. Bears will keep cats away. Still, Loon didn't stay long at any berry patches. The berries were nearly goners anyway.

He came on a bare knob of rock protruding from a low ridge crossing the plateau, and he went to it and found a break on its far side that served as a way up it. The broad top of the knob gave him a view down into a short curve of the river in its gorge, and some canyons dropping to the river on its other side. He could see where the two big loops in the river seamed the plateau; his pack's camp was hidden beyond them, on the other side of the Stone Bison, also invisible from this vantage. The plateau behind him was revealed from here to be a snowy moor, its point-and-bowl edge dropping toward the river. Many of the most dangerous animals would not go up onto the moor. And there were big boulders up there scattered about. Almost certainly there would be one he could crawl under, into a space too small and low for wolves or big cats to fit. It would also be possible to cross the moor westward, uphill toward the Ice Tits, a particular pair of the ice caps out that way, and then descend into the western head of Upper Valley, and from there drop down to his pack's camp, when the time came.

So he walked north onto the moor. The snow on it was old and hard, and held his weight even in the afternoon. Up there he could look back south across many ridges and valleys, like gray hands cupping the river gorge. Lines of green, patches of white. Crouch was really barking now, crying Hi! Hi! Hi! with every step. Loon had his deerskin cape rolled and tied around his waist, Prong in one hand, a clutch of needled branches in the other. He limped along, looking at the hollows under each big boulder he passed.

In the sunset he found a hollow that he liked the look of, and crawled under the boulder into it, through a gap just big enough to let him pass. The open space under the boulder was just taller than his prone body. The boulder rested on the stone ground on four big points, like a giant tooth. He pulled his branches in after him and arranged them into a bed. It was going to be cold up here. Prong was now a spear to defend him in his rocky burrow. The moon was full gibbous, bright in the mid-twilight. It cast distinct shadows.

Wolves howled somewhere again that night, and his sleep was often disturbed by them; but when he woke and listened, he liked hearing how far away they sounded. He also liked how much their presence would discourage other hunters, especially old ones. Old ones mostly stayed off the moor anyway, people said. He believed it, as the moor had very little shelter from the wind. So, taken all in all, this was really the right place for him on this night.

During each interval of wolfsong he would wiggle all his muscles, starting with his numb toes and moving up to his jaw, and thus fall back asleep with the weird singing of the wolves as his lullaby, often before he had wiggled his muscles even as high as his rump.

Once, however, the wolves' chorus woke him and he found himself confused. His father was sitting just outside the entry to his hollow, howling along with them quietly. Come out with me, my son, he said, come out and let me show you which star I am now.

Oh but it's too cold, Loon protested, and I'm tired. I don't want to leave the warmth I've made in this hole.

It's all right, I'll make you warm, his father promised. Loon recalled that his father had said these very words to him once before, when he had hauled Loon out of the river under the Stone Bison, spluttering and terrified after he had fallen through thin ice. His father had held him upside down by the ankles and whacked him on the back, as if he were being born, and as Loon retched and wailed in fear, he had laughed and said, It's all right, little one, I'll make you warm. So it really was him.

So Loon pulled himself out from under the boulder and rewrapped himself in his deer hide. The stars were dim in the moonlight, the whole sky as white as the Spurtmilk in summer. His father stood over him, a little transparent, his head touching the sky, his face overlaid on the lopsided grin of the moon. Come walk with me, he said.

Should I bring my things? Loon asked.

No, I'll bring you back by dawn.

Will you take me to mother?

Yes. She's where we're going.

They flew over the moor, down the etched land to a deep valley with a moonbright river. At a tight spot in its canyon the river ran under an arch of stone; it was the Stone Bison, the bridge of rock near where Loon had fallen in as a child.

This is where you saved me, he said.

Yes, his father said.

I have to return to the pack on the night of the full moon, Loon explained. I'm on my wander. I've only got three—he looked up at the moon—three or four nights more.

I know. That's why I brought you here now. Soon you'll be here again. I wanted you to know that I'll be here with you. And your mother too.

Show her to me.

And then he saw her, standing on the stone arch over the river, the water sweeping under the black shadow of the bison arch and rippling moonily downstream. She was naked and her arms were outstretched to greet him.

Mother! Loon cried.

That caused him to wake, and he was surprised to find his father had tucked him back under the boulder in the time it had taken him to cry out. He had frightened their spirits with his cry. Thorn always said you had to speak calmly to spirits when you had the chance. They didn't like noise or hurry; they were beyond that, it offended them.

—Ohhh, Loon said, angry with himself; but then he heard a snuffling around the boulder. Something big, checking it out. Possibly a bear; anyway, too big to get under the boulder. Whatever it was snuffled off, and he was left to sleep again.

When he woke he found a knot in his hand, a twist of hard wood that looked like it had spent quite a bit of time free of its tree. A knob at one end gave it the look of a lion's head; he could see the indentations between the shoulders and the clean bulk of the neck; it was a male lion, there was the little bump of its spurt lying against its underside, but it was standing upright like a man. It would only take a little carving to bring all that out. This was his father's gift from out of the dream. Lions were fearless. From his deerskin belt flap he took the flake of flint he had broken off when he made his choprock. It would be better to set the flake in the end of a shaft, but for now he could scrape away at the knot, make the first cuts. There was just enough dawn light, and just enough warmth in his fingertips, to make it possible to do the work, lying on his side with the knot and flake right in front of his nose. The ragged tip of the flake was almost like a little burin. He scraped away, looking deep into the bloodless white flesh of his fingertips, which would take impressions from the flake and hold them until he rubbed them away. Crouch was humming sleepily, Spit was pulsing with his heart, but only right at the broken skin itself, almost outside of him, not in him. These people were not his friends, and needed to be ignored. What hurts you has to be forgotten. The lion man was emerging from its knot quite nicely.

When the sun was three fists high, he crawled out from under the boulder and hiked west over the moor, on its hard snow, to a low ridge where he could look up to the land farther west. His people were to the south, down at the mouth of Upper Valley, where the Stone Bison arched over the Urdecha. He was due back in camp in three nights. He could subsist on dead berries until then, and he had his deerskin vest and skirt and cape, and some of his cedar bark underclothing. So he needed to attend to his wander, finish it in style. He recited to himself the story as he would tell it: the night out in the storm, his failure to make a fire; next morning a fire started from nothing, while still in the storm; the glories of the fire; the fish and onions, cooked to a turn; the sighting of the deer killed by bears, their fight over the meal; the lions that chased him; the dream appearances of his dead parents; the disastrous encounter with the old ones, the arrival of Crouch and Spit, his escape; the interval in the tree nest; the time on the moor, under a rock.

Now he needed to add the story's spurt: the vision. And up here in the hollows of the moor were little sprigs of ground artemisia, and certain old piles of bison dung, not too fresh and not too dry, in which grew the little gray mushrooms called witch's nightcaps. He wandered around, gathering some of these sprigs and nightcaps and putting them in his belt flap. He would eat them together on the morning of the day before he was to return. Thorn would be impressed despite himself. They would taste bitter, and were best washed down in a big slug of water. After that one needed to chew a sprig of anise, and be prepared to vomit a fist or so later. Loon touched a nightcap to his tongue, and just the touch put a quiver of dread down his throat, right through him to his pizzle and asshole. It shook him. This wander had already been hard enough: should he do this? Would he be making it too hard? He didn't even want to be a shaman, that was Thorn's idea. It was his father who was supposed to have been Thorn's apprentice. Heather didn't like Loon doing it. If his parents hadn't died, Thorn would never have taken him on. He had always been away from camp as a boy, out in the canyons absorbed in the animals, looking for Heather's herbs. After his parents' deaths he had almost become a wolf child, brought up by the woods themselves, as if stolen by a woodsman. He followed horses whenever he saw them, they were his animal, he was entranced by their beauty. Heather had had to tempt him back in to camp like she did her camp cat. Thorn had never noticed him by the fire, and

Loon never remembered any verses to Thorn's songs. None of this would have happened if his father hadn't died.

But it had happened. Thorn and Heather had raised him and taught him, and his wood carvings and slate paintings had all come to him by way of Thorn. These Loon loved. Of course the endless verses also came from Thorn, and Loon hated those. But they were all part of what a shaman did. But Loon did not want to be a shaman. It was too intense, too lonely, too scary, too hard. Thorn's shaman had been a bad shaman because all shamans were bad.

On the other hand, Loon had left on his wander accepting the challenge. To renounce it during the wander would be a shameful thing, an act of fear. If he had wanted out he should have said so before he left. That would have taken cold blood indeed. But he hadn't done it. Embarrassing not to have acted on his desires, done something he didn't want to do and then gotten stuck with it. But there he was.

So on the morning of his last full day out, he sat facing the sun and ate the combination of nightcaps and artemisia sprigs. The aftertaste was as bitter as always, so much so that it made his skin crawl. His stomach began to grumble and burn. Something in the mix rebelled inside him more even than usual, and before too long his body rejected it, he had to vomit. He didn't want to so soon, it felt like his body was taking over and reversing his decision, but he had no choice; he fell to his hands and knees, arched over, and vomited like a cat spitting up grass, his whole body clenching to eject the offensive stuff, a mass of burning spit littered with chunks of mushroom and little leaves, as bitter coming up as going down; the taste itself made him retch some more, made him run at the mouth and nose and eyes, coughing until he was empty and his belly sore.

Perhaps not a good idea to play these crazy shaman tricks on himself.

I am the third wind
I come to you

He lay there for a while, feeling his body pulse with his heart's knocking. Crouch yelped in his ankle, Spit was silent. His throat and mouth burned with stomach spit. This was what happened to Thorn too when he ate the mix. Shamans poisoned themselves to launch their spirits out of their bodies, that was what it came down to, and Loon could feel his head throbbing as his spirit tried to burst out of the top of his skull. For a moment he could see himself from above, lying down there on the edge of the plateau puking his guts out. And yet his feet were still numb with cold. He tried to shift the heat around in him. Miserably he chanted one of the hot songs, aching all over, pulsing like the bag of blood he was. There was more blood in him than there was really room for, that was true of every creature; when you hit certain veins blood spurted out like spurts of spurtmilk, released from a confinement that had squeezed it hard. That was why he so often felt like he was bursting. Now he could feel all that blood inside him, pulsing to get out. It was strange really that Spit had ever stopped spitting, that any cut ever stopped bleeding, given that squeeze of the body. Sometimes you saw speared animals spurt blood from the eyes, mouth, asshole; he felt how that could happen, had to close his eyes and rub them hard to keep them from bursting out of his head. That set off a wild shower of sparking red dots and squiggles. Ah yes—he had seen these red stars and squiggles painted in the cave. Dots red and yellow and black, oh yes. Zigzag lines, squiggling right and left all over his sight. He traced them in the dirt under him, as the shamans had on the wet insides of the cave. He remembered the first time he had gone in a cave, right after his parents had died, and Thorn had shown him the wet wall and put his hand against it, leaving its impression there, then led him through his first squiggles, each finger a narrow trough, between them parallel little ridges, the clay of the walls firm but pliable. A hard press made a trough to the depth of a fingertip, and the mark remained.

Not so this dirt under him now, so friable and full of roots and dead leaves. Suddenly he felt hungry, not as a pinch in the gut but as a general weakness, and he wondered if there was any sustenance in this dirt or these dead leaves. Surely the leaves would give him something. Normally it was not thought to be so, but they did eat certain succulent leaves, and all manner of roots and tubers and shoots and flowers and fruits, so surely these dead leaves had something good in them, or anyway would fill his belly. Although when he tried to eat them, he found his belly did not seem to want filling. No, there was nothing to eat here. He needed to shift his burning skin heat down into his feet without food to help him. Best now to stand and chant the hot song, and think about Sage and her big new tits, down by the riverside swinging together as she leaned over washing, like a ewe's udder magically doubled. Big dark udders hanging down, sloshing side to side, banging together as Sage washed clothes, her ribs as big as any man's, her back hard and muscled in a way that made her hanging tits more than ever like bags of milk a-swing under her. Oh yes; he was warming up at the thought of her, the heat moving around in him, rising even into his chilled spurt, which warmed as it antlered. He clasped it and squeezed till it felt like a flesh stick, hard as a stick, almost, oh but his hands were so cold, it was only the sight of Sage's naked body there moving in his eye that could keep him hard, and thus help him overcome the cold. Dance a sex song, mix the hot song he had been chanting with a sex song, seeing how she would look if they were joined in sex, or so it seemed; Loon had never done it with her, or any girl. Both Thorn and Heather made it clear to him, as did all the women in the pack, that it was better to mate with girls from other packs. So the summer festivals were good for that. Your pack was too close, the girls in it like sisters. Except they weren't, especially if they were from other clans. Loon had been his parents' only child, and he was a raven, like his mother had been. The girls in the pack included eagles and salmon, and had been only girls to him, and he only a boy to them. Now they were young women and he a young man. They bled and were painted red at their moon time, they had perfect tits and asses and legs and furry soft kolbies, everything really: they were perfect and beautiful. Actually only Sage was perfect in all possible ways, something that everyone saw and remarked on, but in the end they all looked good, and Loon loved them. And Sage was an eagle. To be a shaman was to have a distance from women, but also a closeness; he would be involved with the life of their bodies in ways he wouldn't as a normal man of the pack, a hunter married to one woman. But not to have a wife! Well, that remained to be seen.

Loon danced holding his hard spurt, thinking of Sage naked, and decided then and there that he would not be that kind of shaman. He collapsed to his knees and fucked the dirt, spurted calling out at the sensation of coming, the bolts of pure pleasure streaming out of him onto the ground, and when he was done, still holding himself and pulsing, he scooped up the spurtmilk with some leaves and ate all of it. He would feed himself. It was like a mushroom soup, congealed although still warm with his warmth.

Ah, the slow pulsing of afterglow. He staggered around in a bliss. Vomiting, spurting, they were all part of it. To feel so good in his body; he should have been spurting in Mother Earth as often as he could manage it. Well, maybe he had been; maybe this was the first time in the whole fortnight he had had the time and warmth and strength and spirit. Of course; or else he would have. Afterglow buzzing down his legs from his spurt, up his belly from his spurt, then out his arms to his fingers. A subtle but distinct flow of goodness, there to do battle with all the nicks and scrapes, with Spit and Crouch, and all the days of throbbing cold feet. Well, down at the very ends of his legs it was hard to penetrate with the goodness. Too cold down there. Best to hop again, dance and chant again, say good-bye to Sage for a while and focus his attention on the moment. The sun was high, it was mid-morning and the air was warming up. Time to be out and about.

He rolled up his cape and tied it around his waist, retied his belt and skirt, and headed down the plateau's edge toward the top of his home valley. Upper Valley dropped to the river, past Cave Hill onto Loop Meadow, the filled dry river course that ran around Loop Hill and the Stone Bison, which straddled the river. He was not a great distance away from home, it would be only a day's walk on the ridge trail between Upper and Lower Valleys. Going down the valley cleft itself it would take much longer, but it would be good to avoid the ridge trail, he judged, to reduce the chances of running into anyone. As he walked he found he had decided to stay just under the ridge trail, on the Upper Valley side.

He limped down the easiest traverse as it presented itself. There were faint trails traversing the slope where animals had chosen, like he had, to make their way without risking a ridge trail encounter, also without descending into the alder thickets filling the valley floor. Up here he could often see over the west ridge of Upper Valley to the distant horizon, a white haze obscuring the ice caps, which were sometimes visible. Many of the hilltops around Upper Valley were white knobs and protuberances, so that the land looked like an immense boneyard. Now it was breathing a little under him, undulating like the back of a living thing. He had to slow down to keep his balance, using Prong more than ever.

He began to feel exhilarated. His afterglow had turned into a benign tingling all through him. It emanated from his stomach and gut. He found he could walk without actually putting his weight down, which caused Crouch to sigh contentedly. Anywhere he looked sprang right to him and resolved as if he were close to it, which was part of what was making him sway as he walked; it was hard to keep his balance when things kept jumping at him. The blue of the sky throbbed with different blues, each more blue than the next. The clouds in the blue were scalloped and articulated like driftwood, and crawled around in themselves like otters at play. He could see everything at once. His spirit kept tugging at the top of his head, lifting him so that he had to concentrate to keep his balance. The problem made him laugh. The world was so great, so beautiful. Something like a lion: it would kill you if it could, but in the meantime it was so very, very beautiful. He would have cried at how beautiful it was, but he was laughing too much, he was too happy at being there walking in it. All right, this was what he had not known: Thorn poisoned himself to get to this feeling. Once you got to it, you saw the puking was worth it, oh yes no doubt about it: well worth it. You would die for this feeling. He reeled a little, trying to turn and take it all in at once, but then Crouch complained, and he went back to traipsing along, as in a slow dance, winding along the narrow ledges that allowed him to walk just a few body lengths below the ridge trail.

Then he heard a noise on the ridge, and he dropped under a fallen log and froze before he had time to think a single thing. Musky smoke smell: the old ones.

Terror ripped through him, and he snuggled farther under the log, trying to shrink to the size of a mushroom cap. They would stick their mammoth spears through him and he would die in a squeal of horrible agony, like a rabbit. His feet went ice cold again at the idea, and the leaf mat under the log disintegrated into whorls of blotchy color, like pebbles seen at the bottom of a swift stream, everything breaking up and bouncing in his eyes.

The sounds above him moved downridge, in the direction he had been going. He heard the old ones croaking to each other in their raven voices. Over any distance they whistled to talk. These two were moving down the ridge trail pretty quickly. If he tracked them he would know where they were, and then when night came he could move away from where they were. As long as there weren't any others, he would then be safe. It seemed like a good plan.

He floated down through the trees and rocks under the ridge, on the hunt and never more so, not ever in his whole life. He caught sight of them below him from time to time, by putting just one eye around trees to have a look; each sight of them made him tingle. The little trees on this broad ridge rustled and clicked in their own bird-like language, waving their branches to snag his attention. Clouds were swirling out of nowhere into existence overhead. One had to hope it would not rain. Although it felt like rain would only hiss and steam off him. He found he wanted to kill the old ones; that would make him safer, and he could see what they owned. But this was not a good idea, in fact he was surprised it had come to him. One didn't kill old ones; they were people in their way, almost-people, and never dangerous to humans properly in a pack. Although as he was alone, ordinary conduct did not obtain. But it was still a bad idea.

There was a shallow rill running off the ridge down into Upper Valley; the old ones dropped into the ravine holding this rivulet. Loon wondered what they would do when they came to his pack's camp, whether they would stop and visit his people or not. In camp people seldom saw old ones, or had any trouble with them if they did drop by. They sometimes showed up at the edges of the eight eight festival, whistling and chirping and clicking curiously, talking to shamans who knew their speech, staying clumped together a little defensively. No, his pack would be all right, no matter what these two did. So he could stay on the ridge above them, come down on the ridge to the gorge overlook, at one of the points on the cliff's edge where a chute of scree ran down to the river. There he could see if anything approached him, and ride out his spirit wander in peace. Then if his spirit left his body, as it was still trying to do, banging against the top of his skull to get out, then he could deposit his body in a safe tuck, and take flight above the sky. That would be much better than killing some passing old ones. Even if they were the ones who had tried to kill him. Although he didn't think they were. There had been three of them. A jolt of fear flooded him at that thought, and he regarded the ridge above carefully, listened and sniffed and watched. No one around.

So he stayed on the ridge and sneaked down its trail, peering down the slope into Upper Valley, where the old ones were still descending, clearly in view. There was a lot of open rocky and snowy land here, only broken by the creek's line of trees, and some isolated groves on the slopes dotting the rest of the valley, with some tilted meadows and scrub here and there.

The other side of the ridge had a short cliff right near the top, then the long forested slope into Lower Valley. As he was feeling exposed on the ridge, spooked by a presence he couldn't see, he changed his plan again; he decided to take the first chute through the cliff that would allow him to drop into Lower Valley, and then go downvalley to the river, meeting it one big loop downstream from the Stone Bison, then work his way back to camp on the river path. Tonight was not the full moon anyway, but the last night before it, unless he was mistaken. So he needed to find one more good tuck, and he knew of a small cave over the river. He could spend the night there. The old ones were in Upper Valley, he would be in Lower. That was good.

Clouds puffed into existence as the sun went down, inspiraling like fern tips, their whites turning pink in the pulsing blue of the sky. As the sun winked away the moon was big in the east, and slightly red. It was a little less bright on its left side than its right, or so it seemed to Loon. He worried about it: there had been boys who came in from their hunter's wander a night too early, which made them look eager to return, so that people had laughed at them. On the other hand Moss had come in a night too late, which had made him look tentative. The problem was that full moons were not all alike; they grew a little bigger and smaller, and their glow also shifted a little, so that the perfect ring of bright light sometimes did not surround a full moon until midnight, rather than right after sunset. Worse, the perfect ring of glow sometimes happened a bit before the moon rose in the east. So mistakes were possible, even when examining it most carefully.

On this night the fat bright moon was growing and shrinking with his every heartbeat, jumping in every blink of the eye, but at all times brilliantly huge. By its light he could see down Lower Valley into the gorge in perfect detail, though everything was in shades of gray frosted with moony white. Otherwise it all lay below him like a ghost version of the daytime world, Mother Earth in all her loveliness, and he floated along looking into the gorge, watching moonlight glitter on the open black riffles in the part of the icy river he could see. The gorge walls seemed to glow from within, and yet the shadows were charcoal black, giving the land a decisively hewn look, as if the gorge had been hacked into the hilly landscape by a great sharp blade. Ah moonlight!

The ridge came to a point that gave him a view of the big loop in the river one loop downstream from their camp. It was just the shape of the loop their camp was in, but filled with water instead of meadow. He saw that when the river wore the upstream turn of this loop's bank away and broke through, there would be another stone bison standing over the flow, and this loop would dry out and become another meadow. Curve of the water around its icy bend, pouring out of shadow into the moonlight. It made little wet noises, audible even up here. The river was singing to itself, as it always did, even now when it was still mostly iced over. Black leads were like long narrow ponds in the gleaming white flat surface, sometimes seeming higher than the ice, other times black holes in white ermine.

In the shadows under the alders at the curve of the bank, some-thing moved and caught his eye. It looked like a person, but when it walked into the white moonlight and stood on the snowy riverbank, Loon could see it had an animal's head, dark and rounded: huge owl eyes over a feline muzzle, antlers curved like ibex horns...Loon had never seen anything like it, and he reeled a little at the sight. Its eyes were surely owl eyes, they were so big and round; everything would be visible to it. Loon froze against the tree behind him, hoped that he would become part of its blackness. But the thing stared right up at him, and kept its gaze fixed on him as it walked upstream on the riverbank. It raised its right arm, and he saw its hand was a paw, a cat's paw; and it had a lion's head, he now saw, but owl-eyed, and with horns that curved above cat ears; the ears turned up at him, listening to his heart pounding loudly at the back of his throat. Then the creature disappeared into the shadow of the gorge wall.

Loon found himself walking backwards without knowing it, up the ridge. Terror had stuck him like a spear through the throat; he could scarcely breathe, and was hot all over. He could feel he was about to shit, like a steppe beast preparing to flee. He had to clench his butt muscles, clench his gut.

Then he turned with a whimper and ran without a thought in his head, without seeing where he was going, without feeling his legs. It was extremely dangerous to flee through the night like that, but I could not help him; in that moment of terror there was nowhere in him for me to enter.

By accident he found himself on the ridge trail again. He stopped because he had to, he was panting so hard. He looked around, afraid of what he might see. And he was right to fear: there was the owl-eyed lion man again, but now above him on the ridge trail, as if he had flown to get there ahead of Loon. With a bleat Loon turned and limped down the ridge, still terrified but back within himself, feel-ing the pain in his left leg, sobbing as he ran.

There was nothing else to do but follow the ridge trail to the gorge overlook at its lower end. This brought him to the intersection with the trail that ran along the north side of the gorge from Loop Meadow, but he didn't want to take that trail, as it was exposed. Instead he dropped down a little cleft he knew in the gorge wall, a break furred with shrubs, which forced him to proceed on his hands and knees to get under the lowest branches. Soon he came to a ledge that hung over the gorge wall proper. He crawled onto the ledge. When the ledge narrowed and disappeared into the cliff, there was a narrow slide on which one could lower oneself to another ledge below the first one. He had been here before.

At the far end of the second ledge he came to the entry of a little cave, a vertical notch in the white stone. Yes, this was a spot he knew. His father had first showed it to him. The notch incised the cliff to a certain depth, where there was a short drop to a little platform. Beyond that the cave was unfortunately bottomless, a hole dropping into blackness. In a crack at the back, beyond the hole, a little water trickled down.

His father had showed him this cave to warn him about it; the hole inside it went right down to the river. His father had found this out, he said, by dropping a walnut etched with a sign down into the blackness, and then finding the walnut later down in the river, turning in an eddy.

Now Loon sat on the platform, in the dark, behind a rock. He could still look out the cave opening, which gave him a view across to the south wall of the gorge, its moony white all mottled with lichen streaks and ledges of its own. Black sky over it pricked with stars, faint in the milky moonlight. The night was young.

From behind and above him, on the first ledge, there came a clatter. Loon, shivering now, feeling like he did after getting stung by a bee, crawled to the hole at the edge of the platform and reached down into it. The wall of the hole was damp, but broken. There was a knob sticking out he could step on. No way to tell what else might be down there. But now there was a snuffling from the second ledge, outside the cave, so Loon slithered feet first into the hole and stepped with both feet on the knob he had felt. He toed into the rocks below the knob, really felt them. At this point Spit was his best scout, being sensitive even when cold. More snuffling from above caused him to grope around faster. He found another knob he could grab, squeezed it as hard as he could, lowered himself farther into the hole. He would have to remember where all these knobs were, and with his eyes closed he painted the two knobs he knew of in their positions. With his right foot he toed down, hunting for another knob. There was one, though it was a bit too far down; by the time he had the arch of his foot on it, his left leg was so bent his knee was above his hip. This wasn't good, the ankle hurt more than it had in a while, but he ignored that and searched for a lower handhold. If he could find another good one, he could take the left foot off and seek something lower for it. There was a crack, discovered blindly by hand, a good crack; he could make a fist in it and the fist would not come out no matter how hard he pulled. That was a hold he could swell or shrink as he wanted, so he let his left foot slip off and probe around next to the one already down there. In the end he discovered that both feet fit well on the same knob, which now felt more like a shelf.

Now he was well down in the hole. He would not be visible even from the little platform, unless the thing hunting him could see in the dark. Or if it smelled him. A lion's head on a man's body, with owl eyes, with antlers: no way to guess how well it could smell. A thrill of terror bee-stinged through him again, as he remembered what it had looked like looking up at him. Well, but even if it smelled him, even if it saw him in the pure black, would it climb down into this hole? Without fingers, with paws on its forelegs, would it be able to descend? Maybe not. This was all he could hope for. He could see on his eyelids his way back up, left right, left right. He didn't want to descend farther. Maybe he would if the thing snuffled at the top of the hole. But in fact he heard nothing but his breathing, and the tock of his heart at the back of his throat. No way to know what the antlered owl-eyed lion man was doing. If it didn't have a bear's nose too, possibly it would have lost him. Lions hunted mostly by eye, owls too.

He hung there. It got cold, and his legs grew stiff. He couldn't feel his feet, except for a little burn from Spit. He let go with his right hand and carefully untied his deerhide cape and arranged it over his head and around his shoulders. He eased his body up and down, up and down, and shifted which hand he had in the fist crack, and hung from each as long as he could. Inside himself he called on the third wind to help him. But that one always came late, if at all. He rubbed himself against the dark rough rock. He was down in a cave. Small though it was, it was still an earth womb, a passage to the spirit world. In their painted caves, one pressed one's hands through the walls into the underworld, and saw the animals' spirits dance. So he tried to believe now, but really it was just a cold hole at the back of a little whitestone cave, a hole his father had warned him to stay out of. It was too cold to be a womb, too cold to birth him through to the other side. He could only hang there and endure.

In the blackness before him, the rectangular grids of red dots turned slowly into squiggles, into blobs, into side views of bison and mammoth and horse and ibex, all there hanging before him just as clearly as if they had been snatched off a ridge in the sun. His brothers and sisters. Maybe he had passed through the wall of this hole. Only the three points of it that he touched still seemed real to him. It was as if he held three cold hands, clasping him as he hung in the starless skies of the animal spirits. They pulsed as they floated before him.

He grew weak. I held him to the wall of that hole for a while.

I am the third wind
I come to you
When you have nothing left

Some twentytwentytwenty breaths later, it seemed lighter above. It was as if the blackness now had one drop of white diffused in it, like blood dripped into a river. More drips of gray followed, and then there was a tint, a gray somewhat like the blood in his eyelids when he squeezed his eyes shut hard. He seemed to see the trickle of water that had been dripping down the wall behind him, when he turned his head to look.

Ah yes: he could remember the way up. First the knob he had had to raise his knee above his hip to get his left foot onto; then the other handhold; and the higher foothold; and then he could grasp a knob at the very edge of the hole, and reach over and curl his fingers like hooks of cedar root, into cracks on the cave floor. And pull himself up, up into the fist before dawn. Crawl out to the ledge, look down into the gray gorge. It was empty except for the iced river, which snaked through it like the big live thing it was. On this quiet morning it was slipping along under its blanket of ice and old snow. Black leads flowing flatly. Nothing else moving. A squirrel, talking to itself: nothing big and terrible could be prowling around this morning. The sky had lost its stars, and was that gray that could be either clouds or clear sky, in that brief time before you could tell which.

Down the gorge a touch of pink indicated the sun was coming soon. Suddenly it could be seen that it was a clear sky, a cloudless sky. Loon clenched the right fist, the one that had held him the most, and felt its flesh groan. He stretched the hand open, wiggled the fingers, twisted one hand with the other. That right hand had gotten him through the night. And as the day grew brighter, the lion man with the owl eyes seemed less and less likely to be out and about; or even to be real. Although in the night it had most definitely been real.

Now that he could see, the ledges he had used to get to his hole were scarily narrow. Stiff as he was, he crawled over them like a lizard, a red water lizard, every limb plopped deliberately in its place. Then up the bushy cleft to the gorge edge. Now he could walk back to the ridge trail, and down into Upper Valley. He needed to take the whole day to get to camp, so he could come in after dark, at full moon. There was lots of time. He knew right where he was.

Daylight chased off the night's fears. The air was cool and clear. He felt a buzzing in all his skin, all his flesh and bones. Trees were leafing right before his eyes, and the colors of the day flooded him as they grew brighter. A breeze bounced everything up and down in the air, and something inside him opened. He knew he would survive to be a man, a man on Mother Earth, so big and beautiful. There was terror out there too, oh yes, but this day was huge, bigger than terror. Clouds in his chest swelled like thunderheads. Squirrels celebrated the day with their chitters and chirps, and Upper Valley's creek clattered and splooshed down its icy defile, sunlit moss greening its banks with bright spring greens, vivid against the old snow.

He passed a trickle of snowmelt in the sun, and crouched to drink, and Crouch crouched with him. Crouch was in a bad mood. He had retrieved Prong from above the first ledge, and now it and another walking stick he picked up became part of his arms. He had become one of the four-legged animals again, with very long, double-jointed forelegs. Snowmelt cold in his empty belly, flooding him from the inside, stilling the buzz in him until he could float again, could walk as lazily as a leopard, flowing with the bump and tilt of the rocks underfoot. He moved so slowly that he didn't move, and the sky's blue billowed and lofted over him, higher and higher, bluer and bluer. What clouds there were that day were all inside him.

It was a day for animals. Fourteenth day of the fourth month, the days getting longer fast, the sun higher in the sky, the warmth of spring finally burnishing the air of the world. Snow melting everywhere it was left. Everyone felt good on a day like this, they all came out to forage and look around. The gods inside them pushed out into their pelts.

Four-pointing down the valley, floating a little. There was a narrow lane in Upper Valley, above the creekbed so choked by alder, below the valley wall so rocky and snowy. Loon descended to this lane, he floated down onto it. When he got to it, he sat and rested, and felt Mother Earth spin a little under him, undulate up and down with her breathing. The narrow lane was mostly grassy, and where side creeks tumbled across it, the darker greens of sedge and moss striped it. Every creature walking up- or downvalley used this lane, and in the muddy patches Loon saw hoof and paw prints of all kinds.

Around noon he came to a broad open flat, a meadow where the creek slowed down and snaked through grass-green reeds. Loon kept against the eastern wall of the valley, which was here a stack of setback cliffs, with trees on every ledge. He felt safe here, and when a little herd of bison appeared at the top of the meadow and wandered downstream, he hid behind a tree and watched. They were wary and skittish, as if being hunted, and soon they passed out of sight downstream. The bison was Thorn's animal, which was just right, they were so big-headed and full of themselves.

Now the valley was peaceful again, and the squirrels chirped and dashed about. Overhead a hawk spiraled lazily, one of the few birds to be here so early in the spring; a sprucetopper, seeming too high to be on the hunt, though it wasn't true. They sometimes dove from so high they only became visible as a dot already diving. A quiet warm afternoon, not as clear as the morning had been, but almost cloudless still. His stomach pinched, and he felt a little weak. He floated not so much from relief as from light-headedness. With every heartbeat the trees moved away and then back at him, and a cloud of bees around a beehive roared in a way that told him he did not want their honey. Although some honey...if he threw rock after rock, blasted them away, knocked the hollow tree apart, splashed them and smoked them...but no. Only smoke would do it. Otherwise they would get angry and attack him in a swarm, he had had it happen before. One more bee sting added to the buzzing already in him and he would burst out of his skin.

Regretfully he left the beehive alone and continued downstream, slower than the water flowing through the meadow. After the stream left the meadow and fell down a forested slope he moved from tree to tree, resting against them as if against friends. They propped him up the way friends did.

The afternoon shadows lengthened in their leisurely way. He was close enough to the pack's abri that he could stop and crawl under a log. His sleepless night suddenly caught up with him, and he had to give in to sleep, hoping that nothing hungry would come upvalley while he did. On a journey of twentytwenty days you can still fuck up on the last step. Yes, but there was nothing for it, he was helpless to hold it off. Sleep with one eye open.

When he woke it was just a fist above sundown. He pulled himself up, brushed himself off. He went to the river and washed his face, then spotted a chunk of earthblood in the stream and plucked it out happily. A little scraping with a harder rock would yield enough red for some facepaint. He still had his deer tooth necklace, and his knot carved into a lion man, which now gave him a little shiver of dread as he pondered it; also his deerhide clothes and cape. He would use the earthblood to spot his hide cape like his cheeks and forehead. Make a leopard pattern on both, come into camp in style. He would be thin and weak and injured, but clothed and well. Alive. He considered casting aside Prong and the other pole; but if he did he would have to limp, because Crouch was now objecting loudly to every single step he took. He could lose the poles at the last moment, and stop himself from limping for his walk in, if he chose to.

In the last light of the sun he crossed Loop Meadow and slowly climbed Loop Hill. From its top he could see down into the bowl of land they lived in, and up the river gorge to the ridges all round, to the sunset and the moonrise. Camp was down there under the abri that seamed Cave Hill. When night fell he could walk right down to it. It was all coming together just as he had planned in the sleepless nights of his wander. Looking down he saw the smoke from their campfire, curling up through the trees. Ah yes.

In the last part of that day, sunlight slanting down the gorge of the river, there was a motion on the first ridge to the west of him. He saw it was a black horse, standing there looking around. The sacred animal, the most beautiful animal.

The horse stood alone, watching the sunset just like Loon. Loon took the chunk of earthblood from his belt flap and scraped its friable surface with his foreclaw until he had some of it nubbled in his palm. He spit on it and rubbed it around until he had a paste, then applied it in streaks across his forehead and under his eyes. Then he bowed to the horse, and the horse bowed back, nodding his head and lifting it up, nodding and lifting. The god animal was lit by the sun almost from below. Long black head, so etched and fine. The land's witness to the end of his wander, pawing once, then nodding and lifting. Throwing his great head side to side, his black eyes observing Loon across the gulf of air between them. Black mane short and upright, black body rounded and strong.

Then without warning the horse tossed his long head up at the sky, off toward the sun, and this movement popped in Loon's eye and bulged out across the space between them, scoring his eyes such that he could close them and see it again; Loon's eyes spilled over, the tears ran down his face, his throat clamped down and his chest went tight and quivered. He put his hands on his heart. The horse turned away and cantered over the ridge out of sight, disappearing with a final flash of sun on its black upright mane. Loon looked away, still blinking out tears, and for a time he was almost afraid to look west again. He squeezed his eyes shut, saw it all happen on his eyelids. The head leading the body through its turn away, so graceful, so smooth. Last of the sun flooding the gorge, gleaming off the black body as if off a crow's wing. Rounded shoulders and long legs.

The sun touched the horizon and began to set. At the same moment a spot on the eastern horizon gleamed brilliant white, spread left and right: the moon was rising. In the same time the sun took to set, the moon rose; watching the two, looking back and forth, Loon felt himself expand between them, felt the sky rolling over Mother Earth. Sun down, moon up, all part of one big flight. So it must indeed be the night of full moon.

And as the moon cleared the horizon and hung in the blue sky, it showed the brilliant white glow all the way around it, confirming the true full. It was a huge one, much bigger than the setting sun had been. The last sunset of his wander; as he realized that, a pang pierced him, the world grew to something more immense than he could grasp. Oh that it had to end! Would he ever be this alive again, would the world ever again be so beautiful as in this moment?

No. Never. It was not possible. This was his moment, his alone, the end of his wander, the peak of his gyre. It would never come again. Now he was a man, and a horse had blessed him. Tomorrow he would be back in his pack, Thorn's apprentice. This huge new feeling, could he hold to it then? Could he remember it?

It seemed very unlikely. He would see when it happened. He had
to go home. And it was true he was hungry.

In the dusk he arranged his things, and repainted his face and the
palms of his hands. He pronged down the slope of the hill to camp,
the full moon pouring its light over everything he saw. At the last
moment he decided to discard only the second walking stick. Prong
was too much of a friend, sturdy and reliable, stained at the top with
the sweat of his hand, the wood at its bottom perfectly rounded by
all the times he had stuck it onto the stony ground. He would come
in showing how he had got along despite Crouch, showing that
nothing had stopped him on his wandering way.

He saw the fire almost the entire hike down the hill. They had
made it big to welcome him back. The bee buzz filled him again,
and he burned as he floated down the hill, adjusting his clothing and
hoping that his facepaint had been applied neatly. If not he might
only look as if he had been recently murdered. If so, that too would
be fine. He had indeed died, and was returning as someone else. He
felt that so strongly he was sure they would see it.

The black trees marking the curve of the meadow's loop were pulsing upward as if trying to float away, held to the earth by their trunks,
but tugging up against them with all their branches. He himself was
floating with a nearly perfect buoyancy through the air, pegging
down with Prong in a perfect balance for his feet, halfway between
landing and flying into the sky. Crouch said to him, I am all right, I
will do whatever you ask, I am not really here tonight, good-bye for
now. Pleased at that, Loon focused on keeping the three points of his
walking in a smooth flow, a dance down to his pack in their camp.
The fire flickered through the trees, trying like everything else that
night to fly up and away. The moon over the trees was still immense,
and superbly white all around its edge: a fuller moon could not exist.
Full moon of the fourth month: here they were again. The hunger
month was over, summer not that far away. The rabbit in the moon,
stirring her bowl of earthblood with which to paint the dawn, was

putting her whole body into the stir, and though her head was in profile, he could see she was looking to her left to watch him walk down the hill. She would indeed paint the coming dawn for him, for they would stay up all night to celebrate.

He came into camp and realized at the last moment that he had not announced himself, that he might surprise them, and so he hooted the little roop roop greeting that loons made when they came up after a dive and were locating their friends.

His people heard it and cheered. The men howled like wolves and came out to greet him, grinning hugely and shouting his name. Loon dropped Prong and they lifted him up under his legs and around his back and carried him to the fireside on their shoulders. Loon was glad he was all cried out; he was full but empty, he could see them all with a calm little smile. It was a big bonfire. All the women and girls and boys called his name and hugged him one by one, many hands always touching him, and then the women brought their finest fur robes to drape him.

Even Heather smiled for a moment, then ducked her toothless head and darted away, returned with a bowl of hot spruce tea and some little honey seedcakes.

—Don't eat too much too fast, she warned him in her ordinary voice. —How did you do out there, are you all right?

—I twisted my ankle, he confessed at once. —There's something still not right in there.

—Ah. She shot an evil glance at Thorn. She did not like the men's wanders, nor any unnecessary danger of any kind.

Thorn ignored her, caught up as he was in his own close inspection of Loon. Loon could not guess what the old man was thinking, and turned to the others; but that didn't feel right, that was too much like before. He didn't want to fall back into the old habits of his life in the pack, least of all with Thorn. Even though it was a huge relief to be among them again. What a life it would be to be a woodsman or a traveler, hunted night and day, unable ever to let down one's guard, and no one to talk to!

—Tell us about it! they were saying. —Tell us what you did, what happened to you!

—Wait a moment, he said, casting himself across what seemed an immense gulf of time, back into the present instant by the fire. It was hard. He had to collect himself. There were so many faces, and he knew each one like the palm of his hand.

—Well, I couldn't get a fire started that first night in the storm.

They groaned and laughed to hear this.

—So I had to dance all night to stay warm.

—Oh too bad! A lot of the men were laughing at him, or with him. —I hate it when that happens!

—Then the next day I got a fire going. He took a deep breath, and they saw it and fell silent, all their eyes on his:

And I stayed with that fire three days.
I ate fish and old berries and meadow onions,
And I saw two bears attack a deer,
And they fought over it and I got part of it away,
Not much, when they were done.
Then I had something to work with,
But an ibex broke my first snare
And I didn't get anything till later.
Third time I set a snare that held a deer
And I killed it. I used its skin for clothes,
And did pretty well after that.
But I ran into some old ones,
There are old ones around up there, you know—

And some of the men nodded, and Heather too, their eyes round. Loon kept glancing at Sage, he was telling this story to Sage most of all, Sage and Heather, and Thorn of course:

—they hunted me and I had to run for my life,
And walk in the creek to Lower's Upper,
And I got away, but I hurt my ankle,

So I had to find a good tuck, and I did.
Up in a broken tree it was.
When my leg felt better I left there
And started back to here,
And when I saw there were two more nights to go
I ate a witch's nightcap, and artemisia leaves.

This he said to Thorn, but here Thorn shook his head. —Tell me about that later, he said. —That's shaman stuff.

—All right, Loon said. Although what followed had been the biggest night of the wander by far, and would have made a good story. Later he would tell it, he decided: now wasn't a good time to defy the old man. Or was it?

Loon pondered this. But yes, now he could see what Thorn meant. He didn't want to tell just how afraid he had been of the thing on the riverbank; he wouldn't have been able to convey it, and so he would have had to lie about it, one way or another. And so far he had not lied.

He could see Thorn watching him closely, watching to see if he understood why he should stay quiet about the thing in the night, and the terror; looking to see if he had changed or not, and if so, in what ways. But two could play at stone face, and so Loon merely returned his gaze, happy at the warmth of the bonfire, and the sight of Sage there in the firelight. He was still seeing everything bounce and bloom before him, trying to fly up into the sky, and now the people of Wolf pack were all of them bouncing, on fire with themselves, every face the perfect image of that person's character, bursting with his or her particular self, and he was among them; and although that meant trouble, it was the best trouble in the world.

Even Heather in her irritable way was pleased to have him back, he saw, and at some point, by the bonfire when she was passing nearby, on one of her perpetual errands, he put out an arm to stop her and give her a hug, as she was the only one who had not hugged him, but only touched his arm. —I made it, he said.

—Yes, yes, you made it, she replied, squeezing him briefly before she moved on. —Now you are twelve.

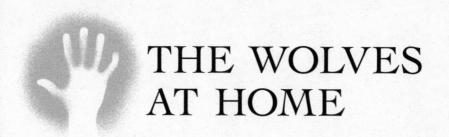

THE WOLVES
AT HOME

In the chill dawn Loon woke under a blanket of ash flecks, mouth parched and head aching. His wander was over, he was back in his pack. Thorn was groaning and calling for water. The old man's gray braids hung over his dark face, their broken hairs sticking out everywhere. His eyes when he opened them were red and gooey. He stared at Loon suspiciously; he looked like he was still wondering what had happened to Loon on his wander. Loon decided never to tell him. His wander was his. One of Heather's sayings finally came clear to him: no one else can live your life for you. He felt the solitude of it, the loneliness. Another lesson of his wander.

Thorn growled, as if seeing Loon's secretiveness and disapproving it. Then he grunted like a rhino and crawled across camp to its sunrise end, where Heather kept her nest. All her stuff was tucked around her on wooden shelves which made a tight little wind shelter. She was in there now, and when she saw Thorn she moved to stand in her entry, blocking him. Thorn reached between her legs for her water gourd and she kicked his forearm.

—I don't speak to unspeakables, she said, —but everyone knows to stay out of my nest.

—I just want a drink of water, he whined.

—No one touches my things. They stay away from my nest. I've dusted it with poisons that will make you sick, everyone knows that.

Thorn lay there defeated. —Loon, he said, —get me a bucket of water, please. You can take it from Heather here.

—You get it, Loon said. —I'm not your apprentice anymore.

—You just became my apprentice, didn't you notice? Do what I say and don't be insolent. He laid a red eyeful of command on Loon. —That's what your wander should have taught you.

Loon dug in a net bag for his real clothes, which Heather had kept for him. —It taught me I'm not your apprentice.

But of course that was just what he was. Unless he quit the shaman's way entirely, which would probably mean leaving the pack. Thorn's heavy red scorn speared the point home.

Loon got dressed and stumped around camp doing things for the old sorcerer, feeling like he had let himself get snared in a snare he had known to avoid. It made him sick as he saw it happening. Mornings after a big night could be like that, just a raven–shitted kill site, sunlight slivering the eyes, the camp all ashy and sordid, its people disgusting. Best to get out of camp on mornings like that, go down to the river and jump in.

So Loon did that. The one lead of open water had iced over in the night, but it was easy to crack through the thin clear layer and make a hole into the black water below. What a luxury it was to plunge into the sandy shallows of the lead, rub himself until he began to shiver under the shock of the black water, all the while knowing that the campfire would be there to warm him back up, and his clothes right there on the bank. Ah the luxury of home!

Except for the people. Although it was true that last night he had been very glad to see them. People are more wolf than wolverine, people are more lion than leopard, because they run in packs. Seeing all their faces in the firelight: he had to remember the feel of that, so intense and comforting. Where had it gone already? There was so much to remember from his wander. He would be asked to tell the rest of it, and he wouldn't; but he had to remember it. It was his, it was what he had. And it had taught him some things. If he could remember them. Already it was getting to be like a dream he had had.

He limped up the side of Loop Hill to the flat spot that ledged around to the tail of the Stone Bison. This was a fine prospect, with views up and down the river gorge, and over Loop Meadow to the gray rise behind it, where their camp was tucked at the bottom of a little abri.

From here their camp was as small as a child's toy. The pack house was a neat round thing of spruce logs and hides, smoke rising from the hole in the high point of the roof. People were still coming out of it, stunned by the day, or rather the previous night. In the doorway of the women's house Chamois and Bluejay sat where they always did. His friends Hawk and Moss were still asleep in their furs, on the ramp under the abri. There were Thorn and Heather, and across the camp Schist and Ibex, putting wood on the big campfire. Every person down there was known to him so well that if he could see them at all, no matter how small they were, he knew just who it was, also what they were likely to be doing, and what they would say if you spoke to them. It was enough to make you scream.

Heather was holding up her blowdart tube and aiming it at Thorn. Her darts were tipped with poisons that would kill in just a few heartbeats. Thorn had his hands up, but was clearly berating her. His words could be as poisonous as her darts. He had cursed people to death at the festivals.

Loon stared down now as if looking at some other pack. Rising smoke, people grubbing in the morning chill. Out on his wander he had wanted to be home, now he wanted to be back on his wander. But of course, Heather would say if he told her this. You only want things you don't have. Things you do have, you forget to want. We're stupid that way.

Their camp was laid out like most abri camps Loon had ever seen. Quite a few had cliff overhangs even better than theirs, many of them upstream and down on the gorge walls of the Urdecha, others in other river canyons east and west and south. The cliffs backing these camps were usually painted, as theirs was. From the Stone Bison the paintings were tiny, a jumble of red and black spots. Loon could just make out the long stretch of painted wolves on the hunt, something like four score of them overlapping in a run toward the camp. They were the Wolf pack. Two score and two of them, this spring.

Schist was standing by the fire telling Ibex something. Schist was broad-shouldered and deep-chested, not tall but nevertheless big, shaped like a river stone but light on his feet. A very clever hunter, and very accurate with the javelin. A mild friendly look, attentive to everyone in the pack, an easy manner. He made jokes often but at heart was very serious, because he took on himself the task of making sure they had enough food to get through the winters and springs. That was his version of being a headman, and it was something women usually did, but he joined them in their work and suggested what everybody do. So every summer when the birds returned and they had not starved, he became briefly cheerful; but after midsummer day he returned to his beavering.

Now the birds had not yet returned, and their saved food was getting low, and he was very intent as he talked to Ibex. He was always talking food: cooking and fishing with Thunder and the women, hunting and trapping with the men. He had dug their storage pits himself, and was always lining them with new things. He spoke with people from other packs to see what they knew. He and Thorn had worked out an accounting system similar to Thorn's yearsticks, using clean lengths of driftwood to notch marks for their pokes of animal fat, bags of nuts, dried salmon steaks, smoked caribou steaks; everything they gathered to eat in the cold months was stored and marked down. He knew how much every person in the pack would eat, based on the previous winter's markings and adjusted by everyone's summer health, by how much fat they had put on, and so on. He knew better than you how hungry you would be.

The thing that made Schist complicated was that he was married to Thunder, sitting there by the women's house. She along with her sister Bluejay were the headwomen of the pack, as involved as Schist in the running of things. And Thunder was a bruiser. She and Schist had grown up together in Wolf pack and married young, which was said to explain everything about them. But Schist was relaxed and agreeable, while Thunder was so intense and overbearing it was said her mother had eaten otter meat while pregnant. And her sister Bluejay was even worse, and the two of them were close. People joked that Schist had married two women, both meaner than him. How could he be headman of the pack when he wasn't even headman in his bed? But somehow the necessary things got done. Their pack didn't really want a headman anyway, he was always suggesting with his manner. They were better off this way. Except when it came to food. With food he was a boulder that could not be moved. Thunder and Bluejay left that to him, to avoid a push coming to a shove they would not win. And so he spent his days going from one task to the next, asking for help when he needed it, and people gave it when he asked. It looked like he was asking Ibex for help right now, although he was more agitated than usual. People said he had been good to Loon's father when Tulik had married into the pack.

Looking down at the tiny people, Loon realized he could close his eyes and still see them all. Everybody knew everybody. The adults were married, the children were not, the young people were in between, thus on the lookout. Their bodies had begun to bleed or spurt, the older ones were putting them through their initiations. There was no way out of that, no place to hide.

Hunger shoved him back down to camp. He was not happy.

Hawk and Moss were sitting in the sun, straightening their tusk javelin tips with a bone-point straightener, Hawk laughing as he inserted the white point into the hole, miming a spurt into a kolby, in and out, in and out. Then a gentle twist on the bone handle to lever the point back into true. Mammoth tusk was strong and light, but it warped as it dried, also when it got wet. Point straightening was always a pleasure, it meant they were about to go out on the hunt again. But Loon was too hurt to go.

When you know a man you know his face, not his heart. Never help a person who doesn't help anyone else. The more you give, the more you get.

To Loon these sayings seemed to suggest he should spend most of his time helping women. Heather often said it: find the right woman and do what she says. A woman will cook for you, and then you can hunt. And he dearly wanted to go with his friends on the hunt.

Heather told him he would only hurt his leg worse. —Real friends wouldn't let you go, she said. She didn't like the pack's men. In her constant muttering Loon sometimes heard her quite clearly, though he didn't always understand her: —Bunch of drunken old spelunkers, you shamans, and you hunters mere pig-stickers and jerk-offs, all your splendiferous vainglorious buffooneries and ass-holeries, hootenanies and corroborees, wandering around thinking you're men, just get the meat! Get the nuts! Get the firewood! Do your work! Quit with the lies and the boasts and the tall tales, the flat-out undeniable fucking stupidity! Do your work and then brag if you have to, otherwise I shit on all your brave talk, it's just the slubgullion left at the bottom of the bucket!

The people of Wolf pack had long ago stopped listening to Heather, as she knew very well. Sometimes she would shout at them just to see them turn their backs and move away. But Loon had to stay. After his parents' deaths Heather and Thorn had raised him, and now, between them they had him trapped. —All these widows and orphans, I'm tired of it! Heather told him whenever he complained about this. —Quit getting killed and then it won't happen! Heather the midwife, the herb woman, the loudmouth, the witch, the crone, the horrible hag, the deadly poisoner. A very busy and bossy old woman, small and bent and proud to have three teeth left, two opposed. The spider was her animal, and it was said she turned into one sometimes.

Now she was dismissing him with a wave, staring up into the hemlock over her nest. The cat that hung around their camp, enticed by Heather's gifts, had climbed into the branches over her and was daintily eating the tree's new spring leaves, even the new twigs. It seemed uncatlike.

—Get out of here, I have to talk to Schist.

He couldn't go out on the hunt. All that day and in the days after, a feeling of doom grew in him, the weight of the sky weighed on him.

If he killed everybody in the pack he would be able to go out on his own, find a high place to sleep at night, and have a fire always, everything he needed, a cave to paint, new people when he wanted them; come and go, drop in on festivals, no duties to a pack or to anything at all. A traveler, a woodsman, a green man. He could do the deed in the night before dawn, before Heather woke up; kill her first because she would be the one to know, the hardest to surprise, catch her asleep, a blow with a chopper to the back of the head or to the temple, go around to those who were always first to wake, then to the heavy sleepers, the late sleepers, they would be late indeed on that morning! And in the sunrise, with all of them dead, walk out on a wander that would never end. Live a lifetime every month.

B etter to be lucky than good. The cat had seen that many times. A sound snapped in her head like a thunderclap and she was far up the tree overhanging camp before she understood it was one of the humans stepping on a dry twig. Better to be safe than sorry. The humans would kill anyone, and then not only eat their kill but tear off its fur and tear out its teeth and wear them afterward, macabre trophies that were part of what made humans so awful, along with their smell, and their ability to kill at a distance by throwing rocks and sticks. None of the other animals could do that. The cat disliked all the other animals, including her own kind. Cats at least liked to stay away from each other, they had that basic courtesy. All except for the lions. Lions acted like they were wolves, it was sickening. The biggest of every kind of animal were gregarious, which the cat found mysterious. All the littler wolves were solitaries: fox, coyote, mink, weasel. So were all the littler cats. But the biggest of both kinds, wolves and lions, roamed in groups. There's safety in numbers. So they clumped and safe they were. And their prey, the big herd animals, clumped together too. The lions should have known better.

Bears left their little sisters alone, wolves likewise, but big cats would eat little cats. Anyone would eat a little cat if they could catch one. Thus her jumpiness. To see the biggest cats ganging up in packs was a little disgusting, a little embarrassing, also terrifying. They looked like cats in every other way, then there they were, hanging around like wolves. How could they do it?

All the animals had been the same in the beginning, then things happened and they became sun and moon, northern lights and thunderstorms, and all the various animals, still the same inside and sharing an outlook on things. But some killed and some got killed, and many did both, like cat. Best be careful. Hiss at the storms and they might go elsewhere.

Another thunder crack of a twig snap and cat's fur stood, her tail grew fat with unease. Another pair of humans were now under the tree. These were the two dominant males in the herb woman's pack, deadly men with rock or stick. Cat peeked over the side of the branch to observe, and saw that the two humans were talking to another pair of them, from the pack that cut off their little fingers and gave them to the cats. Naturally cat liked these humans better, but they did not have an herb woman like cat's, so she stayed mostly around the woman. It was a pack with a lot of camp mice, and the oddments left out by the old woman were interesting. The old woman teased cat with weird gifts.

Now the men were arguing, pointing up- and downcanyon. It was territorial, and they were chest to chest and swelled up. In such a state they would never notice cat, and she poked her head out to see better. Possibly they would drop something in a fight, or something would remain after to be scavenged, anything from drops of blood to dead bodies.

But the finger cutters were backing down. They did not want a fight. Their territory was off under the sunset, they indicated that with their gestures. The herb woman's pack leaders accepted this and the finger cutters left, heading upcanyon.

Then the two men remaining argued with each other. Something about the meeting had left them at odds. Cat followed them as they went toward their fire, hopping nervously from branch to branch. Best be careful. Curiosity killed the cat. Despite which she was curious enough to watch from afar as the men entered camp and went to the dominant male's wife. This big woman listened to them with a scowl that did not spare either of them. When they were done she cursed them and they slunk away abashed.

Once when they were boys Loon and Hawk and Moss had gone out on a hunt and come upon a pack of lions in a meadow, eating a big horse they had killed. As the boys had watched from the shelter of a rocky ridge above, a flock of ravens had swirled in on the wind from the west and begun swooping and shitting on the lions, and even more so on the open dismembered body of the horse, as became obvious when the snarling lions backed away to get out of the spew. The ravens kept shitting and peeing on the dead horse until it was little more than an uneven mound under the curdled white of their shit. The lions padded sullenly off. After that the ravens descended to beak through their mess and eat the body of the horse themselves.

The boys had crowed themselves at such a great opportunity, and when the lions were gone they charged down and drove the ravens off, and then threw rocks at the black birds when they dove back in their counterattacks. The boys were more dangerous to the ravens than the lions had been, and after a brief skirmish, filled with curses in both languages, the ravens had flown off heavy-winged, hoarse with unhappiness.

The three boys had been very pleased with themselves, and had quickly hacked chunks of the horse free, and carried the two rear legs and the head down to the river to wash them off. They had washed them and rubbed them with sand in the cold flow of the upper Ordech for more than a fist of the afternoon, then carried them home and on Hawk's urging told the people at camp that they had killed the horse woman themselves and brought back this meat. Thorn had taken up one of the rear legs and sniffed it and nibbled it like Heather's cat, and then whacked Hawk with it as if swinging a branch, knocking Hawk to the ground. Hawk cried out and everyone gathered and Thorn picked up the leg and gave it to Heather. Heather bit into it and scowled. —When ravens shit on a kill the meat changes, she told the boys. —You can't just wash it off.

—Oh, Hawk said.

The three boys must have looked pretty foolish, because all of a sudden Thorn started laughing at them, and then everyone was laughing. Although then the boys had been slapped around a bit too.

Today you mix paint, Thorn croaked one morning.

—I always mix paint.

—Then clean up my spot.

—No! Loon said, frowning.

Thorn grinned in a way that revealed he had wanted to get a rise out of Loon. —So mix paint. I'll teach you how to make it so it won't run in the rain.

This was just what Loon wanted to know, so he stared at Thorn suspiciously, and Thorn laughed at him.

Heather watched the two of them unsmiling.

—How is your leg? she asked.

Loon shrugged. —All right.

Although he worried about that. Next month they would head north to the caribou, and by then he would have to have his legs.

Now he limped after the old man to his nest, picked up his leather sack of earthblood and charcoal, and followed the shaman to the painted part of their cliff.

Thorn stood in the morning sun squinting at a wall of the cliff that had been drawn over many times. He ignored the many erect spurts and open kolbies, including a pretty great series depicting a man whose spurt was so long that he had to bend it back down to his mouth to be able to suck himself off. Instead Thorn regarded a grouping of ten russet cave bears. He liked these bears: they were clumped in a pack, in a way they never gathered on the land, with some of them standing, some shambling, some sniffing the air with their incredible noses. Each bear revealed its mood or purpose by a deft turn of eye or ear, or furrows on their sloped foreheads. A few of the bears were three-liners, but most had been painted fully, with charcoal stumped and smudged over underlying red paint, making precisely the russet shade one saw when the bears wore their late summer coats. And they were all fat. So in the painting it was autumn; and by the looks on their faces, it seemed something down by the river had caught their attention. Bumps and hollows in the stone of the wall were incorporated into several of their shoulders and rumps and foreheads. It was as if the painters, whoever they had been, had seen these bears emerging from the cliff and then drawn them on the surface. The paintings were beginning to chip away, and Thorn had talked about recoloring them. Now he pointed at the rearmost bear.

—Fixing that one was your first day of painting! Loon preempted him.

Thorn tossed a pebble at him. —Be quiet. I'm still your master. I'll beat you and you'll have to take it. Even though you're strong enough now to beat me. You'll hate that but you'll have to take it to stay in the pack. So shut up and let me show you something you don't know.

—For once, Loon said, and dodged another pebble.

As Thorn pulled out a few chunks of earthblood, and a selection of chopflints and burins, Loon settled down and stopped the needling. He had hungered for this, and now the old man was willing to feed his hunger.

Earthblood was friable, like sand soaked in something's blood, which then had dried and turned into a rock. You could scrape a little of its surface off under the curve of your claw, but underneath that first scrape it got much harder. You needed to scrape that part with a flint burin, using the pointed edge of the burin to scrape off chips and granules until you had a pile of them, then grind the pile under a flint pestle, in a granite grinding cup or on a slate metate. So: scrape away with one of the biggest burins, its sharp flint point and edge turned as needed. Push where the red stone was weakest, which was where the darkest earthblood clumped like scabs within the sandier parts of the rock, which were also red, but mixed with blacks and browns. The rock broke best where scabby and sandy met. Once broken away, the scabs were softer than the sandy parts, like a very hard mud.

—You want mostly that, Thorn said, pointing at the finer powder from the scabs. —The sandy part makes the paint too grainy. You can have a little, but not too much. It has to be just the right thickness for wall work, like a thick soup, or a very thin paste. It has to be thin enough to spread, of course, but not so thin that it runs.

—So you add water to the powder.

—Of course, don't be such an insolent youth. You also add something to bind the water and the powder together, and that's what you don't know. It has to bind it without clumping it. There's a number of binders will do it, some for body paint, some for wall paint. Today we need a little spit and some deer marrow fat, which I brought along for the occasion.

He pulled a gooseskin bag from his belt pouch and untied it carefully, then poured a little of the semi-liquid fat into a wooden bowl.

Loon stared at the bag; he had not known there were binders.

—It's better if your powder is even finer than this you have here. You haven't done a very good job, but let's use it so you'll see.

He picked up Loon's metate and tipped the powdered earthblood on it into the bowl. —Swirl that around, then wait twenty beats, and in that time all the biggest grains of sand will sink to the bottom of the bowl. Then pour the paint into another bowl, but stop in time to leave the dregs in the first one. Like this.

He poured. —See, the coarsest red stays in the first bowl. Now we'll let a finer powder settle to the bottom of the second bowl. That will take a while. Most of the red will just float forever. So, when it's ready, pour off that water carefully. Later when these dregs in the bowls dry, they will be two cakes of earthblood powder, one coarse, one fine. You can cut the dried cakes into sticks and draw with them, like you draw with a stick of charcoal, only red. Or you can put a dried cake back in some water and break it up while adding more marrow fat, or spit, or pee, or hide glue, or spurtmilk. Then you'll have it back to paint again. Or you can crumble a cake and mix it into beeswax, and that's how you make the crayons you see some people using.

Loon nodded. —Heather makes a good glue. He had often watched her cook down the last remains of butchered animals into a white goo in a bucket, combining cartilage, fat, sinews and ligaments, and little bits of bone and muscle, along with some dried and crushed plants known only to her.

Thorn nodded. —She must put something special in her glue, it dries so hard. I add a few drops of it to my cliff paint. Won't run in the rain later. Here, stir this fat in, then grind some more rock.

Grind the chunk of earthblood with the burin. Scrape scrape scrape. Warm morning air. He liked this part: the redness of the rock, its friability. Hold the block to his nose: it even smelled like blood. Sun hot on his neck.

The morning passed while he ground the rock. So pleasant to sit in the sun, soaking in its heat. He made sure Crouch and Spit were in the sun, it made them happier. It got so nice he fell asleep and sat there scraping earthblood in his dream just as he would have been if he had been awake, so that he could hardly tell which world he was in, and it wouldn't matter if he couldn't. Oh give thanks for the warmth of the sun!

All the time as he worked, Thorn moved around muttering to himself. He and Heather were a matched pair in that regard. In so many ways it was a contest between them. They were like a bad marriage, indeed some people said they had been a bad marriage, had split back before anyone else in the pack had even been born. True or not, Loon saw their ongoing fight up close. Indeed he worked them against each other, to crack a space for himself.

Neither of them ever stopped talking. If Thorn stopped it was almost always because he had fallen asleep. This morning he was retelling the story of the long winter, one of his favorites. All the awfulest stories were his favorites, but only told in their right time. Loon listened as he scraped, or rather let it wash over him, like the sound of the squirrels chittering in the trees.

Thorn's croaky low voice was much like a raven's hoarse cawing:

Back in the old time we lived like birds,
We pecked and shivered and did what we could
In every season, rain snow or shine.
But once there was a time, they say,
Once in that time when we lived so far south
That the sun stood in the north of the sky,
Came a year when summer failed to return.

Spring didn't come nor summer after it,
It stayed bad cold though the days got long,
Cold and stormy through spring summer and fall,
Cold right through to the following winter
With never a chance to gather food.
And then it happened the next year too,
And the year after that, yes, never a summer,
No, nothing but winter, yes winter for TEN LONG YEARS.
And if it were not for the great salt sea
Everybody everywhere would have died and been dead
And no more people on this Mother Earth.

The grimness of Thorn's croak as he intoned these phrases was something to hear. This part he always said the same, standing upright and facing the sun.

Then he moved around again as he continued, listing with morbid gusto all the ways those poor summerless people had starved, the suffering and hurt, and all the strange things they had been forced to eat to survive. Thorn loved lists at all times, their threes of threes of threes, all the names he mouthed as if spitting out stones, tasting each name with evident satisfaction. So he spoke the lists in the hunger stories, naming foods of every kind, and of course right in the month when they themselves were down to their last bags of nuts and fat, and out every day checking empty traps and hunting snowshoe hares and ptarmigans, and eyeing the sky to the south hoping to see the ducks return. When the ducks came back the hunger months would be over, but that was usually late in the fifth month, sometimes the sixth. Until then they would be doling out their food by the mouthful, and feeling a little pinch in the gut all the time.

—You like to hurt us, Loon observed.

—Yes! That's what a shaman does! You tell the hunger stories when they're hungry. That's when you really have them seized in your grip. It's never easier to make them weep than when they're on the brink already. I've seen that many times. Now, tell me the list of what they had to eat during the ten-year winter.

Loon could never remember the poems except in the very moment he heard Thorn saying them, when he recognized them, even though he could not find them in himself. So now he sighed heavily to indicate his protest and said,

> We ate what lived through ten years of winter,
> Meaning whelks and clams and mussels and sea snails,
> Meaning seaweed and sandcrabs and limpets and eels.
> We ate fish when we could catch them,
> We ate shit when we couldn't.

Thorn nodded, his mind somewhere else already, which was good, as Loon's list was so woefully short compared to any of Thorn's. Loon scraped the earthblood to powder and stretched in the sun, feeling the sunlight penetrate his leg, where it began to make Crouch happier.

He saw that this was his life he was scraping, his fate. The world would scrape him down just like he scraped this chunk of rock. It would go on until Thorn died, and then the pile of granules that was Loon would replace him, and do all things Thorn had done, including scraping down some apprentice of his own; then he would die, and the apprentice would go on and do it to his apprentice, and on and on and on and on and on and on and on and on and on and on and on it would go, the earthblood and their own blood ground up together under the sun.

The thought of that, when held up against the memory of his wander, was like Crouch moving up into his chest and flexing there. Oh the pain suddenly squeezing his chest! How could it be? In the fourteen days of his wander, entire months and even years of life had sometimes crushed into every beat of his heart! Surely that was how one should always live, surely it would be better to make every fortnight a wander, and thereby live for scores and scores and scores of years.

Scrape the rock to powder, sitting in the sun.

Restless nights by the fire and in his bed, remembering his wander and wanting it back. Came to him the terrified eye of the deer he had killed, in the moment of her death. Was there ever a moment they ought not live in that fear, not quiver with a desperate hope to live on? That deer, how he had loved it. Loon loved to see deer almost as much as he loved to see horses. He kept the teeth of the deer he had killed around his neck, and kept her hide among his bed furs, though it had not been properly dried.

All the young men had necklaces crowded with the teeth of animals they had killed. Heather said it was always that way until the first time a necklace tooth punctured face or neck in some accident, and then the teeth went away. And it was true none of the older men wore them.

One morning Loon woke from a dream in which he had been sleeping with his deer in her lay-by. His chest and belly had been against her back, and his hard spurt was pressed against her fur; he had had his arm across her belly. Very slowly and delicately he had slipped his thumb up into her slightly damp and slippery kolby, moving very carefully, so that she still slept. He could have stayed like that forever, the two of them together, but with his spurt pronging so hard against the top of her rump, he had finally tried to thrust down and up into her; but in removing his thumb from her to make room for his spurt, he had woken her up, and she had looked over her shoulder and then leaped out of the lay-by with a single convulsion of her body. Looking back down at him with her giant wide-set brown eyes full of alarm and disbelief, she said to him, —You want too much, and then deered off through the forest, white rump flashing.

Awake, remembering the dream, the feel of her body, he felt bad. He wondered if he had managed to succeed in mating with her, if she would have gotten pregnant and given birth to a stag-headed person. Thorn had shown him a painting of one of those on a shaman cliff on the other side of the ice caps. Maybe that was what had happened out there to the west. He ached with love for the deer he had killed.

The light in the hour before sunrise. He woke to see the sky had gone gray, the eastern horizon a dull red topped by a band of yellow, and knowing day was coming he promptly fell back asleep, warmed by the thought. It was in those dawn sleeps that he dreamed most of the dreams he remembered. All through the night he dreamed, as he knew because whenever he happened to wake up it was from some busy effort in the dream world, which could range from lovely sexual encounters with girls or cats or horses or deer, to convoluted efforts to escape being eaten by cats or girls, sometimes even horses or deer.

If Thorn woke him in the morning, it was usually with the quiet question: —What are you dreaming? And as Loon pulled himself up into the waking world, he would look back into the dream world and tell Thorn what had been happening there. These were his best moments with the old man, who was more relaxed in the early morning, and would sit there nodding as he watched Loon's face, prodding him with questions, clearly interested, no matter how trivial or strange Loon's dreams got.

—The dream world is different, Thorn would remark when Loon finished. —It's writhing with our wishes and our fears, but we lack good judgment in that world, and that's why so many odd things happen. If you can, try to dream your dreams without any desires. Just watch. Except if you see a chance to fly in a dream, then fly. That's the first thing you should want. There's no point in wanting sex in a dream, because the people in dreams never really touch you. You might come but usually you won't, and if you do it's because you're fucking the ground. You can do that anytime. In dreams you should focus on flying, because you can't fly in this world, but you can in the dream world. And when you fly in the dream world, that gives you practice for when you fly in the spirit world. The spirit world and the dream world aren't the same, but they come together in the sky. The dream world is inside this world, the spirit world is outside it, but you can fly in both. And they meet, too, out beyond the sky. So you can fly back and forth. The spirit world is where all the worlds meet, that's why shamans go there. So when you're there you can be in all of them at once.

Loon would nod as if he followed this, still caught up in the dreams he had been dreaming, or simply falling back asleep. But with Thorn's questions he got better at remembering his dreams, and when he woke in the night, he could often look back into them without confusion, and even fall back asleep intending to resume where he had left off, and it would happen. And when he flew he knew it was good, and so tried to fly more, tried to enjoy it, even if in the dream he was flying for his life somehow, as it so often seemed to be.

Afternoons after painting they wandered back to camp gathering armfuls of firewood from the slope below the painted cliff. Heather had saved some midday nuts for Loon, and their winterover taste reminded him that summer was almost on them. He was running out of time for his leg to heal.

He limped around the riverbank to the beach under the Stone Bison, following Moss and Sage. They fanned through the shallows plucking new sedges for baskets. The tender white sedge bases in the mud broke off with a snap. Female stems were required by the basket weavers; male stems would be thrown back at you.

Sitting under the great stone span over the river, they processed the leaves so there would be less to carry home. Remove the outer leaves, peel off the inner ones, split the inner ones lengthwise in half by running a thumbnail down the midrib. Pieces not split right down the middle had to be discarded. Squeeze the half leaves between the fingers until they were flat and flexible. Be careful not to cut one's fingers on the sharp edges. Tie the processed leaves in bundles of a few score, then take them back to the weavers in camp, who would spread them to dry, dye, and ply. Their women made very fine baskets, very highly regarded at the eight eight festival. Heather had a lot to do with that, being good with dyes.

Heather's spirit animal was not actually the spider but the wolverine, and this was so right for her. Wolverines were very solitary, and demonstrated an intelligence and rancor second to no other animal. Same with Heather. She did have her good moods, and it was probable that wolverines did too, but in both cases it was a private feeling, because company itself dispelled it.

Although Heather was not completely predictable in that regard. Sometimes she would breathe in some of Thorn's pipe smoke and slump down by the fire baking herself like a cat, chatting with whoever was next to her. Sometimes when it was raining, in that heavy gray way that said nothing different was going to happen the rest of that day, it was she who would begin to sing some happy song, in a bright tone completely inappropriate to the moment; thus obviously sarcastic, sung to make fun of them; but as they all sat under the abri watching the rain piss down, eventually it could make you laugh.

Loon's spirit animal was the loon, of course. Apparently he had gotten so excited when he was a little baby, hearing a loon singing one night out on the river and waving his little arms, going red-faced as he tried to sing their weird songs with them, that they had given him his name that very night. And all his life since, at night when the loons talked to each other in their unearthly language, which outdid even the wolves' for liquid strangeness, Loon still felt a sizzle down his spine, and tears would start hotly in his eyes, and he would get up out of bed and stand at the edge of camp and cry back, ooping and looping in the hopes that the big gorgeous black-and-white birds with the red eyes would hear him, and understand that even though he didn't know their language, he loved them. And in fact sometimes they did hear him and reply to him, which Thorn said was one of the greatest honors a man could be given, as a loon's cry was the greatest voice a human could hear. How lucky to have your spirit animal sing back to you in the night, and fling your spirit up into the stars!

Crouch kept complaining, so it was best to stick around camp and pray to the sun for faster healing. Flex it in the sun bath over and over, ask Heather for one more rubbing. Rest it, she would say. Massage it, and feel exactly where it hurts, and how. Press starting from where it feels good, and very slowly press into the hurt. And keep it in the sun as much as you can.

So he went down to the riverside, where the sun blazed down and bounced off the water too. The sand was warm under him, and it felt like the sun was kissing him.

So when Sage showed up on the bank by herself, and sat by him, he tried kissing her too. He leaned toward her, and saw she saw what he was up to, and then saw the eager look come into her eye, and seeing that he fell in love with her. Again. So many times it had happened, ever since they were little children, and this time his spurt was hard, and she rubbed it as they kissed until he spurted, and in the moments of kissing, when he could remember to do it, he rubbed her little vixen until she too spasmed, scrunched over her pulsing belly and squeaking into his neck.

—Do you spurt inside? he asked.

—I clutch.

She grabbed his arm in her hand and squeezed rhythmically to show him, and at that his spurt started to harden again. Women bison and deer clutched like that when they wanted a bull or a stag, their kolbies pulsing pinkly. The way Loon and Sage would fit together was extremely clear: finger in glove, antler in cleft, heron and vixen. But Sage was very strict, having recently been red-dotted in the women's house. She would never allow his spurt into her. So they only kissed some more and then sat talking in the sun, feeling pleased and generous. The glitter of the current off the river sparkled in his eyes and he could feel himself glowing in his afterglow. He knew he was healing fast. Even Crouch was healing.

—Did you hear Schist is going to give some of our food to the Lions?

—No!

—He is. Bluejay is really mad at him. He says there's enough, but he didn't ask anyone else about it, he just did it.

—But we're down to eating ten nuts a day!

—I know. Bluejay and Thunder are really mad at him. His sister Moony married into the Lions, they say it's all because of her, that he doesn't care about us.

—The ducks better come on time.

—No lie. If they don't they'll be cooking him over their fire.

And they laughed. The ducks would come.

So that was good, but meanwhile his friends were going out hunting, and he couldn't go with them, not yet. He would make up for it later.

But he could see that Hawk was growing fast. At the end of almost every hunt Hawk came back with something, even now in the hunger month. He was getting good at it. When they were kids, Loon had been better than him at all the things it took to be a good hunter. They had raced and chased together, played and wrestled, threw rocks and little javelins they made, and he knew he had been better at these things because they tried them so many times. Hawk knew it too. But now, maybe not. Now Hawk was broad-shouldered and lean around the waist now that all his fat was gone; he stood tall and had a fine head with tightly curled hair and a squarish set of teeth, very handsome. Very strong and graceful.

Then one night across the fire he saw Hawk and Sage slip away in the night, and his throat went tight and his feet cold. Well, she wouldn't let Hawk do very much either. Still, it meant what it meant. He would have to fool around with Ducky and make Sage jealous too. Little looks, bad jokes, sharing food or braiding hair.

Stuck in camp, he helped Heather and Bluejay make shoes. This was meticulous work, and Loon plied the bone needle slowly, following Heather's awl punches, which were all at the same angle and distance from each other, in a curving line that would sew together the bearskin bottoms and the deerskin uppers.

One day when Bluejay wasn't around, Loon muttered something about Sage going off with Hawk.

—So what's your problem? Heather asked.

—I guess I'm jealous.

—Jealousy is when you don't want someone else to have what you have. Envy is when you want something that someone else does have. So it sounds like you're feeling envious rather than jealous. Because Sage is not yours.

—It doesn't matter what you call it, Loon muttered unhappily.

—Yes it does. You'd best know all the words and what they mean, or else your thinking will just be mush.

Heather returned their attention to the shoes. She thought marmot fur uppers were worth trying for winter boots. She liked to try out new things that occurred to her. She made things backwards sometimes, especially for Thorn. She seldom spoke directly to

Thorn, and looked at him as she would look at a hyena or one of the other worthless animals.

He would glare back at her as if looking at a wolverine.

Now when he walked past she grinned horribly at him and said, —Here, unspeakable one, have this gift from me!

It was a pair of shoes made of porcupine skin. Porcupine mothers had the easiest births of all, so little toy porcupines were slipped carefully down the front of a pregnant girl's dress for good luck. Now Heather had made shoes of a porcupine's skin, with the smooth side outward and all the needles pointing into the foot. They were finished, so had to have taken a fist or two of work, and yet completely useless except for this moment of her sharp laughter.

—All yours! she cried to Thorn. —May they lend wings to your travels!

Thorn glared at her, then took the shoes from her and looked inside them. —Wait, I see something, he said. —You made your vixen into shoes for me!

He fingered one of the bear claws on his necklace and thrust it in and out of the shoe in a copulatory manner. —That was us, he said, and threw the shoes back at her.

—At least you got the size of your prick right, she said as she dodged the shoes.

—I was just keeping it proportionate, since you shrank your mammoth kolby as much as you did.

And they glared at each other before Thorn stalked away.

Another morning in the sun, grinding earthblood. Thorn sitting nearby, sewing something or other. When not biting off ends of the sinews, his face a mere thumb away from the hides as he needled them, he talked as always. From time to time he told Loon to recite one of the stories he was supposed to know.

—Start with the seasons to get your mind going. You've known that one since before you had a name.

Or not known it. Loon sighed and tried:

In autumn we eat till the birds go away,
And dance in the light of the moon.
In winter we sleep and wait for spring,
And watch for the turn of the stars.
In spring we starve till the birds come back,
And pray for the heat of the sun.
In summer we dance at the festivals,
And lie in twos on the ground.

—No no, Thorn said. —It's,

In summer we dance at festival,
And lay our bones in the ground.

—Why would you get that part wrong, of all things? Also, it's

In winter we sleep and watch for spring
In the turn of the nighttime stars.

—Try it again.

Loon repeated it, keeping it the way he had said it the first time. —Summer is when people lie in twos, he pointed out. —I like it better that way.

—But that's not the way it goes!

—I've heard it that way lots of times.

Thorn gave up and went back to talking to himself. —Ah, see how this shirt I'm wearing is something I made the year before last, it was in the ninth month and we were back home, and I was sitting right in this very spot. So I can know an action from the past. And here it is now. And when I come back here next summer, the shirt will be here again. So now is now, but in this now there is some mix of the past and future, right there inside things, and blowing around in our thoughts. Everything keeps rolling around. Because there will be a now next year at this same day of the year. Nineteenth day of the fifth month. We know that. So every day is the birthday of all the days in the years to come that are this day.

—I don't understand you, Loon said. —Have I got enough powder here yet?

—No, Thorn said without looking. —Of course you understand me. Because I'm talking to the you in you that is the birthday of the yous that will follow. So if you understand me then, you understand me now. By then I'll be dead and just a white point in the night sky. I'll wolf your heels, boy, like Fools the Wolves wolfs the Firestarter.

—So I'm going to be the Firestarter? I thought Firestarter was Firestarter.

—I'm not talking to the you that is here right now, you are too insolent.

—Just tell me how to etch a curve like that bison's neck you did. How do you get the line to curve so smoothly when it's stone cutting stone?

—It's not stone cutting stone, it's flint cutting whitestone, and that's how. You chisel it out grain by grain. Just keep your eye on the line you want, and make it happen.

—So you have to see it before it's there, is that it? No wonder you need birthdays from the future.

—Well exactly. See, you did understand me.

—No. Not at all. Show me how to make the line. Show me how to start it.

—Let your future self show you.

—Is that why you keep your yearsticks? To tell your future time what you were actually doing when you did it?

—Yes, exactly.

—But that's silly. Stupid. Backwards.

—That's why I'm the shaman and you're not.

Thorn was very insistent about the importance of his yearsticks. Every morning he took one of the obsidian blades that had been glued into sticks to make fine cutters, and cut a line in his yearstick, which was always a nice piece of river-worn oak driftwood. On every new moon day, he cut a loop on the top of the line marking that day. At the eight eight festival he would get together with the other shamans, a very crazy and obnoxious gathering, and during the days they would do their corroborations. Thorn already had Loon marking a yearstick of his own, supposedly separate from Thorn's, but as Thorn never forgot and Loon sometimes did, it was not a very happy arrangement. Thorn thought that Heather should join them in doing it, to provide a third so they could corroborate within the pack, but she declined to do it. To Loon the yearsticks resembled many of Heather's other pursuits, but she didn't like doing anything that would please Thorn, so it didn't happen. And so Loon was always wrong, and if by chance he wasn't the one who was wrong, then they would really have problems when it came time for the corroboree.

—I don't think Firestarter is starting a fire, Loon said. —I think that's his antler pronging down at us. He's on his back trying to mate with Mother Earth, and he can't get close enough, and the Spurtmilk came from him.

—But the Spurtmilk is in the summer sky, Thorn pointed out.

—That's right, he came so hard that his spurtmilk flew right around into summer.

Thorn laughed in a way he had never laughed at Loon before, truly amused.

—I don't think so, he said at last, shaking his head. —The firestick is just at the right angle. And then there's the base too. Those stars can't be his nuts, they're too far apart.

—Those are his hip bones, Loon explained.

Again Thorn laughed. —All right, good, he said. —A new story to tell.

The eyes speak what the tongue can't say. Force begets resistance. Even a mouse has anger. After dark every cat is a lion. In spring Mother Earth is pregnant, in summer she gives birth. Children are the true human beings. The good-looking boy may just be good in the face. Danger comes without warning. Every fire is the same size when it starts.

Such an itch for something different to happen. How he wanted his wander back. The ducks kept not showing up, and Thunder and Bluejay began to roast Schist daily for giving away some of their food to the Lion pack. Schist ignored them, his face hard. He turned his back on them and walked away. No one got to complain to him about their food, even though they were the ones feeling the pinch in their guts.

Eventually Loon just had to go back out on the hunt again, Crouch or no Crouch.

—You'll be all right, I think, Heather said doubtfully. —If not just come back. You can't push the river. Hurry the break-up and bring on a flood. So be careful. Let your good leg carry you. If you can do it at all, it will be good for you. You need to get out there for it to go completely away.

So he went off with Hawk and Moss and they went upstream, over the low ridge between Loop Meadow and the confluence where the Ordech ran into the Urdecha.

Hawk and Moss were happy to have him back with them on the hunt, and after asking once or twice about his leg they stopped mentioning it, as being an unwelcome reminder. This was the usual courtesy among men on the hunt. They went neither slower nor faster than normal, and when they came to Mother Muskrat Meadow on the Ordech, they went silent and took the west ridgeline around it, single file and heads down. Loon focused on the ground, and on dancing over it in a way where good leg carried bad. His javelin served as Prong had in his wander, and its cupped back end took a little beating; hopefully it would still fit onto his spear thrower cleanly when the time came.

Best not to jam it down onto rocks, and to hit the ground cleanly with the whole rim of the cup. Ah yes, it was going to work. His friends were happy and he was happy.

Above the meadow they came on some of Mother Muskrat's children, splashing in the inlet turn. Their black heads swam around in the water, their whiskers cutting little curls in the sides of the nose wave. If they thought the three young men were interested in them, they would dive and take refuge in a muskrat house emerging from the water near the far bank. Possibly the humans could have descended behind trees close enough to throw a javelin, but it would be a long throw. Better to remember and come back and set a trap underwater. They wanted something bigger anyway.

Bigger, they said to each other, and hiked onto the upland at the top of the Ordech saying bigger, bigger, bigger. And today luck was with them; the hunger month was almost over, and some of Mother Earth's creatures were in trouble. On the rim of the upland stood an elg, thin under its enormous splayed antlers, looking out of place on the broad moor, where you could see so far that the Ice Tits were visible over the horizon to the west.

The three hunters had frozen on seeing this elg, and after that they moved without moving, flowing like snakes into a alder brake that filled a wet seam in the moor. Inside the brake they had to move over the alder branches without moving any of them enough to squeak, or even quiver. The elg themselves were unexpectedly good at this complicated procedure, despite their immense size, so it would be a coup to use the method to creep up on one. And it would also be a coup to bring back to camp that much meat and hide. Indeed they might have to make two trips home with it all, and hope for the best concerning what got left behind.

But this was getting ahead of the game. For now they had to flow through the brake toward the elg without revealing themselves to it. Elgs didn't have much of a nose, and the hunters were downwind of it. So for a long time they slithered through the net of alder branches, making sure their javelins never got hung up. Sometimes finding a spear's way was harder than getting through oneself. Some of the thorny vines that grew under alder were so intensely thorny that they could pass over one's skin without pricking it at any point, the many tips making a surface of sorts. If one could pass these without snagging...but so often they snagged. One had to accept the poisoned little scraping and slip on, indomitable as an otter.

Loon came to the edge of the brake, and through the last net of branches saw the elg still where it had been. Its hide was unbroken, free of sores on the back, and yet it was gaunt. Probably sick, or old. It would still be well worth bringing back. Hawk and Moss appeared to his left and right, and they had a little eye conference. The problem was clear: how to get the javelins deployed on their spear throwers, and then throw them, without revealing themselves to the elg. It wouldn't be possible unless it had its back to them, in which case it would be hard to kill with javelins. If they hit it and then it ran off, they would lose their spears to it. So, two of them should throw, hope to wound it, and the third chase it and rush in for a more direct throw or thrust. Hawk wanted that part, so Loon and Moss twisted and contorted until they had their javelins cupped on their throwers, and aimed. Loon eyed his throw space, got ready to throw; the convulsive jerk would have to be just right. Looking into each other's eyes one last time with a mad glee of anticipation, they counted it out with their moving lips—one, two, three, throw!

Hawk immediately burst out onto the moor and ran toward the elg, which was trotting away, both spears hanging from his right haunch. So they had both hit him, but now they had to get him. Loon and Moss crawled out of the brake and followed Hawk, who was chasing down the elg with his javelin held in his right hand just over his right shoulder, ready to throw. It would take a thrust to the gut to bring him down, so Hawk would have to outrun it, and to Loon's surprise he was actually doing that, running faster than Loon had ever seen any human run.

Then the elg suddenly stopped and kicked back at Hawk, who had to tuck and roll over his spear, then stop on one knee and thrust the tip up into the exposed gut and roll away, dodging a kick of the elg's foreleg. That too missed, and Hawk had stuck him deeply in the gut. For a time the beast stood there, breathing heavily and bleeding from Hawk's puncture, which was so close to the ribs that it might have hit a lung.

—Die brother die, they implored it, looking around for rocks of the right size to make a useful blow to the head. It might also be possible to withdraw one of their spears from the right haunch, but that would risk another vicious kick, and backward rear leg kicks were dangerous. And the last kick is the worst.

There were rocks ready to hand almost everywhere on the moor, and as soon as they all three had both hands full, they threw six rocks in a flurry, and Loon's first throw caught the elg right on the ear, causing him to bellow and turn as if to charge, but this was too much for him. He stood there quivering and bleeding more than ever from the gut stick, as the spear was dragging on the ground. Moss dashed around him like a mink and darted in to pull out one of the spears from his haunch. The elg did indeed kick at him, but feebly. Moss got his spear out and prodded briefly to spur another weak kick, and after Moss ducked away from that he came back in with the returning leg and stabbed deep at the gut just in front of the haunch, twisting it at the end of the thrust and then leaping back to avoid another kick. It was just like when they had fought as kids: Moss was a counterpuncher.

The elg began to bleed from the mouth and nose, which meant one of them had punctured a lung. They cheered as the elg went to his knees and snorted out his last breaths. —Ha! they shouted, slapping each other with a huge delight. —Thank you brother! they shouted at the dying beast.

The elg crashed onto his side and gurgled his last breaths. When he was gone they could tell; there was always a noticeable difference when the spirit departed a living thing. Immediately it was as inert as a stone. The spirits sometimes stayed nearby, and there were certain proprieties and taboos about eating creatures too soon after they had died, just to respect these hovering spirits. But the bodies were empty. And none of the taboos obtained when it came to getting meat back to camp before scavengers arrived to complicate things. Indeed this was a time to hurry.

They had to work hard to cut up such a big brother. Their spear tips could be used as cutters, and though they weren't as good as real meat blades, they were immensely better than the choprock Loon had used to break down his deer. Even so it was hard sweaty work, and they huffed and puffed as they speared the joints apart and cut hard at the ligaments.

They cut the haunches entirely away and then gutted the body, then cut the head and neck off just in front of the forelegs. The head would be the most awkward of the three pieces they wanted to carry back to camp.

As they were working the sun went down and quickly darkness fell, as always on the moors of the upland. And they were covered with elg blood. So they were not comfortable being out there, as several wolf packs regularly passed by here. The closest pack to their camp ran a ten-day circuit around its land, and had not been seen for most of a fortnight, so they were due back anytime.

When the waning half moon rose they hefted their pieces of the elg and began to run toward the mouth of the Ordech. They traded the elg parts during brief rests, to alter the kind of load they had to carry. It had already been a long day and night, and at a certain point Loon felt the weariness in his thighs and calves, and all through him. He had to limp pretty hard to keep his bad leg quiet. He breathed deep and fast, working to call up his second wind. There was a period between when you called for the second wind and it came, when you felt like shit and simply had to bear down and slog through the weakness; that bearing down was the call for the second wind, and the sign that it was on its way. And as often happened, when the second wind came he forgot he had ever been tired at all; the night could go on for as long as it wanted, it didn't matter. He was eating his own body at that point, Heather said, so there was food enough for a long haul.

But Loon had to admit, as the night wore on, that his bad leg was bad. He also had a good one, however, and because the good leg was so good, he could do it; he could favor the bad leg and in time it would get better. So tonight, the trick was to see how well he could get along on the good leg, and not hurt the bad leg further in this run home.

They came into camp around a fist before dawn, and most of the pack woke up and cheered them, and built up the fire and ate a little roasted meat, while breaking down the elg into parts that would preserve better. Hawk and Moss and Loon were congratulated and cosseted as they told the story of the hunt, and Loon didn't say anything about his leg, but he couldn't help protecting it around the fire, and both Heather and Thorn saw it, and glared at each other as if each thought it was the other's fault. It almost made Loon laugh, but he was too worried to laugh.

The next day Loon looked down at his body and pinched the skin over his hip bones. The lobs of fat that had been there through the winter were completely gone. His skin was the same brown as certain horses' manes, a particular brown lighter than most of his pack's skin color. People said he had some lunkhead in him, that that was why he was so stupid. There was no fat in the ring around his belly button either. He couldn't have packed on much more fat last fall or it would have slowed him down. Some men got so that they almost looked pregnant, but of course they never really did, because they carried the weight low and looked like dropstones in the river, whereas women carried their kids right under their ribs and looked beautiful. It was a stark contrast, and sometimes struck Loon's eye very strongly when he saw a bag-bellied old man; which was rare, as usually he only had eyes for the women. Men he evaluated with the same dispassion he gave to himself; how was that one doing, how was his body faring in the daily struggle? Not bodies but motions he admired in men, in the way he would admire his own leaps and jumps when they surprised him, coming so fast he could only witness them after the fact, as memories. Things happened so fast he could only remember them. When he saw the other men move like that it was beautiful. They were capable creatures, tough animals among the other animals. They could outlast any animal in a long chase, and that said a lot.

But the women—the women were beautiful. They were as beautiful as horses. Their hair, either braided or flying free from their heads, looked like manes. They tossed their manes like horses, they worked in groups and chattered like squirrels and looked at you; they looked at you, they looked at everything with a most piercing glance. They were the most curious animals of all, even more than their sisters fox and cat. They could spear you with a look.

There was a grove with some soap trees scattered among the spruces, just over the pass at the head of Upper Valley, in the north-trending canyon they called the Lir. Loon spent some days after their hunt walking slowly over there and cutting off some straight soap-tree branches. It was a hard wood, but filling the core of new shoots was a soft pulp that could be hollowed out. The hollow stick that remained could be used as a dart blower, or made into a flute. Other pieces could be split into four lengths, and each quarter polished and its ends sharpened and fire-hardened and polished again, and the result be two pair of knitting needles, one for Heather, the other for Sage.

Doing that took a few days of sitting in the sun, back against a warm boulder, talking with the kids and eating elg steaks and elg head stew. The moon was almost gone, and they worked by firelight on the things they were going to take to the eight eight festival. The soap-tree leaves he had brought back with him were mashed in a log trough, and on the sunniest mornings they washed their clothes in the foamy water. After that the smell of spring cleaning was in the air, and they knew their summer trek and then the eight eight were coming soon. The hungry month would end, the ducks would be here any day. Their remaining nuts had their overwinter flavor worse than ever, but they were still there at the bottom of their bags. Schist could have pointed this out to the complainers, but that was not his style. Besides, it wasn't over yet. Until the ducks came out of the south he would definitely not be telling anyone I told you so. When they came, the hard care in his face would finally relax, replaced by a satisfied gleam in the eye, almost a smile.

Thorn showed Loon where to cut the holes to make a flute sound right, and how to blow in the upper end of it to make the notes. After that Loon was like a baby owl hooting, or like a jay squawking if he blew too hard. He would have liked to sound like a loon, but the sounds broke differently inside the flute. Every night in his bed he played. After half a fortnight or so he could make the notes reliably. He wanted to play it inside their cave.

They went out on the hunt again, looking for more animals suffering the long hunger month, in a larger group that included Spear-thrower and Nevermind and Thorn. Thorn always brought up the rear, but was smart about the animals, and interesting to have along.

Loon thought he might be out there as a drag on the group to help Loon's leg, but of course he would never admit to that, and Loon didn't show any sign that he suspected it.

They killed an old bison hiding alone in a brake, and were near the end of the task of breaking it apart for carrying, and had buried its bones and guts in the deepest part of the creek, and jumped in upstream themselves to wash up, when they started teasing Nevermind about his recent marriage to Rose, a good-looking eagle girl from the Lion pack. Moss made one of the usual cracks about getting less of the vixen after marriage than before, and Nevermind parried by claiming he was getting more than ever. When they all laughed disbelievingly at this he got huffy and said that when he wanted it he took it. She didn't really mind.

A dubious silence followed this assertion. —And how did you find out this would work? Thorn asked.

Nevermind was nervous answering Thorn about a matter like this, but his friends were around him listening, so he said, —Because I just did it! She said no one night when I wanted to, and I said, Oh no you don't, and made her. After a while she liked it.

Another silence.

Finally Thorn said, —Why would you be so stupid? Now you've given her all the power in your marriage, don't you see?

—What do you mean? Nevermind asked, sullen and offended.

—You have to do what she tells you now, Thorn explained, —or she'll tell the other women what you did. And if she does that, they'll kill you. So now she has all the power between you.

—The women can't kill me.

—Of course they can, Thorn said. He stared at Nevermind with his chin tucked back into his neck, miming a look of exaggerated astonishment. The younger men all stared at him. He said, —How could you say such an ignorant thing? They cook your food and put what they want in it. They give you life they give you death. They bleed and they make you bleed. Talk about the monthlies, they can make you bleed daily, bleed from your pizzle and your asshole and your ears and your nose, even your eyes. Maybe it's poison in your food, maybe just from the way they look at you. After a bit of that look you'll wish you'd never been born. You'll jump off the cliff into the gorge to be out of your misery. That's the kind of power they have. They have the sky behind their eyes, you can see it when they look at you. So now you have to do just what Rose says, or she'll tell them, and then you're a dead man. I'm surprised you would give over that kind of power to anyone, especially just to get a spurt. You could have done it yourself, or just been polite and waited your turn. Even husbands only get their turn.

—How would you know? Nevermind asked, trying his best to fend off the old man.

Thorn waved this weak riposte aside. —I was married. Back in the dream time, before you boys were even born. Now I don't have that burden or that blanket. You should enjoy it while you have it, be thankful. Mother Earth speaks through those silly girls. I'm surprised you weren't taught that, growing up in this pack. Mama mia, if Heather ever hears of this! Shit. Really, the way it is now, any of us could get you killed with a word to the old hag. So you are the weakest lunkhead in the whole pack.

With that Thorn hefted his chunk of the bison meat and headed toward home. The others followed, at first subdued, then enjoying the prospect of bringing such a load back to camp. Even Nevermind cheered up; he was well named. And killer goddesses or not, their women would be pleased to see this much meat, and the cooking and smoking and drying would go on long into the night. Some of the young hunters would give meat to young women who didn't have it, and some of those would give them a spurt in return, that was just the way it was. So in the slant light of late afternoon they got more cheerful, and ran back to camp dancing with their own long shadows, singing a particularly rude song to irritate Thorn, who after his outburst had retreated to wolverine silence, surly and brow-furrowed. Then as they came over the last low pass and dropped into camp, they heard the women singing the sunset song. And their hearts were filled with a fearful joy.

The wolverine nearby lived under a boulder in a south-facing tilt of boulders overlooking the river. His home was warm and dry, and over the years had been made into a comfortable nest of a home. It had four entrances, uphill, downhill, upstream, and downstream.

No one bothered the wolverine. This was not because of his size but because of his ferocity. Besides which, if you did manage to kill him without getting killed yourself, his flesh was fatless and tough as roots. He wasn't worth the trouble. Only very hungry wolves or lions would even consider it.

So wolverine walked the gorge by day, or under the moon when it was big, looking around for food. Berries were just green dots now, but he ate a few just to get their taste to start the day. Berries in the morning and meat in the evening, this was wolverine's routine. Bears were big fools who bumbled along eating whatever they found, they didn't bother with a plan. Wolverines had plans. This one was going to walk his big walk. He would go down the river gorge, up the second loop creek, up that creek's left fork, and then over the pass at the top of the fork, and down the first loop to the river gorge again, after which a short stroll would bring him back to his boulder.

This circuit provided his food and allowed him to view his territory. Of all the animals he shared it with, all the cats, raccoons, weasels, foxes, bears, horses, porcupines, beavers, muskrats, ibex, chamois, elg, skelk, rhinos, hyenas, lions, leopards, mammoths, squirrels, and all the rest of the various beasts, the pack of humans was by far the most dangerous, to him as to everyone else. But they were also the most interesting. Not interesting enough to take him near their camp, but he knew all their traps and snares, although it was true he had to keep sniffing out new ones, which they kept making because of the other animals they caught. He kept his distance. Regularly, however, he would walk the gorge wall at a part that allowed him to look down onto their warren, and sometimes he tracked them when they left it. As with all pack animals, they were not as dangerous on their own as they were in groups. A single one would avoid him on sight, unless it was a young male with a spear, in which case the wolverine definitely kept his distance. The rest were just as happy to keep their distance from him. No one bothers wolverine.

On this morning, near the ridge at the top of second loop's west fork, he was surprised to hear a small moan. He stopped and sniffed, then smelled one of the long-headed humans, who were mostly heavier and slower than the ones from the warren, and mostly lived toward the sunset, except for some solitaries. This one's arm emerged from a thicket as if reaching for him, and wolverine hopped upslope, landing on all four paws in his usual way, ready to bite and claw. But it was not necessary. The human male held only a loop of birch bark in his long-fingered hand. His blunt flat claws were useless compared to wolverine's. The arm hung there out of the thicket forlornly. Behind it, through the leaves of the brush, he could see the human's eyes looking at him, watery and sad. It was hurt. In a day or two it might be an easy meal. Trying to trap a wolverine with birch bark: it was desperate. Its wound smelled bad.

The human whistled a perfect imitation of a female wolverine's hello. Wolverine, startled at first, then impressed, stepped closer to see if the human would do it again. He did: a truly inviting hello. The long-headed humans were really good vocal mimics, wolverine had heard that before. Now this one shifted into a whistle like a lark's, liquid and burbling. Again very impressive. Wolverine sat up on his haunches like a big marmot, settling in to hear more.

The human whistled and hummed for quite some time, giving wolverine the calls of several birds and animals—even the wet smack of a beaver tail on the water.

Finally it quit.

Wolverine got up and went on his way, wondering what would become of the human, and if it would be worth returning on the following day before moving on in his big walk. Humans tasted strange, but that made for an interesting change. The long-headed sunset people were exceptionally dense and heavy in their meat.

Well, he could decide the next morning, depending on hunger, weather, the little sprain in his right foreclaw. On whim.

But then he came on a female human he knew. He smelled her before he saw her, and that was enough to be sure. Old female often out alone, now wandering upslope with a basket hung over one arm. Herb woman; no one else in the forest smelled like her.

Today she appeared to be interested in the new mushrooms. First mushrooms were thin and bland. She fell to her knees in front of them and plucked them up and sniffed them, then either put them in her basket or dropped them. She got up by putting a hand down on the grass and shoving herself up, like a three-legged thing. No other creature did this.

When she straightened she saw him and raised her basket above her head, then pulled up her dress and displayed her sex to him. This was her usual hello. Wolverine stopped and raised his head to sniff hard two or three times, which always made her laugh. She put down her dress and looked around the hillside above her, confident that wolverine would go on his way. And usually he would have. He had seen this human kill a bobcat that was leaping at her by putting a hollow stick to her mouth and blowing something into the cat's face; the cat had run off howling, and over the next hill died, writhing and frothing from the mouth. Wolverine had been afraid to eat it.

So he left this human alone. When they happened to pass each other in the forest, they always said their brief hellos, and she laughed, and that was that. But today wolverine was still thinking of the male human who could sound like so many other animals, and he thought the herb woman would be interested to know about him. So he stood up on his rear legs like a marmot again, and caught her eye, and then jerked his head toward the pass, just a short stroll above them.

The woman laughed at this and said something agreeable. Wolverine led her up the slope of the forest to the pass, ignoring the switchbacks that she used, but always making sure she could see him. When she reached the pass he whistled her down the western slope, which was thick with trees, to the little copse holding the longhead. When he saw that she had seen this person in the thicket, whose eyes were round at the sight of his return, he veered back up the slope, working his away around her. For a moment he tarried, peering down to see how the two humans were getting along. They were whistling back and forth in a friendly manner. Wolverine strolled back up to the pass and wabbled off on his way.

Heather came into camp and asked Thorn and Loon and Hawk and Moss to help her, that she was treating a wounded old one over Lower Upper Pass.

She didn't want the old one moved into their camp, she told them. Everyone was relieved to hear that, because she had brought all kinds of wounded creatures into camp before, which was why her nest was located out on the edge away from the fire. This time she just wanted their help getting this wounded old one into a protected spot.

What that turned out to mean was building a shelter right over him, because he was too hurt to be moved. So they wove a spruce shelter around and over him, while he stared at the ground and occasionally glanced at them, sometimes emitting a cooing whistle.

—We say, thank you, Heather told him.

—Tank oo, he said.

Weaving the spruce branches into position took them a while, and during that time Heather sat Loon down beside her to help her care for the old one.

He was broad-shouldered and squat. Once he had been strong, but now he was emaciated. It gave Loon a quease of disgust to be so close to him. He smelled like an old one, and had that old face, a real saiga of a face, distended and foolish. His skin was mushroom pale, so much lighter than normal skin that it apparently was translucent, as Loon could see blue veins under his pale skin. This was truly disgusting. One or both of his legs was badly hurt. His coat was roughly sewn, his fur skirt made of a fur Loon couldn't identify. His shoes were simple bearskin wraps.

He did not meet their eyes, but while looking at the ground, glanced up at them from time to time. He had a huge beak of a nose, big furry eyebrows, and a forehead that receded to a balding head, somewhat like Thorn's but much longer and paler. His ugly face, which might have somewhat resembled a beaver's if it were not for the great nose, held an expression attentive, intelligent, concerned. In a speechless face the eyes do all the talking. What these eyes said was clear

enough: this old one was sick and in trouble, but trying to be hope-
ful about their intentions.

They finished building the shelter over him. He whistled and
clicked and hummed at them, and Heather said reassuring things in
return, and even whistled something he appeared to understand, one
of his words it seemed. Immediately he whistled away at Heather,
but she shook her head and repeated a few low warbles, and words in
their language. Eat, drink.

—Tank oo, he said.

After that Heather sent the boys up to guard him and give him some
of the worst overwintered nuts, and she worked her medicine on one
of his legs. It was mostly a matter of rest, she told Loon. —Injury needs
rest, you can't take things too fast. Healing happens, but it takes time.
So you have to give it time. A moon and fortnight for that hurt you
had, and him too.

She appeared to whistle a similar message to the old one, for he
did lie around for most of a moon, eating and drinking what Heather
and Loon brought him. She taught him a number of words in that
time, but the one she said the most was, —Slowly, slowly, with her
hands and movements illustrating what she meant by it. He nodded
from the waist when assenting to her, and with a visible effort said,
—So-ly, so-ly.

When he was finally getting around on his feet pretty well, he
came to her one morning after dawn and held her hand in both of
his, whistled briefly, and took off toward Lower Upper Pass. After
that they saw him from time to time in the distance, in the way they
occasionally spotted other local woodsmen, who mostly tried never
to be seen, but sometimes got careless. And from time to time there
was an offering of snow hare or baby goat, or flowers, left in front of
Heather's nest. And she left things out there near the old one's broken
shelter as well, in the same way that she left things out for her cat.

Because Loon slept near Heather and helped her, he got more of
a chance to see the old one than many of the group; and because
he went out with Thorn, or on Thorn's behalf, to gather chunks of

earthblood from the spot under Northerly ridge called the Giants' Knapsite he continued to see the old one out on the land. The old one was like a woodsman, it seemed: cut off from his pack, if he had ever had one. He bumbled through his rounds like a bear, setting traps for little animals and birds, eating berries and grass seed along the way. He moved strangely, and his smell was as if a little fermented. His beard was like a saiga's beard, straggling under his chin, providing a point to balance the massive shelf of his eyebrows. His beaky nose had perhaps been smashed to the side at some point. His hair was held back by a leather band, and hung down freely over his shoulders. He wore a fur cape all the time, and now went barefoot, as if his bearskin shoes had worn out and he could not make new ones.

Thorn believed one could not become a good engraver without learning to make good tools. A good straight burin, some good blades, and a nicely edged scraper made all the difference. When it was rock against rock, you wanted your cutter as hard and sharp as possible.

So they sat in the sun and hit blocks of flint with choprocks of granite and schist.

Thorn stretched like a cat in the sun, and said, —Wait, I see something.

—Not another one of your riddles.

—They are not my riddles. They are the world's riddles. Listen:

Silent my clothes when I walk on ground
Or stay at home or cross a stream.
Sometimes my life and the lift of the wind
Raise me above the place where people walk
And then the power of clouds carries me far
Above the human world and my clothes
Loudly echo and send forth a song.
They clearly sing when I am not in touch
With earth or water but a flying spirit.
Now find out what I am.

—You are the second wind, Loon said, thinking of his recent night return from the hunt with Hawk and Moss, and pleased to have seen the answer so readily.

Thorn laughed.

—What, aren't I right?

Thorn tipped his head left then right, which was his sign for yes and no. —It's like the second wind, he allowed, —but you think small.

—The second wind is never small, Loon objected.

People said Thorn had been a very strong hunter in his youth, but Loon had not seen it. Maybe he had forgotten what the second wind felt like when it came into you.

—Granted, Thorn allowed. —The second wind is big. But it's even bigger than that.

—I'll think about it.

—And smaller too, don't forget. Most boys posed that riddle say it's about a grasshopper. And he laughed at the look on Loon's face.

Thorn spent a lot of his mornings taking care of the kids on the flat at the east end of camp, where the trees gave them a mix of sun and shade. He was much different with the little ones than he was with adults. He sat among them playing with their toys and goofing around, while also running them through their lessons. —They're so much easier than you, he would say to Heather and Loon.

—Children are the true human beings, Heather intoned, whether sarcastic or not Loon could not tell.

—Well, it's true. They're not old enough to have problems. I'm so tired of you all and your problems. Men and women are just big bags of problems.

—You should know, Heather said.

—Indeed I should, watching you and all the rest. My time is much better used with the kids.

—A pinch of mother is worth a pack of shaman, Heather reminded him.

Thorn only waved her away with the back of his hand.

But with the kids in the morning sun it was different.

—Wait, I see something: little dots in the distance.

—The birds are coming back! the kids would say.

—That's right. Our summer friends. We'll see that again real soon. But wait, I see something: little wood crumbs falling out of a tree.

—The grouse is up there eating, one of them said. If just one of them spoke up, it was usually Thunder's daughter Starry.

—That's right. Some people call them rock pounders because of the funny whirr they make when they run. You've heard that sound. On the coldest nights they sleep under a blanket of snow. You can walk around on a snowy morning and surprise them sometimes, catch one for breakfast. But you have to be fast.

The kids assured him they were fast, and he agreed.

—Wait, I see something: tiny bits of charcoal scattered on the snow.

Silence.

—No? It's one of the white-in-winters. The beaks of ptarmigans. They're so white in the winter, all you can see is their beaks. It looks funny. Wait, I see something: we are wide open in the bushes.

Again silence.

—Another white-in-winter! It's the eyes of the snowshoe hare. They watch you when they're hiding, and their eyes are the only part of them you can see. How about this; wait, I see something: a bit of charred wood waving around in the air.

—Same again! Starry said triumphantly. —The ermine's tail in winter.

—Very good! And then wait, I see something more: far away yonder, a fire flash comes down.

—Fox in the summer, Starry declared.

Thorn tousled her head. —You're going to be a handful, kid. All right, last one. Wait, I see that the river is tearing away things around me.

—Is it you? Starry asked, eyes round.

Thorn laughed. —Yes, you bad girl. But it can be an island too. But we're all islands.

And they decided to make a toy village on a puddle island and then drown it all in a terrible flood from a bucket. They all loved that game, Thorn most of all.

Out with Sage, at the bog where the Edich dropped into the Urdecha, to collect herbs for Heather.

Sage filled her basket slowly, distracted by thoughts of her own. She had long legs, and the hair on them was a fine black down, nearly invisible against her dark skin. Her shirt was loose, and when she bent over to pick a sprig of mint or thyme her breasts were revealed, swinging together like udders. Loon hummed happily and begged a kiss, but she wasn't in the mood. She picked green moss for the two babies' diapers, but it was also for the next full moon, when the women's house was crowded, and so Loon pretended not to notice. Full moon was an odd time, because so many women would retire to their shelter and do things on their own, while at the same time the young men gulped down berry mash and went out to see things in the full moon's pale but revealing light. In other packs it wasn't like that; in some, most women bled at new moon, and huddled together in the starry nights around the fire, waiting it out. Either way they would need a lot of dried moss.

They watched a mother porcupine lead four little balls of needles across a patch of open ground. Bears and porcupines were cousins. They lived alike, and helped each other. Otters had no relatives, they would kill anything. Otters were very intense. Farther down river a family of them slid around on the mudbank that dropped into the river, and even in their play they were intense. Women couldn't eat any part of otters, or else their children might become nervous and uncontrollable. Once Loon had passed a beaver pond with its beaver house just behind the dam of logs they had felled. It all looked fine, but strangely quiet. Then an otter emerged from the water next to the beaver house, sleek and round-eyed as it looked around, its muzzle still bloody. Loon had shuddered, imagining the carnage in that round house, a whole pack comfortably at home and then a swift black thing swimming in and killing everyone with bites.

But everyone had to eat.

Up on the ridge above the big cave Loon saw a flicker between trees. Not red, so not a fox. Could have been a woodsman. Every once in a while they appeared in the distance, usually in forests, which was why they had their name. Most of them had lost their luck, Thorn said, lost it so bad they had lost their pack too. Because luck was real.

Thorn always said that he didn't have any luck anymore, nor any spirit powers of his own, but had learned to ask the spirit powers out there to visit him and take him over. It didn't look like a comfortable thing. Sometimes he sighed heavily on the days when he woke to realize it was a day for one of his spirit travels. He drank berry mash all day and trembled as the time came for the visitation. He would flick Loon on the ear for no reason. The spirits who visited him were Bison Man, Birch Woman, the Night Colors, and another he would never name. Telling others about one's abilities could sometimes make them go away, so Thorn was usually reticent and even secretive about that part of his life. But Loon was his apprentice, and although Thorn did not think much of Loon in that regard, he had to train him or find someone else. It would have pleased Loon to be rejected and allowed to go his way. He kept trying to make that happen, just on the off chance it might work. As the ducks kept not coming and everyone got more stretched and thin, Loon was ruder and ruder to Thorn, or he just left camp all day, every day, just as he had so often as a child. But Thorn seemed determined to keep him, and the truth was that Loon liked etching stones, and carving wood and antler and tusk, and making the paints and painting. He wanted to paint the big animals inside their cave when the time came for him. In that way he wanted to be a shaman. And Thorn knew that and used it against him. And he reminded Loon that being a shaman was a good way to know lots of women too, even if they were sick when you knew them. Loon found that idea horrible. A lot of what shamans had to do frightened and disgusted him.

Not only did the ducks not come, but one day the air went so cold that the sun showed its ears, and everyone returned to camp and began to prepare for a cold snap. It was the worst time of year for one, because the last snow was melting and all the little creatures' tunnels between the snow and ground were flooded. It was already

the most dangerous time of the year for every animal, much worse
than winter itself; to add a freeze at the end was a hard thing. But
the sky was frosted, and the sun's ears gleamed in a circle around it.
Cold was surely coming. At this point firewood was more important
than food.

Cold enough to frost your face, cold enough to freeze your pizzle;
everyone got into the big house, even Heather.

Two days later, with frozen little creatures all over the land, it
warmed back up again. The day after that it got very warm. They
heard the first mosquito, and when you can hear one mosquito there
are sure to be ten more around. The day was coming when the river
was going to break up.

They gathered on the Stone Bison, where they could see up and
down the gorge of the Urdecha a long way, and the flat discolored
ice with all its leads against the banks ran right under their feet.
Thorn put on his bison head and led them in the prayers to the river,
asking it to break up cleanly so that it wouldn't get dammed and
flood Loop Meadow and drown their camp. That had happened.
Just in case it did again, everyone had their most valuable small possessions in their belts, and were dressed in all their finest clothes. It
was a hot day to be wearing so much, but they would soon be able to
swim in the open river and wash off all their sweat and body paint. It
was one of the biggest days of the year. And surely after break-up the
ducks would have to come.

Upstream and downstream, the river was groaning. In the fall
when it froze and made these noises, it was crying out for its blanket
of snow. Now it was crying out for release, for the chance to run free
and see the sun again. Loon recognized in these low booms and sizzling cracks the very words his own spirit had been crying out inside
him since his wander. He sat on the back of the Stone Bison and
moaned with the river, as many of the pack did.

Big jagged plates were rising out of the shattered patches of river
ice, as if something underneath was pushing up to be free. Some
leads were resolving into eddies, with small ice plates jumbling in

their downstream ends. Many shards of ice were half black with bottom mud. The booms and cracks became very frequent and loud.

Thorn approached Loon. He looked oddly small under his bison head. He said loudly to Loon, —Let's say the break-up story together, right here watching it.

—No, Loon said without thinking. He didn't know that poem.

Thorn's right hand leaped out and flicked Loon on the ear, the first time he had managed it since Loon's wander. Loon howled and stood up to walk away.

—No, Thorn shouted, standing in front of Loon and pointing at the ground. His eyes were fixed on Loon like little suns. —Say it now, when it's happening right before your eyes, and remember! Remember!

After a while Loon bowed his head. He rubbed his throbbing ear and looked at the stony ground of the Stone Bison's back. Well, when memorizing this one his ear had always been throbbing, it seemed. With a big sigh he began:

Frost has to freeze and ice build bridges,
Water support you and hide the seeds.
One alone shall unbind the frost
And drive away the long winter.
Good weather will come again,
Summer hot with sun.

Great salt sea deep trail of the dead,
We burn holly for you to break the ice.
Take it back we do not need it,
Tip the sun up toast the air,
Hurry the water under the ice,
Fill the meadows with snowmelt.
Flow water flow,
Fill the ravines fill the ravines,
Fall down the cliffs black in the sun,
Fall water fall.

—No no, Thorn said. —That's Fill water fill.

Fill water fill,
Push from below
The old ice and snow,
Fill from above
Like finger in glove,
Like baby born
With a push from inside.
The moment comes to push and push,
Mother Earth knows   Mother Earth squeezes,
A spasm   a cramp   a knot   a push.

Break ice break now,
Break ice break now.

Loon tried to remember what came next. Below them the deepest canyon of the gorge was groaning hugely, as if a big woman in a spasm of birthing pain.

Suddenly Thorn spoke, and Loon listened gratefully, because he had never remembered what came next.

As it happened, Thorn shifted to a different story, one Loon knew much better.

One spring a great storm came out of the west,
Destroying the homes of the people by the river.
They lashed their skin boats together for safety
And sat in them as water rose up all the valleys
And covered the land completely.
They drifted unable to save themselves,
In the bitter night many of them froze
And their bodies fell into the sea.
Then wind and sea calmed and the sun beat down,
The sun was so intense some died of its heat.
Finally a shaman struck the water with his spear,

Crying, Enough! Enough! We've had enough!
Then the man tossed his earrings into the sea
And again cried out, Enough!
And soon the water began receding,
And after a time formed the rivers and streams
And retreated to the west where it still remains.

—That must have happened right around this time of year, Loon
joked when Thorn was done.
—What do you mean?
—I mean, it didn't matter what the shaman said or did. The water
was going to recede anyway, its time had come.
Thorn stared at him. —Repeat the part I said.
Loon stood and spoke as loudly as he could:

One spring a storm came out of the west,
Destroying the homes of the folk by the river.
They lashed their boats together for safety
And the sea rose up and covered all the land.
They drifted terrified unable to do anything,
In the bitter nights many of them froze
And their bodies were thrown overboard.
Then wind and sea calmed and the sun came out,
It was so intense that some died of its heat.
And so a shaman stuck his spear in the sea
And woefully cried, Enough! Enough!
And threw his earrings into the sea,
Whether as gift or killstone even he didn't know.
And as the water was already receding
It didn't matter   the land returned
With the rivers and streams we know today
And the great salt sea off where it belongs.

Thorn had raised a fist during Loon's changes to indicate his dis-
pleasure, but the gorge was now cracking and roaring under them very

loudly, sounding very much like the cracks and rumblings of thunder overhead. Loon hoped that one day that would happen, that the break-up would come in the midst of a giant thunderstorm, and he had an idea for a poem that hopefully would be ready to tell, if it ever did happen.

Now, in the cloudless sky, with the sound originating below them, it was too awesome a thing to persist in stories, or anything else human, except just to watch and bear witness. The white surface of the river ice was fracturing downstream in a jumble, starting on the outsides of the river's curves, then flowing downstream from where they began, until big sections of the river were all cracked open, and black open water visible riffling below. Ice plates were detaching from their banks or each other and moving downstream, white rafts crashing into each other and reforming immense masses that flowed downstream until they ran into a bank, or another raft of ice, when plates of ice slid over each other, or broke up and tilted at the sky. Sometimes big ice dams crossed the whole flow from bank to bank, and water built up behind them, floating more ice rafts into them so that they quickly grew, and more water bulged up and pressed higher on them, until with roars louder than thunder the whole white mass roiled down the black chaotic stream, ice plates tumbling and rolling wetly until another dam snagged and held them all again.

Everyone was standing arms outstretched on the downstream side of the Stone Bison, looking down at the spectacle; everyone was shouting and yet no one could be heard. Even Heather was open-mouthed and red-cheeked, grinning hugely. The whole pack of them howled like wolves, and not a voice was heard in the stupendous break-up. When it came upstream, and was happening right under the Stone Bison itself, they danced and hugged each other and spun in circles until they were facing the upstream side, well away from the edge, for it would not do to fall in now; and when the break-up showed under them, and proceeded upstream away from them, they howled louder than ever, and still could not hear themselves in the giant roar of the world.

And then someone spotted a line of ducks in the sky.

Summer was here.

So they had not starved. They had felt the pinch, and as the very first ducks to arrive were never taken, they had a bit more pinching to go. They devoured the last of the winterover nuts and went out to set the snares that would catch the ducks that came in the following days. But it felt different when you knew it was only going to go on for a while longer: sharper, but less frightening.

With the success of the last four winters, their pack was getting rather large. Two score two was a still good number: not so small that they had to worry about defending themselves, not so big that the food required to feed them was impossible to gather.

Still, the way everyone knew everyone else. Relations, habits, likes, dislikes, abilities, weaknesses, tendencies. Everything. Smells, digestive habits, turns of phrase. They knew each other so well that they were no longer interesting to each other. Part of the excitement of the coming of summer had to do with the prospect of seeing other people again.

After the duck snares were set on the still parts of the river, Loon went out with Heather to help her hunt for her special herbs. Some of them grew only down in wet-bottomed hollows, and Loon could help by getting down into places Heather was too stiff to reach.

Heather's cat followed at a discreet distance. Heather had found it as an orphaned kitten and kept it alive, but at a certain age it had gone off on its own, and now only came back in the winters to skulk around for food. They had several camp robbers like that, mostly jays and squirrels, but also a minx, some marmots and foxes, even a nearby beaver family who made quick raids on them from the river.

Heather used her cat as an herb tester. She would leave some meats the cat liked most with a sprig of a strange new plant in it, and when the cat ate it Heather would watch to see what happened. She didn't think any plant would kill the cat, because if it did not agree with the little beast it would quickly cough it back up.

When Heather saw this happen, she would shoo the cat away and go to the vomit and inspect it closely, even take dabs of it between finger and thumb and taste it with her tongue.

Now as she did this Loon said, —Heather, you're eating cat vomit.

—So what? I can taste tastes that are like other tastes I know. It gives me ideas how this flower might be put to use.

—What if it kills you?

—Cats have very delicate stomachs. It won't kill me.

Loon said, —I dreamed about some lions last night, a gang of them going after some bison.

Heather wasn't interested. —I don't know about dreams. Maybe it's one of those worlds we don't see very well. We only see snatches of them. I don't know what they are. It's this world I know. Well, know. It's this world I look at.

—So you eat cat vomit.

—Better than eating shit.

—Well sure, but who would do that?

Heather shook her head darkly. —We all have to eat shit sometime.

Loon didn't know what to say to this.

Heather gave him a look, laughed her brief hag's laugh. —When you get hungry enough, you'll eat anything. And the first time it goes through you, not all of the food in food gets eaten. You shit some of it out uneaten. So there's some food to be had in shit. Second time through is pretty bad, I admit. You get gas, the runs, it tastes like shit, you bet. But you get something out of it. You can tell that's true because you do it again.

—Again?

—Not with the same stuff. I mean later. A third time through you wouldn't work. Your body knows that and wouldn't let it in you anyway.

—So you didn't have any other food?

—That's right. Some winters are hard. Heather frowned as she stared at the western sky. —Harder than any you've ever seen.

She picked more of the herb sprigs the cat had thrown up, inspecting them for undamaged flowers. —Hopefully harder than you'll ever see, she added. —But they do seem to come along every once in a while.

As the seventh day of the seventh month approached, they began to sort through their gear and decide what to take on their summer trip and what to bury. They would collapse their big house and the women's house flat, and cover them with big rocks; leaving them intact always got them ransacked. Even when flattened and covered, sometimes it looked like other people or some bigheads had dug into them, and other times it was clear that bears had clawed some rocks away and rooted around, no doubt interested in the scents. But by their leaving the camp as clean as possible, marauders would find nothing but old hides to eat, and although hungry bears would eat old hide, as they would anything that lived or had ever lived, still their downed camp was often left alone, and could be reconstructed that much easier on their return.

Loon's clothes were well made and clean. Loon had stitched them, but for the most part Heather had cut the parts, and she had her own style. Loon liked the way his clothes felt and looked, and when compared to the makeshift equipment of his wander, he felt superbly comfortable and well dressed.

He wore a woven reed cap that had a good sun brim, and a strap to tie it under his chin in a wind. He had made it himself and would wear it until his abuse wrecked it, after which he would weave another one.

On his back, outside everything else, he wore a woven reed cape, which took such a beating from water and sun that he needed a new one every summer. He folded and stuffed it in his sack when he did not need it, and that too was hard on it.

Under that he wore a parka made of caribou hide, with ruffs of marten and marmot fur around the hood and bottom and sleeve ends.

His middle was covered by a skirt of deer hide turned inward, with a crotchpiece of rabbit fur cradling his pizzle when it was cold.

He had chaps of caribou hide, but kept them in his pack except during the bitterest cold or the thorniest brakes; he liked his legs free as much as possible.

He often went barefoot, but his shoes, worn on rough ground or during long walks, were some of Heather's best, with bearskin bottoms and deerskin uppers, big enough to take a layer of fine straw stuffed in their tops when he wanted that warmth.

Over his arms were the hide straps of his backsack, and in his sack were his fire kit, some duff and punk and fungus tinder, an ember bole, and some bearskin butt pads. In the fold of his waist belt were flint and antler points and needles, a burin, some blades, a tassel of leather strings looped in a bone ring, a blade retoucher, and some assorted lucky pebbles and teeth, including his deer's teeth.

These things were really all one needed, along with a javelin and spear thrower. One could become a traveler with just them. They took all that away from a boy going out on his wander, supposedly to make him prove he could get by on his own; but now it occurred to Loon that if the boys were allowed to leave with their things, a lot of them might never come back again.

Loon made up a riddle of his own:

Wait, I see something:
My head is covered by reeds.
Marten and marmot make my fur.
Reindeer and saiga cover my legs.
I walk on a bear's back with deer on my feet.
I can break stone   cut wood   start fire,
Etch bone   paint cliffs   glue cuts,
Kill any animal   except one,
Sing like a bird   drum like thunder.
What am I?
I am Loon the wanderer.

ELGA

On the seventh day of the seventh month they began their summer trek, walking up Upper Valley and over its head onto the moor to the north, then over three low divides into the valley of the Lir. Everyone carried a sack on their back; some of these were lashed to wooden frames strapped over their shoulders, to take on heavier loads and the new kids too small to have a name.

River valleys and their feeder canyons were often thick with brush or blocked by boulder fields, so they walked almost entirely on ridge trails. These had obviously been used forever, they were so well marked. Always in the land they crossed, when you succeeded in finding the best way you would find a trail there already, in some places trod ankle deep. When the trail ran over rocks it would be a matter of cairns marking the way, cairns ranging from two or three stacked stones to rockpiles taller than a person, and including many carefully stacked stone figures of one sort or another. One also saw bits of colored yarn tied to branches, in places where there were trees.

On the last pass before the head of the Lir, they came to a spring that poured out of a broad spot in the pass itself. In most of the summers they visited it, its water ran down into the valleys on both sides. Around this double outlet spring the meadow was trampled by hoofprints and paw prints. They drank there, and then dropped into the Lir valley, for the spring was considered dangerous to camp at.

So in the waning of the day, near the end of the long summer evening, they came to their traditional first night's camp. It was the same every year, unless something untoward happened to slow them down. This first camp had an open prospect to the north and west, and the late sun slanted off the nearest ice cap, which from here loomed well over the ridge to the west. This was the northernmost of the four ice caps that rested on the highest parts of the highland to the west of the Urdecha. Even in summer these ice caps stood there, smooth snowy white hills, with parts of them the creamy blue of bare ice. The two smallest ones farther south they called the Ice Tits, the larger ones to the west and north, the Big Ice Caps. Whenever the people of Wolf pack saw these big ones, they knew they were on the way to the salmon and caribou, so the sight always filled them with the sudden thrill of distance, of knowing they were in that moment of the year and on their trek over the great big world, like all the other animals in summer, journeying from one place to another in search of their livelihoods.

On the third day of their journey, low dark clouds poured over the western horizon on a cold wind. The ridge trails were headed mostly downhill now, and mainly northward. Once they got to the north end of these ridges they would be on the open land of the steppe, but now they were still in the hills, on an exposed ridge trail, and this summer storm was coming in on a raw wet wind. So they stopped early that afternoon and dropped into a protected high canyon to the east, and chopped up branches and made a shelter in a grove of oak and hemlock and white spruce and yew. It was a big storm for summertime, but these things happened.

When they were all tucked out of the wind, under a woven spruce branch shelter, they rekindled their fire from embers they had carried from the previous night's fire, and huddled and ate some of the last of their nuts and the newly caught ducks of this summer, delicious straight from the fire. Schist and Ibex and several other men went out setting snares and looking in likely dens. Thorn and Heather took over the fire, and, given the look of the night to come, laid it long and hot, to build up a bed of embers to sleep by. The clouds rolled in thicker and thicker, until it looked like evening all afternoon. When night finally fell, little chips of snow flew sideways on the wind, sailing over the branches of their grove and the smoke of the fire. It was going to be a stormy night.

—The unspeakable one should tell the story of how the animals got summer, Heather said to Thorn. —That's one he always tells on this walk.

—You tell it, Thorn said unhappily. His bones hurt him in any unexpected cold.

—In the beginning the sky came right down to water, Heather said in her clipped harsh tones, as if she were recounting a story she didn't approve of.

It was winter all the time.
Squirrel mama came out of the tree crying.
Went down to the forest floor to collect her frozen babies.
That kept on happening to her.
Winter is too cold, she said to the other animals.
Every once in a while all my babies just freeze.

Raven said, we should steal summer from the summer people.
Summer is on the other side of the sky.
We only have to break through the sky
And take a bag with us,
And kidnap summer and bring it back.
So they decided to do that.
To break a hole in the sky
They put a leech to it, to bite that first hole.
Then next wolverine clawed through that little hole,
And while he was at it
He pulled through a seal skin to use as a bag.
Once on the summer side, wolverine found
All the people were away from home,
And he started to stuff summer into the seal bag
To take it back to the animal side.
But there was an old man there tending the fire,
An old man not as stupid as some I know,
And he said to wolverine, Don't take all of it
Or it will be winter all the time here,
And all the people here will freeze.
Just take part of it with you, then it will go back and forth.

So wolverine brought back part of summer to the animal side,
And broke the bag open and all the summer things came out.
Pretty soon the snow melted and they had a summer too.
So now when the animals have summer,
The people have winter. But when people have summer,
The animals have their winter again.
So it goes, back and forth, winter on one side,
Summer on the other. Every time the animals bust the bag,
All the summer comes out.

—Fine for them, Thorn remarked. But tonight we're just going
to be cold.

—You still have to tell the story, Heather said. —What kind of a
shaman are you?

Thorn did not reply.

As they took a day's rest to wait out the storm, Loon saw Sage talking to Hawk again, and he could see the interest there in both of
them. After that, when they continued north and west down the
Lir valley's east ridge, he thought about it, and what Heather had
said about jealousy and envy, and when they came to the next river
crossing, he helped Ducky across. She was the best-looking of their
women after Sage, indeed many called her the beauty, because of her
rounded figure, which was indeed a little ducklike, even now that
she had grown up. Sage would not care about this, he judged; but
it would be possible also to ask Ducky to take Moss's spear thrower
back to him, now that Loon was finished carving a horse's head into
it. Moss always camped next to Hawk, and when Ducky took him
his spear thrower, Hawk would see her, and they would talk for a
while. And indeed it happened just that way. This pleased Loon. He
thought something might come of it.

The ridges got lower, and the ridge trails passed now between valley
bogs that were often covered with moss. The women plucked a lot
of it and took it with them.

Then it got stormy again, a warmer storm, wet and windy. Weather really mattered when they were on their trek. They didn't want to lay by any more days, so they put their capes over their sacks, and over the kids being carried, and hiked on underneath ever-taller black-bottomed thunderheads, enduring the wind and the occasional pummeling of hail. When thunder rumbled to the west they made camp fast and hunkered down in it. Getting the fire going was hard, keeping their beds dry was hard. In so many ways, rain was worse than snow.

Thorn, perhaps stung by Heather's words, held his hands out to the fire when it got going and intoned,

The shadow of the night spreads gloom,
It blows from the north.
The ground is wet and cold.
Hail, coldest of seeds,
Falls upon the earth
And makes life miserable for poor puny people.

The next day, walking north and west, they came to where a knob on the ridge they were walking gave them a view to the great salt sea. Always so vast, with a sunbeaten blue unlike the sky or anything else. An awesome sight.

The ridge trail turned right and headed straight north, running along the hills edging a flat coastal plain that stretched to the great salt sea. The hill route was easy walking, with occasional knolls providing high points to camp on and keep a good lookout. The biggest problem was crossing the rivers that here and there cut between the hills, flowing west toward the great salt sea. But over the years a number of rafts had been built, used, and then pulled up on these rivers' banks at the best crossing points. So they could usually paddle across on these.

This year when they came to the first big river, they found that their crossing point had been dammed by a log jam, a truly enormous log jam consisting of many scores of logs, most of them giant tree trunks, and all wedged together like the branches of a beaver dam, but much bigger.

—Big Beaver must have done this, Thorn said.

There were many stories about Big Mother Muskrat, the mother of all the muskrats, who lived in her lake on the way to the ice caps; and the log jam did look like the work of a beaver twenty times normal size, so they laughed at Thorn's joke. However this log jam had gotten started, now it was snagging every floating tree swept downstream, so that it was always growing on its upstream side. It was hard to see what would ever move it, except the rotting of the trees, and since new ones were arriving so much faster than the old ones could rot, it seemed like it might last forever, like the Stone Bison over their river.

Carefully they walked over this new dam, stepping from one stripped battered log to the next: up, down, over, holding the little ones by the hand, hefting them over branches that blocked the way. They followed Schist's lead, which he marked with ties of red yarn, and the route was solid; not a single log moved under them. They might as well have been walking on fallen logs on the forest floor, even though through the many holes underfoot they could see the river bubbling west. It was strange and beautiful, and they talked about it all that night by their fire.

Still farther north, out on the coastal plain itself, the kind of landscape features they used around their home camp to locate themselves were no longer to be found, so they spoke of their route in ways that at home they would only use to talk about the wind: they headed north, on low land to the east of the great salt sea.

Overhead, shifting lines of geese spear-tipped the way for them, also heading north. It was the twelfth day of the seventh month now, and every living thing on earth was moving, it seemed, including them. There was a thrill in that you could feel in your spine. SUMMER. They woke at dawn and ate by the fire, packed up, went downstream to shit and pee, gathered the little ones up one way or another, and headed north. The morning moment of taking off was as effortful and squawky as the geese when they flapped and ran over a lake to get off water into the air. There were many sharp words from Schist as he got them on their way, but also encouragements, and direct help to those who were lagging. Something about him made his encouragements more encouraging than other people's. He was good at making you want to do what you hadn't wanted to do.

The rest of the day was a matter of walking north, with some young men tapped to bring up the rear. Loon was happy to do that. His bad leg was not so bad when going at the pace of the pack, across a coastal steppe. Clumps of grass and stretches of bog covered the flat land, with shallow ravines full of low bushes and gnarled little trees. There was a lot of old snow still on the ground, so soft and suncupped in the afternoons that it was hard to walk on it. The trail stayed slightly higher than the bogs, sometimes on low bluffs overlooking the great salt sea, other times inland at the first real rise, running from ford to ford over the rivers. It had been a snowy year, and some of these fords were running too high to walk across, and they had to find the old rafts if they could. This year the rivers here seemed to have swept them all away, so they had to make new ones. While some of them made these rafts out of driftwood, a few of the young men would run upstream to see if they could find something to eat; this was so seldom successful that they came to understand how much they relied on traps and snares at home. So they set snares every night, but snares worked better when they had more time. During the day hunts, they tried to come back with some eggs or mushrooms at least. The truth was, they were all still hungry. The ducks, delicious though they were, were not enough.

But the farther north they walked, the less the land held. The rivers had to provide, if anything was going to; but these rivers were not yet full of their salmon and sea trout, coming back home to die. One of the fords worked as a fish weir, and there were signs on both banks that it was often frequented; but they saw no one this time.

When the seventh full moon came, they were at the river called

Deer Ford. This was the moon when the caribou were going to arrive nearby, at the western end of their annual trek. In effect these caribou and the people of Wolf pack made treks from different winter homes and converged here.

This year the caribou were nowhere to be seen, however. Thorn warned the pack that it might take longer in such a snowy year, and they would just have to be patient and spend the time making a good chute to run their caribou through. That was all very well, and they set to the task with spirit, but they were again getting down to the last of their food. It was just as well when it came to the nuts, as they were beginning to go beyond the satisfying oddness of their winter fermentation, to something truly rancid; and the pungent liquid fat they had in their sealskin bags was taking on the taste of the bags. They needed fresh meat, like the ducks but more of it. Hopefully it would be coming soon.

One night while they huddled around in the smoke of the smudge fire of birch fungus, which was the only thing that would hold off the mosquitoes, Thorn went into one of his vision trances, first eating his mushroom and artemisia preparation, then vomiting like Heather's cat, then lying back in the beginning of his trance, snorting and muttering. No one bothered him as he lay there spirit traveling.

He came back to them the next morning, and said the caribou appeared to be less than a week away, but it was hard to judge when looking down from so high in the sky. In any case they only had to get through a few more days.

Then wolves began to appear on the ridgelines of the low hills upstream. —See, Thorn said. —They're here to tell us the caribou have almost arrived.

—They're here in hope, Heather said. —They're saying to themselves, the humans are here, so the caribou must be coming.

—Well of course, Thorn said. —That's only right.

Wolves and humans were cousins, just like bears and porcupines, or beavers and muskrats. Wolves had taught people to hunt and to talk. They were still the better singers by far, and hunters too for that matter. What people had taught wolves in return was a matter of dispute, and depended on what stories were told. How to be friends? How to double-cross and backstab? The stories were divided on this.

Then one evening at the end of the twilight, with the ribbon of the river next to them the lightest thing on the dark land, a great horned owl flew over hooting its hoo, hoo, which means yes.

Thorn stood and shouted, —They're here! The owl saw them, and I can feel their hooves in the ground!

No one else felt anything, and the land remained dark and empty, the light band of the river pouring through it. The moony band on the river surface was the only movement, the river's chuckling the only sound. Thorn sat back down grumbling. —You'll see, you'll see. The owl always knows.

And in the morning they came. The first ones ran up and crashed into the river and swam to the other side, then some stopped in the big meadow inside the swing of the river to nuzzle into old grass and new, both revealed by the melting snow. Caribou ate better in winter than summer, and so now were fat, and still wearing their long winter coats.

While on their summer trek, the caribou were always in a terrible hurry. They followed each other in loose lines, speeding up in sudden little panics, and hesitating impatiently if another line cut in front of them, or just surging into them, impelled to keep moving. There were many scores of them, filling the meadow and the low hills around it, hurrying and hurrying, as if they had lost all restraint and could do nothing else. When they finally did stop to forage and look around, they seemed surprised and uneasy to find themselves not in a hurry. But here was their summer home. They migrated west and east, unlike the birds who migrated north and south. And when they arrived at their summer destination, there to meet them every summer were mosquitoes, deer flies, wolves, and humans, each of these packs dangerous and full of pain for the caribou, and therefore to be flicked away, or avoided, or faced up to, in lines of broad-chested bulls with lowered heads and sharp antlers. Why they came nobody was sure, but it was said that their summer food grew first here and they came for that.

*   *   *

The Wolf pack's method for trapping and killing caribou almost always happened in the same area and the same way. Thorn sometimes said this was the way it had been done since the old time, but on other occasions claimed it had been his own idea, which had come to him as a child, watching the men running around the steppe chasing down the beasts one by one.

In this region the steppe was flat as always, but with low lines of hills running north, and boulders scattered all over. Many were too big to move, but there were lines of smaller stones, and these lines sometimes came in twos. The Wolves chose one of these paired rubble lines, as they always did, and cleaned up the ground between the two knee-high walls until they had made an inviting passageway.

The caribou as they arrived in their scores crossed the land somewhat like flocks of geese, in loose ribbons of twenty or so. They joined other ribbons or separated as the land shoved them this way or that. They were all rushing to get somewhere, and none of them knew where. Considering the distance they had come, which was many days to the north and east, so far that no one knew for sure where they wintered, it looked to the humans like they were hoofing along as fast as they possibly could, maybe even faster than could be sustained. They were strong and fast creatures, fore-weighted like a rhinoceros or hyena or bison, with heavy shoulders and a long heavy neck and head, and big antlers on the males. They seemed to hurry at least in part to catch up with their heads before they tipped and fell forward.

In that hasty careless state, so unlike their usual wariness, indeed as if they were possessed by some spirit not theirs, it was relatively easy to spook a ribbon of them into the chute the pack had made with its paired walls. And at the western end of the chute, under a small drop which the caribou normally would have jumped down without any problem, and so would not be afraid of, the pack had placed some poles across rocks, then also some antlers, until they had built a trap line that was certain to trip some of the beasts when they tried to pass over it.

When the trap was ready, the men went out with wolf skins on their heads in groups of three, and began running around trying to spook a line of running caribou into the eastern end of the chute. This took some crouched running and frenzied leaping on the part of these men, wolf heads flopping on their foreheads to give the caribou that first alarming profile on which they made their snap judgments, like every other animal. Meanwhile the people not out there hid behind the low rock walls, listening for the thump of hooves on the sod that would announce the beasts' arrival. Loon stayed with this second group, as his bad leg was hurting a little, and the runners often had to get crazy to spook the beasts. So he sat there with the rest of the pack in ambush, salivating heavily as he listened for the signal whistles or the thumping in the sod.

Then the thumping sound came, and the hoarse breathing that one always forgot year to year, and the unhappy neighing of the first beasts as they tried to stop rather than risk a jump down onto the poles, and their squeals as they were pushed over from behind by other beasts; then Loon stood with the rest who were in ambush, his javelin end cupped onto his spear thrower and his arm raised.

Panicked caribou were being pushed from behind and pitching over onto the beasts already below. Loon chose one beast teetering on the brink and threw his spear as hard as he could. It was a very close throw, but downward, so he had to adjust accordingly, and he did: the spear slammed deep into the beast right behind its ribs, and Loon shouted to see it. Quickly all the men cast their spears into the mass of struggling beasts, and the women and children threw rocks at them, and the big beasts thrashed and bled and screamed, the air filled with the smell of their blood and shit and piss. The human screams were as loud as the caribou.

In a matter of twenty or two score heartbeats they had about twenty dead caribou lying at their feet, which was as much as they could deal with at once, or more. It was a bizarre and awful sight, shocking and exciting. Everyone was cast into a kind of blood lust; their mouths ran and their faces were red and pop-eyed. Some of the boys and girls were sent racing to the chute's eastern end, to drive away any beasts that might run into the trap. Thorn went with them to help them construct a block.

Loon limped up to the top of the little hill overlooking their trap, and saw columns of smoke in the distance, rising from the distant fires of other packs of people. They were all out there doing the same thing. The smoke from every fire was black with burned caribou fat.

Some of them started a fire from their embers, and the kids were sent out to find old caribou dung to add to the fire, as the steppe had so little wood. The rest of them set to breaking down the animals. But before they began, Schist led Loon and Nevermind and Ibex in the performing of the caribou sacrifice, and Thorn tagged along. Never take the first of anything was their constant rule, and so here they took the westernmost body and eviscerated it, then placed a big stone up inside the ribcage, and together carried it down to a deep spot downstream in the nearby river. There they threw the caribou in, chanting the thank you chant, and Thorn threw in some painted stones after the body, asking the caribou to return the following year, and thanking them for this year's gift of themselves. Then they went back to the kill site and the hard work of breaking the animals apart.

Everyone worked for as long as there was light, and ended up with blood all over them; but all the while there was a fire roaring that allowed them to cook favorite bits of the beasts, and burn the parts they could not use, which were admittedly few; but it helped fuel the fire. And disposing of these parts helped to keep scavengers from descending too hard on them in the night. Even after night fell completely, not long before midnight, they continued by firelight.

First they skinned the beasts, chopping out the useful ligaments and tendons as they went, and eating as they worked, getting into a bit of a frenzy, working without clothes on to avoid all the blood, so that the women looked like they were at their coming-out dances, the men from their hunting initiations, all of them streaked with grease and blood, and euphoric with the sudden ingestion of all the fat and muscle of the beasts. They bathed downstream in the narrow but deep river that ran next to the hill they were working on, immersing themselves briefly in the snowmelt water, knowing that with their bonfire they would be able to warm back up, and would stay warm as they kept on butchering. They set a big night watch to guard the meat, and were faced with so much of it that they deboned the legs so they would have less weight to carry when they left. It was a long hard day and night of work. And the next day and night would be much the same.

Schist and Ibex howled when they came back from making the river gift to the caribou, and Thorn grinned to hear it. Loon saw suddenly that Thorn liked the pack's ceremonies that did not require his leadership; this was something Loon had not realized before. Loon put that away to think about, and went back to chopping through hip joints, sitting down as he worked to give his bad leg a break, and trying to be careful as he got more tired. He made each cut like it was a test in a trial, or a contest at a festival, judged by something stricter even than Thorn: which was to say pain. For it would be all too easy, with everything so slippery with blood, and every muscle getting tired, to cut oneself on a turned blade; it often happened on this first night of the slaughter. On a journey of twentytwenty days, that treacherous last step. It was easy on this long night to feel how that could happen.

But no one was hungry anymore, indeed they were all stuffed, and the fire was sizzling and cracking and airily roaring, and between the remaining work, the feasting, the dancing, and, for some, the quick slipping off into the night for a spurt, the entire pack was laughing and singing. Groups went down to the stream to strip off and plunge in screaming, rubbing off the blood and guts, splashing each other, and when clean, hiking gingerly back up to the fire to face it and get warmed up again. It always happened this way; they were at this day of the year again, around full moon of the seventh month; the long winter and the hungry spring were over, and they had reached the time when they were fully fed again, and would be eating well for several months to come. There wasn't another day in the year as giddy as this day, as full of relief. They had made it through another spring.

Loon danced by the bonfire, staying off his bad leg. He fronted the fire and caught its heat, then spun away to laugh at the night, which was very chill, except in the bubble of their fire. But you never feel as warm as when some part of you is still cold.

Sometimes the fire burst with fat exploding. Loon watched all their women, all wearing nothing but skirts, or waist wraps and necklaces, and even knowing every body there, muscle by muscle, move by move, still it was something to see them in the firelight, moving high on the fat in their tummies, swinging around their flat summer breasts, their bodies each known to him curve by curve by curve. His eye was always caught most by whatever seemed at first to make their bodies somehow wrong, but which over time eventually made them right, or made them them, each to her own self. Then too there were the ones who had no flaws or oddities, Sage, Chamois, Thunder, each perfectly proportioned in each her own way.

He danced or sat down from time to time to give the bad leg a break, and wiggled his toes and drummed with the boys for a good long time. Who knew how long these times were, when you were lost in moments that you hoped would go on forever. Although of course the moon always told. Loon drummed away watching Sage dance, and she looked so good his spurt antlered in his wrap, and he stood up and danced with it thwopping side to side, a little pole of pulsing pleasure leading him toward Sage as she danced, her breasts nowhere near as big as they would be in the fall, but even so, their curve and bounce on her ribs as she danced, her arms in the air to left and right of her, her butt dipping and spinning, two big round muscles like the rumps of mountain sheep, known so well to him, their layer of fat hardly there in this month, just pure muscle and the promise of fat, maybe the best look of all; such a long-legged girl, so rangy, so graceful and smooth. Oh yes, Loon would have been very happy to stumble off with Sage into the night, go down by the stream where the chuckle of the water would sing them along and cover their noise as their kissing and rubbing took them away into the realm of helpless cries indulged. It had happened the year before, and this indeed was the thought that was causing his spurt to stand all athrob.

But tonight Sage was not making eye contact with anyone, and was clearly intent to stay in her dance. This was perhaps a response to Hawk as much as to Loon, indeed every man there had a happy eye for Sage, and she by dancing with none of them danced with all of them, which was nice, and appreciated. And no doubt it was the same for the other women, Likes Mash and Chamois and Ducky and Bluejay and Thunder, each of them the favorite perhaps of different men, and Sage by no means the only beauty of the pack's women, but just one of the sisters. Oh yes their pack had such sisters. One had to be fierce to defend such women from the otters of this world; and yet at the same moment one had that worry, one could recall that all the other packs were similarly blessed, and so one could rest easier. It was a world of beautiful women, and the whole world ran for them. A twenty of packs would soon meet for the eight eight festival, and all the men and women would mingle, everyone in their finest clothes, and there would be fires and dances like this one; there many young men and women, and boys and girls too, would find each other for the first time, members of the proper clans for each other or not, and they would stick together afterward, and the packs of the steppe and the highlands and the canyons to the south would mix and become more related yet again. There were packs from the frozen north who stole each other's women, it was said at the festivals, but among the packs who lived south of the caribou steppe, from the great salt sea in the west, to the great salt sea in the south, to as far to the east as anyone had been, they were all inter-related, so there was very little thievery of that kind.

When Loon sat back down, and began to nod off over his little drum, the dancers and bonfire flames blurring together in his eyes, so that he was about to crawl off to sleep, or simply to tip over and sleep where he sat, Sage grabbed him by the arm and pulled him off into the darkness over the hill. He had been just far enough away from the fire that no one would necessarily have seen them going off. They fell onto Sage's fur skirt spread over the cold ground and started kissing wildly, and though Sage didn't let him inside her, which would have shocked him in any case, they rubbed each other as they kissed, and Loon whispered, —I love you, in her ear, and she squeaked, and they came at the same time, laughing a little afterward, immensely pleased with themselves. Sage gave him a last nip and a light slap to the face and pulled her skirt from under him and was off into the night. Loon proceeded to his bedding, and saw she had gone back to the dance by the fire, still full of spirit, indeed it looked not at all unlikely that she would soon drag some other boy off into the night to ravish. Loon was both pleased and displeased at that thought, a little aroused, too tired to see the harm in it. He lay down and fell asleep feeling gloriously empty and full.

It took them many days to cut up their caribou and smoke the meat. They worked hard, because the eight eight was coming soon, and by then they needed to have finished and hiked the way east to the festival grounds. So it was caribou all day and all night.

Favorite parts of roast head while they work:
Jowls, nose, ears, tongue, lips, lower jaw.
The lower lip is forbidden to all but old men
Whose lips already slack in that same way.
Brain for eating or tanning hides.
Neck meat eaten, except for the first joint,
Forbidden to all but old men
Because caribou are so slow to turn their heads.
Scapula dried and used to make the caribou call.
Shoulder meat eaten, leg muscles eaten.
The shinbones used to scrape fat from hides.
Feet boiled and the tissue eaten by old people only.
Leg joints pulverized to make a grease.
Backbone meat eaten, spinal cord eaten.
Back sinews dried and used for sewing
Wherever one had a need for strength.
Pelvis meat cooked or dried for eating,
A real delicacy; tail the same, but for the old only.

Upper hind leg excellent, lower hind legs too sinewy.
Leg marrow eaten, joints used for grease.
Rib meat the best of all, dried or cooked.
Brisket tender, prepared by boiling.
Belly meat dried or boiled a long time,
Another favorite delicacy of some.
Lungs and liver, cooked and eaten with meat.
Omasum boiled and eaten.
Lower intestine turned inside out,
Boiled with the fat inside, happily eaten.
Kidneys and heart, roasted and eaten.
The bag that holds the heart, dried and used as a bag.
Blood boiled with meat and eaten.
Milk in the udders drunk fresh on the spot.
Body fat prized, dried or cooked or rendered,
And eaten as a sauce on meat;
Saved and carried in a sealskin bag.
The fly larvae found in sores on the skins, eaten.
The antlers used for awls, needles, spoons, platters,
Handles, beads, spear throwers, buttons and tabs
And hooks and all kinds of things.
Hides tanned and used for clothing, also winter boots,
Snowshoe lashings, snares, nets, rope.

Smoking the meat was essential to preserve it, and a lot of them worked at building a long fire, creating a hot bed of embers so that green wood or wet dung would burn and their smoke rise with the heat, passing up and through strips of rib and haunch meat strung on thick hide lines, which were completely covered with meat chunks so that they would not themselves burn. They smoked as much meat as they could carry, while also eating as much as they could. It took a bit of care to keep from making oneself sick by eating too much fat at one time, and they all groaned a bit when they had to go downstream to the shitting ground, and on their return. It was hard on the gut to eat so much meat, hard on the asshole to shit so much shit. Despite that they ate with a real will. There is a hunger inside hunger, as the saying had it. This inner hunger kept them eating long past the point where their bellies were round and hard. They all wanted to get some fat on them for the hard months next spring, which right now they remembered so well. They sent the kids out to the berry brambles around their perch to gather berries to add to their meals and stew into the mash that would get them drunk at the festival.

The new moon of the eighth month came on them fast, and they were all anxious to get to the festival. The festival site was a few days' walk away, an immense meadow on the southern edge of the caribou steppe, surrounded by a low ring of hills that became part of the encampment. As always, they now had many big strips of smoked meat, also sinews, ligaments, hides, bags of grease and of liquefied fat: they had more than they could carry. But they were going to drag it.

They found alder thickets in the steppe's shallow river ravines, and cut many three-year-old shoots, long and straight and springy, and lashed them together to make travois, which could haul loads over the steppe much larger than what could be carried on one's back. When the travois were lashed together and loaded, the young men and women got in the harnesses and did the hauling, while the elders dawdled behind them, joking about how easy it was to get kids to haul when the eight eight lay at the end of the path; which led to the jokes about how impossible it would be to keep up with them, if they didn't have travois tied to them to slow them down. Same jokes every year, same everything; and that was very, very satisfying.

They came to the festival site from the west, and from a long way off could see the low hills surrounding the site, each hill topped by a cluster of big spruce trunks, stripped of branches and bark and stood top end down, so that their root balls waved at their tops like hair or antlers, with animal skulls hanging from every other root end. Thorn claimed to remember the emplacement of these tree trunks in the time of his childhood. It was stirring to see them first pop over the horizon, and then as they approached become a strange sight, the mark of their meeting, and of their existence as more than just packs out on their own. They could hear the drumming from a long way off, first the low thunk of hollowed tree trunks, a sound which seemed to come out of the ground, and then the hide drums of various sizes, battering the air and quickening the blood. FESTIVAL!

They always camped at the same spot, on the south side of one of the low hills, next to the Eagle pack whose home was two confluences downstream from them on the Urdecha. Wolf people who ran traps often ran into Eagles out on their own rounds, and now some of these men came over and helped get camp set, around the same fire ring as always. Smells of dung smoke and burning fat lay heavy in the warm and buggy summer air, and the people in the camp next to theirs were playing bone flutes, a little band of them playing as loudly as they could, working against the drumming from the meadow and filling the air with several notes at once, creating harmonies and then dissonances in a rapid oscillation reminiscent of wolf howls or loon cries. The sound of it made Loon's cheeks burn and his blood thump in his fingertips. From the top of their hill, looking down on the meadow from the upended tree trunk, he saw bonfires all over, people all over. There were maybe a twentytwenty people, or even two twentytwenties, anyway far more people than they ever saw together at any other time, which was all by itself astonishing and exhilarating. And then almost all of them were dressed in their finest summer clothes, including many feather capes and skirts; and their faces painted, their hair braided and tied up, and tooth and shell necklaces ringing every neck. Many of them were already dancing around the fires, and those who weren't dancing moved as if they were. Loon and his friends howled at the sight, and that set off more howls from all over the meadow. EIGHT EIGHT!

Some of them stayed in camp to finish setting up and to keep an eye on things. Everyone else went out to look around. Some went to the music circles, or visited clan fellows they always sought out. Some joined little maker's circles, where they shared new tricks and told about their winters. The shamans got together to do their yearstick corroborations, sing songs, and tell stories. The eight eight was not a shaman thing, and the shamans obviously enjoyed that, and took the opportunity to get drunk and make fools of themselves. Traders went to a barter circle to offer things for trade and to look for things they might want, under one of the biggest upside-down tree trunks. Away from this barter tree people mostly gave each other things, or made regular annual exchanges of this for that. People from the Flint pack from the basin in the ice cap highlands called the Giants' Knapsite simply gave away dressed blocks of clean hard flint, the brown gleam of these near-cubes flush with a very handsome dark red. In return the Flints would take whatever people gave them, nodding and smiling to indicate that these return gifts were not necessary but were appreciated, scoops of mash most of all. Good fellowship all around, love all around, human cleverness all around, celebration of their genius compared to the other animals all around; another year passed successfully, the kids mostly fine, no one starving quite. Have another scoop! Eight eight!

Thorn said to Loon, —Come by the corroboree and meet all the shamans as a young shaman. You'll have to tell a story to them.

Loon shook his head at that. —I'm not ready to tell them a story.

—That's too bad, you have to do it anyway. You've had your wander and it's time.

—No, Loon said, and walked away as fast as he could. At the eight eight no shaman would want to be embarrassed by having to punish his apprentice, and so he felt like he could get away with it. The eight eight was like that.

Loon wandered from bonfire to bonfire. This was one of his favorite activities of the entire year: wandering at the eight eight. People dressed up, hair braided and top-knotted, faces painted or just red-cheeked with excitement. Just looking was such a feast for the eyes, he reeled as he walked and saw others doing the same, he tried to dance it and halfway succeeded. The young women were showing a lot of skin, and a lot of it was painted red but a lot of it was just bare brown skin, still summer slender but still knocking him back glance by glance.

He came on the area where they held most of the festival games, which was something else he enjoyed watching. Elders from the local packs set up the games for the boys and girls, from the simplest rock-throwing contests to the very popular throwing of javelins through hoops rolling down a slight hill. This last was a frequent camp game of every pack ever, and so now a great number of boys and girls were throwing light javelins through hoops that rolled and bounced down a gentle hill, and the air was loud with their yelling.

Just as popular were the contests in which men threw javelins with spear throwers. This was the basic young hunter's game, and every boy had thrown twentytwentytwenties of throws to get used to the way a spear thrower lengthened one's arm. This extra reach made for throws so strong that the javelins visibly bowed and flexed under the pressure of the sling. To see such a quivering flight lance into a distant musk ox hide stuffed with grass was a beautiful thing, and Loon cried out with the rest when throws flashed through the air and struck all the way through the targets, which were tradition-ally musk oxen, so much smaller than a mammoth, an easier target to sew but a harder one to hit. When one of these was transfixed from as far away as a javelin could be thrown, a roar went up and the thrower reared in a little dance.

Beyond the throwing meadow rose a steep hill used for hill races, a favorite with all the boys and girls who were swift-footed and strong. Every year the elders set the starting place somewhere new, and from there you could take any route you wanted to the top. The hill was riven by intersecting ravines, so a clever route was crucial to winning the race. Loon with his bad leg could not join this race, though as a boy he had enjoyed it and been good at it. Wistfully he turned his back on the hill and took off in the other direction.

Across the meadow, the bird's eye view makers were shaping their patches of sandy ground to conform to the festival grounds and various areas around it. Loon didn't know the lands outside their home or region well enough to appreciate these contests, which were usually dominated by travelers and shamans, or elders who had traveled for one reason or another.

On a south-facing sunny bank near the bird's eyes, the shamans were having their corroboree, waving their yearsticks at each other and arguing loudly, as usual. Anytime you got more than two shamans together it was not going to be a shaman thing, so it quickly became a drunken mess. So here, by tradition, they tried to get the year straight before they got crooked, as people said.

A good number of the shamans at this eight eight were earless old snakeheads like Thorn, thus either apprentices to that same Pika who had taught Thorn, or to other shamans who had used the same memory strengthener. Heart sinking a little, Loon spotted Heather and a number of other women sitting among the old snakeheads; some of these women were shamans to their packs, others were herb women with an interest in the corroboration, or friends with the shaman women.

—Anyone can end up being a shaman! Thorn had once explained to Loon. —It comes on you and you have no choice! The question is, who can escape it? And the answer is, no one! Nor man nor woman, elder or child, human or animal. Becoming a shaman is a fate that can strike anyone. Even you.

Remembering that remark and Thorn's scowl, regarding all the earless old crazies laughing and hitting at each other with their yearsticks, Loon turned and walked away. Such a bunch of rasty old men, he couldn't stand it. Because of his wander, at some point during this festival he was supposed to join the shamans and receive their congratulations at having become an apprentice to Thorn, and he was then also supposed to recite one of the old stories, as Thorn had demanded. Maybe the swan wife, but he didn't have a line of it in his head. Best to walk away before Thorn saw him.

So, he couldn't run the hill race, couldn't make a bird's eye view, couldn't talk numbers of moons per year, or recite a story. Best to go back to the throwing range and try a few throws with his new spear thrower. This one he had carved in the shape of a ibex's head, and it had a great cast; he felt like he might be able to enter the throw at the longest distance and have a good chance of hitting the musk ox.

Or better yet, he could sit down with the drummers and drink some mash and beat on his drum with the others. That he could always do, it was thoughtless fun, and one of the best parts of the festival. Drink, smoke, drum, laugh right through a beautiful smoky sunset; then, when night fell, go to the bonfires and dance.

At the bonfires in the first dark, some men and women held a contest to see who could make the prettiest fire spectacle. Many circled around to see these players take up very long travois poles and tie little sachets of cloth or leather to the thin end of the pole, then hold their sachets out away from them, into the highest flames of a bonfire, at which point many of them turned their heads away; and all watching would wait, until the sachet caught fire and flared green or blue or purple, sometimes with a quick splash of fire, or a crack like a little touch of thunder. Since everyone spent every night looking into fires, the sight of something new and unexpected flashing out of a blaze was enough to make them laugh with surprise and delight, and when the whole crowd did that together and as one, it was exhilarating. All the firebangers saved their biggest ones for last and poled them into the fire together, and the quick sequence of bright loud colorful cracks was enough to hurt the ears and provoke a huge cheer.

After that it was drinking, drumming, and dancing. Loon wandered over to a bonfire circled by dancers. Because of Badleg, as he had started naming it during the trek north, he first sat with the drummers and put his little wood and hide drum between his knees and drummed. The farther people traveled to get to the eight eight, the smaller the drums they brought. These little drums took the fastest parts, and Loon quickly got into the groove of the fives, and then switched between the fives, fours, and threes, as the spirit of the piece moved them all around to different emphases. These drum sessions were led by no one and yet could make quite sudden shifts in pace and flow, like flocking birds in the sky. Those moments were really something to be part of, to feel so clearly that there was a group spirit that could seize them all and take them off in a new direction. Time after time it happened. That it could be so easy was astonishing to feel, right there in hands and ear and body. And they drummed this astonishment too! And so it would go, all night long.

Sometime before midnight Loon came out of his drumming trance and could see everything from all the way around. It was like the way owls must see, with the distance to everything much more exact than usual. And so much more than usual was dancing before him: the flames in the fire, the sparks and smoke pouring up, the danc-ing people dressed like birds. The scene flowed in bumps tied to his pulse, a palpable bump moving one fire-flick moment to the next. Mother Owl was inside him, it seemed, and he watched the dance flicker in a way he had never watched before, not just at this eight eight, but in his whole life.

There were young women dancing, of course, wearing their furs and feathers, their necklaces and bracelets and anklets, all bouncing up and down barefoot in time to the drums, across the flicker of the firelight, snapping hand clacks and weaving circles with each other as they circled the fire. Red and white body paint had been applied to their skin in dots or snakes or weaves, and their birdskin hats or cloaks usually came from the most beautiful parts of birds, such as the heads of mallards or the chests of flickers, many such sewn together so that the cloak or headdress was much bigger than any actual bird's. There before him spun a cloak of flicker chests, rising over breasts painted white with red nipples. The sight flickered like a flicker. Another dancer wore a cloak of loons' backs and necks, and that dense superb weave of black and white was so striking and beautiful that Loon could not look elsewhere.

The young woman wearing it was someone he had never seen before. She was tall and heavy-boned; the elg would be her animal, and her dancing was correspondingly slow and simple. Slimmer faster women were dancing circles around her, she was ungainly in that company, and this was precisely what snagged Loon's eye and quickly became her most beautiful feature, the thing that arrested him and compelled him to watch. She knew what she could do, and did it. She was enjoying the dance. She was big and slow, but had excellent proportions, long legs, strong rump, nice tits, broad shoulders. Hair the color of the flints from the Giants' Knapsite, gleams of firelight glancing off it. Thick triple-braid of it down her back, tied with a strip of loon neck feathers at the tip: her friends had done well by her hair. She clumped around and slapped at people freely as they passed her. She had a carefree smile, unselfconscious and relaxed. She had no cares at that moment, she was herself and wanted nothing. So it seemed looking at her.

Loon hung his drum on its loop on the back of his coat and stood up. It was time to dance.

He joined in next to her. Even favoring Badleg a little he could dance rings around her, and he did.

—Hi there, he said to her, —my name is Loon, so I like your cloak. Who are you?

—I'm Elga, she said.

—Ah good, he said. —That's good.

—It is good, she said, drawing herself up with elgish dignity and taking a neat little turn. —And Loon, is Loon good too?

Though no human could really imitate a loon's arching of its wings to the sun, Loon put his arms out and stretched, stretched, stretched, and Elga laughed to see it. It was actually quite a fun dance style, and fit the firelight's blink-blink-blink, so Loon kept it up for a while, thinking about how birds courted, the cranes, the doves, yes even the loons, such a display! He relaxed to get it to a more human style as he circled around her. She rotated inside his circles with a dreamy smile, like an elg chewing on a sunny day. She was taller than Loon, and heavier too. Her loon cloak was gorgeous, and yet the body it was draped over, the shoulders, collarbones, breasts, ribs, belly and hips, arms, back, legs, all of them were much more gorgeous even than a loon's back. With his owl sight he could see that her face was a perfect image of her self, just as it was with all the people in his pack. People's faces were three-liners of their nature, that was all there was to it; somehow their essential natures got stamped on the front of their heads, as if it was a game Raven played when he put them all in their mothers to be born. Their natures were there for all to see. And now Loon was seeing with owl sight, and here dancing before him was a woman calm, straightforward, maybe a little dreamy and withdrawn, all right there to be seen in her eyes and the set of her mouth, and the whole shape of her face, oval and big-eyed. A little mouth, lips thick and rounded when in repose or suppressing a smile, but now she was smiling, so he only caught glimpses of her mouth at rest, as she thought over a dance move or looked out at the night thinking about something. Her teeth when she smiled were neat and small, more otter than elg, which was nice too. No, she was herself; he loved the way she looked, loved her slow neat dancing inside his circles. And she seemed content to stay there, she danced to face him and circled the fire at a speed that accommodated his looning around.

—Where do you come from? he asked.

—From north of here, she said, and saying this caused a little frown to crease her brow, and he saw better than ever the little flower her lips made when she was thinking.

—North? Loon said. —Are you an ice person?

—No, she said, but looked away as if this weren't the whole story, and added —Not anymore. My pack winters to the sunrise, but we take our caribou north of here, caribou and saiga. What about you?

—We take our caribou two rivers to sunset, and winter down south of the ice caps.

—What's your clan?

—Raven, Loon said proudly. —And you?

—Eagle, said Elga, looking pleased; it was best if couples were from different clans. Seeing her expression, Loon danced in and pecked her on the cheek with a kiss.

—Well met, eagle woman, he declared, smiling, and when he saw the pleased look still there in her eyes, he smiled for real, he could feel the difference in his face.

—Let's dance, she said, as if they weren't already, and raised her hands over her head and shimmied. She was more graceful than an elg, and her loon cloak bounced and flickered in the firelight, and Loon with his owl vision danced with her with his gaze cast down, watching her legs and hips and hands, keeping his gaze from hers as she kept hers from his, except for a moment now and then, when a move made them laugh or they bumped together hard. Right now they couldn't look at each other, but once in a while they would both look up and their eyes would meet. Are you here too? their gazes asked, and then answered, Yes, I am here. We are here, together in a bubble of our own, which has all of a sudden popped out of nowhere around us. Isn't it exciting? Yes it is! And then they would look down and dance, almost as if abashed, or a little shocked, needing a little time to take it in.

And there was no hurry. The night was young, midnight had not yet come overhead, the bonfires were still growing their big mounds of embers, with immense heaps of steppe dung piled around them to be burned. Most of the people there were going to dance the night through and then sit watching the sunrise together. This was the eight eight, peak of the year, it was meant to be like this, and Loon found himself comforted by that, it made the strength of the sudden new feeling in him all right. This was the place where this kind of thing happened. He glanced up at her face again, watched her looking into the fire; he knew he didn't know her, and yet at the same time it felt like the look on her face told him everything about her. Everything he needed to know. A northern woman, she would be tough and hard and hot. She would enjoy the south and its mild air.

On they danced. A pack from the east formed a dance line, each of them holding a stout stick in each hand, and their drummers took over the rhythm and moved it to a heavy four beat. Their dancers began to dance with all their footwork the same, a kick left kick right, while they smacked their sticks together, mostly hitting their own but also trading hits with others in their group when they all spun around at once, a beautiful sight and sound, nimble and clacky and quick. While they all watched, Elga came to a stop beside Loon, and the sides of their upper arms touched, and Loon felt the touch like a beam of sunlight on a cold morning. A big howl of approval went up when the stick dancers brought their routine to a sudden halt, and they clacked their sticks lightly in return and took the ladles and cups of mash offered them. The drummers shifted back into a four-and-five, and the general dancing took off again.

Loon and Elga went back into their bubble and danced with the rest until well past midnight. Loon's feet were getting tired, and Badleg was asking for relief. When the drummers switched to a big heavy two-three beat, Elga turned to him and put her arms over his shoulders. She was distinctly taller than he was, and in feeling that a sizzle started at his ears and ran down the back of his neck and up around through his guts to his spurt, which began to rise heartbeat by heartbeat. She leaned down to him and kissed him on the ear, and the sizzle turned to a little bolt of lightning running right down his spine to his prong.

—I'm tired, she said, —and I have to pee. Come with me to the stream and then let's find some place to rest.

—All right, Loon said. —I have to pee too.

—I've eaten so much this week, she said as they stumbled across the meadow away from the firelight, to the slow looping river that drained the festival meadow. Down this way were the shitting grounds, and they had to go slowly to dodge the holes and trenches dug into the wet ground. Elga stepped down to the streamside by herself, and Loon went behind a tree and managed to pee successfully through what was more spurt than pizzle, peeing up at the stars as he began, which made him laugh.

That done they wandered back toward the camps, and Elga stopped at hers, and rejoined him with a bearskin rolled up over her shoulder. She was also wearing a long fur coat with a wolverine-fur collar. Off into the night then, upstream into the hills. On the south-facing sides of these hills, low tangles of brush made for many small lay-bys. It was only necessary to find a good one that was not already occupied. During the last couple of eight eights Loon had taken a look at these hillsides in the mornings, wondering if he would ever have reason to want such a shelter, telling himself it might happen, it might happen. And here it was. He could not find the nook he had discovered two summers before, but then Elga saw a knot of white spruce that she liked, a little tuck of stunted trees, such that they had to crawl to get into it. They paused as they did to make sure no one else was already in there; but it was empty.

And then they were inside their lay-by and on Elga's bear hide, on the thick fur lying together kissing and getting their clothes off, squeezing and caressing each other, and then he was on her and her legs were open to him, and with a couple of thrusts he was up and into her. They were both gasping. Loon, who had mated only with Mother Earth, was shocked at the incredible smoothness and warmth of her, the way they fit together and slid against each other with no drag; it felt so good he couldn't really tell where he ended and she began, it was just a big blur of good feeling down there, a back-and-forth sizzle of good feeling.

She stopped him with a hand over his mouth. —Don't come in me, she said.

—Oh. All right. But I'm about to.

Indeed at the very thought the glow of pleasure flooded back from his spurt all through him, his whole body one great thrusting mass of pleasure, he was thrumming with it, and then bursting. Her knees were up to each side of his ribs and she was squeezing him between them, and as he felt himself begin to spurt he pulled out of her and thrust himself convulsively against her belly, and feeling that she grabbed him by the hair and kissed him again and again as he moaned.

They lay there for a while and then she rolled over onto him. He grew hard again faster than he had realized was possible, but she rubbed her vixen over the length of his prong this time, kneeling on him and kissing him as she did, until she too moaned and pressed herself down on him, crushing him down into the bear fur and the lumpy ground under his back. The female covering the male! He had never seen any animals do that, so it had never occurred to him. Now he thought it might be the best way of all.

They lay there and kissed and petted. Her belly was gooey with his mushroomy spurtmilk but she did not care, she rubbed it into her skin and into his skin, she kissed him and caressed him, rubbed herself against him, humming; when he got hard again she kissed his chest and his belly and then took his spurt in her mouth and sucked on him until he came again, feeling it more powerfully than ever. She hummed approvingly throughout, and then stretched out and kissed him again, and he tasted his own seed there in her mouth, shocking to his tongue and then he wanted to taste it again. She turned and rolled and presented her vixen to his face, all wet and musky, and he licked her in the way he had seen wolves lick their mates, it was obvious what to do, but also shocking in the new way it felt, the slick smoothness of that interior skin, the tight curl of the hair around it under his tongue, the taste of her.

They lay there again, wrapping up to stay warm. They kissed, they made love. The sky turned gray in the east, then the red flush of dawn lined the horizon.

—No, Loon protested. —I don't want this night to end.

She hummed her agreement, burrowed her face into his neck. She appeared to fall asleep for a while, and Loon lay there feeling her breast rise and fall on his arm, her leg thrown over his middle. He was not even the slightest bit sleepy; in fact he wanted to wake her up and slip inside her again. He did not, however. He let her sleep, and watched sunrise with his head lying right on the ground, cradling her head and feeling her body's weight and warmth, smelling her, soaking her in. This was what he wanted. He had never wanted anything the way he wanted this.

In the warmth of the morning sun, he too fell asleep for a while. When he woke she had her loon cloak rolled and tied with a thong. She looked him in the eyes, in a way she hadn't during their dance.

—Can I come with you? she said.

—What do you mean?

—I just joined my pack last year. I ran away from the one before, because they took me from the one I grew up in. But I can't find that first one anymore. I lived like a woodsman trying to find them, but when I couldn't, I joined the pack I'm in now. But I don't really fit there, and a lot of them wish I wasn't there. It makes some problems I guess. Anyway I don't like it.

—Sure you can, he said. —Sure you can come with me.

They went to his camp together, and he went straight to Heather and told her about it. She hissed and said, —You wait a minute before you talk to Thorn.

After a quick hard look at Elga, she turned her back on them, clearly displeased with the situation, and dug around in her traveling selection of baskets and bowls and gourds and boxes. No one carried more around in her backsack than Heather did, it was always taut with its internal weight, and hung from a tumpline that pressed a livid mark on her forehead when she hiked. Now it looked like she was having trouble finding what she wanted, knocking things around like a jay beaking through leaves. —I knew this was going to happen, she muttered.

When Thorn came into camp he was mashed and smoked, red-eyed and roaring. Loon might have chosen some other time to tell him, but Thorn immediately saw Elga and stared at her and said, —Who's this then?

—We're getting married, Loon said. —She's joining us. Her name is Elga.

—No, Thorn said, and with a snarl he leaped at Loon and hit him on the ear and then in the gut. After that Loon held him off with straight-arms and shoves, until during one shove Thorn grabbed Loon's right hand in both of his and quickly twisted Loon's little finger. Loon felt the bone break, and after that it hurt so sharply that he stepped back and kicked Thorn hard in the belly. Thorn fell back and picked up a burin and was about to attack Loon with it when Heather screamed, —STOP IT!

She was slightly crouched over Thorn's stuff, and peeing on it.

—Hey! Thorn shouted in outrage, and turned to leap at her, raising the burin; but instantly she was holding up her little blowdart
tube to her lips and aiming it right at him.

He stopped in his tracks.

Tipping it slightly away from her mouth, she said, —Stop it or I'll
kill you right now. You'll die inside twenty breaths. You've seen me
do it before, don't think I won't do it to you, because I will, and you
know it.

—Fucking hag.

Thorn stood there, eyeing the blowdart uneasily. The little darts
were tipped with a poison Heather made which definitely killed
animals fast, even lynxes and hyenas, her chief victims. They had
all seen it. And when she was angry she was capable of anything.
Thorn knew that best of them all, and he stood there pushing his
lips out into a disgusted knot. He said sidelong to Loon, —You're on
the shaman path and you can't get married now, you have too much
to do, it would be wrong. You didn't even come to the corroboree!

—I'm not going to do it the way you did it, Loon said. —I'm
going to do it better. You had a bad shaman, and I didn't. So I know
better than you what to do.

He held up his right hand up to Thorn and straightened the little
finger with his left hand, feeling the bone in there grind against itself,
a gut-wrenching moment that caused a wave of light-headedness to
pass through him, but after that the finger only throbbed, and his
head came back to him, though his forehead was dripping sweat. He
would have to make a splint and get someone to tie it on for him. He
kept his voice steady and cold as he said, —I'm going to marry Elga,
and be a married shaman. There's no reason not to. Lots of packs
have them.

—They're not real shamans.

—Yes they are.

—As to the girl, Heather put in sharply, —it's the women's decision whether she joins the pack or not. Neither of you have anything
to do with that, or with who marries whom in this pack for that
matter! Those are women's decisions.

Thorn stood there glowering. His boxes were wet with pee, he had to wash them soon. Meanwhile Loon stood there nursing a broken little finger, which was the new leader of all the hurts in his body, although he could tell already that it was not a serious thing like Badleg, because a little finger could be splinted and left alone to heal. The pain itself didn't matter now that he had his head back. The main thing here, he saw, was that Elga be accepted by Heather, which now she seemed likely to do, even if it was just to put Thorn in his place. And so Loon began to feel happy.

Of course it was complicated, Heather having peed on Thorn's stuff and threatened to dart him to death. Their ancient reverse-marriage would no doubt snarl worse than ever. On the other hand, how much worse could it get? And Loon didn't care anyway. Indeed the worse Thorn and Heather were getting along, the less time either of them would have to tell him what to do. They would focus on each other, and Loon would slip to the side. And he would have his Elga.

He looked at her, smiling to try to convey all this to her. She had been staring at him uncertainly, but when she saw the way he was looking at her, she relaxed. She glanced around at the Wolf women with a beseeching look.

At that moment Sage came back into camp. —Who's this? she said.

All eyes fell on Loon. —This is Elga, he said, moving to her side. —She's going to join us, if the women agree. We are to be married, if the women agree.

That gave Sage a start, and for a moment her eyes flashed. Elga meanwhile was looking serenely at something in the sky, as if not really there. Loon saw suddenly that this would be her way, that she would slide away from trouble if she could. That the struggle might be to keep her around.

In the last days of the festival, around the eighth month's full moon, many had been celebrating for so long that they now lay prostrate right through the day, and the drumming and dancing was mostly taken up by boys and girls. Many men stretched out in camp or with clan friends, stuffed with mash and steak, and even the women sat around preparing the meals a little stunned. They had proved yet again that too much feast is worse than famine, that enough is as good as a feast, and so on. But there were very few who could resist throwing off all restraint just once in the year. Sometimes you just had to let go.

In the wreckage of that particular morning's light, Loon built himself a finger splint, and with Heather's help attached it to his hand. She said he hadn't set the bone between the two knuckles straight, which he could see, and feel too, but he didn't want to do the pulling and twisting it would take to straighten it properly, knowing how it would hurt. Heather offered to do it, but he shook his head. —It will be all right.

—It will heal crooked.

—That's all right. That will mark this fine occasion! And he smiled at her, feeling the prospect of Elga staying with him.

Here and there among the exhausted celebrants, some hoarse arguments were breaking the peace that had finally descended after the drumming had been reduced to a few boys trying a slow four beat. Mash headaches made people irritable. But the arguments were only put-down contests, even if people were truly angry. Curses lashed the air, and shocking insults were traded, but blows were not. Because fights were too dangerous to indulge in. Everyone had seen the battles of the male antlered animals in rut, all the clashing and kicking and blood, and although these too were supposed to be put-down contests, accidents often happened, and animals got gored, or broke a leg, and many later died or were killed. From time to time men would fall into the same kind of folly at a festival, usually when drunk, but these too ended in dangerous injuries, and only served to prove how stupid fighting was. Life was dangerous enough; everyone got injured accidentally one time or another, no matter how careful they were. As the saying put it, every path leads to misfortune. Also: when you're injured, your pack is injured. What it came to was that everyone had enough experience of injury to want to avoid it.

So festival fights were almost always shouting matches. This was part of what made Thorn's attack on Loon's hand so shocking. It was almost as if Thorn had been trying to end his painting, to take away the part of being a shaman Loon wanted the most. It didn't make sense to Loon, and he sucked down bowls of Heather's spruce tea, and rubbed the finger with a salve she gave him, and thought it over.

To get what you want, get what you need. When the fire is hot enough, there is no smoke. No fear when in your place. Do not allow anger to poison you. Each person is his own judge. It is not good for anyone to be alone. Everyone who does well must have dreamed something. The one who tells the stories rules the world. Burnt child, fire dread. A starving man will eat the wolf. A wily mouse should breed in the cat's ear. Naught venture naught gain. A friend is never known until a man have need.

Wait, I see something: two red eyes. A frightened old man.

Well, there were so many old sayings, and many of them cut against each other, like blades on the opposite sides of a tree. Eventually the tree falls one way or the other. But in the meantime you still don't know what to do.

After a while Loon found what he thought might be a way forward. He gathered himself to attempt it, and wandered over to the low hilltop where the shamans always met.

The mass of ash in their bonfire was nearly out, mere pink gleams poking out from strange clinkers, remnants of the weird things that shamans threw into their fire. There were about a dozen of the old men there now, looking even more shattered than everyone else at the festival. They had more endurance for excess, having practiced it more, but as they mashed hard at the eight eight, and dosed themselves with smoke and mushrooms and dancing and flagellation and sleeplessness, they eventually overwhelmed even their own great endurance. Now they were lying around still wearing their animal heads, canted over their faces to cover them from the sun, so that they looked more than ever clowns and fools, frazzled, drunk, splayed out like lions after a kill. Thorn was among them, as flattened as the rest under his bison head. He stared at Loon stone-faced from beneath it.

He and his fellow sorcerers had so painted their bodies with red dots and crescents and wavy ribbons and basketry patterns that they were hard to look at. Their spirit voyages the night before would have cast them out into unions with Wood Frog, Birch Woman, Raven, the Northern Lights, and so on; they had all left their bodies and flown far above or below, become mixes of themselves and their animal spirits. Now it looked like they had not yet completely returned.

Some of them were croaking out an insult contest while still lying flat as moss.

—He's worth just as much as a hole in the snow.

—He's so full of shit, if you pinched him your fingers would get brown.

—He's so lazy he married a pregnant woman.

In the scattered laughter at that last, Loon sat down among them. He stirred their fire, put on a few dung patties and a branch or two.

—Welcome, youth, one of the shamans growled.

Loon nodded his thanks. —This is the story of the swan wife, he said, and stood up and began immediately with the first lines of the old story, which was one of the first Thorn had ever taught him, and thus the one he remembered best. Those first twenty lines seemed to have filled his entire capacity for remembering stories. But his flute was carved with images from the rest of the story, and they would help him remember. He could stop to blow a few notes, and see right where he was.

A man was son of the chief no one knew
And he had no marten skins to wear.
He went out from his village one day
Following a loon that called to him,
And over the ridge he came on a lake
And there on the bank lay a loon's feathers
And in the water a girl was bathing.

He sat on the loonfleck of black and white
And said he would not give the girl her clothes
Unless she agreed to marry him, which she did.
And he took her back to the village
Where no one knew his father was chief
And introduced his new wife to them all.

And she was welcomed but would eat nothing,
Bear lips, deer marrow, none would do for her
Until an old grandmother steamed some marsh grass
And the girl happily gulped it all down.
The villagers were hungry too, and seeing that,
The girl promised them food, but every day
She brought them piles of marsh grass
Wet from the lake bottom, and she was wet too.
And people said, She thinks very highly of goose food
And instantly she decided to leave.

She put on the loon skin and flew away,
Looning the cry loons cry when they're sad.
Hearing it her husband was desolated.

He wandered the village crying all the time,
And asked the old man who lived out of camp,
What can I do to get my wife back?
That old man told him, You have married
A woman whose mother and father
Are not of this world, as you should have known.

Loon went on to describe the three helpers the old man then sent
the husband to find, to help him get the things that he needed to
rescue his wife. Loon particularly emphasized the encounter with
Mouse Woman, enjoying how the little creature scuttling around the
fallen leaves on the floor of the forest was actually a big headwoman

when you got inside her house, a power bigger than the old man, or indeed anyone else in the story. He knew quite a few of the shamans there would recognize Heather in this description of Mouse Woman, Thorn foremost among them: all the little things she knew that made her bigger, like knowledge of poisons, or what roots you could eat. In so many ways it was Heather who kept them all alive, and not these raven-shitted sorcerers sweating in the light of day.

Loon made sure that point was made clear in all the trials the husband successfully overcame, with Mouse Woman crucial to each, until finally the husband was reunited with his wife, in the loon village on the lake above the sky, in the next world over. The various parts of the story came to Loon well, he hardly had to look at his flute; all the threes of threes pulsed through him in a chant, until he came to a good end:

She was happy to see him,
And after that they did everything together.

And as to whether they stayed that way,
Or whether the husband tired of the sky
And fell back to earth,
Dropped by a raven who didn't care where he landed,
That is a story for the next eight eight
Or some other eight eight in the time to come.

And then he stopped and nodded to them, clapping lightly to thank them for listening.

—Ha, Thorn, one of the other old men croaked, raising his head from the ground. —Your apprentice is well taught, he sounds just like you! Always the heavy moral, always the cliffhanger ending!

The others laughed. Thorn mimed a glower, but he was pleased too, Loon could see. —The highest trees catch the most wind, he reminded his needlers with scorn, and all the shamans groaned appreciatively. It looked like none of them wanted to take on Thorn in a put-down contest, as his tongue could be truly blistering. And his apprentice had just made an adequate entry into their misbegotten little clan, so no one would badger him much on that day.

Loon kept his eyes on the ground. Possibly it was going to work out. His bleary-eyed audience was now grinning their horrible pleasure.

Then full moon was past and the festival too, and people packed their travois until the poles bowed under the weight, and set out every way the wind blows. The Wolves went south and east, toward the ice caps and home beyond.

Elga was quiet on their trek, and spent more time with Heather and the women than with Loon. Often Loon saw her talking to Heather. She woke as early as anyone, and made fires and washed and cooked and cleaned and carried the babies whenever she could get a turn; she worked like a beaver woman. She seldom met the eyes of the pack's men, but answered and smiled when spoken to. She took her turn in the harnesses of the travois and hauled longer than anyone else, and not in any suffering way, or as if to prove a point, but just because she didn't seem to notice the travois dragging behind her. Strong. She was bigger than most of them, and although fatless in the way of midsummer, still solid. She's like an elg, they said, they must have named her after her animal, it really fits. Hearing that made Loon happy: they saw her as he saw her, at least to that extent. But only he knew what she was like at night under the stars. So: Thorn was not happy; Sage was not happy; but Loon was happy.

On the trip home they stopped at the ford over the Joins-Lir river, and found the red salmon had already arrived. —Let your food come to you, the women sang as they wove and tied together some pole frameworks, and dug out the leather nets they kept buried under rocks near that ford, and the following day they netted twenties of salmon, a big catch. While they were drying their meat they killed three bears, including a stayawayfromit, as a warning to the other bears in the area to keep their distance. Loon helped Ibex and Hawk and a few others to break up the bears, while most of the rest of the pack chopped and dried the fish. The men who had killed the bears gave Loon a bear penis to eat, laughing at him and saying it was clear he needed it. —You're looking pretty haggard man, she's sucking you dry, you need to save some for the trail. The penis was chewy and tasted like kidneys.

Hawk was happy for him, and happy too, Loon supposed, at the removal of a rival for Sage. When they left the Joins-Lir, their travois heavier than ever, they trudged south and upstream on the trails running along the Lir. The travois were as heavy as could be pulled, and everyone over five years old pulled one. But that was the right way to come back from the summer trek, down off the moor into Loop Camp again, where they howled and got the houses back up and began settling back in.

THE HUNGER
SPRING

Now they could occupy their fall days in eating, in finishing the smoking and drying of the caribou and salmon meat, in gathering and leaching nuts, plucking seeds and berries and leaves, and getting all the food properly stored. Also, while they sat around the fire, they made new clothes and tools, and new toys for the kids. Also went out trapping and hunting, especially for the ducks before they left. And did the fall initiations.

Once again Schist took on his most intent air. Pine nuts were spread on old deerskins in the sun for three days before being bagged for storage in cedar boxes, and every nut had to be inspected to see if there were any little breaks or insect holes marring their smooth surfaces. Dried meat and bags of oil were stored in pits floored with pine needles and covered with bark, dirt, and then stones. Thorn helped Schist and Thunder pack these supplies away, marking a stick like a yearstick with his counts, and calculating what they had against their needs for the coming winter. Schist would not be satisfied unless they had stored up an amount that would feed them all to the end of next spring. Almost certainly they would be able to trap some winter animals, indeed in some years the snowshoe hares were so common that they could almost have lived on them alone. But other years it wasn't so. They had been through some hard springs, as Schist often reminded them. Thorn and Heather and all the older people of the pack were in agreement: better safe than sorry. Store is no sore. If they happened to waste some nuts by having too many, and could not eat them before they went bad, then they would have something to give if other packs came asking, or they could give them to the ravens at the end of the spring, with thanks for another year passed without hunger. Besides, it was more likely that they were going to end up counting nuts next spring, just as they had in this last one. Two score and three people ate a lot of food.

The women declared full moon of the tenth month to be Loon and Elga's wedding day, and on that morning when the sun came over the hills they were all down by the river on the sand bank, Elga dressed in something from each of the other women in the pack, with her hair braided around her head, so that she looked immensely taller than Loon, and more elgish than ever. Thunder and Bluejay and Heather and Sage presided, running the two through their oaths to each other and the pack in a quick singsong that nevertheless included the pack women's promise to the groom that they would stab him to death if he ever mistreated his wife; and this was spoken by Sage, standing right in front of Loon and looking him in the eye with something like the wolves' long stare. Loon shook that off, and also noted with relief that while Thorn had not said anything at all about this marriage, and wore a black look throughout the ceremony, he still put on his bison head and played his flute at the end, and through the day of dancing.

That night Loon and Elga took their bearskins to the edge of camp beyond Heather's bed and mated through the night, pausing to nap or to talk.

After that Loon was completely lost in the night world of Elga and their mating. It was all that mattered to him. He ignored Thorn during the days, and went out on short hunts or to check traps, but often Elga came with him, and they interrupted whatever they were doing to lie down and kiss and get their clothes off and mate. Loon fell directly into a dream at certain things Elga did or said, things like her murmured, —I'm hungry for you. They got better and better at pleasuring each other, and he learned to feel the differences between his spurts through the course of the night, the way the first was so prongy and tingly, the third so deep and profound, a kind of soul-slinging into her. He could scarcely believe the seizure of love that came on them when they came together, the spurt and clench pulling them together so tightly, something that happened in their eyes looking at each other, in the way they clutched each other, the way they felt they were meant for each other, had found each other among all of Mother Earth's many creatures, and would be happy in each other for as long as they lived, and were only sorry they would not live longer in such bliss, and each hoped to die first so as not to live beyond the other.

After moments like those, they lay next to each other intertwined, and sometimes talked. Loon felt a need to tell her everything that had ever happened to him that mattered, and he wanted to learn the same from her; and although she was still a quiet person, she sometimes pleased him by falling under a similar compulsion to tell her stories. She had been born into a pack that lived far to the east, she didn't know how far, but had on the appearance of her monthlies been married out to a pack farther west, still well to the north and east of the Urdecha.

—Some bad things happened in that pack, she said once, looking away and frowning. —I don't want to talk about that. There's no need. I plan on forgetting it. My life begins with you. With a sleepy little smile she would pull him back into her.

Loon's story was a bit more complicated, at least to him.

—My father Tulik was Thorn's real apprentice, he told her. —He was the one who was supposed to be the next shaman, not me. If he had lived, Thorn might already have given it over to him, and gone off to be a woodsman or something. But my dad was killed by a skelg kick during a hunt, and my mother died that following spring, some say because she was too sad to get fat enough for winter. But Heather says it was a fever. Anyway, with both of them gone, Heather and Thorn took care of me more than anyone else. So eventually Thorn started treating me like his apprentice, although I never asked him, and I don't like it. But everyone just seems to assume that's what I am. They know I don't like it. Moss would be better at it. But now I'm stuck with it. But now I have you, so it doesn't matter. I'll be a lot better at it with you, I hope.

Elga smiled her little smile and kissed him. —That's right, she said.

In the eleventh month they hurried around every day as if forestalling a doom. Which was true, as the swiftly shortening days made clear. It was getting colder, leaves swirled east on winds that filled the gorge at night with their fateful chorus. How big the world grows in a wind!

Stinging nettles for net twine. Lily bulbs. Birch bark. Cedar roots. Pine pitch. Spruce gum, spruce inner bark. Mistletoe berries. All these had to be gathered in the fall.

Often while out gathering, Loon and the others would bring the kids along. To keep the kids amused when they weren't gathering, Loon would bend and weave a hoop, and roll it along for them to throw sticks through, or set up targets for throwing rocks. He carved knots into toys, and hid them for the kids to try to find. He had to think like a squirrel or a jay to recall where he had hidden these things, because often the kids would not find them. There was no point to making something and then hiding it where no one could see. Don't hide your gift in the forest, they said, don't tell your story to the forest. Though he often did just that, even if he never spoke.

Full moon of the eleventh month was the time for the pack to make its annual visit into the cave in the hill above them, after which it would be abandoned to the bears for their winter sleep. It was one of the smaller ceremonies of the year, but as it came at the end of the fall, an important one: a time to say thanks to Mother Earth for the year's bounty, and weave themselves together for the long winter to come.

This time, when the ceremony in the big room was done and the other members of the pack had left, Loon was supposed to stay in the cave with Thorn, and for the first time penetrate farther inside, down the shaman's passages to the secret rooms that only shamans entered. All fall Loon had wondered if Thorn would do it, he seemed so disgusted with him for marrying. As the eleventh moon approached, Thorn had said nothing about it. Loon was tempted to ask him but did not want to show that he was concerned, so he didn't.

On the morning of the eleventh full moon, Thorn said, —Do you have the paints and brushes ready, and your lamps?

—Yes.

—Remember you're not going to be painting anything in there this time, and for many years to come.

—I know.

He would only help Thorn. Possibly Thorn would let him etch

some old painted lines. It didn't matter. He had Elga, and he was going down into the shaman's part of the cave. All was well and more than well.

In the twilight of the eleventh full moon the pack made its way up from Loop Meadow to the clay ramp that was incised into the cliff as if by a giant burin. The paintings on the back wall of this abri ramp welcomed them, the animals leading visitors up to the cave entrance. The entrance was a wide gap in the cliff, about a man's height above the bench, and fringed by a brush overhang. The animal paintings on both sides of the entry showed the animals returning to the underworld that had birthed them. They were mostly red to the left and black to the right, with some red and black mixed in every animal, in a way that the colors were not mixed inside.

Though night was falling, the remaining twilight and the rising full moon illuminated the cave for a good distance in, and the first big chamber's walls were still clear to their sight. This chamber was left unpainted; it was not yet considered to be in the cave, but rather the last part of the outside. In Mother Earth's body, it was not the sabelean but the baginaren.

When they were all in the big dim room sitting on the floor, Thorn spoke to them in an almost conversational tone, unlike his more usual shaman's voice.

We had a bad shaman, he pinched us
And beat us with sticks till we bled,
He stuck bone pins through our ears
And pulled them out sideways to make us remember.
You see what I have on the sides of my head,
Nothing but holes straight into my brain.
It wasn't right but I'll admit this:
I do remember things very well.

One thing I remember is how he led us
Into this cave for the first time

To paint the sacred animals.
It was one of his sorcerer things.
He had us all painting the cliffs
Under the abri at Ordech-Meets-Urdecha,
Using charcoal and bloodstone
To paint just like he did,
Not just lame tries like kids on a lark,
But true three-liners and colored paintings,
And all the tricks you see in here now,
To make the brothers and sisters look real,
And move in the light like they'll jump in your face.

I remember he took me and his other boys
And made us eat his sorcerer's dust,
A ghastly mix so bitter we puked
And afterward walked knee high off the ground,
Which is very hard to do without falling.
And he hauled us into the depths of the cave
Singing a spirit song announcing our presence
To the great mother goddess whose body we stand on,
Whom he said we were mating by walking inside her.
We were the spurtmilk that night, he said.
A full moon it was, and Pika the shaman took an oil lamp
And led the way into the kolby of Mother Earth,
Warm and damp just as you might expect,
All opened to us, and pulsing not so much pink as orange.

Thorn paused, looking around at the cave walls surrounding them.
—And here we are again, he finished abruptly. —Let me show you.

They lit the pine torches they had brought along, and by their big wavery light walked deeper into the cave. In the next chamber it was dark, and they saw only by the yellow of the torches, a light which caught the red of the animals on the walls of this first painted room. Here the animals were dominated by red lions, and so this room was called either the lion room or the red room, or sometimes simply the first painted room. Thorn said every pack who visited this cave had its own names for the chambers, and the shamans involved couldn't corroborate them.

When they were all in the first room, they gathered in a circle around Thorn, and he passed around his lit pipe for everyone to breathe in on. Through the smoking and coughing some of the men shook rattles and huffed into big gourds. The women sang the thanksgiving for the year which they always sang during this visit, and then Thorn set the torches together in the middle of the floor, so that as they danced around them their shadows were cast out onto the walls, black figures moving over the red animals, who after a while themselves began to move. So they danced with the animals in there, slowly so as not to spook the beasts' spirits, then approached the walls and touched the animals' flanks and their own shadows' hands, connecting thereby with their cave spirits.

Then they all sat down near the torches and watched the walls pulse around them in silence, holding hands. It got so quiet that they could hear each other breathing, hear their own heartbeats tocking at the back of their open mouths. All the oh-so-busy year came to a still moment of silent thanks. It went on for a long time; watching the animals pulsing redly around them, looking as if they were in their women's initiation, it felt like the longest moment of the year, something like the spindle the stars turn around.

Then Thorn set a tone, by humming it loudly, and they all hummed it with him; and humming their good-byes, the rest of the pack stood up and filed out of the chamber, back up to the day room and the cave opening, through the baginaren of the world to be reborn yet again into Loop Meadow. They left their shamans Thorn and Loon inside to speak further for them.

Thorn used their torches to light oil lamps, and when the little wick flames were burning, he ground the torches out in the wet clay underfoot. For a while it was shockingly dark, and then Loon could see again, although never as clearly as he had when the torches were lit.

They continued down into the cave, Loon following Thorn's black back. Their lamps flickered in their hands with every step, so that their shadows danced on the flickering walls, and the whole cave seemed to tremble.

As Loon's eyes adjusted to this, he saw the walls more clearly. The whitish rock often glistened wetly, and it bulged or receded away from him, making the stone appear glittery or darker. In places the stone looked to be coated with a thin clear layer of wet stone, like ice; in others it was covered with smooth sheens of mud; in yet others it was spalled as cleanly as if it had been recently knapped.

Suddenly a black lion appeared out of the wall to his right, leaping right at him, and he started back in fear. He could hear Thorn's low laughter ahead of him; Thorn had seen his lamplight jump.

Now black animals drawn in full emerged from the walls on both sides of their passage. Stepping slowly through them, Thorn and Loon came into a big irregular room where clusters of animals were drawn on all the walls, from about chest height to easy arm's reach above, making for a kind of belt of paintings around them. Thorn stopped in the middle of this room and turned in a slow circle, and Loon turned with him.

Underfoot the floor of the room was damp, in a few places muddy. Depending on the flickering of the lamplight and shadows, different animals seemed to shift or slide. There was a black hole at the foot of one wall, from which a faint gurgling sound came. Otherwise it was very quiet.

For a long time they looked at the paintings, some of them three-liners, most fully fleshed. All the sacred animals were there, bear and lion, bison and horse, mammoth and rhino; they all both stood still and moved a little, and as they were overlaid one over the next, and at very different sizes, there was an intense quivering movement inside their stillness. In the end every beast held its place, and only quivered a little with the lamplight.

Thorn laughed shortly and moved on. Loon followed him, staying in his line of footprints as instructed, which was apparently out of respect to the goddess, although it also allowed him to avoid sinking into the mud covering much of the floor.

The passageways between rooms were narrow. The rooms were big in comparison, bigger than any house's interior. Though irregular, and thus full of black shadows, they were fully present to the eye, flickering with the flicker of the lamps. Red lines and spirals marked some walls, and when Loon looked closely at these, they crawled under his gaze until they detached from the wall and floated out ahead of him among the shadows, like floating bubbles of paint lodged right on his eyeballs. Even when he closed his eyes he still saw these dots, and a web of red lines connecting them, all jigging up and down with his pulse. When he opened his eyes again, everything had become a matter of woven red and black patterns, variously fine or large in their weave. Mother Earth's womb was woven like a basket.

They walked on, very slowly, for what seemed to Loon like a long time. Going down in a twisty passage, they stepped once onto a big square stone that had obviously been placed there by someone who had come before, to break a big drop into two parts. Farther along it briefly got so narrow they had to squeeze through sideways, feeling the earth give them a clammy squeeze before allowing them passage.

Now they were truly in the womb of Mother Earth, the kolbos, the sabelean. I like her kolby, men would sometimes say, adding things like, It's just like a deer's, so inviting. But down here was too deep and dark and cold for that. This was the womb of Mother Earth, who had birthed the sky along with everything else. They were moving inside her. The walls around them were slightly slick with damp, just as it was in Elga's vixen. Their paintings were impregnating Mother Earth with her most sacred animals; it was as clear as could be. Thorn would paint her kolby's walls with his paint, and she would birth the animals he painted, and on they would go.

Thorn sang a song that said something much like what Loon had been thinking:

Now we come to you, mother, sister
Singing and bringing you some of your people
Bison and horses, favored by the sun
Hunters and hunted, cats and mammoths
Every manner of brother and sister
The ones you love, the ones we love
Talk to me, mother. You are the one I listen to
You are the one I want to speak. Not me
But you. You speak to me and through me

Thorn sounded more relaxed in the singing of this song than Loon had ever heard him. It was almost like a different voice, or a different person inside the voice. Apparently this was Thorn happy; Loon had never seen it before.

—You're making them come to us, Loon said. —Mother Earth gives birth from here. We're in her womb.

—I'm telling the great mama that we love these animals in particular, Thorn said. —She gives birth to all the creatures of the sun, no matter what we do. But we can show what we love. So in here we paint only the sacred animals. It's nice to hang them up there on the wall like they're floating, as if you're spearing them to the sky. That's what Pika used to do. He would even paint them with their legs hanging and their hooves round. The heavier they are in the world, the more he would do that. He had a lot of little tricks like that, little jokes for himself and whoever might see them.

Thorn's voice was relaxed even now, when he was speaking of his bad shaman. His shadow jiggled against the wall like a living painting, or as if his spirit was dancing before them. The echoes of his voice seemed to indicate a space around them much bigger than what the lamps' light revealed. The walls of the room were pulsing in and out, very distinctly, and not in the rhythm of Loon's pulse, which beat much faster inside him. The sounds and sights around him did not cohere in the way they would have in the world outside. The cold mud sometimes squished under his feet, then firmed to cold wet stone again. When it went soft it felt like he would slide down into the rock, and once, looking down fearfully, he saw he was in the floor up to his ankles; somewhat desperately he hopped from one foot to the other to free himself.

Thorn noticed this, and he reached out and took Loon's right hand and pulled him by it over to the wall, and put his hand against the cave wall.

—Touch it. Hold still.

He put a little hollowed bird bone to his lips, like Heather's blow-dart branch, and blew a cloud of black powder over the back of Loon's hand. It disappeared into the new black splotch on the wall, and Loon felt the stone swallow his hand, felt himself jerked forward, pulled by the hand. The wall could suck in his whole body; his wrist had been pulled in, and now he started pulling back hard. He was too frightened even to cry out.

Thorn put an arm around Loon's middle, and together, with some difficulty, they pulled Loon back out of the wall, grunting and heaving. When Loon popped free he held his pale palm up to his face amazed, staring at it and trembling with relief to have it back. Thorn led him away with uncharacteristic gentleness. There on the cave wall behind them, an open hole the shape of Loon's hand showed where he had almost been sucked in.

—Now a part of you will always be here, Thorn chanted.

Loon thought, So now I really am a shaman, and immediately he had to contain a little ember of fear burning at the center of that thought, trying to flare to a blaze in his chest.

Thorn kept holding Loon's hand, and pulled him deeper into the cave. —Duck your head here, we're almost to the black room.

The descending passage soon opened up again, and they walked into a large chamber, with a ceiling that was low and obvious in some places, sheer black emptiness in others. Thorn set their lamps carefully on the floor, illuminating a bare part of the cave wall curving to the left of a big crack that might have been a passage to yet deeper rooms, but was too narrow for a human to pass through. Cool air wafted out of it. There was a sound like distant voices reverberating up from chambers below them through another hole in the floor. Loon shivered hard as he set to helping Thorn unpack their gear, putting things around the paint bowl. Thorn picked up the charcoal sticks and inspected them closely; the burnt ends of these sticks were so black they did not appear to Loon's eye in the lamplight, but were rather holes in his vision of the cave floor.

Farther down the wall, to the right of the crack, a stone in the shape of a bison's pizzle hung from the ceiling. Drawn on the side of it was a woman's kolby, again so black it was another hole in the rock, triangular this time, the black wedge tucked between legs that went pointy below the knee. The vertical slit of the kolbos was an intense white; it had been cut into the bottom of the triangle, etched with a burin, so that against the solid black of the vixen it was a glowing white line. The crack, the slit, the kolby, the baginaren, the way-to-bliss.

To the right, hovering over this naked woman's legs, loomed a bison man about to mount her, his left leg hooking at her left leg, about to pull her legs apart and plunge into her. It was clear as could be.

Thorn laughed when he saw Loon goggling at it.

—That was Pika, he explained. —He would do anything.

Thorn lit a spill of dry pine needles from his lamp flame, and straightened up and used the flare to light his pipe. He breathed in his smoke deeply, then breathed it out onto a blank part of the wall. He hugged that part of the wall with his arms spread wide, and Loon feared he would merge into it and leave Loon all alone. But he came back and sat down, and they prepared the paint in a bowl, mixing some black powder Thorn carried in a sachet with water from his water bag. He was going to use black paint and charcoal sticks both, he explained. He began humming a deep resonant hum, which seemed to resound from first one part of the recess and then another.

He stood again and kissed the rock wall, then rubbed his hands over a bulge he declared to be a lion's shoulder, feeling each little crack and declivity with his fingertips, then his lips. The wall was covered with fine cracks, but otherwise it was a very clean face.

Thorn sang his exhales: —Ahhhhhh, ahhhhhh, ahhhhh, always in a steady tone. The cave hummed back, —Ahhhhhhhhhhhh. Loon felt the sound in his skin, and then his bones. He too hummed, it seemed involuntarily, as if he were a drumskin helplessly vibrating. It was like a kind of shivering, as if the chill of the cave was penetrating him and making a sound like river ice in the sun. Everything in the cave at that moment was humming that same Ahhhhh, and the vibration helped Loon to fight the cold, which flowed up from the floor into his feet like a flood of water. Ahhhhhh, ahhhhhh, ahhhhhh...

Thorn was still attending to the wall, head cocked to the side. He drew a line with his charcoal stick, stepped back and took a huge breath in, exhaled loudly. —Ha, he said. —Good. Let's get started then. Oh now we come to you, mother, sister! A hunt I saw myself, on a midsummer day.

He chose the stick he wanted to start with, and flattened one side of it with his blade, working gingerly so that he wouldn't break the brittle charcoal. When he was done he dipped the tip in their bowl of black paint and stood up.

When he pressed the charcoal end of the stick over the blank wall, he sang, —Ahhhh. The wall sang back, —Arrrr. Thorn's head tilted to the left as he drew, and his whole body tensed like a cat on the hunt, then relaxed, then bunched up again as he drew some more. He moved smoothly, made each line in a single continous motion. The round bulge in the wall became the shoulder of a lion. Then a head, as in a three-liner. Ears were blacked on their insides, rounded and pointed forward: the big cat was listening. Both eyes were visible at the front of his face, gaze very intent to the left. Then another head in front and beneath that one, long and scowling, ears flattened back on the head, a foreleg reaching ahead. Then a foreleg almost horizontal ahead of that, detached and by itself; clearly the same foreleg in the next instant. The lion was making her dash for the kill.

Loon gaped as he watched Thorn work. Another head emerged before the charging lion, mouth open and eye round, pupil placed most carefully to show where the lion was looking. Then a giant head, the biggest of them all, leading the way: this one slobbered with hunger as he stared ahead. Then a three-liner of a smaller head, and another one.

When those were completed, Thorn sat on the ground behind the lamps and stared at what he had done. Then he jumped up with a newly prepared stick and began again. —Ahhhhhh.

More lions, and some smudging with both fingers and stick ends, to darken certain parts of the heads. He dipped his fingers, or a little pad of moss, into the black paint, then applied it very gently. Now the lions were flowing left in their dash, six lion heads, bigger and smaller, blacked or three-lined, with some free squiggles and detached forelegs to emphasize the flow. In the lamplight they all quivered together.

Above these Thorn added two lions who were ignoring the hunt, touching noses the way cats in a pack did. Above them then, a lion with a snout almost elongated into a cave bear shape, slobbering eyelessly. That was the hungriest lion. To its right another one appeared both in profile, as was normal, and yet also turned toward the observer, both in the same head space.

Thorn then did some scraping with a burin to get the space around the black heads even whiter. One big lion head had three rows of whisker spots dotting its muzzle, over a tight mouth. They looked just that way out in the world; when hunting they were very intent and serious people, and pursed their mouths like unhappy old men thinking something over. Now Thorn dotted whiskers on the one above also, an afterthought it appeared.

—Wait, I see something, Thorn said.

—The animals they're hunting, Loon guessed.

—Exactly. They were hunting eight bison.

As far as Loon could tell there was not room for eight bison on the left end of the lions' wall, where a fold tilted away into darkness. Loon watched curiously as Thorn worked, first taking a caribou shinbone and scraping the lower part of the space left, then drawing a bison with a rhino's horn, some kind of joke or odd perspective. Above that a clutch of bison heads, all in profile except for the one to the farthest left, who looked straight out at the viewer with a suspicious round white eye. All the bisons' nostrils were pinched shut unhappily, and they squinted, except for that one looking out at Loon from under its sweet curve of horns. Animals were seldom painted front on, but Loon enjoyed seeing the characteristic double curve of horns one saw when a bison was regarding you: out, in, out.

Now Thorn was almost climbing into the wall as he used a pad of moss to stump-black some of the bison heads. His nose appeared to touch what he was doing, as if he were blacking with it. The three bison heads at the top were the darkest masses on the whole wall, it almost seemed as if they were coming out of the wall, perhaps to evade the lions, whose flowing pursuit seemed to dive slightly into the wall. Yes, they were making their escape: it was as clear as could be.

At the far left edge of his painting, Thorn took up a new charcoal stick and quickly blacked the entire wall where it curved away, giving the whole scene something like a black riverbank containing it. Now the vision of the hunt hung in space before them, melting into Mother Earth, emerging from Mother Earth. Loon found he was standing; he couldn't remember standing up. His arms were wrapped around his chest.

Thorn moved back beside him and regarded his work.

—Ah, good, he said. —They were really coming tonight. What a thing, eh? Lions on the hunt.

—I can see them move, Loon said.

—Yes, good. Do you see how I did that? It's a thing you can learn. They have to be each in their own space, and a little stretched in the way you want them to move. Different sizes, and a little elongation, and some extra lines.

—And like that foreleg. Just there by themselves, I mean.

—Yes, that's right.

—Those two lions touching noses don't make sense.

—But cats are like that, Thorn said. —You know how they are. There are always some in a pack who aren't paying any attention to what the others are doing. Raven messed them up, they're not very good at being pack animals. They have a hard time staying on the hunt long enough, and they don't care what the rest of the pack thinks of them.

—That's true, Loon said, remembering lions flopping around in their meadows ignoring each other.

—So, that helps make it look real. I did it just as it came to me. It always has to be more than just your idea of what you want. It's not just your plan. You have to think how it would really be. Also, see how that lion and the bison just to its left are on the same bulge? They're like a combined animal, looking like both at once. Of course if the lion catches the bison, that's what would happen. And at the moment of attack you often see both tells at once, mixed together. Like a two-headed sheep in a herd. Or bison man over there, about to mount the woman. See how the left leg could belong to either one of them? Things overlap.

—It really moves, Loon said, growing a little fearful when he couldn't make the lions stop moving. —I feel like I might trip and fall.

—Good. That's what you want to feel. It's the painter's trap. They'll try to move forever and they never will. People will come in here and see them move. How I wish I could see Quartz when he sees this! He's always wearing his lion head cloak. This will blow the top of his head off. He will shit in his pants, he will run away blubbering, maybe knock his head on that bull pizzle over there, slam his head right into that girl's big old kolby. He wouldn't be the first man to knock himself senseless on a woman's pubic bone. Come on, let's get out of here. I'm hungry.

L oon in the days after that:

Mix up a batch of charcoal dust and water and go down to the river cliff to three-line some animals, working on the curves that marked each kind of beast, their proportion and flow. Spring's high water washed the wall clean most years.

More detailed drawings he reserved for flat pieces of sandstone he collected for their surfaces—flat, rippled, crackled, each had their possibilities. He spent a lot of time knapping blades he liked enough to mount on sticks and use to etch, continually seeking a finer burin tip and edge to cut into things. There were so many ways flint could break wrong, it was a little maddening. There was no such thing as a perfectly edged burin. The angles involved were not flint's natural angles. You could get a good point or a good edge, but not both on the same rock.

Still it was interesting to try. The trick was patience. It was like throwing spears through a hoop; you had to do it twentytwenty twenties, until you knew what would happen when you did it, if you could.

Silence is a prayer.

Sit in the morning and whack rock on rock, careful to squint and look away at the moment of the strike. A single splinter can blind you. Check the results in the light of the sun, fingering shards and chips and splinters. Sometimes the most remarkable blades would lie there in the dust after a lucky knock. Girls would give you a caress and a friendly look forever in exchange for blades perfect for what they needed. He already had needles he liked enough. So knapping was good. The better you make things, the better they are to you.

Heather would tax him with plant lore. Every little twig she put before him was bursting with its life story, its uses and dangers, twig after twig, until it began to seem to him that their variety was infinite, that no two plants in the world were the same. Of course this was not true, there were lots of samples of every type out there to be found when walking around, often bunched by type in their favorite places, like thin soils, or shady areas, or whatever might be their characteristic ways. Loon saw that better as he learned more with Heather, and it gave him some pleasure, these habits in the way living things made their living. They grew, they flourished, they died and fed their descendants, who used them as ground and food. Plants were mute people, stuck in their one spot.

It was in tasting that Heather went too far. She wanted him to accompany her to all these places and bring back samples of everything, and then she wanted him to help her eat them! He might as well be her camp robber of a cat, vomiting strange meals she set out. Added to what Thorn demanded that he learn, it was almost too much.

Although he liked it better. He was more interested in what Heather wanted him to know than in what Thorn wanted him to know, all except for the painting. He could see her things, touch them, put them cautiously to his tongue. Thorn on the other hand was always going off into the realm of numbers, stories, poems, songs, and all of it to be memorized, sometimes word for word. Words words words! That was what made it too much.

But even Heather wanted him to memorize words. She would have him recite the qualities of three different twigs as he looked at them, following her lead, and the next day ask him to do it by himself, and he would stare at them and try to remember what they were. It didn't always come to him.

—You are not very good at this, Heather observed one time.

Another: —Why are you so bad at this?

—I don't like it! Loon said. —You can't make me do everything.

—Everyone does everything, haven't you noticed?

—No they don't. No one else does the shaman stuff. And not many people have the plant knowledge. Mostly women at that.

She stared at him. —Well, but are you a shaman or not?

He heaved a sigh.

—So, she said. —You need to know all this stuff. The plant stuff you will need if you are going to try taking care of sick people, and that's what shamans do. Maybe our unspeakable one doesn't like that part, but believe me, it is shaman work. What I do for sick people would go a lot better if they had a shaman teaching them what to try for. So, stick it in your head! Put it in there as a song or something! Practice! You memorize things by associating them in strings and clusters, like tunes. Pick your own method, or try more than one. See something like the riverbank, and put each thing in a different spot on the riverbank, that's what I do. It's a skill as well as a talent, so you can get better at it if you try.

Another big sigh.

—Go away you big baby, you'll huff out my fire. Go cry in the river.

She would let him off, in effect. With Thorn it was never like that.

—Tell me the story of bison man, Thorn would demand.

Loon gritted his teeth and took a deep breath. Thorn was a bison man, Pika had been a bison man. They were all assholes. Making your wife mate with a bison, trapping the son that resulted in the cave, sending girls in to find him, it was all bad news, therefore one of Thorn's favorites. If Loon told it in a way that made it sound as bad as it really was, Thorn would flick him hard on the ears. Loon was getting tired of that.

I t's forbidden!
—Oh, sorry, I didn't know.

Twentytwenty prohibitions in Wolf pack. Elga was sick of them. The pack she had grown up in had had them also, but not so many. You can't eat sucker fish, they're such thieves! You can't eat pike, they're too mean! Although you can ward off bad spirits with a ring of pike jaws and teeth hung over the door. Hang a goose wing in a golden spruce to show respect to the birds. Never eat newly killed fish when you're bleeding, they're not yet all the way dead and it will make you bleed more. Never butcher an animal when you're bleeding. If you want a baby and it won't come, eat a bear penis, it works every time. Catching sight of a weasel or a flicker means good luck. Don't ever touch a raven! Ravens will take away your luck.

In other words: be afraid! Everyone in the forest knows more than you do! Elga knew from her first pack that it wasn't right. All these Wolf women were too much like their leaders Thunder and Bluejay. The fish rots from the head.

If you really want to know someone, find out what animal they are cousin to. The strong spirits are bear, wolverine, lynx, wolf, and otter. Don't drink too much water, it makes you heavy-footed.

This was true. Elga nodded and listened, nodded and listened some more. She asked questions even when she knew the answers. She asked all the women one thing or another, even Thunder who usually spoke before there was time to ask her a question. How do you make that sauce? What is the moon?

The sun is a young woman, the moon her brother who slept with her and turned to stone. If the northern lights are strong in the fall, there will be many caribou the following spring. Dreaming of a bear means a storm is coming. But don't call them bears, women call them black places.

—Do you ever hunt boars?

—Don't ever say the names of bad things! What, are you crazy?

And so they called poisonleaf the evil shrub, bitterroot the one not used, shit-soon the ugly one, boar the unspeakable, lynx black tail, or something-going-around; otter was the black thing, hyena the one-beneath-notice.

Beneath notice because they acted too much like people, Elga thought when she heard this one.

—Never eat fish with porcupine! Thunder yelled at her. The fish will be offended!

—Oh, sorry. I didn't know.

Glacier milk will give you the runs. When the fuzz from willow catkins floats in the air, the salmon are coming. You catch the first salmon and brush it with willow, while asking for more salmon in the days to come.

They had twentytwenty recipes for preserving salmon, all delicious. Different kinds of salmon were better with different sauces applied. When they went to the salmon rivers to wait for the salmon to arrive, she was told, the Wolf women would sing them up from the ocean, naming all the rivers and streams the fish would have to swim to get to their rendezvous with Wolf pack. The oldest women would eat the first salmon caught, while doing their best not to move a single bone of it, and the way the bones moved or didn't would tell them things about the year to come.

Thunder was as mean as a pike or a leopard. Cats were the fastest of the hunters, they struck faster than you could see the strike. When a red fox is heard barking near camp, a death will come soon.

Elga didn't like Thunder or Bluejay, and she saw that none of the women did, but only endured the two of them, and worked around them as they could. Elga was used to this kind of situation; she hadn't liked the Jende pack either, and their women had been horrible to her. Thunder and Bluejay were better than that, but they had under them a cowed and unhappy group of women. So Elga kept to herself and worked very hard for them. It would take many months to become a silent counterweight to the headwomen, if she did it right. It would happen one question at a time, one sympathetic glance at a time, after someone got yelled at.

So she worked and she asked questions. When others asked her questions, she asked what the questioner thought of the matter. This always worked to turn the talk around. She could see that Thunder and Bluejay considered her pliant, even a little slow. It was only later they would see which way the wind was blowing. By then it would be too late.

Never fall asleep when your meat is on the fire.

Loon saw that Elga appeared to be on good terms with Sage, which made him a little uneasy. Once he approached Sage alone by the river, even tried giving her a kiss, as he would have before, and with a quick scowl she smacked him on the ear and knocked him back a few steps. —No!

—I just wanted to.

—You want too much!

Hearing that, he remembered the dream in which the deer had said that very thing to him. Shocked by the echo, he stared at Sage. —You were the deer! he said aloud, and then left her alone, feeling a pang of loss.

But all that was a kind of spillover of his feelings for Elga, and left him when he was with her. In her presence he had a hard time taking his eyes off her, and during the day, if he spotted her down below in camp, he would watch her and prong at just the sight of her walking, so long-legged and slow. His wife. It was the oddness in her proportions that drew his eye, as with all the women he watched so lustfully, their particular oddities exactly what caught him and drew him to them. A woman was never bad-looking, as far as he could tell. If they were round, like Ducky, roundness was good. If they were mannish, like Thunder, then their mannishness was exactly what made them a more attractive woman. And so on. He was hopeless in that regard.

By day Elga only occasionally glanced his way, with a little hello in her eye before she returned to her affairs. From a distance Loon saw her talking with one person at a time, usually the girls, but also Thorn and Hawk and Schist. He didn't like her talking to Hawk, but there was no sign that anything was going on there. And the pack was the pack, after all. You had to be able to talk to everyone, or there would be trouble. And enough trouble could split things up, and that would really be trouble. Like when the Fox pack split and many of their younger people moved west of the ice caps.

At night Loon and Elga met at their bed, behind Heather's place against the backing cliff, and got under their furs and took off each other's clothes, first one stripping the other naked, then the naked one stripping the one still clothed; either way was great, a time filled with kisses and caresses; and then he would slide into her and off they would go.

One day in the twelfth month, warmer than most, he found her down by the river alone. The last birds around were singing in the low midday sun, giving the news that there were no cats or bears in the area. Elga saw him approaching and simply pulled her cloak off, untied her skirt and let it fall. Her dark skin gleamed like flint in the sun. She stepped back into the stream and immersed herself in the water and stood again, and the water beaded and fell from her sparking with sunlight, all her fall curves there for him to see as he hurried to her untying his jacket. He took her in his arms, embraced her and lifted her, made her laugh with his eagerness. She tore his pants down his legs and squeezed his spurt with both hands, and then fell into the sandy shallows tucked in the outer bank of the river behind a snag. Ah blessed union. He kissed her all over, intent to kiss every surface and crevice of her body. He licked at her like a stag licking a deer, licked her until she gasped and helplessly rocked her hips, the sign she was about to come. What he liked then was to have his tongue as far up her as possible. The squeeze of her clenching on his tongue was the best feeling of all, better even than his own spurt, because while spurting he was gone from himself, whereas when her kolby was squeezing his tongue he was still there to feel it. Nothing else in the world made him feel as alive as that. His own spurt, which she so easily drew out of him afterward, was a kind of excess of happiness. After that his body glowed, and he wanted to nuzzle her dark skin, feel her heat, smell her on his muzzle. Crawl over to the creek and plunge his face in the stream and suck down swallows of clean cold water that still tasted like her when he licked his lips. This winter would not be so bad with Elga to warm him.

—It's so good with you.

—Because you love me. She said this with a fond look at him. —You love me and I love you.

—Yes. I didn't know it could be like this.

—Neither did I.

It made him so happy that he could barely stand to be with Thorn, all his stinky dishevelment, his reproaches and remonstrations and orders, his picky and convoluted lessons. Learn how to calculate the relation of the months to the year, so many scores of days, all the ugly little slash marks on the yearsticks and the tally sticks. Recite one of the five great poems or one of the ten lesser poems, and always the one he was weakest at. Ducking away to avoid the swift middle finger snapping off the thumb onto his poor ears. Ending long fists of nonstop effort with his ears buzzing nevertheless.

—Quit it! he would complain.

—You quit it. Start thinking, start remembering.

—I am already. Just leave me alone!

But he seldom ran off, because then the night by the fire would be bad, and the next day as well, until he apologized and got back to it. Painfully he had learned that his least bad option was to sit there and try to get through his lessons.

—Wait, I see something. Thorn was not impressed by his unhappiness. —A face looking left and down turns his head until he's looking up and right.

—The man in the moon, Loon said, —looking around every month.

—Yes. And full moon is when the moon's face is looking right at us. How many days in a month?

—Twenty-nine and a half days, new moon to new moon.

—Yes. So what do we do about that?

—We alternate the months and call them either hollow or full, meaning either twenty-nine days or thirty days. Twelve of those in alternation leaves us short of the winter solstice by eleven or twelve days, so the shamans at the corroboration add a thirteenth month every two or three years.

—Yes. And it still doesn't work, Thorn added with a gloomy frown. —The error builds up fast. Vole thinks he has a splitter that makes it better, two score and nineteen over two, but even that loses a day every three years or so, and besides, what kind of a split is that? It has no shape, no one can see it. It's cat vomit.

—Maybe Heather should taste it.

Thorn laughed. —I wish she would. I would be interested to hear what she thought of all that, but she doesn't care about matching the sky to the seasons. Month to month is fine for her. People think just like they fuck, women inward and men outward. And women are naturally very monthly because of their bleeding.

—Everyone is monthly, Loon pointed out, thinking of their nights under the full moon, that world of light so clear and pale, a different world, almost like the world of dreams, but one they were awake in.

Thorn shook his head. —Everyone is yearly. Monthly is a matter of more or less.

—But the way you can see on full moon nights! It's so bright you can even see the colors still, a little bit.

—There you are, thinking outward. You don't think inward when it comes to the moon, but women do. So it's different. I should have thought that as a married man you would have figured that out by now.

Jays while bathing grew ever more disheveled as they managed to get their feathers wetter and wetter. Never did you see a bird's feathers in such disarray, except in their bath. It was as if they took their jacket off by briefly disassembling the weave of it. The blue of a jay will go away. Soon all the jays would be gone for the winter. There were only a few left now.

Sitting with Heather, splitting cedar roots for basket making. Being with Heather was far more relaxing than being with Thorn. She went out for a walk every day, to seek out her own plants in their little tucks. She joined the nut-gathering groups and helped them, then took Loon as a lookout and helper, on rambles even farther away. He often came back laden with small fragrant twigs or entire plants, and she crushed the leaves under his nose so he would learn the scents. Indeed a smell was a very distinct thing, seemingly right there inside his head, so that it almost always called up a name from him.

—When you need to memorize something, she said to him, —sniff this rosemary. It will help you remember, you'll see.

Loon took from her the fragrant brittle twig with its short pale green needles. It had a very particular scent, part of the smell of the south-facing slopes. —Thanks, I'll try it.

—Bears have by far the best sense of smell, she told him.

—Is it true you should never eat a bear's small stomach?

—Who says that?

—Hawk and Moss. They say that if you eat it, you'll end up slipping and sliding around in your shoes when you walk in forests. They say they tried it and Nevermind and Spearthrower didn't, and they started slipping and falling when the others didn't have any problem.

Heather shook her head. —I don't know. It's possible something about that small stomach might make you a little sick, hurt your balance somehow.

—So it's true?

—It could be, I guess.

Loon made a fire with his firestarter, and they heated water in cedar cups held in the forks of branches and brewed spruce tea. Taste of spruce filling his throat and making his insides bigger. Watery eyes. Spruce had a big spirit, it helped them in all sorts of ways. Thorn wore a spruce top in his hair when he went into the caves, to bring a little luck in there with him.

Different firestarter kits used different woods: red cedar, bitter rose, elderberry tree, alder root.

—Find out which kind works best, Heather instructed him, gesturing at several kits she had assembled.

—How?

—Try them all and see which one goes fastest! She stared at him as if he were feeble-minded.

He nodded. —All right then, I will. When did you think of this?

—Last winter.

—And how long were you alive before you thought of this?

—Go. Do it.

He took the kits out into the low sun and put them each to the test, using the same starter in every case, made from a dried duff and moss mix commonly used by the pack. Thorn could drill up a fire almost as fast as you could sit down and get comfortable. Loon was not that fast, but he was good at it, as indeed most people were. It was that which made his failure on the first night of his wander still rankle. What a night that first night had been.

All Heather's kits worked about the same speed, it seemed to him. The alder root was almost black, its firestick much lighter. The elderberry stick was made of a dried tip of new growth. The hearths had to be hard and with a tight stubborn grain to their wood, so the cup for the firestick tip would hold. The firesticks had to be hard enough to hold their tips as they were spun, but soft enough to make them hot. Putting a little sand in the cup would make them hotter too, but for the sake of the test Heather didn't want him to do that.

—They're close to the same, he told her when he was done trying them.

She frowned. —Do it again, I'll sing the time. So as he lit fires, his arms beginning to burn with the effort, she turned away from him and sang the reed-splitting song, which was very short and repetitive, sticking out her fingers every time she did it five times, and marking the results on a tally stick with a blade. When they were done, she looked at her tally stick and nodded. —The cedar is fastest. We can tell people at the next festival.

—They won't believe it.

—They will have to believe it. She gestured at the kits. —They can try it and they'll see we're right.

She grinned fiercely at this thought. She liked to be right about things, he saw, and in ways no one could argue with. Like hitting a rabbit with a thrown rock and killing it dead. No arguing it had been a good throw.

Thorn only snorted when Loon mentioned this later. —Hers

aren't the interesting things to be right or wrong about. Those are just the way things are.

—But that's what she wants to know.

—Sure. So does everyone. But things we can know in that way are a very small part of what matters. So it's a form of looking away. You get to the hard questions, Heather just looks away.

—I wonder what she would say to that.

—Ask her! But I'll tell you what she'll say, because she's always saying the same things; she'll say, first things first. First know what you can know, then take a look at the harder things.

—Isn't that right, though?

—Not at all. The hard questions press on us the whole time, youth, no matter what we know or don't know. You have to face up to Narsook. The hard questions can't be avoided, not if you want to really be alive.

The flexible young cedar withes could be woven into strong ropes, and that was one of the things people did around the fire during the long nights, weaving and tugging them and making sure they were strong. They could be even stronger than rawhide cord. Any withes that were brought in would be put to quick use. When Loon went with Hawk and Moss out to check their snares, he brought a hand blade and cut as many of the new young branches as he could fit in his backsack. Everyone tried to come back from their day's walk with something useful for the handwork at night around the fire.

That end of the year Loon became a five-strand rope maker under Ibex's guidance. —What did you do to that finger? Ibex said, pointing to Fatty.

—Caught it knapping.

—Ow. I bet you won't do that again.

—It wasn't so bad, Loon lied.

They went out on the hunt one morning, headed downstream and then across Lower Valley and up its east ridge trail. On the ridge they had to stop and retreat, as a bear was devastating a beehive, and looked like she would be a while. Between the bear woman and the angry bees it was not worth waiting for it to be over. Spearthrower wanted to try to kill the bear, but a ridge was not a good place to try, and the others already had all the bear claws they wanted and did not want to risk harm to get more. Spearthrower gave them a hard time about it, but the others ignored him and descended to the Lower Valley floor by way of a deer trail Loon had not noticed before. Spearthrower still had a neck cord hung with a great number of bear and lion claws.

On the valley floor the creek's flow had dropped enough to make walking up the creekbed easy. And near the head of the creek they saw a herd of horses. They stopped and bowed to the creatures, then stood and watched for a while.

The horses were beautiful, as always. About half of them were spotted, either black on white, or white on black; the rest were brown. Their colors were as vivid as birds' colors, and they had a little of that same fastidious quality, so much finer than caribou or saiga or elg. Their footwork was light and neat, like a cross between women dancing and the swift trotting of the unspeakables in the forest. Big glossy haunches, short stiff manes. Lower Valley was pinched to a gorge at its top, so it wasn't clear whether they would pass through the gorge or return downstream to continue their grazing in the Urdecha.

Again Spearthrower wanted to kill one, and again the others declined. Horses were only to be killed when people were really hungry. Not to mention they were hard to get near.

—Spearthrower wants to kill. Let's find him a wolverine and let him do it.

They laughed at Spearthrower, and he said, —All right then, let's find a deer, if that's what you want.

—That is what we want.

They traversed above the horses in order not to disturb them, and crossed Quick Pass into the top of Upper Valley. As they came over the rib of rock that marked the Lower side of the pass, they were hailed from the ridge trail across the valley.

—Look, he's short-handed, Spearthrower said.

Loon saw it. All of the men in the Raven pack, who lived south of the biggest ice cap, were missing their left little fingers. This was a little worrisome, but other than that they seemed like any other people. Loon recognized the man they were approaching, a traveler named Pippiloette, which was the Ravens' name for red squirrels.

Pippiloette waved as he approached. —Well met! he called.

—Well met, they all said.

He was much friendlier than a squirrel, but quick and inquisitive in their way. —Have you seen a pack of spotted horses? He said his words farther back in his mouth than they did, so that they came out of his nose a little.

—Yes, they're just over the pass in the first meadow. Why, do you want one?

Pippiloette grinned. —I do. Our big mama wants one of their spotted hides. I'm trying to find out their grazing circuit, so we can set up an ambush.

This was the only way to kill horses; they were very fast and had good endurance, and stuck together in packs very hard to split. And they saw traps that caribou would run right into. No, horses were hard, and being sacred, were only hunted for sacred reasons.

—We're hunting deer, Hawk said. —Do you want to join us?

This took Loon by surprise; Schist would not have asked, nor Heather. But Pippiloette was pleased.

—Yes, thanks, he said. —Those horses will be there tomorrow too, I'm pretty sure.

So they were five, and they discussed where deer had last been seen. Pippiloette had seen some that morning down by the top ford on Lower's Upper Creek, so they made a plan as they went over there, and Hawk and Spearthrower slipped ahead to get downstream and get settled into an ambush. Loon was left with the traveler, to beat downvalley after a fist of sun had passed.

—You're Thorn's apprentice? Pippiloette asked.

—Yes, that's right.

—Hard work! the traveler said, and laughed at Loon's expression. —Our shaman likes him a lot. But he's a handful even for other shamans.

—Your shaman is Quartz?

—That's right, Quartz the magnificent. A very good shaman. Well, odd. A little scary. But I had a sickness last winter, and he made a steam that almost choked me, but he pulled the bad thing right out of me, I could feel it leave me, right here.

He pointed to his diaphragm.

—You're lucky, Loon said. —It's good when that happens.

—Can Thorn do that? Are you going to be able to do that one day?

—I hope so, Loon lied. —I've been on my wander, and gone with him to the end of the cave.

The man nodded. He was happy for Loon, interested. He had a lot of stories about the Raven pack and Quartz, and Loon offered that he had recently married a girl he had met at the eight eight festival.

—Oh very nice, congratulations on that. Where did she come from?

—From north of the caribou.

—North of the caribou! Those people, well, you tell me, I shouldn't presume, but I hear they are wild?

—She's actually pretty quiet, Loon said. —But maybe wild is still the right word.

The man grinned at Loon's expression, such that Loon couldn't help grinning himself.

When a fist had passed they clomped down the creekbed whacking things with their javelins, and Pippiloette emitted some very realistic lion roars. Any deer in the brakes below would surely have bolted downvalley to avoid either lions or, worse, humans acting like lions. Although if the deer heard the falsity they would know it was a trap, and take off sideways on a traverse over the ridges bounding the valley.

Lower's Upper was steep and narrow, with not much in the way of meadows, curving out to the west so that it caught a good afternoon light. The wind was picking up, the pine trees roaring in their big airy needle chorus. Pippiloette sang and yet Loon could barely hear him.

Then they heard a frightened bleat cut short, and after that the triumphant cries of their brothers of the hunt, who clearly were celebrating a kill. Loon and Pippiloette ran down to join them, saw it was true; the men were standing around a stag splayed on its side, two spears stuck through his ribs and the men busy trying to catch some of his leaking blood in gooseskin bags. When he had stopped bleeding they started a fire and began to break down his body for carrying back to camp. Pippiloette knew the proper disposal rituals for the parts of the body they weren't going to be taking back, and he chatted amiably before they burned the guts, then chanted the deer death chant, and took the unusable bones and set them at the bottom of a little eddy in the creek, stuck in a little circle so they would have fish for company. This was Pippiloette's version of the water burial, and one he assured them would result in much better luck with deer afterward. So the others did it willingly, and the bone circle looked good there in the water, like something beavers might do.

After that they had the quarters and body and head, and they were five, so all was well, and Pippiloette joined them cheerfully. —I'm almost going that way anyway. It will be good to see your people.

He came by once or twice a year, as he spent much of his time walking a circuit, like a wolverine's but much larger. He liked to drop in on packs in a particular order, trading for things people elsewhere would like, moving them along region to region and holding on to a few things for his return home. —It can be lonely, it's often dangerous, but it's interesting, he said. —I get to talk to so many people, in so many packs. There are salmon people everywhere you go, so I've always got my clan's people to look out for me, and they help me make my trades. And then in between visits I'm out and about, just like the rest of the animals.

—Always alone? Loon asked.

—Almost always.

—But isn't that dangerous, to go alone?

—No, not so much. Best be quick at making fire, of course. I try to always carry a live ember, kind of go from fire to fire to make that happen. But if you're good with fire, and keep an eye out, you'll be left alone.

—Even when you sleep?

—It depends where you sleep, right? Don't you think so?

—I was out on my wander back in the spring. It seemed hard to find a safe place to sleep, especially with a fire. Sometimes I slept in trees. Other times I made a huge fire. I would even sleep by day and stay awake all night.

—I've done all that, Pippiloette agreed. —You have to take care.

—What about woodsmen, or old ones?

—You have to take care. It depends what you think is worse, the animals or the woodsmen. In different areas it's different. Woodsmen are skittish, they're almost all up on the plateau, or in the ravines of the highlands, up where no one else will live. The lunkheads aren't like that. They have their own regular camps, usually at the top of kolby canyons, or else on islands in rivers. They're not very dangerous, compared to lions or hyenas. They're not real happy around people, but they are polite. Woodsmen are usually crazy, and most want to keep their distance. They're out there because they killed someone, or ate a dead person when they were hungry or something. Lots of times when I've run into one, it's seemed like they forgot how to talk. A couple of them talked all the time, but never to me. They had invisible friends. They spoke languages I've never heard.

He shook his head. —It wouldn't be good to be alone all the time. I like it when I'm out on a trip, but I like it because I know I'll be talking to someone soon. If it were to go on forever, I wouldn't like it.

I don't think the woodsmen are any different in that way, or not much. It's true that a few I've met seemed really happy. Although it's the happy ones you're most likely to run into. The other kind, you hope you don't.

He came with them to their camp and joined the evening by the fire. They cut up the stag and the women stuck some herbs into the brisket, and marinated the ribs and haunches and coated them with spiced fats. Everyone ate well that night.

As they sat watching the fire bank down, Pippiloette gave out some gifts from his sack, shells and carved sticks of antler and tusk and black wood. Those in the pack who had handcrafts to trade at the eight eight gave him some of their littler things as something to pass along to other packs. In this way people knew what to look for at the festivals. So they gave him things that would fit in his sack, like baskets, spoons, waterproof bags, fur liners, or hats.

Loon gave him an antler carved to have a man's body and a lion's head, much like the knot he had carved in his wander, and Pippiloette laughed out loud as he inspected it and shook Loon's hand, saying —I'll keep this myself, I tell you, but I'll show it to everyone and tell them you made it.

—Thank you, Loon said.

Several of the girls clustered around Pippiloette, and because of that a number of the women did as well, some keeping the girls in hand, others just joining the general pleasure, because the traveler was a good-looking man, and his stories often brought news. Even Heather was relaxed around him, which was a good sign, because usually she regarded such men and muttered, —A face is just a face, what do you do in your place?

But Pippiloette seemed to do quite a lot in his place. And also he was good at being friendly without actually coming on to the women; he was charming but a little distant, and intent to speak also to the men he had hunted with. If there was ever an awkwardness, he took his flute from his sack and played them his tunes, which were the same every time he visited, and ones they only heard from him. He had a haunting way with the flute, different than Thorn's.

He sang their songs with them in a high nasal voice, buzzy and penetrating, but perfectly pitched. A really musical person. A spirit took him up when he sang or played, just as one saw in certain morning birds. He even stood up when these moments came.

Tonight he agreed to tell them a story, and they settled in around the fire happily. He stood by the fire, and looked at them as he spoke.

> I am a traveler as you know,
> I walk the surface of Mother Earth
> And so do my fellow travelers,
> Each of us on his own path.
> And some of us repeat our paths
> As long as we can find them,
> And nothing makes us take a different way.
> I am one of those myself,
> Having a wife with my brother,
> And he goes out when I'm at home,
> And he doesn't like it when I'm overly late
> Although both of us have been delayed
> Once or twice through the years.
> What this means for me is I go out east
> To the gate between worlds
> And then turn north and walk for a fortnight,
> Right up to the edge of the great ice cap,
> And come back just under that great white wall
> Or sometimes up on the ice itself
> If the summer melt has made the land next to the ice
> Impassable. West I return and south
> Across the steppes to home, using paths
> Of my own that no one knows, the best ways of all.
>
> That's the way it is for me, but in my travels
> I meet other men out walking the world,
> And some of them have neither circuit nor home
> But wander always a new way. These men

Are curious people, odd in their ways and speech,
But interesting for that, and we talk.
Always when travelers get together over a fire
We talk. You can see that right now, I know.
And travelers together talk about traveling. Where have
    you been?
What have you seen? What are people like?
What's out there in this world we live on?
These are the questions we ask and the stories we tell,
And some travelers travel to find the answers
And tell new stories to those they meet.

One such I met this summer, at the farthest east
Of all the places I go. This man looked like
The northers and I could barely understand him,
But I could, and it got easier as we talked
Because he had only one thing to talk about,
Which was this world we live on, its shape and size.
All travelers agree, for we've seen it ourselves:
There is ice to the north, wherever you go,
And to the west is the great salt sea,
And to the south, again the salt sea,
Although warmer and more calm,
More in and out, and dotted with islands.
We all agree on this, we travelers,
As between us we have seen it all,
And some travelers claim to have seen it all
Themselves alone. Good. Maybe they are even
Telling the truth. I can't say. But here's the thing:
What about east? This norther man
Was like a lot of us, he had that question,
And more than that: he wanted to know the answer.
And no one had it.
So he took off walking east, he said.
He walked for days, he walked for months,

He walked for years. He walked east from the time
This question had come to him, in his youth,
And kept on walking until he was a man in the middle of life.
Seventeen years, he said, he walked east.
I asked him what he had seen on this life walk.
He told me of steppes that went on forever.
There were mountains like those to the west of here,
And some lakes bigger than any I've seen,
Little salt seas even, their water was salt, he said,
But mostly it was steppes.
You know what that's like. The walking is good
If it isn't too wet, and there are always animals to eat.
So there really was no impediment to him.
Yet there he sat, across a fire from me,
As far to the east as I had ever been,
But it was only the gate of worlds, a nice broad pass
Between low mountains to north and south.
It had taken him twelve years to walk back
To where we were. This he told me.
Finally I had to ask him: why did you come back?
Having gone so far, why turn around?
Why not keep going for the rest of your life?

He stared into the fire for a long, long time
Before he met my eye and answered me.
When I was as far east as I got, he said,
I came to a hill and went up it to look.
I was feeling poorly and my feet hurt,
And no person I had met for several years
Spoke any word I understood. All my dealings
Were done by sign, and you can do that
And still get by, but after a while you want a word
With the people you see. I Pippi could only agree to that!
And so, he said, he stood on that hill, and all to the east
Was just the same. There was no sign at all it would ever change.

I realized, he said, that this world is just too big.
You can't have it all, no matter how much you want it.
It's bigger than any man can walk in one life.
Possibly it just keeps going on forever.
Possibly our Mother Earth is round, he said then, like a
    pregnant woman
Or the moon, and if you walked long enough
You would come around to where you started,
Assuming the great salt sea did not stop you,
But really there is no way to know for sure.
And so I turned back, he said, because the world is too big,
And most of all, I wanted to talk to somebody again
Before I died. Having said that, having told his tale,
We stood and hugged, and he cried so hard
I thought he would choke. I had to hold him up.
Whether he had succeeded or failed in his life walk
He did not know, and I didn't either.
After that he calmed down, and we looked at the fire
Until long in the night, telling other stories we knew.
Before bed I asked him, So what's for you now?
What will you do, now that you're back?
Well, he said, to tell the truth,
I'm thinking I may take off east again.

—That is my story for tonight's fire, Pippiloette said. —I have chewed off a bit of this long fall night for you.

After that they talked some more, and it seemed to Loon that Pippiloette had a way of not looking at Sage that seemed to indicate that the two of them had an understanding. Late in the night, when the fire had died down and everyone was asleep, Loon wondered if those two did not find each other. Also, if it might not be that Pippiloette had a similar arrangement with women in each of the packs he regularly visited. Heather had suggested as much one time with a remark under the breath.

When he thought what that must be like, Loon wanted to be a traveler too. Sage was the best-looking woman in their pack, the most desirable, with her big autumn tits ploshing together at her every move. It was not chance Pippiloette had made his arrangement with her. What would it be like to lie with a woman like that in every pack, each one different?

But these were just the spillovers of his feelings for Elga, which were so filled with spurting that the feeling extended from him in every direction. He loved all the women of the pack, and all the women of other packs as well. They were all people he wanted, and so were the female animals. He wanted the deer and the vixen and the ibex and the bear women, and the horse women of course. It was simply a world of desirable females. Sometimes the feeling flooded him, like the break-up of the river in spring. So when the nights came and he pulled all these feelings back together and poured them into the body of his wife, there in their bed and the whole world nothing but Elga, he felt like he had fallen into a dream where love was all in all.

And one night after they had fused and melted into each other in their nightly way, she nuzzled his ear and said, —I'm going to have a baby. Heather says it's true.

Loon sat up and stared down at her. —You are?

—Yes.

—So. We did it.

—Yes. She grinned at him and he suddenly felt his face was already doing that. They kissed.

—We have to take care of it, she said.

—Does Heather know if it's a boy or a girl?

—Not yet. She said she will in a few months.

—When will it come?

—Six months from now. So, the end of the fifth month. Right in the spring, the best time. Unless it's a bad spring.

Loon tried to understand it, but couldn't. It felt as if clouds were filling his chest. Or as if he had plunged over a waterfall he had not seen, into a deep pool. This Elga was his. The night when she had shown up at the eight eight bonfire, everything had changed—not just at once, although that too, but also more and more over the months since, with everything else that had happened, each step along the way finally leading to this entirely new place.

As Elga grew bigger with child that winter, she gained in influence among the women, like the moon over the stars. Sage didn't like it, Thunder neither, but Elga had a way, even with them, of calming people. They felt her power in a reassuring way. Her silence could have been a withholding, but it wasn't; it was more like an assent to the other person and her story. Often they told her things while she was helping them with their work, because she asked questions, and remembered the answers too. It was hard to resent such a person.

And now she was bringing a new child into the pack, which was a big thing. Normally the grandparents would be celebrating such an arrival, so there would be two or even four strong advocates of the new pack member, and there would be a discussion lasting through the whole winter as to which clan the new babe would become part of. In this case there were no grandparents, but as Heather and Thorn between them had taken Loon in when he was orphaned, it was their role to be like grandparents to this child.

Heather, however, was not interested in such things, and Thorn didn't like Loon's marriage to begin with. So it was a matter of Elga's ability to put the other women under a telling, and she did this without looking like she was trying; it was just her being herself. And so in her last few months the other women helped her in the way she helped them. And a pregnant woman in the end of her time was the focus of all their efforts.

The short days, the cold; the storms rolling in from the west, low and snowy. Ice on the river and the creeks, snow over that. The white world. The midday sun just peeking over the southern gorge wall. All the birds gone except for the snow birds; all the animals sleeping or hiding under the snow, or caught in the people's traps, quietly enduring. White fur. The pack in its house, sleeping away. They were used to snow, they liked snow. They had their stored food and the daily tasks, the long nights sleeping like bears. The long stories told around the fire.

*   *   *

Heather would be the midwife for the birth, as always. She grumbled about this in the way she did about every task she performed for the pack, but in this case she seemed to really mean it. She didn't like being the midwife.

—It will be fine, she told Elga gruffly. —You're a big girl, there won't be any problems. I'll give you the right teas and infusions and we'll have that kid out of you before you know it. There's some work you have to do to push it out, of course, but we'll help you. Mostly the work does you. You just have to ride it out.

And so the end of the winter passed with something for them to think about, and to watch happening. Tucked in their house or under the abri, they ate their food and watched the sky, went out on clear windless days to check the traps. The strike of the sun's warmth on a body cut through all but the coldest days. But even the sunniest days were short, and in the afternoons they scurried back to their big house like muskrats or mice.

One morning Loon went out with Moss to look at some of their traps downriver, set in the ravines off the canyon one loop downstream.

They made good time on the trail climbing the ridge between the two loops, and were on the ridge by sunrise. All the sky to the east was orange, and they agreed this meant it would probably snow two mornings later. Then Moss laughed and said, —Does it ever happen that way?

Loon laughed too. Moss's laugh was particularly infectious. He was slighter than Hawk, with a narrow handsome face under a thick tangle of black curls. His face was very flexible and expressive, one moment as sharp as if knapped, the next slack-lipped and foolish.

—I do think snow comes after the sun shows its ears, Loon said.

—Or the moon, Moss agreed. —It's the snow in the air getting lit up. The light bounces off the snow in the air just like off any other snow.

The light was definitely bouncing off the snow on the ground. They pulled down their caps to their eyebrows and tilted their heads down and to the side to hike up the ridge into the low winter sun. Loon's cap was edged with marten fur, Moss's with wolf.

When the snow warmed up in the sunlight enough to soften a little, they stopped and tied their snowshoes to their shoes and continued on to the first traps, set in the ravine mouth where Steep Creek ran into the main creek of Next Loop Down. There was a giant rock called the Robin's Nest standing in the little meadow at the confluence of these two creeks, sticking out of the blanket of snow so tall that its top was still over their heads as they passed it. The creeks under the dips in the snow were frozen, the land silent. No birds, no animals; snow everywhere, except on the rock faces too steep to hold snow. These ragged gray walls breaking the snow blanket here and there were just begging to be painted, Loon felt, and two or three they passed were: the sight of the sacred animals in red or black, vivid in all the white and blue of snow and sky, caught his breath in his throat. The air was cold, and Moss was singing a little hunter's ditty to himself. In places the snow was so feathery they sank knee deep even with their snowshoes on. Big lumps of soft snow balanced on every bunch of pine needles in the trees around them. —You should bring some of this feathery snow back for Elga, Moss said.

Drinking water melted from such snow would make her child light-footed. Loon laughed and said, —Good idea.

They came to the first trap, which was a pit Moss and Nevermind had dug the summer before, down into the soft dirt of the meadow. At the bottom of the pit they had put sharpened sticks and blades of knapped rock, and then covered the hole with light poles and leaves. It was only under a blanket of snow that this kind of trap was likely to catch an animal, and now as they snowshoed into the meadow, they could see that something had crashed through the roof of the pit, leaving an odd hole in the land. They rushed to the edge of the hole and looked down. A big red stag had fallen through and broken a foreleg at the bottom of the pit, and after that frozen to death. Now its dead eyes looked up at the sky as if the beast's spirit were nearby, and using its old eyes to get its bearings.

—What is he doing here! Loon exclaimed.

—Helping us out. Thanks old man! But couldn't you have jumped out of this pit and died up here?

Moss clapped Loon on the arm. It was an excellent bit of luck, though it meant a hard afternoon for them, first getting down safely into the pit, and then hauling the stiff body onto a frame made of trap poles that held it barely chest high, from which position they could get under it and shove it up together, out of the pit. They were just strong enough to push it up, and in their first try the stag's body crashed back down into the pit and they had to skip away through the stone shards like squirrels to get out of its way. It stared up at them with its fixed cloudy gaze. The second time they were more careful and it went better. All the while the beast kept looking at them.

—What do you think he was thinking at the end? Loon asked.

Moss shook his head and frowned. Loon only said things like this when he was alone with Moss; the others would just joke at such questions. But Moss regarded the stag's big weird eyes, which somehow conveyed so clearly its mute endurance, and pushed his mobile face through any number of expressions to show he was thinking, before venturing, —Maybe he was just thinking he should have been walking one leg at a time to test the snow. That's probably what I would be thinking.

—But not only that.

—No. No, he was probably sad. Maybe thinking of his wives. It's strange how deer have rectangular pupils, isn't it? They look like they're from somewhere else.

—Thorn says animals' eyes show they don't have human souls. There's no flutter or movement, they're always just stuck there in one position looking.

—So our soul is in the whites of our eyes? I don't believe it. This deer looked at you just like you looked at him. There's no difference except the square pupils, but even so you can see just what he's thinking, I mean look at him! Hey, we're sorry about this, brother, he said to the frozen deer, —but we need to eat. So thanks for helping us out!

And with that he plunged his spear between two neckbones and began to slice between them. After that they took turns in the low sun skinning the body and cutting it up with their spears. Under the spear tips the frozen meat had its usual hardness, crystalline yet flexible; they thrust between joints, bent them apart with twists from the end of the spear, cut back and forth at the meat. The blood still frozen in the beast's veins was going to be much prized by their women back at camp. It took hard work for most of that short day to get the body into pieces they could carry in their sacks and haul behind them through the snow, using its own halved skin as a rough rope to drag them along.

By the time they were ready and on their way, the sun was low in the west, casting long black shadows over the snow, which was hardening quickly back to a surface they could walk on without snowshoes. They were a long way from home, and when the sun went down behind the hills to the west, the air quickly got much colder. But there's always heat in hurry, as the saying had it, and without discussing it they picked up their pace and cronched over the snow side by side. It was only when it was this cold that they could hike this hard without overheating. It came on them again; they were made to run in cold like this.

Behind them the moon rose. It was the first night after full, and the fat moon turned the sky a thick twilight blue, which then infused the white snow under their feet. A world of blues: when they came to the broad ridge between loops, and could see far up and down the gorge of the Urdecha, and over the hills on both sides of it, the sky and the land were still so lit by the blue moonlight that they felt they could see everything. It was Mother Earth at her most beautiful, her every curve and declivity glowing distinctly; though blanketed by snow, it was in these moony nights that she looked most naked, the bare blue flesh of her hillsides smooth and curvaceous.

Before the last drop to Loop Meadow they stopped and looked around wordlessly at it for a while. Nothing moved, no wind, no sound. It was like a spirit world, a world beyond the sky, where the stillness quivered with a mystery. The few stars were fat and blurry, and they swam about as Loon blinked and blinked in the cold. They stood inside a black starry bag, on a white body, and everything was much bigger than could be grasped. So many times they had gone out at night during full moons to see things look like this, all the way back to when they were little boys, slipping out of the big house when most of the women were in the women's house and there was no one to catch them. Loon and Moss were the two who liked it most.

Now they glanced at each other, smiled and nodded: time to go. The cold air was chilling them quickly. They dropped toward camp almost at a run, skidding down the hard snow where it was steepest. As they came into Loop Meadow, Loon smelled the fire, and realized he was returning to Elga, who was pregnant with their child, and they were bringing in some unexpected meat, so that most of them would stay up late, eating some meat while the women worked on the rest of it. The cold air expanded in his chest, and he let it out of him in little loon cries that Moss laughed to hear.

Late that winter Elga got huge, and her time came one morning and the women took her off to their birthing hut, which was a shelter they had built next to their monthly house. They all gathered there and shooed the men away, and Thorn gathered the men around the fire and started a round of smoking his pipe, even though it was not yet noon. —New kid in the pack, he explained with his snaky grin, —our duty to welcome it.

He did not congratulate Loon as the father, but he didn't glower at him either. Loon took up a blade and stick and carved it with nervous precision, making a little birthday toy for the newborn, in this case an ibex, which used a couple of knobs at one end of the stick for its horns. From time to time they heard the women singing, and then for a while they heard some yelps, which were hard to believe came from Elga; Loon's scrotum tightened and he felt a flash of pain in his gut, as if his body were feeling what Elga felt.

—Getting the head out, Thorn said. —It'll be over soon.

—So, what clan? Hawk asked.

Thorn stood. —The new one should be from the eagle clan. That will give us an eagle in a few years, and we need one. And Elga is an eagle. So eagle it is.

—Don't the women have to agree? Hawk asked.

—No, Thorn said, glaring at him. —I'm the one who sees the clans in this pack. I had a vision the other night that showed me which one this one was.

—I'm an eagle too, Moss offered.

—That's right, but you and Schist are the only adult eagle men in the pack. We need younger ones. You and Schist will have to get together to choose the newborn's clan name, if it's a boy.

Moss laughed and came over to give Loon an embrace. —Now I'm your kid's clan uncle. Did Heather ever say whether it will be a boy or a girl?

—She wasn't sure, but she said probably a boy, Loon replied.

—Either way, we're brothers more than ever now.

Loon nodded, his stomach still tight. —That's good.

He finished the birth stick, which as it turned out was only the ibex's head, to take advantage of a whorl that could be made into its eye.

It was Sage who came down to give them the news, with a sly smile. —Elga's child is born. It's a boy.

The men cheered.

Later Heather said to Loon, —It was harder on her than I expected, because your child has a big head. I had to scare her into pushing him out. There's a point that sometimes comes, where if the babe doesn't come out, there's going to be trouble. The mom's getting tired, losing heart, and the babe's neither in nor out, which is a bad place to be caught. So before I have to do anything worse, I try to scare the mom into pushing harder than she has up to that point. I tell her what will happen to her and to the babe if I have to get drastic, and how wrong that could go, and usually by the time I'm done telling them that, they're so scared that they are really pushing hard. That's what happened with Elga.

Every once in a while when out on a hunt, they would run into hunters from the packs that lived nearby. The Lions were downstream where the Urdecha ran into the big river, and the Lynxes were up under the ice caps, the Foxes and Ravens south and west of that. Meeting any of them was cause for a quick little party. They would share some food and a pipe of smoke, and sit by a stream and drink and talk for a while before heading on their way. If they were both trailing the same animals they would sometimes join forces to finish the hunt, but that seldom happened. The Lynxes were very easygoing and even a little sleepy, more like cheetahs than Lynxes, and they liked to travel with little sacks of mash to tipple from, so some said it was because of that.

Once Loon was out gathering plants with Heather when they encountered two Ravens, who had been walking along hand in hand on the plateau's edge trail. After they had gone on their way, Loon said, —I've seen those two before.

—They're always together, Heather said.

—What do you mean? Loon said.

—They're a pair, like swans.

Loon looked through the forest after them. —Really?

—It's just their way, Heather said. She gave him a look. —Like Hawk and Moss, right?

—What?

—Or Thunder and Bluejay.

—What?

She stared at him. Finally she said, —You and Elga are lucky, right?

—Yes.

—A lot of people feel that way.

—But...

She dismissed his puzzled frown with a wave. —We're deeper than we can see. There are other people down inside us doing things. We get carried along by what they do. That's what it looks like to me.

—I was in love with a deer once, Loon confessed, blurting it out with a sudden flush of relief, even pride.

Heather nodded. —Once I loved a bison, when I was a girl. It didn't work out.

Loon stared at her. —Thorn?

Heather shook her head. —No, Pika.

Now Loon was even more amazed. —Old Pika? Thorn's shaman?

Heather nodded.

—What was he like?

Heather considered it. —Well, he was kind of like Thorn. Only more so.

—Mama mia. That must have been...

—It wasn't good. Like I said, it didn't work out. And Thorn was there too, so it was messy. She looked at her hand, sighed a sigh. —But I was there when Pika first started painting in the cave. We went in there and mated and then he jumped up and said he was going to paint me, paint what we had done. I was supposed to be Mother Earth. But then he turned it into the bison man again. He had that bison in him. No, what Thorn says is mainly right. We had a bad shaman.

He came on a good-looking chert in the open water of the high pond's outlet lead. The black water was slicing away from it on both sides in a way that showed it was balanced. He took it out of the creek and set it down in his camp on the ridge, between the two big boulders.

One day he ate the last of a boar's fat from a bag he carried, and slept in the sun for a while and then picked up the creek rock and a knapping rock he had been using for many days, very fine-grained and hard, seemingly unbreakable. He held it in his right hand, and hit things held on the ground with his left hand. Tap until feeling the kind of hit that was going to be needed to make a clean break in the chert, and then: whack.

It took some whacks to find out how brittle the creek stone was. After he got a good sense of that, almost every whack did what he wanted it to.

Breathe in, breathe out, whack.

Breathe in, breathe out, whack.

Warmth in a sunny winter morning. The sheen of the river ice, the chuckle of the little open rapids in the creek, the bubbles swirling downstream. Two breaths and a whack, then three. Three against two was the cross beat of day. Four and three for the dark of night.

The whacking lines were tighter together now, and at slighter angles to what he already had done. He could see the way it was shaping up. It would be like an alder leaf, pointed at its stem and rounded with a little dip on the side farthest from the stem. The balance would be very good, if he could get the last whacks right.

Breathe in, breathe out, breathe in, whack.

Breathe in, breathe out, breathe in, whack.

The winter air was warming, strike by strike. His fur lifted a little on the river breeze, his sweaty skin cooled with the waft. The love of stone work, the bliss of it.

Two of the fast ones came by and stopped to visit with him. The old woman and her boy. They were not on the hunt and he regarded them without fear. The old woman had been good to him, and the boy was not on the hunt. They jabbered at him in their hoarse nasal voices, not like any of the other animals' voices, various and expressive like certain birds. By now he had learned some of the old woman's words, how are you, good, hurt, hungry, thank you, and he listened to her and tried to make out more, and told her he was good. He showed them his new stone blade and they were suitably impressed. It was almost perfectly balanced, and had as many facets as the grain of the stone could take.

The old woman hefted it and asked him a question. It seemed she was asking him what he did with the blade, or what it was for. And yet there she was hefting it. Shyly he took it back from her and held it in his fingers, turned it over, felt the edge, eyed it edge on to see the balance. He handed it back to her. That was what it was for.

—It's just to look at, he whistled at her. —I made it just to look at. Our women like to see such things.

She shook her head, not understanding him.

—Good, he said in her tongue. She nodded, glancing at him uncertainly.

Spear tips were also good to make, but he liked these show blades most. It was true you could throw one into a herd, and if it hit an animal and caused them to stampede, smaller members of the herd might get hurt and be easy to track and kill. Boys did that before they learned to spear. But you didn't need the facets and the balance for that. Any rock with an edge would do.

He knew the fast ones did things similar to this blade. Their clothes were painted and fringed with loops of leather, and they wore leather strings around their necks from which they hung teeth and shells. They painted their skin with bloodstone and char. They painted cliff walls. All that, and yet they did not see what he was doing with the blade. It was too bad they didn't whistle.

All the things they did. So active around their camp, always bustling around doing things. Going out on the hunt. All kinds of different sizes of group, different directions, different kinds of hunts.

They were always in a hurry. Hurry slowly, his mother had always whistled. It was an old tune mothers whistled to children. He had heard his grandmother whistle it to his mother once.

Now the old woman wanted him to accompany them down to the riverbank. He got up and followed them, taking the new blade with him.

They wanted his help in moving a boulder from the bank into the shallows. He couldn't understand why they wanted it, but after the boy showed him the motion several times, he couldn't see any other explanation. He got behind the boulder with the boy and together they rolled it into the stream, where it knocked up a mighty splash.

—Thank you! they said to him, and made motions as if eating from the river. Ah: the boulder might be the start of a fish trap. They were changing the river to make it easier to catch the fish. Some kind of trap.

—Thank you! he said, and whistled, —Good idea! He ate fish when he could catch them. Mostly it was the red ones who swam upstream to die. Before they died they were still good to eat. After they died they fell apart very quickly.

One day he would go back west to his people, who were at the red fish river west of the ice caps. He would bring them the best blades ever knapped, and show them things to do that he had learned from the fast people. Then his wife might take him back again. Then his father might forgive him. If they were still alive.

It turned out Elga and Loon's child had been born in a bad spring. The freeze-no-more moth never showed up, and not long after the child was born they ran out of their winter stores, all the nuts and skin bags of fat, the frozen ducks and smoked fish, the edible roots and dried caribou meat, everything in the final weeks measured out in pinches or one by one. Schist again took on this task, and Hawk and Moss did not presume to interfere or criticize. The shortage was damaging enough to Schist, they did not have to refer to it or add to it, and indeed they could not have done any better themselves: a bad spring was a bad spring.

It meant the men needed to be out hunting more than ever, hoping their snares and traps would catch someone to eat. But this winter the land was bare. In some winters there were enough snow hares to feed an entire pack, all the snow-white little people getting fatter as the rising snowpack lifted them to higher and higher forage on the willow bushes. Snow hares actually got fat in winter, and they were easy to trap. Wait, I see something: two eyes in a bush, caught in a trap.

But this year there were no snow hares to be found. Some years were that way, Heather said. They would be better off looking for ptarmigan and grouse. Wait, I see something: black sticks moving. Walk around in the early morning with a net in hand, ready to cast it as the white birds burst out of their snow beds. You had to be fast, but if you were ready there was just enough time. But this year, no ptarmigan or grouse.

Loon went out with his friends on the hunt, and he went out on his own or with others to check traps, ranging as far as he could. After the stag he found with Moss, no one else seemed to be around. Sometimes he found broken traps, and once a vixen, once a muskrat. Without the snow hares all the little hunter people were just as hungry as the big hunters, and easier to catch. Anything at all was worth bringing back to camp; once he found a dead mouse and brought it back, and no one laughed. But there were two score and four people in the pack, and finding enough food for all of them every day was becoming the only thing anyone thought about. It was the only thing one felt, a sucking of the stomach up and in, until it pressed hard against the backbone, and deep into one's thoughts.

But it stayed cold. The hunters began to lack the strength to range as far as before, they had to conserve their efforts and save them for what really mattered. The other men considered Loon lucky because Elga could breastfeed him from time to time, to give him a little help keeping going. And it was true that it was a huge comfort to suck her thin sweet warm milk from her, while their baby sucked from the other breast. Once the babe reached out with his eyes closed and patted Loon on the head, as if to bless his participation. —I guess that's why I have two, Elga said with a little smile.

But Badleg impeded him, and he was no more successful than any of the rest of the hunters. Once he came on a muskrat dead in one of their tree traps, but it looked empty somehow, and it was: the muskrat's head had been touching the ground, and ground shrews had eaten up through the face and devoured all of its meat and intestines, leaving it a fur bag filled with nothing but bones. Loon brought this remnant back to camp anyway; they would eat the marrow out of the bones, and use the fur.

Another time he went out on a trap circle and came on a wolverine biting through the sinews of a snare in order to release a marten who had been caught. As Loon ran toward the scene, the wolverine cut its little cousin free and they both scampered off on the snow, the marten like an elongated squirrel, the wolverine in its big hops, all four feet landing together under him. Quickly they both disappeared among the trees. Loon had heard of this happening, but had never seen it himself. Wolverines and martens were family. Bear and beaver were similarly family. The bigger ones always left their little cousins alone.

Today, it was really too bad. Nothing to be done about it but repair the snare and set it again, and hope for a better result next time. You get what you get and you don't throw a fit. No cure for disappointment but to try again. Obviously it would be best to visit every trap every day, but that made for a lot of walking. The days were getting longer, but the trap circle seemed to be getting longer too. It was a relief to lie down with Elga and the babe and suckle a little from the breast not taken by the boy. Of course most of the milk had to be saved for their child. But the rich flavor went right to his stomach and quelled his pangs for a while, and made it possible for him to ignore Badleg's throbbing.

They got so hungry that two of the pack fell sick at the same time, Ducky and Windy. Thorn and Heather laid them in beds at opposite ends of the camps, and went back and forth tending them. Thorn told Loon to come along, and there was in his eyes such a stony look that Loon gulped and decided his insubordinations could be resumed some other time.

Their diseases were very different, as Ducky had a fever and boils, while Windy was simply exhausted all the time, to the point where she could barely move. It could have been just that she was so old. So when they were at Ducky's bed under the west end of the abri, Loon shivered in fear and watched agog as Thorn put on his bison head, so absurdly big compared to Thorn's real head; it looked like a black snake was eating a bison's head from below, like the shrews had eaten the muskrat. To see and talk under this bison head, Thorn had to cant it back so the bison appeared to be examining the sky. Nevertheless, as Thorn staggered about Ducky, and peered down her throat and fingered her in the armpit, then played his flute over her body, he was in such a deliberate flow, like an eddy in a slow river, that Ducky seemed entranced, and Loon felt the pull too. He wanted to help, but kept his distance. He was afraid.

At Windy's bed, up in the morning nook, he was just sad. Windy's lassitude was so unlike her manner when Loon had been a child. She had been always rushing around camp tending to little particulars. In his sadness he would think of how later that night he would be with Elga and be so happy. It was strange to feel both these feelings, he felt like he might break from being too full. Windy had been that same frisky woman she had always been, up until this winter. So Loon sat at the foot of her bed with his head on his knees, and thought about

Elga, or the black horse, or the herd of bison filing down Lower's Upper, all of them as big-headed as Thorn, their bodies lean with the work of carrying all that head around. Lions were the same, and he saw in his mind suddenly how they were brothers, lion and bison, the same form made into hunter and hunted, either fast or big. He saw on his eyelids the sweet curves of an ibex horn and an ibex rump, different kinds of curve entirely, both very fine. He wanted to carve.

Heather all this time sat by the sick women, sniffed their breath, put her ear to their chests to hear their hearts, tasted their pee and came back from the shitting grounds with them, shaking her head and thinking things over. She brewed many cups of tea for both women; she dripped it into Windy's mouth from a hollow reed. Mostly it was artemisia tea, bitter and brown. To Windy's tea she added mistletoe pollen, and a pinch of wolf lichen. This bright green moss stained Heather's fingers and made the tea greener than it seemed it should have; the browns it mixed with went entirely away. Wolf lichen was poisonous to wolves, but Heather often fed her people noxious things in small quantities.

With Ducky, on the other hand, she covered the boils with a balm made of bear grease mixed with alder bark powder, and other grits and dried flowers she had in her collection of little colored bags. She fed both women a mash made of honey, berries, and herbs, slighty rotted like the festival mashes. These tasted bad, but seemed to give the sufferers some relief.

One night Thorn put on the bison head and danced around Ducky singing. All of a sudden he shouted and leaped on her and held her by the throat as if strangling her, reached down her throat and pulled out a white mass that he threw down toward the river. Ducky stared at him amazed.

With Windy he only sat by her side and played his flute. One morning when they were walking up to do this, he dismissed Loon with a slap to the shoulder. —Go hunt, he said. —There's nothing more you can do here.

And there never had been, Loon refrained from pointing out, happy to get away. Windy died the next night. But Ducky lived.

They carried Windy's wrapped body out to the raven platform, put up the ladders and carried her up, and laid her body out to be eaten. The ravens were as hungry as anyone else, and Windy's flesh would soon be gone. When her bones were clean they would collect them for their burial in the river, that summer before going on their trek.

Before they left Windy the whole pack sat around her body and cried while Thorn played his flute. They were too hungry for this, their feelings were flayed raw, and everyone had loved Windy and been mothered by her. It was a painful disappearance of one of them from the pack. They were all part of Mother Earth, Thorn said between his flute pieces. Birth, sex, death, they were all petals on the same flower. The goddess eventually pulled all these petals off: birthed them, mated them, took them back in death.

Loon heard inside him the sound like a loon crying in the night. This was his heart's song, this was the song no one else heard.

So a few lucky ravens had a little respite, but the rest of the people of the river gorge got hungrier. Finally a freeze-no-more moth flew out of one of the brakes near the river, and the sixth month came. At the dark of the sixth moon, Thorn stayed up all night chanting, asking the summer spirit to come, and just as he sang what Loon thought was his most haunting song, the one about the voyage between worlds, the night colors appeared up there among the stars, lighting up the black sky with shimmering waves of green and blue, so beautiful that Thorn woke everyone to see it, and announced that this was a sign that the summer spirit was returning, coming back from the other side of the sky. They all watched for as long as the lights spilled through the stars and poured through the black sky like waves made of dragonfly wings. When the lights went away they fell back asleep.

—Summer had better come, Heather muttered as she stumped back to her bed. —You can't eat ptarmigan droppings when there are no ptarmigan.

Passing by Loon, she said, —Don't you drink too much of your wife's milk. Your boy needs it to grow.

—I know, Loon said. —But if I can bring something back.

Heather nodded. —But do it soon.

They got so hungry that finally Schist and Thorn went upstream to the south side of the biggest ice cap to visit the Raven pack and ask if they had any food they could share. Neither man wanted to talk about it when they returned, but their sacks were heavy with bags of nuts and fat, and they dragged between them a bag of frozen ducks.

—They're tight there too, Schist said somberly. —This was a good thing they did for us. We owe them now. We'll have to give them something good at the eight eight, or in the fall.

Then the ducks showed up overhead, quacking their news: summer! summer! summer! The Wolves waited a day and then quickly netted a twenty or two of them. As they did that the geese too appeared overhead, in waves of long ragged Vs, feathers creaking, complainers honking, clonking, ooking, acking, eeking.

The pack's hungry times were over. Both men and women went out with nets and javelins to hunt geese. Never take the first of anything, of course, but when twentytwenties of a creature arrived at once, you weren't going to be taking the first. Summer was here. Many of them went out on the hunt weeping with relief. They had been scraped raw by that hunger spring.

UNDER
THE ICE

It was on the second night of that summer's eight eight festival, during the dancing just after the bonfire flares, when Loon noticed that
Elga was not among the women dancers anywhere around the main
bonfire. He danced widdershins to be sure, and then wandered back to
their camp to find her. Heather was there, the babe and several other of
the youngsters with her, but not Elga. He went to ask Heather about it.

Heather scowled in a way that caused Loon's heart to flutter.

—What? he demanded.

—Find her. Heather glanced at the kids. —Find her, or send
Thorn back to me right quick.

—Why? What's wrong?

—Just go find her. I'll explain later.

Loon ran off, alarmed by her manner. He quickly circled the main
fire again, and all the subsidiary fires, and then the whole circle of
encampments. No Elga. He had spotted Thorn with his little pack
of shaman friends at one of the smaller fires, and panting now with
fear he ran back to him and pulled him aside.

—I can't find Elga anywhere, and Heather said I should get you.

—What do you mean? He sounded a little drunk.

—Elga! We left the little one with Heather at camp, and went to
the dance, and she stopped to talk to somebody, and I kept going
around the circle, and after that I didn't see her for a while, but I
thought she was just on the other side of the fire, in the women's
line. Then when I didn't see her I figured she had gone back to our
camp for something, so I went back but she wasn't there either. And
Heather, I don't know, she didn't like it.

—Let's go see what she wants, Thorn said, his brow furrowed.

Heather saw them entering their camp and came right to them.
—The girl came from the north, she said to Thorn. —She was a runaway from one of those packs up there. I'm afraid they've taken her back.

—Oh, no, Thorn said, voice rich with disgust. He glanced darkly
at Loon and said, —Which pack?

—One of the northers. One that doesn't come to this festival.

—Then why were they here?

—I don't know, how would I know? Go find Pippiloette, and Schist, see what they say.

Thorn took Loon by the shoulder, squeezing it hard. —Go find Schist and Ibex, and your friends. Get everyone back here. Tell them I said we've got a problem.

Loon ran off toward the big fires, and in short order found Schist and Ibex and gave them the news. Within a fist they were all regathered at their camp's little fire. Thorn came back with Pippiloette in tow, and the traveler sat next to the fire with them, warming his hands and watching the Wolf pack discuss their situation. He took a bag of water from Sage and drank from it, then splashed some of it over his face, shaking his head as if trying to clear the festival out of it. The noise of the crowd around the bonfires didn't help any of them with that.

It suddenly became clear to Loon that Schist and Ibex, but also Hawk and Moss and Nevermind, had no desire to go after Elga.

—We have to save her! he exclaimed when he saw this. —We can't let them do it!

—Be quiet, Schist told him. —This isn't your decision to make.

—We do need to defend ourselves, Thorn pointed out. —Word will get around if we don't.

—She was a runaway. She wasn't ours, she just came.

—We let her in, Heather said. —You don't get to decide that. She's been ours all winter, and she helped us get through it, and she's married to Loon and has his baby. So don't talk about her that way.

Schist took heed of Heather's black withering look and extended a hand. —All right, but she was a runaway from another pack, you said. And we don't know where she is now.

—And you want to keep dancing, Heather said contemptuously.

Schist glared at her. No doubt he wanted to silence her, but he knew that trying to silence Heather often splashed back on one. No one could lay curses like Heather, not even Thorn. This was not the moment for that kind of scene. And he had not become the leader of their pack without a quick sense of what they needed.

So now he sat down next to Pippiloette. —Do you know who they are?

—Maybe. I don't know for sure who took her. But I've heard the stories about where she came from, and if those are the people who took her, I know who they are.

—Are they a big pack?

—Northern packs are usually bigger than southern ones.

—Could you track them?

—Maybe. Depends if they've gone straight home or not.

—Why wouldn't they?

Pippiloette stared at him.

Schist got to his feet and looked into the fire. He spoke without looking at Loon.

—We can't go running off to the north after a woman. We just barely made it through this spring, we're still weak, and we need to be here finishing our caribou, and getting back to Cedar Salmon River in time for the run, and putting enough together to give the Ravens something in return for what they gave us. We don't have the food or the strength for a chase. That's just the way it is. We can't do it. Maybe next year we can steal her back.

Loon left the fire. He stood outside the light of it, on a low rise above the festival. The drumming around the big fire pounded inside him. He was numb; he couldn't take it in. He understood what was happening, he sensed the enormity of it, but it was so big and sudden he couldn't feel it yet. He was stunned in the way he had been once after running straight into a tree while looking behind himself as he ran. He had never done that again; he knew the truth of the saying Watch where you're going. Now the buzzing in him suddenly resolved to a quick clutch of nausea, and he put his hands to his knees and hung his head for a while.

I am the third wind
I come to you
When you have lost everything
When you can't go on

Pippiloette left their camp, and Loon took off after him. He made sure to catch up to him well away from camp.

—Pippi! I need your help!

—What do you mean? the traveler asked carefully.

—Can you show me where those northers live? And which way they go to get there?

—I could show you that, Pippiloette allowed. —But look, youth. I don't want to take on the northers. It won't be easy to steal your woman back from them, especially on your own. And a second person is no help either.

—I'll do it, Loon said. —Just show me where they are, and you can leave.

Pippiloette frowned. —I will leave, he said after a long pause. —Understand that. You'll be on your own. I'll be headed east.

—Fine, I understand. That's good enough. I wouldn't expect any more.

—I should hope not.

The summer nights up on the steppe were so short that by the time Pippiloette had made his enquiries with friends around the festival, the eastern sky was growing light. Loon hurried past the bonfires and slipped back into their camp and sat down next to Heather, who was hunched over, drowsing by the little one's bed. She started awake and sat up to look at him.

—I'm going after her, he said.

She hissed. —I don't think you can do it on your own.

—I'm going. Take care of the baby. I'll be careful.

—You'd better be, she said darkly. —And you'll have to be more than that. It will take trickery, and patience. Go in by night when you get your chance.

—I will.

Suddenly she reached out and clutched his arm. —I don't think you should go.

—I have to.

And he took off in the predawn gray to meet Pippiloette.

★   ★   ★

The eight eight festival site was south of an area that Pippiloette called Five Rivers, where several creeks met the Lir. The northers, Pippi told Loon as they hustled out of the festival camp, would almost certainly head up the valley of the Maya, a tributary of the Lir that ascended a gentle straight valley that trended north, often so much so that its river pointed right at the Spindle Star. At the head of the Maya there was an easy broad pass, and then a drop to a broad flat valley that sloped from east to west, where its river emptied into the great salt sea. On the northern side of this broad valley, Pippi said, was the big ice wall that covered everything to the north and in effect ended the world in that direction, just as the great salt sea ended it on its western side. The northers lived at this meeting of ice and land and the great salt sea.

—Does anything else live up there? What do they eat?

—The usual people. Salmon and caribou, geese and ducks, seals on the winter sea ice. Actually they eat very well. It's just that it's always cold.

—I couldn't stand it.

—Don't say that, Pippiloette said. —Never say aloud what you don't want, didn't your people teach you that one?

Loon didn't reply. He hiked on the traveler's swift heels, still feeling sick. His guts were knotting so badly they bent him as he walked. He wanted to run, but Pippi set the pace at a walk. A fast walk, it was true; Loon gritted his teeth and followed his guide, watching the ground closely in the predawn light of the steppe. It felt like it would have been easier to run.

Pippiloette breathed hard through his teeth as he walked, making a whistling sound that was like a little song, the song of himself walking at speed. A traveler provided himself with his own company, and Loon had seen a number of different ways they did that; some of them talked all the time, commenting on things no one from Wolf pack would have mentioned aloud; others sang, others beat their walking sticks together in between stabs into the earth. Luckily Pippi was not like any of those, he only had his little whistling, and he was proving to be fast, indeed very fast: Loon had to focus to match his pace.

They followed a riverside path for a long time, then a big tributary forced their trail upstream, to a bend in the tributary, and a ridge that bordered the Maya river valley on its west side. Up there a typical ridge trail broadened, and in the dawn light it was easy to hurry.

But now they had to be careful; the ridge was bare in the usual way, and in the gray they could see up it for a long way; meaning anyone up there could see down. It was crucial not to be spotted. And given that these people had stolen a woman, it was also possible they might leave behind some men to slow down any pursuit that might appear. A quick little ambush and no one would be following them anymore. So as the sky lightened, leaving only the morning star and a few others to prick the gray dome, they got off the ridge and hiked the border of trees and rocks on the Maya side of the ridge. This was hard ground to traverse fast, but they could slip between the little spruces and birches, and stay out of the willow tangles in the streambeds, and check the skyline of the ridge ahead as they proceeded upstream. It was safer, but slower, and so they pushed when they were concealed, to make up time.

They went very hard all that day, stopping only twice to sit and eat some food from their packs, and drink deeply from two of the little tributaries they crossed on fallen logs. Pippi ate fast. His long loping stride did not seem fast at any given moment, but covered ground with surprising speed. Over the course of the day Loon had seen that he had his own ways, cutting across the land in lines Loon would not have seen, but which revealed themselves when right under his feet to be slight trails.

—I'm a straightwalker, Pippi said when Loon asked about the trails. —I mean, I run a nice clean route. I don't go straight at the land if it doesn't make sense, but I don't like extravagance. Ups and downs are usually not bad enough to justify a divagation. Anyway I look for the best way. I'm always looking to see if there's a better way than the one I've used before, if I'm where I've gone before. And if I'm in new land, well, it's the best thing there is, finding a good way.

—Do you remember everywhere you've ever been?

—Oh yes. Of course.

—And have you been this way before?

—Oh yes. Otherwise we wouldn't be able to go this fast. We'd have to track for sign. But as it is, I know where they're going. And I've seen some signs that they've been by, and not so long ago. So we can catch up to them, hopefully. It would be ever so much better for your chances if you were to catch up to them when they're on the move rather than in their encampment.

—Do they do this kind of thing often, then?

Pippi shrugged. —They fight the other northers from time to time. And there's some wife stealing. As you have seen. Yes, there's been bad blood up there for a while between some of those packs. Some say the great ice wall scares them and makes them angry, others that they get too cold to think straight. But they act hot, so I don't know. They're like otters.

—Ah, Loon said, feeling a shiver of fear. The indomitable otter, the murderous otter. —It seems strange to me.

Pippi looked over his shoulder at Loon, then turned and walked on.

—You come from a good pack. A good pack in a good pays. All the packs in the south are very friendly. But in some pays it's not that way. The northers are tough. They fight for their lives up there.

—But why?

—What do you mean? There is no why. They like it. They like to fight, because the ones who survive think it's not so bad. It gets them things, and up there maybe that matters.

Loon sighed, and tried to put the matter of the northers out of his mind. For the moment the task was to follow Pippi close and never slow the traveler down. Be his shadow, as one said when on the hunt. They would see what the situation was with Elga when they caught up to them. But thinking of her was even worse than thinking about these northern otter people. He felt his gut shrinking, and walked like a starved wolf, backbone hunched gingerly over its taut pain. He tried to watch the ground under Pippi's feet and walk on it neatly.

Here in this long valley the soil was thin. In many places big broken flats of bare rock were furred in their cracks and low points by moss and ground-hugging willows. The rocks were covered with lichen that looked like splashes of paint. In the pass at the head of the Maya, a pale green lichen grew in big circles and then died from the inside out, clearing the rock of other lichens and leaving behind circles of clean pink stone. Briefly Loon glimpsed these things and then fell back into his fear.

He and Pippi crouched behind boulders among the pink and green splotches, inspecting the long prospect to the north. They saw nothing, and during the course of the rest of the day descended a ridge into the big flat valley running west. Pippi wanted to cross this valley's river at a ford he knew, which was a bit to the west, he said. He headed that way.

Near sunset Pippi stopped. —Let's eat, then see if we can go on by moonlight. They won't do that, so we might catch them.

He pulled his food bag out of his backsack and rooted in it. He had a gooseskin bag of marmot fat in there, and offered it to Loon, who fingered a little of the liquid fat into his mouth. Ordinarily marmot fat was so rich that no one ate it by itself; if you did it would make you sick. Usually it was heated into a broth, and morsels of meat dipped into it. Out on the hunt, however, it could be downed in little sips, and after a little wave of nausea passed through one, it would expand in the gut and give a pulse of energy after. Little sips, fist after fist; it was the main hunting food in certain packs, and Pippi must have come from one of those.

It was the twelfth day of the eighth month, and so the waxing moon hung in the eastern sky at sunset, lighting the land as the sunlight drained from it. Pippi led the way to a low ridge and hiked north on it. He was slower now, and as they came up the ridge to certain knobs he crouched behind boulders and kept off the skyline, looking up the ridge carefully, then down into the valley next to them. Loon did likewise, heart beating hard; but they never saw anything below. Most of the night passed, the moon was setting in the west; they both moved slowly in the cold air. Loon felt the long walk in his feet. But as the moon set and the night blackened accordingly, Pippi topped a knob on the ridge and sat down quickly. —Keep down.

Loon sat and rested.

—Look, Pippi said, gesturing ahead. —Their fire.

Far downvalley to the north was a tiny yellow flicker.

—Ah yes, Loon said. Hope and fear made a furious crosschop in him. —What now?

Pippi was silent for a long time. Then he said, —They will probably have a night watch. And the day is coming. I don't think we can do it tonight without being seen. Tomorrow night, if we come on them earlier, we can study them in the moonlight, then move when the moon sets. So I think maybe we should get some sleep now, while we can, and follow them at a good distance tomorrow. Keep out of their sight while watching them.

Loon was weary enough to accede to this. They found flat spots among the rocks, looked for moss to make a quick bed. They both had fur wraps in their backsacks; Loon's was made of muskrat pelts sewn together so the fur overlapped the sewing lines, Pippi's was a flank of a bear. They rolled up into these wraps and were quickly asleep. You have to be able to sleep on stone.

At sunrise Loon woke briefly; Pippiloette was sleeping. After a moment of welcoming the rays of the sun on his face, Loon fell asleep again.

He woke as he was being jerked to his feet. He was in the grasp of two big northers, with three more holding spears and surrounding them. Pippiloette was nowhere to be seen.

The northers held their spear tips right to him, a frightful thing, and then after he went still, they pulled them back and indicated with them that he was to walk north with them on the ridge trail, or be speared on the spot. Soon they joined a larger group.

Off they all went. The ridge dropped until it disappeared into a steppe. Here shallow streams looped across plains of grass and scree. Sometimes exposed flat rock was split in warp and weft fashion, so that the streams pooled and poured in rectangular patterns.

All that day they walked north over the flat stony plain. During their first stop they indicated that Loon was to give them everything on him except his clothes. Most of what he had was in his backsack, which they already had, but he gave them his belt with all the things in its pouch. They tied his hands behind his back with what felt like a leather braid. While they were doing that, he saw that Elga was there, standing among their women with her head and shoulders down. She turned her head and saw him, then turned her head away. He flinched and did likewise, feeling in agreement with her, that it might go better for them if their captors did not know they knew each other.

Although perhaps the northers were already aware. They spoke in a language that sounded almost right, but that Loon often lost the drift of. It resembled how the people of the steppes sounded, but Loon understood the steppe people better. These people didn't reply to Loon when he spoke, and he thought they didn't understand him very well either. Pippiloette would have been useful in such a situation, knowing so many tongues. What had happened to Pippi? Had the traveler betrayed him to the northers, given them a captive for something in return? That didn't seem possible to Loon, but on the other hand, if Pippi had woken to their danger, or known of it before, why hadn't he told Loon about it, so they could have both slipped away? Would it have been that much harder?

In the end he could only suppose that Pippi had been as surprised as he had been by the northers, but had waked just in time to slip off into the dark with his things. Certainly the traveler was quick.

In any case there was no real need for a translator, as the northers' meaning was simple in the end: Go! Ora! And he went.

Possibly they would sacrifice him to their gods, maybe eat him; it was said such things happened in the north. A bad situation, a dreadful possibility.

But Elga was there, and she had seen him. She knew he had come after her. Whatever happened, they at least had that. So he determined to endure, to submit and be a good captive, and to ignore whatever indignities might be inflicted on Elga, if any. She spoke their language, he saw. Back at the festival they had said she was a runaway, that this was her original pack. She didn't look anything like these men, being much taller, and so dark-skinned she was almost black against the snow. The northers were not that dark, though from a distance, against the snow, every person was dark. Not as black as a black horse, but more the color of mud, which was the point of the story of how Raven first made humans, by clawing up some mud into a ball. Thus they were mostly the brown of the winter shag of a bison. These northers were the lightest brown Loon had ever seen, and their eyes were heavily protected by folds of skin. Most of them were short and rounded, although part of the rounding was their thick clothing.

His captors were joined by some of their men carrying parts of a caribou they had killed and cut apart. That night they roasted the head first, and Loon could see that they liked the same parts that other people liked; tongue and brain, but more than that, the jowl, and the pads of fat behind the eyes. After that they roasted the brisket, then the ribs, then the pelvis.

Meanwhile Loon and the two other captives they had with them, neither of whom Loon understood, though they did not sound like the northers, were fed the lungs, the heart, and the entrails, although not the entrail fat, which was scraped off by the women, melted in long-handled antler spoons, and poured into pokes.

Loon chewed the hard muscle of the caribou heart with a dignified lack of expression, as if thinking of something else. It would not do to be among these people like an evil presence or a manifestation of bad luck. He had to accept his standing and perform it as well as he could. He saw how it was that captives helped to capture themselves, just as part of staying safe, of biding one's time, of hoping.

They walked for day after day. The steppe first sloped down to a big river, which looped westward through a broad marsh and grassland, supporting big larch and alder thickets in the loops and along the riverbanks. At the river itself, a leather braid rope crossed the river, tied to tall spruce trees on each bank. There were log rafts floating in the shallows on each side. They got in one, looped two loops of rope over the big rope bridging the river, and pulled themselves across with their hands and arms, moving the loops forward one at a time. Their raft stretched the big rope downstream, so they had to paddle and pull hard as they approached the northern bank.

Back and forth they ferried themselves and their loads. At the end of the crossing, some of their men took both rafts across to the south side, left one, and came back together on the other.

After that they ascended the steppe on the northern side of the valley. For most of the second day of this ascent, they passed through a strange forest, composed of the usual spruce, pine, larch, birch, and alder, but all of them only half as tall as they were to the south, and many tilted this way and that, as though the ground under them had collapsed. And apparently it had, for they passed big ponds sunken deep into moss beds, the water level well below the ground. Sometimes the banks of these sunken ponds were strangely white under the water line, turning the water a sky blue. There was ice down there. The soil and pine spill that made up the floor of this forest, and all the beds of moss and patches of muskeg, even the many ponds— all of them were resting on an underlayer of ice, it seemed, which here and there you could see down to. Whenever this underlayer of ice happened to melt, the trees growing on top of it tilted like festival drunkards. It was a strange forest to walk through.

On the upper edge of this drunken forest, the little trees gave way to low scattered ground willow and pine scrub, and they could see a long way ahead, to a range of hills. Then, as they topped a low ridge that headed northwest, and stayed on it, on a broad trail, they could see above the range of hills a white mass, a mass of ice overtopping all the hills in a stupendous white wall. Ice fingers fell down from this wall, filling the valleys between the hills under it, then splaying out onto the steppe in steep-walled ends, rounded like horse hooves. Some of these ice splays had overrun forests, so that crushed trees lay in a tangle under the bottom of the ice hooves. The big ice mass above looked like the ice caps in the mountains west of the Urdecha, but immensely bigger. Everywhere they could see to the north, ice ruled. Maybe it went north forever, in the same way Pippi had said that the land continued forever to the east, and the great salt sea to the west.

They came to a rise and could see down into a shallow valley under the hills and the ice, running toward the great salt sea in the west, which formed the mouth of the valley. Across the valley, under the hills, lofted columns of campfire smoke. As they got closer, Loon saw that there was a line of poles like bone needles, standing between the great salt sea and the smoke columns. Closer still he could see they were the dead trunks of immense trees, trees taller than any he had ever seen, and much taller than any growing up here. These barkless bare tree trunks were stuck upside down in the ground, their root balls at their tops all white and broken to the sky, with skulls hung on colored string from the outer tips of the roots. They were much like the dead trees at the eight eight, and something in that Loon found reassuring.

The northers lived in a camp of some ten or twelve houses, made of wood, bone, and hide. The houses were tucked in the gap between a hill and the rounded ice wall at the end of a great spill of ice flowing down between the hills from the ice mass. The open end of the gap faced south, with the ice wall to their east. Patches of snow lay everywhere on the ground, even now, in the latter half of the eighth month. A breeze dropped on them from the north, cold even in full sun. A grumbling shallow creek emerged out of the bottom of the ice hoof to the east of their camp and ran southwest toward the great salt sea, which was just visible from camp, a long curve of blue in the distance.

They walked into camp. More giant barkless tree trunks had been used for the corner posts of their houses. As there had been no tall trees at all in the last two days of their trek north, Loon guessed these immense trunks must be driftwood cast up by the great salt sea, suggesting a land somewhere to the west that must be home to giants.

The biggest house of all was about ten strides on a side, and about three times as tall as a person. They entered it through a low cut in the loam before it, a kind of long trap you could walk down a ramp into. When they had walked through this cut and gotten under their big house, the northers took off some of their outer garments, before stepping onto a tall block of wood and pulling themselves up through a person-sized hole, onto an earthen floor cut less deeply than the trap into the ground. Half of it was planked over, and on the planks another tall block of wood gave one a step up through a hole and onto a full plank floor set about head height above the earthen floor.

The captives were urged to climb up through both holes into the house.

Up inside, the only light came from a fire and from a hole made by a hollowed branch set in the roof's high point. The walls were covered with overlapping bare hides. The air on the lowest plank level was cool, but there was a platform above it filling over half the house, and up there was where most of the northers sat. Some children were perched even higher, on raised wooden beds that put them not far from the roof. The children were naked, and the men and women on the upper platform were dressed only in leggings that covered them from the waist to the knees. Up at their level the fire made the air not just warm but hot, and the northers' rounded brown bodies shone with sweat. They handed around ladles of water from wooden buckets, sipping as they talked. The fire was set on a large hearthstone under the roof hole, and it proved to be made up of several big fat lamps, set around a small wood fire burning atop a bed of embers. The fire was so small that it would require constant tending, and Loon saw that the northern women were doing that. They each had different sizes and kinds of breasts, in the usual way.

He counted a score and eleven people in the dim room. Elga was not one of them; she must have been taken into a different house. There were several more houses, so if this was just one pack's camp, it was a very big pack.

They laughed a lot as they talked to each other. To Loon and the other captives they were curt. After spending some time on the first plank floor and getting inspected by some of the men, Loon and the two other new captives were directed to return to the earthen space under the floor, where he found seven other people lying on hides, and a few frozen ducks in cedar root bags.

It was cold down there on the ground floor. There were several caribou skins covering the planked part of the floor farthest from the step-up, and the other captives lay wrapped in these hides, clumped together for warmth. None of them responded when Loon asked what was going on. He couldn't tell if they understood him or not.

The northers above were exchanging news, it seemed, the newly arrived travelers no doubt describing the trip they had just completed. Some of them cut up a frozen caribou and handed the pieces to the cooks by the fire, and the cutters threw the caribou's heart and lungs down to their captives, and later the intestines, scraped of their fat coating. The group below shared this food without fuss, taking a few bites and then passing the chunks along. When they were all sated there was still a good quantity of caribou organs left, neatly piled in the far corner: the least palatable bits, it was true, but they would have eaten them too, if they had still been hungry.

Loon waited until all the other captives were bundled in hides, and then went to an unused half-hide consisting of the rear legs and back of a small caribou, and rolled it around himself. He would be covered if he kept his knees tucked up. He burrowed in and tried to sleep with as little as possible of his side pressing on the hide over the ground. He needed a second hide under him, and got up to use a scrap in the corner for that purpose. The caribou meat was a cold mass in his stomach. His thoughts were as stunned as they had been on the night Elga was taken. He could not quite get a grip on what was happening. It was so bad that he could scarcely move, and even rolled in the hide and lying on the free scrap, he started shivering, more from fear than cold.

I am the third wind
I come to you
When you have nothing left
When you can't go on
But you go on anyway

I stepped in to help him. With my help he would change over between worlds and sleep while waking, wake while sleeping, and live on in the dream world, but nowhere else. And thus endure.

Some of the other captives spoke in ways he somewhat understood. They seemed to say that the northers did not consider the captives to be people. They were just captives, kept alive to help the jende, the real people, by working for them.

So they went out by day, a pair or trio of jende men carrying spears and blades, accompanied by one or two captive men. Usually the jende led the way downstream to the sea shore, to haul back travois and sleds loaded with bags of fish, or entire frozen seals, or blocks of skin and fat cut from giant furred seals, or from beached whales. If there was soft snow on the ground, the captives were given snowshoes to wear. Their travois for hauling loads had antler blades tied to the back ends of their poles, giving them a broader surface to let them ride higher over the snow. Their sleds had runners made of whale rib bones. The jende wore backsacks tied to wooden frames, which they filled on the sea shore and carried back up to camp.

Once back in camp, the captives lifted their loads up onto a wooden platform which was perched on top of a thick dead tree trunk buried in the ground such that its top was well over head high. A platform had been built in a circle around the trunk just under its top, and up on that raised floor lay many twentytwenties of fish, all frozen hard as flint, and set so they formed a wall all around the outside of the platform, with a single open passage in the wall at the top of a ladder. Caribou furs protected them from the sun.

Up on the platform, which reminded Loon of his pack's raven burial platform, he discovered that inside the wall of frozen fish were carefully arranged piles of sealskin bags, each bag made of a whole skin that had been stripped off the animal without cutting the skin much; the holes had been sewn up, and now each skin lay bulbously full of frozen fat, visible through drawstrings. One of the jende opened up the drawstring on one of these bags and scooped out some semi-solid white fat into a bucket. Loon was startled by the sight of all the bags, so startled that he briefly came out of the waking sleep he had fallen into. The food stored on this platform would feed the camp's people for two or even three winters. He had never seen anything like it. These people were rich.

Not only that, but they kept captive wolves, as well as captive people. Loon was again startled to wakefulness when he first saw this: there at the eastern end of their camp, under the groaning ice wall, stood a roofless house of sorts, a circular wall made of a line of tall alder shoots tied together, and inside this enclosure was trapped a small pack of wolves, snarling and snapping whenever the jende opened the short door into it. But when the jende entered, the wolves shrank back and rolled on their backs and peed themselves as they stared up pleading at the northers, licking their own muzzles hungrily. The northers threw them chunks of the same offal they fed to the human captives, and the wolves eagerly snatched the chunks and wolfed them down. Then they crowded around the norther men, heads low, wagging their tails, and the northers reached out and grabbed them by the ears, then tugged their heads this way and that! And the wolves only wagged their tails harder! Loon watched this agape, and marveled again when the men let the wolves out of the enclosure, and snowshoed off with a few of the wolves dashing happily around them. And when they came back to camp late that day, the wolves were still there with them, pulling chunks of wood and bloody meat over the snow, at the end of ropes tied to rope harnesses around the wolves' forelegs, something like the harnesses people put around their waists to pull travois.

Loon could scarcely believe his eyes. These people were... he didn't know what.

He found in the days that followed that the main thing the northers wanted from their human captives was not to carry food up from the great salt sea, which their captive wolves could do, but rather to gather firewood from the ravines to the east of their camp. So the days spent walking down to the shore and bringing back fish and seals and fat turned out to be much less frequent than long hikes to the east along the line of hills, turning up one or another of the short valleys that rose to the great ice wall. These valleys had floors filled with forests that were surprisingly thick, even though the tallest trees were no more than head high. The trees were mostly the same types as those to the south, with more birch and larch, less pine, and no oaks; but all of them small. Walking among these trees all day made Loon feel like he had entered some land on the other side of the sky where living things were smaller, turning ordinary people into giants. Maybe this was part of what had made the northers so strange.

Their jende guides or guards carried stone wedges and blades fixed sideways into branches, and they swung these bladed branches to make a first cut in trees, low to the ground, after which they inserted a stone wedge into the cut and had the captives pound the wedge with rocks, or the thick ends of stout branches, until the tree's trunk cracked across and fell. The captives were also sent farther upstream in the steep valleys to forage for downed wood, or dead branches that could be broken off trees.

The jende made no effort to guard the captives during their forays up these little valleys; there was nowhere to escape to, except to death itself. Nevertheless, Loon found this neglect interesting enough for it to break through his waking sleep and give him something to think about from time to time. Sometimes the jende had some of their captive wolves with them on these forages; that was perhaps another reason they didn't have to guard their human captives. But if he had Elga with him on one of these forage days, and they managed to flee, and if they had sacks with bags of fat in them, and snowshoes, why couldn't they simply run faster than any pursuit could catch them? For he had the growing impression that he and Elga might be faster than these northers over a long run.

Although they wouldn't be faster than the wolves. But if they could hold the wolves off with thrown rocks, drive them away, then who human could catch them? But could you throw and run successfully at the same time?

These questions poked at him, and he pretended to be as insensible as before, but it was a pretense, because he had a little itch now. He was awake again, or at least in a dream that was not so benumbed. He started looking for ways to steal things from the jende and hide them away. At first he didn't find any, but he was looking.

One day he saw which house Elga was kept in, because they both stepped out of their houses at the same time. She didn't see him at first, and he stared at her intently. He couldn't tell how they were treating her. He supposed she was again the wife of some jende in that house. He assumed or hoped she was being treated as jende rather than captive, but he wasn't sure. Maybe the northers' wives were captives too, although they did keep a women's house at the upper end of their valley tuck, for their monthlies he assumed. And the women in his house were cheerful and active around the fire, cooking everything they all ate. How Elga was joining that or not, he could not tell.

Now that he had an itch to know things, it was quite an itch; but it could not be shown.

There was a young man among the captives who spoke like Loon, and who also understood the jende. As they ate at night in the cold trap, he told Loon that he was a member of the eagle clan. None of the jende were eagles, he said; they didn't even have clans.

This youth didn't know how long he had been a captive in the house. Many months, he said, as if it had been more than anyone could count.

While Loon was outside gathering wood, he looked around and told himself stories about how he and Elga would make their escape. All the stories had obvious problems in terms of their actual performance. On some of his days out he would be free to run away for a fist or two, but the jende would soon know he had gone, and set their captive wolves after him, perhaps. Also, during the days he didn't know where Elga was. During the nights he knew which house she was in, but then he too was in a house, under the eye of the jende.

When mornings were orange, they too said a storm was on its way. During stormy days they stayed inside and sat around cooking, eating, making things, sleeping, or telling stories. The jende men quickly grew impatient at staying in. Once they drove Loon out of the house wearing only his leggings, and instructed him to run around the shelter while they threw snowballs at him, shouting happily at the storm to go away. The next day it did. This was the only time they performed anything like a shaman's ceremonies, and really it was more like a joke. Afterward they fed him a chunk of cedar salmon and a roast caribou shank.

In new snow they wore snowshoes. These were bigger and better than the ones the Wolf pack had, made of single long spruce branches bent in a full curve to a point behind the heel, and the ends lashed together. Across the widest part of the bend, two hard sticks had been lashed. An open weave of leather strips was tied to the outer frame, making the surface that rode on the snow. Leather straps were tied to the cross stick and used to tie their boots to the forward cross stick. The snowshoes were light and strong, and floated a walker over all but the softest snow. They were better on flats than on traverses. As when on the cruder snowshoes the Wolf pack used at home, while descending a snowy slope one could slide down on one foot until enough snow piled up under that snowshoe to bring it to a halt, and just before that happened one shifted to the other foot, thus glissading down the slope in long slow steps. In the steep ravines these dreamy glissades added to Loon's sense of being a giant on the land.

Put your head down and get through the days. Eat as much as you can stand to. It was hard to eat, there was a permanent clutch in his belly, though sometimes he also felt a raging hunger. He couldn't tell hunger from nausea, and so ended up getting very cold at night, even to the point of shivering from time to time. No one can shiver for long.

Day followed day. The winter solstice came and went. Around that day, the jende men let one of their captive wolves out of their enclosure and surrounded him and abruptly clubbed him to death, and then skinned the body and ate it, giving one bite to every jende person. Seeing this made the captive humans very quiet, that night in the cold trap.

In the depth of that winter Loon learned the surrounding country-side well, especially the ravines to the east, and the land falling south and west to the great salt sea. On that broad riven slope the jende trapped beaver and marten and fox, and the other furry small people of the marshes and waterways now lying under their thick blanket of snow.

As the winter got colder and colder, despite the lengthening days, they spent more time in the house, and Loon learned more of what could be learned in there. He saw which men were the leaders of this big pack, and which women, and how the group split into its clans, or whatever they had that was like clans. The women ran the house's affairs in a way recognizable from his own pack. Elga still went to the women's shelter during the new moon, as she had at home. That was something to know. On the days when he glimpsed her going there he felt a prick of hope, as if one piece of a riddle had been answered. Anytime he spotted her it was hard not to startle and look away. He still wasn't sure whether the jende knew of his connection to her or not.

L ater in the winter some of the jende men walked out onto the sea ice to hunt seals at their breathing holes. The great salt sea was frozen to an immense distance offshore, even reaching to a few low rocky islands poking over the horizon from the land. So out they went on it, and on certain days Loon was required to follow them, his heart as cold as his feet.

The jende men walked straight to spots where they expected to find seal holes, and there they waited, hiding behind low snow walls they built, to spear seals who came out unsuspecting. They tied leather lines to their javelins so the speared seals couldn't swim off to die. Some of those killed were pregnant, and the unborn seals were a favorite delicacy back in camp.

Loon's task was to haul the sled carrying the kill, which was heavy, and seemed to him therefore to have the most chance of breaking through the ice and pulling him down with it into the great salt sea. But he kept his eyes down and followed.

Big cracks in the ice had sometimes refrozen clear, so that he could look down right to the bottom. Once he saw yellow sand down there, covered by purple starfish like big flowers. On this clear ice the jende speared ahead of themselves frequently to test the ice's solidity. Once, stopping briefly to look down at the purple starfish, the jende called Elhu said, —Too bad! in the particular way the jende had when they were laughing at bad luck. He added something to the effect that the starfish would be prized for something, making a scratching motion as he said it.

Loon nodded, looking around. Out here one could see that the great ice wall looming over the hills extended to the west as far as they could see, covering the great salt sea as it did the land, although on the ocean it did not stand as high. Possibly it rested on the sea floor, like the sea ice nearest shore did; or perhaps it too was floating, like the sea ice farther offshore. One could see where the waves of summer had struck the ice wall to the west and frozen to it in a frolic embroidery of white curlicues and icicles. This white tangle somewhat resembled broken water and spray, but as everything was frozen, the scene was strangely still.

Loon was always scared out on the ice, and he saw the northers were nervous as well, as alert as deer who smell wolves, so that he knew he was right to be scared. The ice under them sometimes bowed down, especially under the sleds, you could feel it behind you. When that happened the jende altered their course and turned in easy curves, never stopping, and one shouted to the slowing Loon not to stop, never to stop: Oma! Oma! Apparently stopping was exactly wrong, as the norther's quick mime of crashing through made clear.

Staying safe was apparently a matter of staying on the whitest ice. New ice was nearly black, and the northers called those areas beltz, and kept away from them. As the new ice thickened it turned gray, and at its thickest, white. The line where gray turned to white would hold a man and a sled. They stayed well away from any open water, no matter how white the ice next to it was. They had with them a long pole with a bone point at one end and a bone hook at the other; this was called an una, and was lighter and longer than any javelin, and used to poke suspect ice ahead, to see if it could be broken enough to let sea water up. Drifts of snow lying on the ice were also probed, to see if there was in fact any ice under them; apparently the winter's sea water was so cold that snow could float on it without melting, looking solid when it wasn't. This slush was called pogaza, and if it had frozen into a solid mass, it was called igini. Igini would hold a man and even a sled, but it was almost impossible to haul a sled over it, or even to walk on it without falling. Also, there was no visible difference between igini and pogaza, so they had to avoid both whenever possible, and treat igini as a great danger if they had to cross it to get to better ice. With gusto they mimed what would happen if you fell into pogaza; nothing to climb out onto, nothing to hold to, so you would quickly freeze and die. They seemed to enjoy miming death's arrival.

One day out there, a short day in the middle of the second month,

Loon was hiding behind a snow wall near a hole in the ice, and a jende named Kaktak, along with Elhu and another friend, were killing the seals that emerged from the hole, when suddenly there was a loud crack to landward. The northers immediately ran off in that direction, leaving their captives to follow or not. By the time Loon and the other two captives had caught up to them, they were standing still, looking at an unjumpable width of open black water. No miming anything now. They were on a floating chunk of ice, sliding out to sea.

The northers conferred briefly among themselves, then returned to the seal hole and made a shelter out of their snow wall, the sleds, and some hides from the sleds. Each of them used a hide to sit on, and the flat rock they carried on the sled for a hearth was placed at their center. They quickly spun up a fat fire, not hugely warm but better than nothing. After that there was nothing to do but sit and wait, and hope that an onshore wind would eventually come out of the west and blow them back to the sea ice still attached to the shore. Meanwhile they were on a raft made of ice, drifting on the great salt sea. One of the jende stood and shouted a prayer to the winds, or a curse; then they huddled in their furs and sat, waiting to either live or die.

Night fell in the middle of the afternoon, and the temperature plummeted. The fat fire's warmth was palpable then, though it was little more than a big lamp, and they blocked the entry to their low shelter with snow and hides, and huddled together around the little flame, pressing against each other in a tight circle to share what warmth they could through the sides of their bodies, and holding hands out to the fire from time to time to warm them a bit before tucking them back into their underarms.

Loon was too cold to think. He sat hunched, pinching his toes, feeling in him a deep sadness that he would be unable to rescue Elga, that it all would end for him so soon. He hadn't felt anything so strongly in a long time.

But sometime in the night the wind seemed to change, and in any case picked up. Though they couldn't be sure of it in the dark, when a gray light crept over the eastern horizon, and they took a look outside the shelter, the wind was clearly coming from the west. They stirred a little under the hides, ate a little frozen fish to give them strength for whatever the day might bring.

With the sun blinking over the horizon, they left their shelter to have a quick look around. In the distance they could see the hills behind their camp, and the ice wall looming over the hills. Their floating island slopped in the great salt sea, getting wet around its edges. Happily it was big enough that they stayed dry in the middle, even though it was getting windier, and broken waves sloshed onto the west side of the ice, throwing up little bursts of spray.

They went back inside to stay as warm as they could. For a long time they sat there in the gloom of their shelter. Finally the raft came to a grinding halt, and they rushed out to find they were well to the south of where they had broken off, and had been blown up against new black sea ice, very thin. —Bad luck! the jende exclaimed, laughing mirthlessly.

The northers walked quickly around their little island, then had a long discussion. Crossing the black ice was going to be hard; the possibility of falling through it was all too obvious.

Kaktak spoke and mimed to Loon and the other captives, in a way that Loon did not find completely clear. It looked like he was mimicking the big white bears who lived out on the sea ice. When confronted with black ice, these ice bears lowered themselves and shoved forward on their chests and bellies, toeing their way forward as fast as possible without kicking downward. Toe pushes and finger sweeps were the most that could be risked when it came to pressure on the ice. The only thing that differed for the humans compared to the ice bears, Kaktak indicated, was that they would also hold an una in each hand, lengthwise right next to their bodies, and would push down on them to help spread their weight over a bigger patch of ice as they slithered forward.

Kaktak spoke briefly to Elhu and the other man, and then with a graceful kneel and dive, he slid onto the black ice and squiggled forward like a big lizard, always moving the unas close to him on both sides. When he had made it to gray ice he quickly stood up, and immediately began to finger water down the fur of his jacket and pants, sweeping it onto the snow under him. He shouted to the rest of them happily. —Omoo! he called, and then slid the poles back over the black ice to them. It goes!

So it would, if you were good. But knowing it could work was the main thing, and Kaktak having tested it, the rest of the stranded jende were quickly across, one at a time, over slightly different places on the ice, trying to stay close to Kaktak's route without repeating it exactly.

When it was Loon's turn, he banished from his mind a vision of the way loons slapped the water when taking off across a lake, and recalled instead a red water lizard he had once seen slither away from an overturned rock in a stream, looking like a live root and quickly disappearing. He crouched and cast himself forward as smoothly as he could, smacking the ice right away with his nose and mouth, so that the salty tang of the coat of water on the ice was in him as he slithered forward on knees and toes and the two clutched unas. It was an awkward kind of crawling, but soon the ice was dirty white under him, and he pushed up to his knees and got to his feet, and began to squeeze the water down and off the front of his clothes before it froze there in the fur. Even though the air was very cold, there was some kind of wetness on the new ice, made of water saltier than the great salt sea itself. —Gatzi! Kaktak said when he saw Loon's face. Salty!

The northers were very pleased at their return to land and their escape from death, so pleased that Loon suddenly realized they had not expected to survive. He had not been able to see that in them during their time at sea, and was impressed at the way they had fronted the situation.

The other captives slithered over to the gray ice and imitated the jende, drying out their furs with their fingers as completely as possible, which left their hands pink and wet and throbbing with cold. Then the jende pulled the sleds off their ice raft by throwing ropes in loops over them, and when they caught them, tugging them over the new ice to them as gently and smoothly as they could. The black ice bowed under them, but did not break.

When they had recovered the sleds, the jende took off toward camp faster than Loon had ever seen the northers move. He soon realized it was because their clothes were damp, despite their best efforts to dry them; the chill was so numbing that they had to run to be warm enough to move at all. The captives followed as best they could. After the running created some warmth in them, they slowed to a walk and caught their breath, but soon chilled and were forced to run again. So it went, run then walk, run then walk, but mostly run, huffing and puffing so hard that their blood should have been burning inside them, though it wasn't; the best they could do was to keep just warm enough to move.

Loon followed the jende, and made no attempt to help the other two captives falling behind him. Surely that was the northers' job. But the northers did not help, did not even look back, and when Loon looked over his shoulder he saw the last man, named Bron, was falling and struggling back to his feet. Loon waited, and when Bron caught up to him, he tied the man's sled to his own, freeing Bron up to make his way back without pulling a sled.

Except a little while after that, he looked back again and saw that Bron had collapsed onto the snow. He circled back and left Bron's sled behind, pulled the man up onto his own sled, then took up his rope again and heaved forward to start. He pulled and pulled on the loop on the end of the rope, and got going at last with his legs burning hot, while the rest of him burned cold; the hot pushed from inside out, the cold from outside in, but both painful. And yet somehow the two together would be enough to see him home. He began to sing one of Thorn's running songs as he approached the northers' camp, and he only stopped singing when he arrived at the tunnel entrance to the big house's cold trap and went in to get help for Bron, still lying on the sled. He was not sure what the northers would make of his rescue of a fellow captive, and he was irritated with himself for standing out to them in any way. He went to his corner of the ground level and stripped to his leggings and stood right over the captive's lamp fire to get warm and dry. Thawing out caused some of the fiercest burning of all, as usual, but it was all on the surface, simply the burn of feeling coming back into his numbed hands, then his face and ears, and, after he had eaten a lot of fish dipped in marmot fat, even his feet. Meanwhile the northers carried Bron up to the middle platform in the house and put him by the fire there, and only when he was coherent did they send him back down to the captives' level to spend the night. Once down there again, he squeezed Loon's arm with a look that Loon did not want to see on any captive's face; he did not want to think of himself as one of them, or as a helpful stranger. But in the nights that followed, Loon sometimes woke to find Bron draped against his back, making of himself a living blanket in the coldest part of the nights. They did not know any words in the same language except for the northers' words, and those words none of them spoke aloud. The ground floor under the big house was a quiet place.

Loon had intended to make himself invisible to the northers, to be a captive beneath notice. Now some of the northers might be aware of him. And he had hidden a sheep shank in the corner of the cold trap, and on every new moon scored its edge with a pebble to mark how many months had passed, and one night it wasn't there anymore. Whether whoever took it had noticed the marks, or knew the bone was his, he could not be sure. There was no overt sign from Kaktak or Elhu or any of the rest of the ice people that they were watching him. But he felt that the men going out earliest and farthest on the day's affairs were calling for him more often. And during their days out, checking traps, or hunting on the sea ice, or foraging for firewood, they gave him as much to eat and drink as they took themselves, and treated him almost like they did each other, except when it came time to pull the sleds home. And of course he was never allowed to have anything to do with the captive wolves they sometimes took with them. They talked among themselves, and Loon only caught part of that, but he was understanding more than he had at first. The northers were content in their life by the great salt sea. It was always cold, and mostly dark in the winter, but they took a good living from the sea and the hills. They never went hungry. They laughed at bad luck. They faced up to Narsook.

One morning Loon left his house and there was Elga right there before him. He said —Hello! but she ignored him, looked away, and then he was cuffed in the back: Kaktak had been behind him, coming into the house from around the corner.

Kaktak glared at him as he regained his footing. —Why did you say anything to her? he said in his tongue, perfectly comprehensible to Loon. —You know you aren't to speak to the women.

Loon nodded, looking down. —She was just there. Sorry.

Kaktak kept staring at him. —Why did you go back for that other captive? That was none of your affair. You leave the other captives to us, understand?

—Yes.

—Good. Because I want to take you out with me. You pull hard. But we'll leave you in the house if you do anything more like this.

—I understand, Loon said, still looking down, his cheeks burning.

Kaktak went into the house, taking a last look at Elga, who had kept walking toward the women's house.

Loon resolved to keep a stone face and do what he was told and nothing more.

Late in the third month of the new year, Kaktak and some of the other northers instructed Loon to haul a sled loaded with firewood and bags and follow them as they climbed up the nearest valley onto the ice wall itself. Now we go up in the wind, they told Loon as they left camp.

To get up the steep side of the ice wall, they ascended one of the hilltops flanking their valley, and followed a ridge from that hilltop north and higher, until they were overlooking the ravines on each side. This ridge ran right up into the massive wall of ice, which stood above them tilted back a bit, gray with rubble and dirt and dust, and riven by cracks and melt lines that were blue in their depths. As high as they were on the ridge, the ice still bulked over their heads, and they could not see the high plateau that must be up there. But here they could see that the ice sloped steeply down into the ravines to each side of them, making fat tongues of ice that the jende called glaciers. These ice slopes ended either in clean walls of ice, like the one east of their camp, or in curving bars of rubble and milky gray ponds.

Now the jende making this ascent led the way in a traverse up the side of the glacier to the east of the ridge, moving up on ice intermixed with rocks of all sizes. It was possible to find good footing on rock after rock, as most of the stones were more than half-buried in the ice; they must have warmed up enough by day to melt the ice under them enough to sink into it a little, and then at night they froze in place, and eventually they sank too deep in the ice to warm up in the sun anymore and stayed stuck where they were. So the men could traverse up the ice slope easily on these rock steps, and after a while, as they got higher, the slope lay back.

Hauling a loaded sled up this traverse after them proved difficult, and the jende came back once to help Loon drag it up an ice channel between two rocks, then lift it up over some others. But soon enough they were all on top of the glacier, where they headed north up a slight rise onto the ice wall proper, with Loon hauling the sled behind them.

When they came onto the ice plateau at the top of the wall, they stopped and looked back south, down to the hills and the steppe and the big snowy valley, and the frozen curve at the edge of the great salt sea, the whitest white of all, with the blue of its water beyond. Loon had never seen the great salt sea look anything like so big, it was stunning to see it from this high up, extending west and south with no sign at all of any shore to the west. The world was huge.

The ice on top of the plateau rose and fell somewhat like the moors north of their home camp. As they walked north over this ice, Loon could hear the ice shift and breathe. Ah: it was alive. A white cold thing of the north, devouring the world. It spoke in low heavy creaks, also cracks, also shuddering booms, as low as any sound he had ever heard.

The ice plateau was not at all like land covered by a winter blanket of snow. The ice was almost all bare ice, mostly white, but in some places blue, in others clear. It undulated in ways that ground never did, nor the great salt sea; the rises and dips were something between hills and waves, but neither. In a few places it was perfectly flat, but mostly it was rounded up or down. Here and there it shattered to a rubble that resembled a close-packed array of smooth-edged ice blades. Little creeks of water cut the ice now and then, and these flowed downward, of course, but curving in ways that creeks on land would never have thought to go. When the jende wanted to cross these streams but they were too wide to jump over, they followed them downstream rather than upstream, because soon enough they always disappeared down a hole in the ice, the creek's water swirling down into icy blue depths with a fearful clatter. The men kept a good distance from these round holes, and spoke apologies to the talkative ice for bothering it with their passing. They also avoided the areas of shattered ice, which came in patches.

Most of the ice surface they walked over was pitted, and about as white as old snow. It was too bright to look at, and indeed Loon had to squint hard to look at anything. As they walked farther north, the ice under them grew cleaner and less nobbled. Here and there boulders and pebbles were heaped up in long curving lines. These grew fewer as they proceeded north, but some still snaked over the ice, about waist high and very strange to see, because they looked like low walls that people had piled up, but were too big and long to be that. Looking back they could see south a great way, but as they walked on, eventually all they saw was ice; even the great salt sea was only a sunbeaten verge to the southwest. It looked like a world covered entirely by ice, a sight to put a pinch in one's throat. But the northers hiked on.

Late that day they hiked on creamy blue ice that was almost too smooth to walk on. Up on a low rounded hill of this blue ice, they could see a long way in every direction. There was only ice as far as they could see. Up here the northers stopped and made a small fire on a hearth rock they had brought with them, and cooked little strips of fish and seal and caribou to black fragments like charcoal. They broke up and dumped the black bits on the ice, while chanting a chant in which the words for ice and cold were frequently repeated. Eeeeesh! Kalt!

After that they smoked a pipe they passed among themselves, and when they were done, Loon was allowed a puff too. It was a harsh bitter smoke, Loon found. The jende coughed as they expelled it, and Loon decided he wouldn't, but he did anyway.

One of the jende men, named Orn, made apologies to the great windy ice. Then he pointed north. There on the horizon was a low black prominence. That was their destination. The nuna, they named it. A rock island in a sea of ice. The pupil of the eye, they called it, pointing at their squinting eyes. It was the reverse of the ice caps on the hills to the west of the Wolf pack's camp.

The jende took off toward the nuna. Loon followed them head down, eyes nearly closed to reduce the glare of beaten sunlight off the ice and the sky. He would have closed his eyes entirely, but he needed to see the ice under his feet to set them properly against the nobbling.

When they came closer to the island of rock, they found that the ice had reared up over its edges, like a wave that was about to crash on a shore, frozen at the last moment. It was not possible to cross the blue trough between the frozen wave and the scraped rock under it; they had to walk around the island to the west, until they came to a break in the ice wave which allowed them access to the rock's edge. Here, however, the rock, which was reddish black, and as smooth as chert, was a short cliff with no obvious way up. The jende led the way left, down what became a flat floor of blue ice separating the rock cliff and a growing ice wave. They descended this little rounded slot, which grew deeper as they hiked, walking on blue ice covered with reddish rubble scattered on it, each bit of rock half-buried in the ice. It was strange to walk down this rubble-floored gorge, with a wall of rock to their right and an overhanging wall of blue ice to their left. It seemed as if the wave of ice would fall on them at any moment, though it never moved, nor groaned, nor scarcely even breathed. Nevertheless the jende walked in silence, and Loon nervously followed their lead, letting his sled down ahead of him. After a fist or so of this uneasy trek, they came around a curve of the island and the rock wall shrank in height until the ice and rock were the same height, and they could simply step from the one to the other.

They walked on flat blocks of dark red stone. The sled's bone runners scraped, but the rock was so smooth that Loon could still pull it behind him. The blocks rose in distinct steps, and the jende helped him lift the sled up each of these knee- or waist-high walls. By the time they reached the center of the nuna, they were two or three trees' height above the ice. The tops of all the red blocks were smoothed to a polish, with straight lines scoring the polish north and south. There were also crescent breaks, the shape of day three or four of the moon, cut into the rock. Small shallow gaps between the red blocks were filled with scree and sand that was dotted with black lichen, the only living thing on the island.

They reached the high point of the rock. From there they could see out over the great windy ice for a great distance in all directions. A turn of the head gave Loon the ring of the whole earth, its western edge blazing with sunblink. The ice below them was a creamy blue marked by patches of white, lined with gray lines of broken stone. That they had walked in a single day onto this new world was astonishing. The stories at home all spoke of three worlds, one inside the earth, one in the sky, one on the surface between them. Loon had had glimpses of all three. But here the northers had simply walked north onto a fourth world, bulking over the earth. A higher realm, a frozen sky.

The northers were looking around attentively. It was not their way to speak much when they were out by day; later, in the evenings around the fire, they would talk at length about the day's happenings, but in the moment itself they did not like to talk.

At the northernmost end of the big block at the top of the island, there was a ring of waist-high stone shards, standing on their ends. The northers walked to this circle of stones, and before they got there, indicated to Loon that he should stay behind.

The highest block had been cleared of any of the small stones that lay scattered on much of the rest of the island: only the ring of standing stones was left on it. These stones were all roughly rectangular, and had been balanced on their ends so that they seemed to stand like short men. There were about a score of them. Gathering them must have been a considerable task, accomplished by a big group of men; the stones were big enough to be very awkward to move.

A squarish boulder lay flat at the center of this circle of standing stones, and on it the northers prepared a fire with branches and twigs they had brought from Loon's sled. They dripped fat from a bag onto them, and soon had a fire sparked to life. On the fire they burned the wing of an eagle and the wing of a raven, while singing in their harsh voices. When the fire was at its biggest, though still nearly invisible in the glare of the sun and the sky and the ice, Orn took a red swath of cloth from his backsack and unwrapped it to reveal a human skull, missing its jaw but otherwise clean and fresh. He held it up to look at the sun one last time, and all of them likewise looked right at the sun, eyes closed, singing together. Then Orn put the skull in the fire, and they watched as it blackened and, when they had poured some fat on it, burned as well, not like wood, but like the tip of a giant lamp wick. As with a wick, it took a long time to burn away. White flame danced in its eye sockets and out of its gaping mouth as if it were comfortable living in fire, but eventually it broke and fell in on itself, and joined the embers under it. As the fire burned itself out, the skull became no more than black chunks, like the other bits of char there in the ash.

When the fire went out, the men stirred the ashes gently, waited again. In the frigid chill of the breeze out of the north, the heat quickly left the ashes, and as soon as they were cool enough to handle, the northers all scooped up double handfuls and carried them outstretched to the ring of stones, where they walked around the outside of the circle and stopped to sing at each of the cardinal points; after which they surrounded one of their company and tossed their ashes into the air, such that the wind caught the ashes and blew them over this man. He held his arms out and his face up, and took the rain of ash on him as if he wanted it.

This was as close to shaman stuff as Loon had ever seen in the northers, and he watched with a pang in his chest as he thought of Thorn, and wondered what Thorn would have made of this, and whether he would ever see Thorn again and thus have a chance to describe the northers' ceremony, their ring of stones, this immense fourth world of ice that they had walked right up onto. He still did not see how getting back to Thorn could happen, and the pain of that made his body weak. His stomach shrank, his knees buckled, he had to collect himself to be able to walk. With all the standing around their feet had gone cold, and they had to proceed carefully as the jende walked west and north, to an edge of the rock island where they had not yet been.

Here the rock stood high over the ice. At their feet a steep cliff of cracked stone dropped away to the creamy blue. All the narrow ledges of this cliff were green with moss, so they saw it as mostly green; then the cliff steepened as it dropped, such that much of it could not be seen from above. The ice beyond the green moss looked a long way down.

The jende had gone quiet on the approach to the cliff's edge, and by signs required that Loon do the same. They stood back from the

edge and looked around them. The great windy ice covered everything they could see, extended to the distant sun-singed horizon.

Suddenly the jende rushed to the cliff's edge as if to cast themselves off, and stopped and screamed as they threw handfuls of small
rocks down the cliff, bouncing from ledge to ledge.

Up and out into the air screeched a great flock of birds, flapping
across each other in wild disarray, some even colliding and tumbling
down before catching the air and flying again. They were crow-
sized black-and-white birds, with big curved orange beaks, twentytwentytwenties of them crisscrossing the air overhead until they
were everywhere over the men.

When they were past their panic and high enough, the birds
flocked and began circling in groups, and either returned to the cliff
below, ignoring the northers who had disturbed them, or flew off.
Black backs, white undersides, ducky feet that were the same orange
as their beaks. Their faces were two big white circles holding little
black eyes. They flew so close together it seemed like they should be
colliding, but now that they were over their fright, they never did.
Birds were good at that.

The jende watched the birds' crisscrossing very intently, hands
on foreheads shading their eyes. When the birds were either gone
or had returned to the cliff, with only a few still circling overhead,
they talked it over for a while, in a way they usually wouldn't. Loon
could see they were interpreting what they had seen in the birds'
splash into the sky, because they sometimes scratched curves on the
rock with their hand blades, or made swooping motions with their
hands. The way the birds had flown off in their panic meant something to them. It was going to be a good year, they were telling each
other.

After that they headed back. Down the many blocks of scraped
rock, back onto the breathing blue ice, once again sliding along
carefully, the sun now blazing off the ice to the west at an angle
that hurt. They had to squint until their eyes were slits nearly closed
shut, and here the jende's eyelids gave them quite an advantage, it
seemed. For Loon the ice was so bright it went black, as if burning at

its edges. It was a light like the fire in the skull on the block. Blindly they walked down the slope of the ice plateau with the wind at their back. Badleg throbbed badly at the growing length of the trek. They were walking back down into the world. Soon the sun would set and they would have to finish their descent in darkness. For now, the world blazed.

Some of their late winter storms lasted a fortnight or longer. They passed these in the big house, eating, sleeping, and sleeping some more. On the upper platforms the jende sat around or lay on their sides. In the dim light coming down through the roof tube, they made things and talked, and their elders told stories, long stories in short rhythmic bursts of speech, the winged words following one on the next in a way that lulled Loon into something between sleep and waking, something that was not exactly dreaming, but like it. When the jende elders finished their stories they were just like Pippilouette, and would say something to effect of, Look, the icicles seem to be melting already, to remind their audience how much time they had eaten up with their story. The more the better, on days like these.

Sometimes Loon made things too. He carved spear throwers from shoulder bones in their food, using not blades, which the captives weren't allowed to have, but broken pebbles. Sometimes after they broke bones for their marrow, there were splinters left over that were easily sharpened into trap stickers; but these could be blades as well, obviously dangerous, and there was no place to hide them, so he usually broke them up when he was done making them. One however he slipped between two hides on the wall where they overlapped, near the floor. No one noticed.

But he couldn't see a way out.

As they waited out the spring storms, they spent more time in their house than in any month of the winter. At dawn one or two of them would dress and look out the entryway, and then report on what the winds told them they could do that day. If it wasn't storming, out they ventured into the cold, and did what could be done. They fed their captive wolves, visited their shitting field, got more frozen fish from the food platform. At sunset they convened in their big beaver den of a house and talked the day over while they ate in the heated air. They sweated freely through the evenings, resting on their highest levels in their highest heat. They slept on the lower levels where it was cooler, just above Loon and the other captives, as they seemed to like to sleep snuggled into their furs. The air flowing in the low entryway's cold trap was the same coldness as the outside air, of course, and if you put your hand down from the captives' level into the tunnel of the entryway, you could feel just how cold it was, very much colder than on the ground floor of the house, so quickly did the air warm as it rose. It always amazed Loon how quickly that happened, but he could feel it with his hand, and also reach up and feel the greater warmth just above him. In the distance from the cold trap to the jende's first level, the air went from freezing cold to mildly cool, indeed almost warm, or in that in-between that was neither warm nor cool. It was like the way air warmed from one's nose to one's lungs, or when the sun hit you in the morning: strangely quick changes in the heat or coldness of air.

In their big house, the warmth had to do mostly with the fire kept burning on the platform level, and the way in which every wall of the house had been covered in leather, making the place windproof and holding in its warmth as if in a bag. The jende's bodies glowed like lamps in the gloom, their plump skin flush with blood and gleaming with sweat. They looked like the rocks they put in their fire, then lifted with stout branches into buckets of water they cooked in: these stones too glowed in the dimness and sizzled the air. On storm days the hollow branch at the top of the house was kept almost completely plugged by a patch of fur, and that held in even more heat. When they retired to their beds in the evening, they pulled out the fur patch and opened the top hole entirely, which let the whole house cool down a little. After that they would curl into their furs and the near darkness of the lowest fire, really just a lamp fire, with three wicks burning through the night.

Before going to bed, they had a final meal. They often ate fishes while they were still frozen, chewing on them with relish. But sometimes they boiled the fish in wooden buckets, using the hot rocks to heat the water. When they did that, they ate the fish and then drank the soup they had been cooked in. The jende women would snatch out the fish, dry them with their fingers, hand them out to every jende in the house, with particular attention to who got what. After the fish were eaten, they passed around ladles of the soup. Then they went to bed. Sometimes they woke at night and peed into their pee buckets. Mostly they slept, with only Loon to ponder sometimes through the long fists of the night, feeling Badleg throb with the cold.

The days began to last longer. They would soon be in the hunger months of spring, and yet the jende were not even close to running out of food. They could have made it through yet another winter with the food frozen on their platforms, Loon judged, and maybe another after that. And yet every day that the winds allowed, the men went out hunting and fishing and trapping. Loon didn't know what to make of that. Probably they just liked to be doing things. They did have more kids in their pack than most packs in the south had. And sometimes they stole wives from other packs, as he very well knew. Maybe having so much food made them want for other things to do. Maybe they wanted a lot of kids, wanted to increase their number. One time he caught a glimpse of Elga in the entry to the women's tent, and she looked well fed, and he wondered if she would get pregnant. Loon sucked air through his teeth at the thought. But he didn't know what to do about it. At night he could only lie wrapped in his hide on the cold floor, eating his cold meat; and if the impulse came to him in the darkness, fucking the cold earth. But the impulse rarely came. His feet were always cold, and a cold lump inside him too. Nothing he could see was going to free them from this place.

Still. He had that bone sticker hidden in the hides on the wall. And whenever he was sent out for firewood, or frozen fish from the food platform, or sealskin bags of fat, he tried to steal things and hide them, first in the hides on the wall, or in snowdrifts around camp, and then, when he went out foraging for firewood, under a boulder in the valley nearest camp, one boulder in a clump of boulders at the bottom of a rockslide. The hole under this boulder was like a marmot house, and of course marmots could get into it, so he did not leave food. But over time he hid stolen bags and backsacks, and later two jackets with hoods, and sticks that could be walking poles or spears. Anything he could steal that was not food, that he thought might be useful for the walk home, he took and put there.

But he still couldn't think of how to get away.

Thorn was crossing Quick Pass when a figure appeared in the meadow at the head of Lower's Upper. Thorn went still and watched for a while. He couldn't see like he used to. Then the figure waved at him. It was Pippiloette. Thorn waved back, and the traveler ascended the headwall under the pass at speed. Thorn tugged at the remnant of his left ear, a stub that he seldom touched. When the traveler appeared in the pass, Thorn went to him and they embraced, then regarded each other holding hands.

—Do you know where Loon is? Thorn said.

—Yes. He was taken by the same northers who took his wife.

Thorn growled. —When?

—Right after they took her. I helped him track them, but their scouts took him in the dawn. I heard them coming and slipped away, but I had to stay quiet to do it.

—And then?

—They went north to their place. I followed them for a while, but then I had to go east. Now I'm on my way home, but I wanted to let you know what happened.

Thorn nodded, frowning. —Come to our camp. You'll be our guest, and you can tell Heather.

Pippiloette nodded.

Back in camp the people gathered around the fire to listen to Pippiloette tell his tale. He stood to do it.

> The youth and I tracked the northers on their way home,
> Keeping our distance, unseen by them,
> For two days, tracking by night and sleeping by day,
> And we were faster than they were,
> And on the second night we stopped in a good ridge hole,
> A place I had used before, a good lookout.
>
> But we both fell asleep, and in the dawn after first light
> I woke to the knowledge that men were nearby,

And they were on us before I could wake Loon,
And as they seized him I slipped under a boulder like a marmot,
And had to stay silent so that they would not know I was there.
All my regular nooks have tucks,
And so should yours if you travel alone,
If you are a person who needs sleep, even just a fist now and then.

After that I followed them from a day's distance,
Only spotting their scouts when they made their
     rearguard inspection,
Late every afternoon. The northers are not very careful
     that way,
Because they don't believe any people would dare follow them,
And are only checking for lions and bears.
So I followed them north to the big river running west
At the bottom of that great plain,
I slipped through the marsh grass
And through willow brambles where I never stepped on
     the ground,
And yet never made a sound or caused any branch to move,
So quick and sure am I.
And I saw them on the other bank of that river,
And saw them head north from there.
A bluff standing over a bend in the river
Gave me sight of them far away,
Headed north and west to their home place.
Out that way some hills plunge into the great salt sea,
And above and behind those hills is a higher world,
A great windy ice that covers everything north of those hills,
Except for the great salt sea.
This ice is sometimes better to cross than the land under it,
Being smooth and not a place animals go,
Except for the great white bears, and they never go far
     from water.

Up on the white heights you can run for days without a care
   for danger,
Except for cracks in the ice so big they would swallow a man,
But these can be seen and avoided.
They who took Loon live at that meeting of ice and land
   and water,
They call themselves the jende, meaning the people,
As ignorant packs often do.

Thorn said, —Could you lead us to them?

—I can describe the way, Pippiloette said, —in a way you can't miss. I myself have to go home now.

The people of Wolf pack talked it over. Schist and Ibex didn't say much, but indicated that they were not interested in taking on the northers for a wife that had been the northers' to begin with, nor for anyone who might have gotten involved with her. The younger men, Moss and Hawk and their friends, spoke with more heat, because they missed their friend, but really, they didn't want to go either. As they urged Schist to act they tried to suggest they were the ones needed at home, to do their part in the pack's work. There was even some truth to this.

Thorn wandered away from the fire, down to the riverside and its view of the sky to the north. It was late; Two Valleys had tipped on its side, and the Ladle was pouring its contents back onto its curving handle.

Later still Thorn returned to camp and went to Heather's nest. He sat by her little fire and warmed his hands. All her helper girls were asleep in their caribou blankets, faces turned to the fire. Heather eventually creaked over and sat down beside him. For a long time neither of them spoke.

—I'm going to go get them, Thorn said finally.

—No.

—Yes.

Heather made a little snort. —We need you here.

—We need them too.

Heather said nothing. She was the one caring for Loon and Elga's child.

—I'll be fast.

Heather regarded him for a long time. —Is Pippiloette going with you?

—No.

—But you'll need help.

—Maybe so.

Heather said nothing.

Thorn said, —Is that old one you cured still hanging around? What was his name?

—Click, Heather said. —I call him Click. It's like the sound he makes for himself. She made a clucking sound by pulling her tongue away from the roof of her mouth. —That's the way he says it. Yes, he's around. Up at Hill In the Middle. He visits with me when I go there looking for hellebore.

—Will you help me find him? And ask him to come with me?

She stared at Thorn and he let her. Finally she said, —Why him?

Thorn shrugged. —He's strong.

She kept staring at him. —And he's the only one who will go with you.

—That too. But he'll be good. He's stronger than any of them.

He went to Pippiloette and said, —Tell me where they are. Show me.

They went to the sand bank by the bend in the river. Pippi scuffed smooth a patch of the sand, and first made a very clear copy of the festival meadow and its surrounding hills, piling up ridges of sand with his bunched fingers and using some pebbles to indicate peaks. He was one of the best bird's eye makers at the eight eight, and when he had finished shaping the festival area, he continued by shaping the sand to the north of that, showing rivers crossing first steppe and then a broad valley running east to west. North of that, right against the sea's edge, drawn with a curving line, were some low hills, and among these hills Pippi stuck a stick.

Thorn nodded. It was a long way north.

*   *   *

At sunrise Thorn rose and finished packing his sack. When it was full, and he had eaten some smoked salmon and a few handfuls of pine nuts, he went to Heather's nest.

She was ready, her sack already on her back. Before they left she gave him a little sachet. —It doesn't work right away. It's fast, but not immediate.

—I'll remember, Thorn said, putting the bag in an inner pocket of his coat.

Together they headed out of camp upstream, toward Quick Pass and Hill In the Middle. Heather led the way at speed. Where Lower's Upper widened and its creek split to go both ways around Hill In the Middle, she stopped at a little cedar grove and whistled a rising note that ended with a triple peep-peep-peep, like a little bird.

After a time a similar whistle floated down on them from the hill. Out of the forest stepped the old one that Heather and Loon had helped when he was hurt. Thorn had visited briefly during the old one's recuperation in Heather's care; he had played a little exorcism tune, while pulling from the old one's throat a mass of spit the size of a toad. So now the old one recognized him, and though it was clear he was surprised, he did not look particularly alarmed. Thorn bobbed his head in the way the old ones had, and made the little roop roop sound that the old ones used when they were trying to locate each other in the forest, sounding just like loons locating their companions when they came up from an underwater swim.

Click repeated the sound.

—A loon to find a loon, Thorn said to Heather, who ignored him and spoke in a slow voice to Click. Click cocked his head to the side and seemed to understand her, though for the most part she used the pack's ordinary words for things.

The old one's face was hairy. His beard, hair, and thick eyebrows all tangled together to a mat like the winter shag of a bear. The skin of his cheeks and forehead and nose was as pale as a mushroom; his nose was big and beaky. His irises were dark brown, the whites of his eyes bloodshot. He stared with a fixity that reminded Thorn of old Pika. Around his neck hung a leather thong with three lion fangs tied to it. He was not quite as tall as Thorn; burly in the chest, short-legged, with a slight limp. His head was long, front to back; it was to a person's head as a cave bear's was to a forest bear's. Under his smoky smell there was a musk like a muskrat's. He carried a spear, and had a big hide bundle slung over his left shoulder. He wore marten and fox furs, and bearhide boots, and looked thoroughly capable, indeed almost like any other woodsman. And there were woodsmen out there who had forgotten how to talk. Still, this one was stranger than a woodsman. The old ones were old.

Now to Heather he made a little honk of assent, onk, onk, clearly a kind of yes, with a fixed look on his face that suggested he was not really sure what he was assenting to, but would find out in good time. Good-natured, perhaps; and yet one didn't want to run into more than one of them when out alone. Somewhat like bears in that respect too. Bears were said to have been people in the old time, before Raven stuck their coats to them by mistake. Maybe the old ones were bears that hadn't gotten the coats.

Heather spoke a mix of old one and human. —Thorn good, oop oop, go look for Loon. Then a series of clicks.

Click nodded. —Onk, he began, and then clicked away for a while.

Heather replied with more clicking sounds.

She turned to Thorn. —He'll go with you and help. He knows you're going north to the ice, to save Loon and the girl.

She clicked at Click, who smiled fearfully, Thorn felt, and then nodded once more. —Tank oo, he said, something he had learned when they healed him.

—No, thank you, Thorn said, and then, to Heather: —How do I say go?

—Hoosh, she said, with an outward flick of the hand.

Thorn nodded and tried it. He looked Click in the eye. —Hoosh, he said, and waved to the north, over the Hill In the Middle. Then the pack's word for it: skai. Possibly in this way he could teach the old one some more of the pack's tongue. —Skai, hoosh, skai.

—Onk, Click said again. Then: —Food. With a wave up Hill In the Middle.

Thorn nodded. —Good idea. Go get food.

Click looked for reassurance at Heather, who clicked to him. He slipped away into the trees.

Thorn and Heather stood there waiting for his return.

Finally Click reappeared through the trees, the bundle over his shoulder bigger than before.

Suddenly Heather clutched Thorn's arm. —You'd better come back. We need you.

—I know. I'll come back.

—As soon as you can.

—It'll be two months or not at all.

They shared a glance, and Heather let go of his arm.

—Hoosh, she said to Click. —Skai. Go with Thorn, do what he says.

The two men traveled fast. It was the fourth month, and the days were now longer than the nights, and getting longer fast. Suncups dimpled the snow on south-facing slopes. In the mornings the snow was so hard that they could almost run on it, and on the north-facing slopes they could slide down on their boot bottoms.

Around the black leads of open water in the river surfaces, it was obvious that many creatures had passed by. Every track on the snow had melted out to three times its original size, so that it looked like they passed through a country of giant animals.

The first part of their trip simply repeated their caribou trek, so Thorn walked and slid as hard as he could all day long, and on the nights around the full moon, continued on till midnight. The snow-blanketed hills glowed in the moonlight such that one could see almost as if by day, though moonlight drained the colors away. But one did not need color to walk. Several times during their night hikes they saw big cats, and when they were trailed one night by a big cat with tufted ears, Thorn shouted at it once to let it know it was being watched. The old one's presence seemed to keep the cat and indeed all animals at a greater distance than they would have kept from Thorn by himself. It might just have been that there were two of them.

Thorn watched Click when he took the lead, watched the way he hiked and how he looked around. Click crossed ground fast, and yet did not appear to be pushing himself very hard. His feet never stumbled, and his boots looked as good as anyone's, their sinew stitching covered with some kind of gum. He hummed a little to himself as he walked, and made little clicking noises, so that he sounded somewhat like a cicada or grasshopper.

When Thorn made a little fire after they stopped, at the coldest part of the night, Click sat close by it, arms out to gather in its warmth, and always mewing and clucking. He had things to say to himself. Thorn sat looking at the flames, listening. From time to time the old one would make a quick double click to get Thorn's attention, then point to things and make the same sound. Thorn would say the name of the thing, and Click would open his mouth and twist his lips, tilt his head, as if on the edge of repeating the word; and yet in the end would not. —Roop, he would say instead. It was almost precisely the loon's little hello on surfacing in a bay, alerting companions. Thorn could only shake his head in reply, and either repeat the word requested, or say roop himself, or remain silently watching the fire. Thorn spoke, the old one spoke, but they did not share a language. One night Thorn played his flute, and the old one whistled the tunes after him, and then continued as Thorn began again, but offset, and so making a round. That was the best conversation they had.

Click always fell asleep while their fire was still burning, so Thorn would dry anything of his own that might have gotten wet during the day's walk, then look into the fire until gray films fluttered over the orange glow of remaining embers, and then lie back in his furs and watch the stars wheel the rest of the way to morning. When he got sleepy he would play a little night song on his flute, and when this roused Click, Thorn would mime keeping an eye out, and Click would click twice, and Thorn would fall asleep almost between the first click and the second, and wake only when the sun cracked the eastern horizon.

Once Click woke him with a very light tap from the base of his spear, and when Thorn sat up, gestured at him to stay still, then slumped forward and mimed a stalking cat to perfection. Thorn picked up his own spear and spear thrower and readied to throw, then rose to his feet, listening all the while. He never heard or saw the beast, and after a while Click wiped his pale face with his pale hand and gave Thorn a look that was perhaps meant to express relief, although his great brow with its perpetual frown was not well suited to doing that. They sat back down to pack their things and drink from their bags of water, and press on.

Out on the broad open land of the steppe it was possible to lope along and really cross ground. They both used their spears to push themselves along at a pace just short of a run, and so they made much faster time than the whole Wolf pack could ever have achieved. The important thing was to stay on the great rock plates of the plain, which in places lay one after another, only slightly broken by flat-bottomed muskeg channels. In the mornings it was easy, because they could walk over even these channels, the snow in them was so hard; after midday it softened, and step-throughs became more frequent. Click was so heavy he plunged thigh deep where Thorn would scarcely sink to his ankles. Under some snow patches it was possible there were hidden melt ponds, so in the afternoons it was best to stay on the rock slabs. Click called these slabs burren, it seemed, humming the word as they hurried over it: —Burren, burren, burren, burren.

North, then, at speed, and with the sun at their backs. They were a fast team. On the fifth day they came to the festival grounds, looking very strange under the snow, but it was definitely the place, all shrouded in suncupped white. By now all their journey's habits were set, and they seldom bothered to try to speak to each other, as there was no need.

Thorn had occasionally consulted a piece of birch bark he had brought with him, on which he had drawn a version of Pippiloette's bird's eye view. Now they were moving into what for Thorn was new land, and the bark drawing thus became their only guide.

The river Pippiloette had indicated as the way to head north beyond the festival grounds was still frozen hard, and they could hurry down its discolored snow surface, poking ahead of them with their spears as they walked. This far north it was still cold even at midday, and the ice on the river still thick and strong. What few leads they passed they welcomed as chances to drink, for in such a land of snow and ice, water itself was scarce. And they were still far south of their destination.

The best response to the growing cold of the days was to hike hard, and they did that, and then huddled around little fires if they could find the wood, or over Thorn's fat lamp if they couldn't. Twice they passed tributaries of their river that were almost as big as it was.

On the third day north of the festival grounds, there came a moment of choice for Thorn. Almost any north-trending valley they now came to might be the one Pippiloette had indicated they should take, as far as Thorn could tell by his birch bark sketch. So with nothing to distinguish them, he took the first big one they came to.

This valley resembled the land surrounding the ice caps west of the Urdecha. There were fewer trees, and they were stunted and gnarled. People had used them; they had few dead branches, and many had been chopped down waist high, and had regrown above the cuts. Thorn and Click had to burn fat and dung on more and more nights, unable to find enough wood for their fires.

After two days up the bare valley, they crossed a pass and found another valley that led downhill in the same northerly direction, and two days farther along, this valley debouched onto a broad plain tilted east to west, just as Pippi's map said there would be. The plain was covered with muskeg and head-high forest, mostly larch and alder swamps, and cedar brakes. It was not easy country to cross, and inevitably they found themselves following animal trails, marked on the land by all the animals who had crossed the plain looking for the easiest way.

—When the way is hard the trail comes clear, Thorn announced to the world every time he ran into one of these animal trails. The trails came and went with baffling frequency. Often they found one only after thrashing through brush for a fist or longer, so they were very welcome, even if they were only deer trails, sure to disappear soon. Each time, Thorn would repeat the old saying, which Pika had repeated often.

—Way har, trail clar, Click said once when he was leading and came on a trail.

—Yes, very good, Thorn said. —Thank you.

—Tank oo.

On the second afternoon crossing the plain they came to its river, now a flat white walkway. Thorn had never seen a river so wide, and was grateful they could walk across it. If the people of this pays managed to rope a raft between riverbanks as far apart as these were, it would be a real accomplishment.

They walked on, north from the frozen river. Thorn often consulted his birch bark map, though it was of little use; in the part indicating this region it was almost bare of features, and he could not recall Pippiloette talking about how many days' walk it took to get from the big river to the ice people's hills.

They found out by walking: three days. At the end of the third day, low hills rose over the northern horizon of the snow-blanketed steppe. The next day the foot of the hills hove over the horizon. Then the tops of the hills separated into two lines, the lower one dark and bumpy, the higher one straight and white. Those hills were overtopped by ice from the north, just as Pippiloette had described. They were getting close.

Thorn turned to the northeast then, and in an alder brake made a little shelter for them to hide in. He started a fire and made it as small as possible, fanned what little smoke was rising from it to disperse it. After they had eaten he let the fire die down, and they lay through the night by the cooling bed of embers. In the morning, when the snow was hard, they walked fast north, right into the hills.

The little ravines between these hills were all filled with boot tracks and footprints, and even wide trails beaten into the old snow. And the little trees in the ravines, and on their walls, were often chopped off. They were near someone's camp, no doubt about it.

Thorn said to Click, —These are the people who have taken Loon and Elga. We have to come on them without letting them see us. I want to watch them for a while to see how they live. Then we will raid them and take Loon and Elga back.

—Roop, Click said.

The hunger months passed without hunger. Loon feasted on the jende's scraps and watched them eat luxuriously as they cheered on summer, which they clearly wanted, though they did not need it like the Wolf pack did, backwards though that seemed. Maybe that was why they lived here. Freeze for ten months of the year, and in the other two months drown in mud and mosquitoes; but always enough to eat, and more than enough. This might also explain all their food prohibitions, so many more than Wolf pack's: they had enough food to be picky about it. Their women were not to eat many things, some only when pregnant, others all the time: otter, lion, mammoth, musk ox; in short, the women said with certain looks, all the best meats. Young people were not to eat the parts of animals that looked like humans in their old age, such as sagging elg jowls or rhino lips. Never eat marmot meat, never hunt the unspeakable one. Don't drink too much water or it will make you slow. On and on it went, far beyond Loon's understanding. Eating only the least-favored foods dulled him to the distinctions they were making on the higher platforms of the shelter, up there in the warmth. They kept the captives cold to keep them stupid, he realized one dismal night when Badleg was throbbing more than usual.

One time near dusk Loon was sent back out to get more frozen fish from the platform. He was allowed to go by himself now, because there was no reason not to. He wasn't going anywhere. He knew the jende had seen this in him, and it gave him a little pleasure to contemplate it as an artifact, like one of his carved sticks, or the wall paintings back home, still so clear in his eye if he thought about them. Sometimes he thought about them on purpose, to get away from the jende at moments when they might be inspecting him. Red bear, black bison.

And so when they sent him out alone to fetch something, or take a meal's refuse out to the midden down the hill, in a snow mound that in summer would melt, carrying all the refuse into the river and out to the great salt sea, he continued to try to take something useful from the house and hide it in his marmot tuck in the boulder field under the hill east of camp. There were twentytwenty boulders at the foot of this hill, and the biggest had rolled farthest. In this great shatter no one would find his tuck.

His runs to his boulder and stashing of stolen things, followed by his return to camp, not to mention the completion of whatever chore he had been sent out to do, all happened so fast, with his heart beating so hard, that only in these moments was he awake as of old. These times felt so rushed and strange that leaving the house became like jumping into a dream.

Then back into the warmth of the big house, breathing slowly and with care, each breath crafted to show a calm spirit. And in fact the breathing helped make it so. Asleep on his feet, just another cold captive.

One time he was sent out with the night bucket to empty it down at the shitting field, another snow-covered space that would melt out of their world come the thaw, and he saw Elga coming back from the same destination, an empty bucket in her hand.

They stopped in their tracks, looked around. They were alone. Loon approached her, his free hand extended.

—We can't let them see that I know you, Elga reminded him sharply. —They'll kill you.

—I know. I'm still looking for our moment. Be ready.

—We'll need snowshoes, she said.

Loon felt his chest expand with a huge in-breath. —So you want to go?

—Yes! she said fiercely. He saw it was true and his throat clamped.

—No more now, she said. —They'll come looking for me soon. I'm only supposed to go out with others.

Loon nodded. —Be ready. And with a light touch to the arm he passed her and went down to the shitting ground.

L ate spring: snow still covered the world, but it was melting everywhere, suncupped everywhere. On some south-facing slopes the suncups were waist deep. In the mornings, when they were frozen hard, it was like walking across upturned blades of rock, and seemed dangerous. Later in the day one could step on the blade edge of a suncup and smash it down just right for walking on it. Later still the snow became so soft and sloppy that it disintegrated underfoot in ways that skidded the walker this way or that, mostly crashing down into the holes of suncups, where sometimes step-throughs took you down right to the hip. Badleg took some horrible blows that way. It was remarkable how in just a fist or two the snow could go from a white rock to a watery mush. After dark it hardened back up fairly quickly also. It was not as fast as air, but fast.

All this time the jende had their platforms of frozen fish and sealskin bags. They had so much fat that they could use it as firewood. And the days were getting longer. Soon the break-up would come, and the earth reappear from under the snows. Summer would be on them.

One night the wind came strong from the west, and in the morning it was blowing so hard that the roar of it was loud even in the big house. Outside the entry tunnel, even the old spring snow was flying east over the ground. They had to block off the entryway to keep air from flying up into the house and blowing it apart like a popped seaweed bladder. Loon went outside with the men dealing with that, and as they put together a door of poles and hides to cover the entryway they were frequently knocked over by strong gusts, after which the wind sometimes had them sliding like seals over ice. They all laughed, shocked to feel just how strong the wind could be.

Later in the day, when the wind had died down a bit, the same men went back out to see if everything was all right around the camp, and also just to be out in such an extraordinary blow. After making sure camp was secure, they pushed down into the wind to the edge of the great salt sea. The sea ice was gone without a trace;

they watched wild broken white waves roar in and surge in a boil up onto the snowy strand, there to launch foam streamers that rolled inland until they snagged on rocks or tufts of grass and were blown to nothingness. All of that was astonishingly loud; they could barely hear each other even when shouting in each other's faces. Some gusts were so strong that they had to sit down with their backs to the wind, and even then were scooted over the sand by the heaviest buffets. They couldn't stop laughing.

In the midst of this, one pointed out at something in the waves, and some of the others stood and leaned into the wind to look, their arms outstretched like birds gliding, or holding their parkas onto their heads. Out in the broken waves floated one of the gigantic tree trunks they used as house posts and markers by the shore. Some of their older standing posts had fallen down in this day's wind, but most withstood it as they had so many previous gales, and held their position without even quivering.

Now a new log was floating in sideways on the white-capped rollers, then crashing onto the beach, where it was nudged and sloshed farther with every big surge, until it lay there like the dead body it was, corpse of a tree bigger than any Loon had ever seen. He wondered what kind of land could be on the far side of the great salt sea, to grow such trees.

Later, when the wind had died, all the jende men and many of the women went out and grabbed ropes they had tied to the new driftwood log, and together they pulled it onto a collection of smoothed branches placed crossways. They pulled the log easier over these branches, and picked up the branches from behind it when they emerged, and moved them to the front. This reduced the pull needed to move it by a great deal. They hauled the log to the line of standing trunks at the back of the strand, and after digging a hole, hauled the broken end into it, and when it tipped in, pulled on the root end with ropes until the log was standing upright among the rest of them at the back at the beach, there to defy the west wind until it too fell down, or was hauled off for use in camp.

⋆   ⋆   ⋆

One night when the jende were boiling fish in buckets using rocks heated in the fire, and the upper levels of the house were at their hottest, two figures draped in furs leaped up out of the cold trap and stuck people with spears and threw fat on the fire, causing it to splash blazing all over the room. In the screaming and smoke and confusion one of the invaders took up the bucket of boiling water and threw it in all their faces and then onto the blazing fat fire, after which fire ran everywhere. Like otters in a beaver's house the invaders stuck anyone they passed while dropping back to the ground floor. One of them grabbed Loon by the arm; only then did he see it was Thorn. Beside him the old one Heather had nursed to health was shrieking like a lynx, teeth bared; the inhuman howl cut through the jende's screams and made the assault even more stunning.

Loon snatched his boots as Thorn hauled him down into the cold trap. They ran out the entry tunnel and Thorn tossed a burning brand back onto an opened bag of fat he had spilled behind him. Soon the whole entryway blazed.

—I'll get snowshoes for all of us, Loon said.

—Good, Thorn said. —Take Click and get them while I get Elga.

—She's in the women's house.

—I know! Get what you have and follow Click, he knows where we're to meet. I'm going to make it so all the men here are putting out fires for a while.

—They've got wolves! They'll set their wolves on us.

—I know! In fact the captive wolves were now howling. —Fuck the wolves, they can't stop us.

He ran off toward the women's house, and Loon led the old one up into the boulder field, found his hole and slipped down into it, handing out the sacks to Click as fast as he could. The opening was smaller than ever as he tried to hurry in the dark, and he didn't feel he was moving as well as he should have, given how often he had told himself the story of this event. After the first shock it had struck him as something he recognized, so now it was happening as in certain dreams, wherein he watched himself act from above or behind.

They ran back down to the jende's camp, and Loon watched himself go to the shelter next to the big house where they kept their outside things and grab four pairs of snowshoes and give them to Click, then take up a stone wedge blade and smash it down on the front curve of all the rest of their snowshoes, breaking each cleanly lengthwise. He was startled to watch himself do this, as he had never thought to do it. But it was a good plan, and he smashed the bent spruce frames as if cracking the jende's skulls. When he was done the old one clicked rapidly and led Loon downstream to a little brake of alder. Thorn was there with Elga; she was draped in a fur cape, but other than that wore only the leggings the jende wore in their houses. The four of them stood there staring at each other, eyes wide. The night was old, the half moon would be setting soon.

—She needs clothes! Loon said.

Thorn said, —We'll make them out of her cape. For now it will have to do.

—I'll be fine, Elga said, and took one of the sacks Loon had hidden. She was wearing soft boots. —Let's hurry, they'll cut their way out of those houses.

They stuffed two backsacks with what Loon had taken, and Loon put his own boots on, and stuck his arms through the straps of one of the sacks. Elga took the other one. Thorn tied the stolen snowshoes onto Loon's pack and the old one's, and then they were off through the night, headed south.

They walked over the frozen snow as fast as they could without actually breaking into a run. When the moon set they had to slow a little, but under the stars the suncupped snow still glowed enough to see it pretty well, and they hurried on at almost full speed. All that night they continued in silence, except for the times when Thorn yelped, —Skai! and they would go hard, running in a kind of wolf lope until one of them would slow down, and then they would all stop running and walk hard again. Across one long descending slope the snow had melted and refrozen so many times that the suncups were flattened out, the hard snow left as slippery as ice. There they stopped to put on the snowshoes Loon had taken. Loon showed Thorn and Click how to tie their boots to the foot platforms. Elga tied hers on, and Loon saw that the snowshoes would give her soft boots some needed support.

Thorn set a pace that the rest of them had to work to keep up with. It got colder as dawn neared, but aside from their noses and ears Loon was warm all through his body, even in his toes and fingers. This could only happen when throwing oneself forward, even breaking into a little run from time to time on level ground or on downhills. Thorn always urged them on by example, and with an occasional look back; to Loon his face was like a slap from a dream, a vision of Otter Man, implacable and intent after killing the beavers in their den and taking one of their women away. The sight sparked Loon, and his body flew after the others without awareness of the effort. It was like a dream and yet he had never been more awake, not ever in his life.

Coming back into himself a little as dawn grayed the eastern sky, he could not help noticing that Badleg had not had a walk this rigorous in many a moon, and was speaking up to voice its protest. He needed a stick, and the first time they passed a lead in a streambed, curving swiftly at a kink in a little gorge, he took a hand blade from his sack and hacked an alder branch that was a bit too short, but otherwise sturdy, and after that used it to lighten all the impacts on Badleg. Being three-legged in such a manner was not as easy as simply walking, but it was worth the extra effort.

When the whole sky lightened to gray, Thorn redoubled his efforts. —We have to be out of their sight all day today. I don't know how much of a lead we got on them, but they'll be fast.

Loon and Elga could only nod at that. Click threw himself onward with a heavy long tread, puffing hard at every exhale, although it also seemed he would be able to carry on like that for a long time. Loon realized he didn't know much about the old ones' abilities. Of course his encounter with them during his wander remained firmly in mind, indeed just the thought of the memory was enough to put an extra thrust in his walking. He had escaped old ones, but he didn't know what that meant about them. He realized that of all the kinds of animals in the world, this one hurrying beside them was the one he knew least. Of course they were the ones who hid most carefully from people, so maybe it was just that: they didn't want people to know them.

The jende, however, Loon knew. They were very fast over snow when they wanted to be. Of course every pack's hunters were fast and could go long; that was part of being a hunter. But the jende, with all their summer treks, and quarrels with their norther neighbors, were both fast and used to the snow. Snow was their home ground, and so anywhere there was snow they were on home ground, and would be faster over it than people from elsewhere. Or so Loon feared.

And they had wolves to set on their prey.

 HUNTED

The eastern sky was red, the sky overhead was that gray that would soon reveal itself to be thin clouds or clear sky. Thorn directed them to stop in a depression in the snow that included a little wall of rock they could hide behind. There they remained until the sky was bright with the coming day, a cloudless day as it turned out, and the sun soon to crack the horizon. Thorn directed the others to stay low, while only he looked back to the north, with a patch of fur placed on his head and held out by his hands to each side, so that he would present a mere bump to anyone looking their way. He held himself motionless as he looked. Then he hissed and pulled his head down slowly.

—They're there, he said. —They're coming this way, with some wolves tied to ropes. They probably have our track. We've got to go.

—Won't they see us?

—Yes. We'll have to outrun them today, and lose them tonight.

He looked at each of them in turn. —We have to go fast. If we go fast all day, they can't catch up to us. We can't be the ones to get tired of the pace. We have to tire them. We have to be fast enough to keep a good distance, even if they charge. We have to outlast them at their charge pace, and then at whatever pace they can keep to after their charge. Understand?

—What if they let their wolves loose on us? Loon asked.

—We'll kill the wolves and they'll have lost their trackers. Anyway they might not be able to let those wolves off their ropes this far away from home without them running away. If we keep our distance, they can probably only use them as trackers.

Loon and Elga nodded. Click saw them and nodded too, humming and then saying, —Skai, skai, skai.

Thorn got out a bag of nuts from his pack and gave them each five. —We'll eat on the run. Let's go.

They took off out of their dip, running on the snowshoes toward the flat snow of the first riverbed. No cries came from behind them, but the way Thorn moved made it clear that he thought they would be seen by their pursuers. Instead of crossing the river's ice he headed upstream on it, then picked a line and took off across the river, headed for the first rise of a ridge that ran south.

They had to show their hunters that it was not possible to catch them, neither in a rush nor over the long haul. With a woman among them it would be hard to do this, but Elga was strong. She had no problem keeping up with the men. It was harder to tell about Click, because of the way he huffed and puffed as he walked, making a song of his breathing. But the old ones were reputed to be made of harder stuff than most people, and Click certainly gave no indication of slowing down or being tired. As for Thorn, it was hard to say whether he would be able to hold this pace. For sure he was setting it now. Some old men had been cured to a kind of leathery toughness that youth could not match, and Loon would not be at all surprised to learn that Thorn was one of them.

So it could be that Loon was the slowest of their little band. It was a galling thought, and yet as they hurried along for fist after fist, it began to seem like it might be true. Badleg was never going to like a full day's running, no matter the aid of the alder walking stick, which Loon had already named Thirdleg, hoping that the feeble joke would prong him along a little. Thirdleg would have to do its part, that was certain.

All that day they ran. At open leads of water they could safely reach, Thorn paused so they could put their faces to the water and drink, and in those moments he passed out some nuts and dried meat and honey seedcake, to eat as they started walking again. They never stopped for long, but Thorn always found something that caused them to pause briefly every fist or two. Their pace was as fast as Loon could keep to; he didn't know if it was the same for the others or not, and he didn't want to ask.

In the afternoon the snow softened, and they stopped to put on their snowshoes again. After that they would certainly be leaving tracks easy for their pursuers to follow. But the jende would be on broken snowshoes, which would slow them down.

Their pursuers were very seldom visible. Once they heard a distant howl, human or lupine, as if their track had been picked up after being lost. Thorn wanted to see them from time to time, to know where they were, so as they crossed the steppe he veered for low hills crowned by trees, or went to the highest parts of the drunken forests they skirted, to find places where trees had crossed in ways that gave them a blind where they could see without being seen. Three times Thorn spotted the jende party, and the third time he said, —They're sending out a pair with the wolves to rush us.

This was the way wolves sometimes chased caribou, tiring them out with a charge until the weakest one fell behind. Their defense now had to be the same as the caribous': stick together and stay ahead. Sometimes, Loon recalled, the lead males in the caribou herd might try to strike fear into the pursuers by turning on them. And Thorn was looking thoughtful as they hustled south through that long afternoon. At each stream crossing he took the most dangerous route, passing over exposed bare ice as near open leads as he dared, as if in hope that their pursuers might be heavier and fall through. Loon followed him over one thin brittle stretch of transparent ice, observing this, and then hustled forward to tell Thorn he was wrong if he thought he could trick the jende into making any mistakes on ice, because the jende were better on ice than anyone. Thorn growled at this, but did not try the trick again. His brow stayed deeply furrowed.

The sun finally sank into the west, and as the stars popped out they crawled into an alder brake, crawling under the weave of branches to do so. Here was where they would be vulnerable to the captive wolves, whom it seemed must have been kept on ropes, or they would have caught up.

When they were wrapped in their furs, Thorn said to Loon, —Stay here with Elga, and took Click by the arm, and the two of them headed back north with their spears.

When they reappeared, a couple of fists later, they were in a hurry to leave.

—Another all-nighter, Thorn said. —We killed one of their lead pair. The other one got away, but he doesn't know how many of us

were there. So they'll be careful tonight. Let's make this the night
we get away.

—They can always track us, Loon said.

—Let's see about that.

The waxing moon was one night farther east, one night fatter; by its
light they walked through the increasing chill of a very cold night.
In the haze of moonlight the stars were dim. The hard sparkly snow
squeaked under their feet. They had reached the muskeg flats of the
big valley's drainage, and the tipping trees and icy black flat spots
speckling the swamps convinced them to put their snowshoes on,
to spread their weight out a little more on what looked like thin
ice, maybe night ice only. If they had had ropes they would have
roped together to cross land like this, but all they could do now
was hope for the best. Click went after Thorn, and was substantially
heavier than the rest of them, so presumably if he passed over a spot,
it would hold Elga and Loon. On the other hand it was possible he
would crush a spot that could only hold two crossings, and the third
person then plunge through. So Loon and Elga stayed close enough
to lunge to each other if they had to.

Happily the black flats proved to be frozen as solid as the white ice,
and it was actually their slipperiness that made them worth avoiding.
Thorn threaded between them when he could. If he crossed one,
they got to feel how much better their footing was with their snowshoes on. One could even skate a little on them. Better however to
stay on white snow, even if it was hard as the ice, and in some places
almost as flat. The whiteness itself seemed to hold the foot.

They followed stream courses when they tended south, and skated
along at a good speed. On land they were not as fast. Thorn cut
a good line up the land southward. Moonlight was really the best
illumination for seeing the shape of the land. Every muscle of the
hills lay there under its blanket of suncupped snow, seeming to glow
faintly under the luminous black sky. Through this white flesh the
black rock outcroppings thrust like erect spurts, and frozen water-
falls slid down clefts like spills of spurtmilk. Male marks on female

curves, the land in intercourse with itself, there in the moonlight and shadow. Always like that, from the beginning in the old time: mother and father first whole and one, split by a fight about how things should be, a fight never resolved. As they scurried under the moon, Loon remembered what he could of Thorn's story about how the world had begun. Once in nothingness there was an egg filled by a person, and this person had all the parts and qualities of the world, and pecked out of its eggshell and poured out and became all things. The sky is the biggest piece of eggshell left behind, the sun what was left of the yolk, the earth and everything on it parts of the white of the egg. Raven pecked the white until everything was itself.

Loon knew he was forgetting most of the story. He wondered if he would ever be able to remember the stories the way Thorn could. It didn't seem like he would. For a long time that truth had been a burden in his chest, a weight like a rock, and now he had to let it go so he could walk better. It was a problem for another time. Now whatever he could remember was enough. Now their walking was the whole story.

Strangely, even while walking at great speed by night, there was still time to think about other things. None of the thoughts seemed to matter very much, and yet they still flitted through his mind, like ghosts he was shedding as he conjured them up, because now they meant nothing. Nothing mattered but their walk, so really it was a question of whether his chittering thoughts helped him to deal with Badleg or not. Sometimes they did, being distractions, like squirrels on a branch overhead. Other times it felt like he had to devote every part of his attention to landing properly on his left foot and getting across its stride with the least amount of weight possible put on it, and quickly getting back onto Goodleg, so foursquare and reliable. If Goodleg were ever to give under these strains he was putting on it... that was a very sharp fear. But for now Goodleg kept on coming through for him, solid and painless. He could rely on Goodleg, push him a little. Then, deep in the rhythms of that altered walking, if his mind did drift to things not present, to other worries, to spin like a firestick, maybe that was all right, even a good thing. Part of the ability to ignore the repeated jab of Badleg's squeaking.

*   *   *

As they continued Loon felt more and more tired. At moonset Thorn stopped at a lead to drink and eat some honey seedcake. After that they hiked on under the stars, pricking out everywhere in the darkening black. It got harder to see. They had to pay more attention to the snow, really look at it, and even when they did it was sometimes not possible to see how it tilted or how slippery it might be. You had to feel the land with your feet.

After a long period of walking blind like this, in the after part of the night when it fell deepest into its icy chill, Loon felt that his second wind had slipped into him when he hadn't noticed. He was stronger now, lighter, tougher; he could go on, and it even felt like he could go on forever, or at least as long as needed. Hike on with these three companions for the rest of his life, and yet never tire. That was how it felt sometimes, when the second wind came on you and someone would say, Let's hike all day and then talk it over.

That was a good feeling. He almost always felt the arrival of the second wind in him with immense gratitude, welcoming it with a little hop and song, and never more than now. It was so good to feel the absence of the light-headedness and weakness, feel their replacement by a deep strength.

So he swung into his pacing, poled hard with Thirdleg; he took over Elga's spot, and then passed Click with a brief hello, and a tilt of the head that indicated his hope that Click would drop back and follow Elga, just to be sure of her. Click rooped his assent to something, anyway, and Loon caught up with Thorn.

Together they came on a river's bend like the big loops in the Urdecha.

As they walked on the frozen stream Thorn said, —We're almost to the big river crossing this valley. I hope the ice there isn't already broken up. It seems like it's almost time. Even these side streams are getting thin. It's eighth day of the sixth month. The rivers down south are broken up by now. These must be close.

—Should we be walking on them then?

—We have to cross them! And I want to know how they are. If

we could get across the big one, and then it broke up ... He hiked on
a little faster.

Loon let Thorn get his lead, followed. Thorn was on the hunt
now, and Loon wanted to leave him to it, as well as nurse his second
wind, pace it to serve the long haul. Behind him he saw that Click
was just behind Elga, and they were close behind. Elga looked intent,
downward, inward: some creature of the night, serious about being
out there, even less inclined to talk than usual. At one brief stop she
looked at Loon and it was as if she were looking right through him.
She had not expected to get to try this escape, he saw; it had surprised her to get this chance, so that she reminded him of the jende
when they had gotten off the ice raft. She had not expected to live.
Now she would escape or die.

Soon after sunrise, in the raw yellows of morning, the stream they had
been descending for the past few fists widened, and they were crossing
a frozen pool or flood meadow, near their stream's confluence with the
big river. Thorn turned and trudged up to the top of a little prominence
overlooking things, and while following him Loon realized how tired
his legs had become; even a slight tilt uphill was close to devastating.
And as soon as they crossed this river, it would all be uphill.

From the knob they could see up and down a broad sweep of the
big river. Its surface was still white, yes, but a great number of giant
white plates stuck up into the air, very striking to the eye. And the
ice was speaking. Low long booms filled the air, like thunder from
below the river, muffled as it came up through the ice. Sharp cracks
punctuated these booms, also long sizzling sounds, zinging away
from them. The river groaned when the zinging sounds ran through
it. Oh yes: this ice was going to break up soon. All these booms and
zings and cracks were announcing it, and rather emphatically at that.
Even though nothing moved.

Thorn looked back to the north, pointed: a gyre of crows wheeled
over something near the horizon in that direction.

—Let's cross now, Thorn said. —No time to rest. Let's cross and
get up on a hill on the other side, then see what we can see.

So they took off across the river. They walked with sliding gentle steps. Crossing lanes of black ice, they saw bubbles trapped below the glistening surface, and below the bubbles caught glimpses of the watery depths, slight suggestions of green grass flexing in the current, perhaps the flicker of a trout. Downstream the cracks and zinging noises were louder than ever, and Loon's breath caught in his throat; this was how break-ups announced themselves, the noise moving upstream well ahead of the break-up itself.

Thorn just put his head down and walked faster. They were still in their snowshoes, and sometimes they walked across black slicks that looked wet, they had frozen so smoothly. The older white ice was much more nobbled. They shuffled and skidded as fast as they could, arms pumping. Loon used Thirdleg to push himself along. The other three stayed as close to Thorn as seemed safe, each a few body lengths behind the one before, Loon bringing up the rear, determined to keep a good distance from Elga but not to drop back too far.

It took a long time to cross the river, it was so wide. When they reached the far bank they were all winded; they had been hurrying for their lives, and now they felt it. After a moment to catch their breath, to slow down the beating of their hearts, Thorn led them to another little headland point, just a man's height doubled above the stream.

Up there they dropped their sacks and pulled out their leather patches, and untied their feet out of their snowshoes and sat on the patches set on the snowshoes. They were still breathing hard. Thorn made them drink from his water bag, and they all fumbled in their sacks and ate nuts, and dried meat, and seedcakes. They saw they did not have much food, although Thorn had a few bags of oil; but that would have to be a problem for later. For now they were famished, and would have to eat a lot to go on at anything like the pace they had been setting. So they ate.

Nothing they could see to the north was moving, except for a pack of otters, frolicking upstream on the far bank as if nothing special was happening that day, as if the river weren't about to break up right under them. Thorn scowled to see that, and after a while he stood, and performed a little dance while singing the break-up song:

Frost has to freeze and ice coat the rivers
One alone shall unbind the frost
And drive away the long winter
Good weather come again
Summer hot with sun!
Great salt sea   land of the dead
We will burn holly for you to break the ice
Take it back we do not need it
Tip the sun up toast the air
Hurry the water under the ice
Fill the ravines
Fall down the cliffs
Fill water fill
Every crevice and spill
Push from below
The old ice and snow
Fill from above
Like finger in glove
Like baby born
With a push from inside
The moment comes to push and push
And push and push and push
Mother Earth knows
Mother Earth squeezes
A spasm a cramp
A knot a push
Go to her cave and tell her to do it
Break ice break now
Break ice break now!

The river was alive, they could hear it throbbing. Under its white blanket of snow, under the bare ice shelving over it, it pushed up, it surged with the spring melt. They could see snow and ice shifting in places, and sudden bucklings where ice tipped up blinking in the sun, or lines of new plates cracked upright as if stitched by invisible sinews. Water sheeted out of these seams, bluing the ice downstream into little skyblinks.

Thorn sang hoarsely, danced without moving his feet, suggesting the dance without actually doing it. Speaking to the sky. The river boomed back. It was loud both upstream and down. But the break-up didn't come.

They all knew that ice in this condition would sometimes hang on for days, holding on for fist after fist, day after day, until the break-up finally happened and it all rushed downstream on a violent spate of black water. It was the river's summer orgasm, a spurt glorious to see. Never before had they cared exactly when it happened. Now, watching it hold despite all, they were in an agony of suspense. Possibly with a river this big, despite all its crashing and snapping, it would take a long time. And now, across the river, far to the northwest, Loon saw dots moving. He pointed them out.

Thorn stopped his dance. —Come on, he said grimly. —Fuck the gods. We have to go.

Loon groaned like the river. He stood and tested Badleg. Still bad. He put his sack on his shoulders, which were sore where the straps ran.

Off they went.

Now their run took them uphill, into the afternoon sun. The glare of the sun's blaze off the wet snow ahead made Loon squint until his eyes were almost closed. It felt like his whole body was squinting, and he had to push forward into the blast of light.

But they kept their pace. Loon found his way back into his second wind, uphill or not. Badleg felt much better going uphill. Loon put his snowshoes right in the tracks left by Click and Thorn; Click almost always stepped in Thorn's tracks, so that it almost looked like a single person's track. When the two sets of tracks separated, Loon began to follow Click's, as having harder snow at their bottoms; then also, as he began to see why Click had deviated from Thorn's tracks, consistently keeping to a higher line, he chose that way to smooth his own ascent. It occurred to Loon at one point that he could understand more of Click's thinking by looking at his tracks in the snow than he ever had by talking with him.

Elga stayed close on his heels. She looked thirsty, and hiked head down, eyes almost shut, fitting her snowshoes carefully into the tracks before her.

Thorn headed for a black hill that popped over the white horizon. As they closed on it, moving more slowly as the snow softened, they could see it was the start of a line of hills that ran south, forming the western ridge of a valley which seemed to be the valley Loon and Elga had come down when the jende had taken them north. It was hard to be sure.

Thorn wanted to run this ridge, so they would stop leaving tracks in the snow. As they got farther south there would be even more snow-free ground, he said, and with luck they would be able to get off the ridge somewhere without leaving any sign, and then keep going tracklessly from there. Loon and Elga nodded and put their heads down again, followed Thorn and Click toward the bare hill.

When they got to the hill's first rise of rock out of snow, however, it became obvious that the ridge was not going to be as easy to hike on as the snowy plain had been. Even getting onto the ridge in the first place involved kicking steps up steep snow to where it met a ramp of rock that would get them on the ridge. Any extra effort now was difficult to give, and Loon could feel cramps sparking in his calves. But it was crucial to get off the snow, so they grunted and hissed and clicked through the necessary steps. The snow next to the rock was especially rotten; one had to be careful not to crash down into a covered gap. Sometimes one step was all it would take. Eyes burning with sweat, Loon struggled to move up in the slush, which pulsed blackly at the edges of its whiteness.

Finally they stood panting and sweating on the edge of the ridge, with an upward walk ahead, and a prospect behind them that extended all the way back to the big river. Lots of snow back that way, but ahead of them, to the south, there was a lot of black patching the suncupped white. Ah yes: they were almost to the steppes, to the edge of the land they knew, where they could run the ridge trails, and melt into the canyon forests with all the rest of their animal brothers and sisters. They sat down and took off their snowshoes, tying them to the backs of their backsacks.

But Click pointed: there the ice men were, little black dots crossing the snowy plain, having crossed the big river. From here the river was still white and noiseless, although as far west as they could see, it was black. But the jende had gotten across, and were still following them. One thing Thorn pointed out was interesting: the captive wolves seemed to be gone. Either they had been taken back, or they had escaped. Thorn liked that thought. But it was also obvious, watching the little black dots, that the jende were the wolves now, or the hyenas, or ravens, or people; they were any of the hunters who followed prey until it was exhausted, then moved in for the kill. Ravens even led wolves or humans to injured animals they had spotted from the air, to be able to scavenge what was left after the hunters killed and ate it.

Loon had never been hunted in this manner. Possibly none of them had been; although when he saw Click's face looking back at the jende, he saw that the old one had lived this before, and was not surprised. Click hummed something short to himself, regarded Thorn and Elga and Loon curiously. He made a gesture with his head: time to go?

Thorn continued to stare at the dots, shading his eyes with a hand. Finally he heaved a big breath in and out.

—Let's see what this ridge can do for us. They have to be getting tired too. If they come up the ridge and don't see us, never see us again, with no tracks to follow, they won't know where we got off the ridge. They'll give up.

Click mimed eating, inspected his empty hand.

—I know, Thorn said to him. —Second wind.

—I've already had my second wind, Loon said.

Thorn regarded him. —Third wind then. Sometimes it has to happen. And this is one of those times.

He smiled a tight little smile. —This is what we live for! Days like this! So come on.

The broad edge of the ridge of hills was indeed harder in some ways to hike on than the snow had been, but it was good to be off snow too, to have secure footing again. There were still snow patches on the ridge, and big slopes of it below them to right and left, but they tried to avoid them all, wending their way from rock to rock.

The ridge went up and down in the usual way, but always a bit more up than down. Sometimes the ridge edge itself narrowed. Mostly it was a broad broken path of black lichenous rock, twenty paces wide or more, but in places it narrowed to a blade of an edge no wider than their feet, with steep drops to both sides. Loon got down on his hands and knees and crawled along these parts, as he didn't trust Badleg to hold him. Sometimes the other three crawled too.

Happily the ridge widened as it got higher, and side ridges began to branch down to both east and west, containing steep little kolby canyons that they looked down into as they passed; these were still snow-choked. Thorn wanted to drop into one of them, if it was possible to stay on dry land or gritrime once down, but none of the canyons offered that. They did have trees, however. The avalanche gullies were snowy chutes, but otherwise the canyon sides were getting more and more forested. Under the trees the ground was still snowy, but the creeks were often open black water. Ground in the sun all day was often free of snow, the black ground steaming between the rocks. The steep slopes to each side steamed to a palpable mist as they hiked the ridge looking for a good way down.

Then Click whistled sharply, pointed behind them. They turned and saw that the black dots pursuing them were on their ridge, still well behind, but on the ridge. Thorn cursed them:

May you trip and fall,
Cramp all over,
Shit your guts out,
Turn an ankle and stab yourself
With your own spear in your belly button,

May a lion ambush you,
Lightning blast you to a burnt cinder,
Avalanche bury you three trees deep,
May you lie with the most beautiful woman ever
And have your prong pizzle out and swing there
Like the guts of a speared unspeakable,

and so on as he led them at speed to the next high point on the ridge, where they could drop again and get out of sight. He could spout curses all day without ever repeating himself, as Loon well knew.

Over the knob, out of sight of the ice men, Thorn stopped to look down a steep headwall into a canyon to the west. The steep slide down looked like it was snow-free ground all the way, although there was a section so steep that they couldn't see it from above, which was never good. Below that drop, trees furred the cleft of the canyon, which curved down and to the south.

Thorn said, —Let's get down this while they can't see us. This looks like it will go.

The other three were willing. The steep section would hopefully be snow-free. It seemed worth trying. It would not do to stay on the ridge; it was beginning to look like the ice men might be faster than they were. And they couldn't go any faster.

So they started the descent off the ridge. As they dropped, it occurred to Loon that another good thing about this canyon was that it was short, and debouched into a valley trending south, so that they would be able to continue more or less toward home.

As it turned out, the part of the slope that had been invisible from above was a steep field still covered by old snow, suncupped heavily in lines that left many long vertical troughs. The whole slope gleamed with waterdrops, it was so wet and soft in the afternoon sun.

Thorn hesitated at the top of this slope for a time. He edged down, stomped on the highest snow: he stepped right through to the rock below. Soft snow indeed. He got out of the hole by hauling himself back onto the rock, thought about it a while, then sat with a grunt on angled rock and took the snowshoes off the back of his sack, then began to tie them back on his feet.

—We have to get down this, he said. —We'll leave tracks, if they come to this spot and take a look, but after that we won't. He gestured briefly downcanyon.

So they sat beside him and tied their snowshoe bindings onto their boots, lashing them down hard. They stood again. Loon bent his knees and felt little crampy pings sparking in his thigh muscles. It was going to be a tough descent.

Loon went last again, and did his best to step down into the snowshoe prints of the other three. They were mostly one set of tracks that all three of his companions had used, sloppily laid over each other, and very deep. Some were thigh deep, and some of these burst under Loon toward their downhill side, forcing him to stop himself from a further slide with an abrupt shift of weight onto his uphill leg. That was Goodleg, thankfully. Actually it would have been better to have Goodleg on the downhill side of him, but the slope was angled such that there was no choice but to traverse to the right as one looked down. Occasionally Thorn had tried to turn left, to carve a little switchback into the slope, but quickly the slope forced him to turn and head down to the right again.

This meant Badleg had to take Loon's weight on the downhill side, and do the real work. Every lead step down had to be made by Badleg; there was no other way, the land itself forced it. As he continued, step after step, the down step on Badleg began to hurt from the ankle up to the hip, stabbing him so that he wobbled, and could not trust the leg not to give under him. But there was no choice: he had to extend down on it straight-legged, stepping into the uncertain support of the deep smeared snowshoe hole the other three had left for him. He dropped into that pain, put his weight on it and ignored the agonizing little crunch inside his ankle, did his best to quickly move Goodleg down into its higher hole, then use it to lift his weight off his left side. Then he held steady for a moment on Goodleg, taking a few breaths, before committing to the biting pain of the next step down. When the lower snowshoe holes burst under his weight he had to ride down the collapsing snow until enough of it gathered to stop his slide; after that, hopefully the higher line of tracks had not become too high for him to step up into, or he would have to kick an in-between step. When getting back up like this he had to stick Thirdleg into the snow as high as he could reach, to help pull himself up.

He kept on, step after plunging step, the pain from Badleg shooting right up through his pizzle to his gut. The traverse down to the forest by the creekbed was less than halfway done.

Loon began to examine the slope below them during his frequent pauses, wondering if it would be possible to sit down on the snow and slide down one of the vertical gullies of linked suncups. The problem with that was there were big rocks at the foot of the slope, the usual spall of boulders big enough to tumble that far down. The snow was so soft now, just possibly he could dig in with his pole and his snowshoes as he slid down. But it was too steep to try it and see. He might slide too fast to stop, right down onto the rocks. Even if he managed to stop himself in the snow above the rocks, he would then be in a hummocky mare's nest of bumps and hollows and big boulders. Getting through that mess, or traversing above it, would be just as hard as what he was doing now, maybe harder. And he couldn't safely slide down there anyway!

He had to stick each left step as well as he could. Step down directly in the hole, then bear down on the pain, make that footing hold if he could; then a quick recovery step onto the right leg, doing everything he could on that side to take all his weight. Step after step, with the penalty for soft snow or a misstep an extra stab.

He was sweating profusely with the effort and pain. He paused from time to time to scoop some of the wettest snow into his mouth, chilling his teeth and the roof of his mouth, briefly wetting the parched dryness rasping in his mouth and throat. He could feel that he was considerably water-short by now, and knew that was part of what was making his legs crampy. When they reached their next source of water he was going to drink till his belly was round. Another six steps, another rest. The suncupped slope blazed. Sweat burned in his eyes, the light burst blackly off the snow; he could hardly see, but there was nothing to see anyway except the snow under him, so it didn't matter. There was nothing now but snow mashed by the double line of snowshoe prints pulsing under him, coated or filled by blackness. The blackness was strange, because the snow was as white as could be, and yet stuffed with blackness. Watery granules of white in black. Blind though he was, he could still see if the next smush of snow was going to hold him or not. That was all the sight he needed.

Then the snow under Badleg gave way as he stepped down, and he slipped and instantly was sliding on his side down the snowy slope, scraping down so quickly that he couldn't stop himself with the edges of the snowshoes, couldn't stick Thirdleg in. He could only try to ride the snowshoes down sideways, try to keep from going any faster. He was headed for a shallow hollow, and he saw it was the best chance he was going to get to stop himself before he ran into the boulders at the bottom, so he tensed himself, waited, and then in the hollow dug in with snowshoes and elbows and Thirdleg, and came to a crunching stop.

He sat there in the snow, gasping for breath, burning with scrapes and cold, sweat pouring down his face. Above him on the slope he could see the mark of his slide, a sloppy trough running straight down to him. Cold and hot, sweaty and trembling, he pushed himself to his feet, using Thirdleg as a support. When he was standing he could see that a gentle traverse would lead him above the boulders to where he could meet up with Thorn and Click and Elga. Elga was calling his name; it came to him that she had been calling him for some time. He waved Thirdleg at them briefly, slowly stomped his way over to them. It was easier than traversing down the slope had been, but Badleg hurt almost too much for him to step on it at all.

When he met them, at the bottom of the slope among the trees at the top of the canyon floor, he collapsed and could not immediately go on.

Thorn stared at Loon as he helped get his snowshoes off his feet. When they had done that he said, —Rest it for a while, but then we have to go.

While Loon rested, Thorn wandered around in the grove filling the head of the canyon, looking among the humps of snow for a spring. As in a lot of kolby canyons, there was indeed a spring near the headwall, although at this time of year the black crease of open water lay at the bottom of a hole in the snow. Thorn had to use all their walking poles to support himself as he knelt, then sprawled, then reached down with his dovekie bag to scoop up some water. When he had a full bag he heaved himself up with a little prayer, uttered like a curse: —Let me up Mother Earth!

He shared the water with Loon and the others. Elga sat on her fur patch, which she had draped over a fallen log. She drank as deeply as Loon did. He was glad to see that she looked much the same as she had in the northern camp, except her eyes were more bloodshot. Now she had her sack on the front of her snowshoes and was rooting through it for a few small handfuls of nuts. She offered some to Loon, but he had to shake his head; he felt sick to his stomach, and could not have forced anything down. —Later, he promised.

Click was sitting on a snowy log and chomping steadily at a length of dried meat, taking it in chunk by chunk until all of it was gone. He drank a few swallows from Thorn's bag and gave it back. —Tank oo, he said absently, the way Heather would have. He did not appear to be entirely there with them.

Thorn was completely there, his sunburned red eyes fixed on Loon. —Are you ready? Can you go?

—Let's see, Loon said, and surged to his feet. He swayed and caught himself on Thirdleg.

—You need two good poles, Thorn said. —Wait there. He took another tour of the copse of trees, returned with a stout branch well over waist high, with a bend at the top end that could be clasped in the hand. —A good walking stick. Put both points down for your left foot, and push up over it. I had to hike for a week with a broken leg, once when I was your age, and after I got used to pushing down on the sticks, it went pretty well.

Loon tried it. —All right, he said. He waited until the others had started, and then followed Elga close.

But it wasn't all right. With the poles he could take a lot of pressure off his left leg, it was true. But they were moving down this new canyon, and there was a lot of back-and-forthing to be done to get between knots of trees, where sometimes they had to slide down little drops in the snow. The other three glissaded down these, and Loon tried to follow them with one-footed glissades, and succeeded sometimes, but more often fell. And getting back on his feet hurt Badleg no matter what he did. He was panting and sweating with the pain of it.

Elga waited for him, and they fell behind the other two. Sun slanted through the pines and birches into their faces; it was a real relief whenever they were in their shade. The smells of the trees cut into Loon's head, so familiar they almost made him cry. The old snow under the trees was mottled with pine needles and tree dust, and in the shadows it was icing up again. It seemed unfair of the snow to go from too soft to too hard with no good time in between. In some canyons like this, or in this one in another season, the walking would have been straightforward, but on this afternoon the canyon floor was becoming a matter of little ice slides dropping between trees. Loon began to sit on his bottom and slide down the steep sections, getting himself wet and cold in the process. If only the canyon had been flat, if only it had been free of icy snow...But really there was no kind of terrain that would have been easy for him on that day.

So he struggled on as the sunlight slanted through the trees. The others stopped and waited for him in whatever lanes of sunlight they could find, stomping their snowshoes to warm themselves. Of course in the snow they were still leaving tracks, slight though they might be. Presumably when this canyon dropped into the valley running south, Thorn would have them run for a while, then look for a snow-free slope they could climb over into another valley. Loon welcomed the idea of climbing again, as a way to keep Bad-

leg from any more downward shocks. Although every up leads to a
down. And it would be more work to go uphill, and he wasn't sure
he had that in him. It would take the coming of his third wind, that
was certain.

Go and rest, go and rest. In the forest dusk the others waited for
him, chilling in shadows. When he reached them he stood leaning
his chest and elbows over his poles. He huffed and puffed as they
rested and talked it over.

—We've got to keep going, Thorn said. His voice had the flinty
sound it took on whenever he was thirsty, or angry, or making a
shaman's command. —We're passing snow-free routes up to the
ridges, so if they come down here at all, they won't know whether
we've stayed in this canyon or not. If we use tonight to get over into
another canyon, we'll lose them.

A wind gusted through the trees around them, and Thorn looked
up. The tallest pines were swaying. All their tops pointed perma-
nently east, and indeed this was another west wind, pushing at them
yet again.

—Could be a storm, Thorn said, sounding surprised. —That
would be good. We could use something good right now. And he
tilted back his head and barked a muffled little fox bark.

They hiked on as the light leaked out of the land. They made Loon
go first, so he could set the pace and they wouldn't lose him.

He put his mind to seeing the best way downcanyon. He could do
this as well as any of them. In all canyons there was a ramp of easiest
travel, inlaid into the jumble of rocks and trees in ways that could be
hard to find. The best way might zigzag from sidewall to sidewall,
or run as straight as a crack. Sometimes it was overgrown by trees or
brush, especially if it was an alder canyon; still it would reveal itself
to the eye if one took the trouble to look for it. So Loon took the
trouble, and the way came clear. He stumped along, his weight on
his sticks as much as possible.

Finally the day's light was gone. It was dark in the shadows of the
trees. The lopsided moon was gazing down, however, so as Loon's

eyes adjusted to its light, he was able to proceed almost as before. Peering down; shuffling over bushes emerging from melting snow; getting to another turn; finding the ramp of fewest drops; feeling, under the pain Badleg was throwing up with every step, the pleasure of finding the right way.

But then the snow under his left snowshoe gave under him, a bad step-through that jarred him when he bottomed on a rock, and he cried out at the pain of it. The others rushed forward and helped him out of the hole, Elga reaching down and flexing his snowshoe sideways to get it up through the snowshoe-shaped gap in the surface crust. As it came through this hole, Badleg twisted in a way that sent a jolt of hot agony up through Loon's nuts and asshole and guts. He cried out before he knew he was going to, then thrust his face into a snowbank and groaned again.

—Shit, Thorn said, arm around his shoulders. —Stand steady there, boy. Put your arm over my shoulder here. Let the bad leg hang free there for a second. There, there. Just let it hang. Now, wiggle the snowshoe. Just a little. Can you do it?

Fearfully Loon tried it. He could indeed move his left foot, although the rocking tweaked the bad point faintly as he did so. —I can move it.

—So maybe you can walk on it.

Loon tried, but he had to keep his weight entirely on his poles.

Thorn hissed to see it. He turned to Click, gestured at Loon. —Click, can you carry him?

He mimed what he meant. Click got it, and his bushy eyebrows lifted his forehead into four distinct furrows. In the shadows of the moonlight, his beaky nose and big brow and wrinkled forehead and bristly little chin resembled one of the wooden masks the western packs carved, expressing one feeling or another; in this case, surprise. He looked Loon up and down as if weighing him. Everyone had had to carry something big from time to time, a deer, a child, a mammoth head, a hurt friend, a log for the fire; so everyone knew it wasn't an easy thing. Couldn't be done for long. And it was night. And they had been going for three days and nights without pause.

Then Click's mask of a face shifted, as if wood were shifting, the mask settling into a new expression: resolve. It was a more than human look, like Thorn on a spirit voyage. —Es, he said.

He shuffled over to Loon. Elga and Thorn got the snowshoes off Loon's feet as gently as they could, and Elga tied them to the back of Thorn's sack. When his feet were clear, Loon reached his arms around Click's neck and clasped his own wrists well down on the old one's massive chest. Click reached back and put his hands under Loon's knees, and between the two of them they lifted Loon onto his back. Click took a step forward and stopped. He shifted Loon back and forth, up and down, took a few short slow steps.

—Roop, he said briefly.

Thorn led the way downcanyon. It was flattening out, which was good. The snow was hardening in the night's cold, and getting slippery, Loon could tell. His front side was warm and his backside was cold. He hoped he could serve Click as a warm cloak at least, and clung to him hard and tried to stay light, to breathe himself upward, to cling to Click well and thus be an easier load, nothing for Click to worry about except for the weight itself, like a heavy sack. Thorn was carrying Click's sack now, and as he strode through the forest's moon shadows he looked something like the bison man in the cave, a big head standing on human legs.

Click was whistling through his teeth. He made a little triple hiss for each step he took, the air forced between his teeth; then a big breath in, then another triple hiss, all in a coordinated rhythm with his slow steps, like a thumping dance around a fire. He did not seem to be breathing particularly hard, nor was he much hunched over, nor slower than Thorn. It seemed like he could keep doing it. Loon tried to loft himself, to become a bird and wing away, to pull the old one up into the air.

Down through the forest. The snow gave way to black soil and washes of sand, also bare expanses of flat rock. Thorn always led them to these bare rock stretches. From time to time Loon fell asleep, and would wake up falling away from Click, grabbing on to him, with the strong impression that he had been asleep for some time without letting go and falling back. He dreamed in these sleeps, and in his dreams the triple hiss from Click sometimes became a bird-song, or someone playing a flute. His back was getting very cold. He wiggled his left foot in quick little tests of what it could do, and tried to confine the resulting pain to its point of origin in the ankle. Keep it trapped there, let his blood flow past it and through the rest of his leg. Let it rest and gain the strength to go on.

The moon was in the west, but still well above the horizon, when the cold penetrated his back so far that he croaked, —I can walk now, I think. Put me down, Click, and let me try it.

—Tank oo, Click said. —Roop roop.

Loon slid down onto Goodleg, and then onto his walking sticks, held out to him by Elga, who had been carrying them. Gingerly he put Badleg down, placed that foot on the ground, shifted his weight that way. A little stab or click of pain; but after that, as it washed up his leg muscles, it diffused to something he could stand. He could still control the leg, around or through that wash of pain. It would work.

—Good man, Thorn said, and they took off again.

Loon hobbled along behind Thorn, and Click dropped back and brought up the rear. Clouds flew under the moon and thickened on their way east, but were still thin enough to light up around the moon, which shone right through them, and lit them all over the sky. Thorn stopped often for short standing rests, and when he did, Elga came up and held Loon by the arm. She was still going strong, but her stride had shortened, as if she were limping with both legs. She stepped like a heron in a marsh. No doubt she was hurting. They were all slowing down. The moon was still a couple of fists above the horizon; the night had a long way to go. Loon wondered if they could make it to dawn. But he was happy to be able to walk. Only that little click of pain in the turn of every stride, and he could almost lift over that with his arms and his sticks. So he could walk. And the walking was warming him up, not completely, but in his middle where it counted. He could feel the skin of his back burning as the feeling came back to it. His fingers too burned with new feeling.

The wind continued to get stronger. Even down in the forest they could feel it. The chorus of trees on the slopes of the valley sang their airy roar as gusts swirled this way and that. The cloud blanket overhead poured in from the west and filled the sky, thickening and then breaking up into puffballs of moonlit white. In the breaks between clouds the black sky swam with fugitive stars, which looked like they had come loose and were sailing westward. A longer glance would steady them and reveal how fast the clouds were flying east. A storm, coming in from the great salt sea. Loon could smell the salt on the wind. Thorn raised his spear and sang his storm welcome. He was clearly happy to see it. It was true that a new blanket of snow would cover all traces of their passing, so Loon had to agree that it was probably a good thing. But it was going to be cold.

Well, cold. He was used to it. He had been cold for months now, and he could endure more of it. The world was a cold place. One breathed and shivered and danced in place to fight it, and it was possible to endure. As long as there was food. And of course a fire would be nice. In a storm no one would be able to see smoke from a fire. Getting one started would of course be a test. Loon grimaced, remembering his failure on the first night of his wander. But Thorn was a real firemaster, like all the old shamans. And he had his kit with him, the firestarter stick and block, flint knockers, bags of duff kept dry in dovekie skin. He could do it and he would. They would make a shelter, make a fire, wait out the storm if they had to. Walk through it if they could. Maybe a little of both. Thorn would decide. He would make their plan, Loon didn't have to do that; which was good, because he was too tired to do anything as hard as thinking. He couldn't think beyond the next click in his ankle.

When the moon set it got a lot darker. The clouds went dark too, and closed up so that no more stars could be seen. Though Loon knew dawn had to be coming, he could see no sign of it. So much black time passed that it began to seem to him that they had fallen into a cave world, that the night would go on forever.

He never did see the eastern sky lighten, but only looked up from the ground under his feet at one point to discover that the whole world had gone gray and was visible again. Neither black nor white intruded on this world of grays. The clouds had lowered in the night, and now skimmed the ridges hemming the valley. Gray snow flurries draped gray forested slopes: this was as much day as they were going to get.

It was so windy they had to stay in the trees. The chorus of pine needles sang a constant roar. How big the world becomes in a wind. They were as ants on Mother Earth now, crawling under grass stalks, grateful for their shelter. Even down there in the trees the wind poured through and slapped them from time to time, ransacking their clothes of any heat they might have held. Even the jende would be taking shelter in a wind like this.

They could not see far in any direction. It was hard to believe their pursuers could still be out in this, and hard to believe they could have followed them into this particular canyon. They themselves didn't know where they were.

Still Thorn hiked on, and Loon put his head down and followed, taking it step by step. Except for the clicks of agony, it seemed like the third wind was still flickering in him, fronting up to the storm. You have to face up to Narsook. He would go until Thorn told him to stop. That was simple enough; it was a thought he could hold on to. Go until Thorn says stop.

The wind roared. It was evening all day. Snow began to pelt them, even in the trees; heavy flakes at first, then icy sand thrown from the side.

Thorn stopped next to a little knot of trees and shrubs that filled a flat spot near a lead in the canyon creek, chuckling blackly as it ate the snow that fell on it. Here the wind was more heard than felt.

—Let's make shelter, Thorn said.

—Oh good, Loon said.

Thorn set about starting a fire while the other three gathered wood, then tangled branches into a shelter wall on the windward side of the knot of trees. Loon hopped around on his poles, gathering wood from the ground, snapping off dead branches from the undersides of trees. He had to keep his weight off Badleg, but he could do that, and it was good to be able to hop around and do something useful without causing himself pain.

Thorn was crouched on the windward side of a flat rock he had prepared for the fire, piling sticks and twigs on one side of the rock and dripping on them some of the fat from his bag. He got out his firestick and spin block, set the duff from his pack around the spin hole and in the cut that ran from the hole to his little pile of fat-soaked twigs. He spun the firestick hard, the shift of his hands from the bottom of the stick back to the top so fast Loon barely saw it. Back and forth he spun the stick, his red eyes bulging out of his black snake's face, his teeth bared in a fierce scowl, hands rubbing down then jumping up and rubbing again.

The tip of his firestick blackened, and little wisps of smoke came from the duff nearest the spin hole. While continuing to spin hard, Thorn also leaned his head around his arms and puffed lightly on the block, contorting his whole body in the effort to call forth flame. When the duff pricked yellow at its edge, and smoked some more, he stopped spinning and crouched even lower, his face right next to the flame, one hand cupping it, the other pushing the duff gently as it burned. The duff's flame remained little more than a tiny glowing ember, and when the twig next to it caught fire, the miracle popping into existence again, he began to puff faster, blowing it up in the way he would play a quick tune on his flute. Loon helped him by getting rocks into position on the windward side of the fire, and then all around it. By the time he had made a proper fire ring, Thorn had a good blaze going in the twig pile, and was carefully balancing small branches over the flames to get them started too. Click came crashing in from time to time with armfuls of wood. Elga was still making a weave of branches between the trees on their windward side, and then around them in a complete circle except for one gap between trees on the lee side. She stuffed so many branches into her barrier that it became a woven wall of wood and leaf and needles.

When they regrouped around Thorn's fire, now a young blaze that no single gust could blow out, they wrapped themselves in their furs and sat like four taller stones in the fire ring, jammed together in a curve around the windward side. Loon sat to the left of the rest and let Badleg lie straight before him. The warmth of the fire helped calm the hurt. Thorn stood up and went out into the storm, and came back with his dovekie bag filled with water from the creek. After they drank from it until they were full, he held it as near to the fire as he could without burning it.

The fire was even more beautiful than usual. Even Loon's first fire during his wander had not comforted him as much as this one. Sometimes gusts blew its heat away for a time, then it slammed back with the full force of its radiance. Loon's face and fingertips and ears burned and itched furiously. Finally he could give Elga a look in reply to her anxious gaze: he was all right. Beside this fire he would be able to rest, warm up, drink water, eat some of their remaining food. It was true that they were running out of food. But if the storm ended and the jende had lost track of them, then they could find food as they hiked on. They could find out where they were, if Thorn didn't know. Loon certainly didn't.

—Do you know where we are? he asked.

Thorn gave him a sharp look. —We're here!

—And you know where here is?

—Close enough, Thorn said. He was looking through the bags in his sack, checking the food left to them, Loon supposed. Instead he pulled out one piece of clothing after another, to hold them up to the flames and dry them out: bits of leather, scraps of fur, mittens... After a while he stood and turned and stuck his rear toward the flames, growling at the heat burning his butt. His clothes quickly started steaming. Inspired by his example, they all stood and did the same. Click still hissed his quick triple whistle, as if dreaming he was still on the march.

When the fire had dried them and they were thoroughly warm, Thorn picked up one of the bags from his sack and took from it his sewing kit. Elga had made the entire hike so far wearing only her leggings and a bearskin robe from the women's hut, and now Thorn offered to help her turn the robe into a proper shirt and coat, and to extend her leggings.

She agreed at once, and while Thorn worked on her robe she stood arched to the fire dressed only in her leggings, like a jende woman. Loon's breath caught in his throat as he stared at her.

Thorn cut her robe up with his sharp blade, putting pieces of the bear hide up against her from time to time as he did so. When he finished the cuts, he punched holes around their edges with his antler awl, biting his lips. Then he sewed the pieces together with a length of leather cord he pulled from his sack, wound around a short stick.

Click stared into the fire as they worked, but Thorn frequently looked up and regarded Elga's body closely, flickering there in the firelight. Her breasts were only half the size they had been the last time Loon had seen them, and in general she was thin, although her thighs were quite a bit thicker than any of the men's, and longer too. And they were all thin now, even Click. Loon could feel his belly button just a finger away from his backbone. There wasn't much left to him. Thorn too was skin and bones; he always was, and now more than ever.

But here they were, warm in the storm, and Elga's body gleamed darkly against the snow and the flames and the trees flickering in the firelight. Thorn worked on, and held up pieces he was sewing against her from time to time. It was night before he had her dressed again. —There, he said when he was done, and added, —You look good. Even now when I've dressed you!

Elga laughed and hugged herself. —It feels wonderfully warm. Thank you Thorn.

That night they lay around the blaze like a fire ring of flesh, just outside the ring of stones. From time to time they fed in branches from their pile. The wind kept blowing, the snow drifted down onto them through the trees. If a snowflake landed on them it melted on their hair or the tips of their furs and quickly burned away. They were more comfortable in this storm than they had been for months now, any of them, and the thrill of that was another kind of warmth.

Loon fell asleep between one breath and the next, and slept hard. When he woke to the cold on his back, and fed the fire, he saw the others were sleeping well also. You have to be able to sleep on snow.

The dawn gray showed it was still snowing, although it was less windy than the day before. Big flakes fell straight down. They had to decide whether to stay or hike on, and Thorn took a brief walk out of their grove to get a better sense of the day. When he came back he said gloomily, —It's walkable. We probably should go.

The others said nothing. The fire hissed and popped on its big bed of embers, inviting them to stay and be warm. It did not seem possible that the northers would be out in this storm hunting them, given how much the falling snow obscured the view. It was flocking down, and up on the ridges it would probably still be windy, with new piles of soft snow ready to avalanche or otherwise give way underfoot. Surely the northers too were tucked around a fire somewhere.

But if they were, then going on would be getting farther from them; and if they weren't, and were out on the hunt, still in pursuit, then going on would be keeping their distance. Either way they should go. They could all see the sense of Thorn's position. But it was a hard thing to leave that fire and go out into the storm.

It snowed all that day. The new snow lay thick and soft on everything, flocking the forest and making the world a dapple of black and white. Summer storms could be like that.

It was lucky they had snowshoes, because without them they would have sunk in thigh deep with every step. As it was, the one breaking trail sank in knee deep, and had to step high. Most of the day Click led, and as he was considerably heavier than the others, they stepped in his tracks and had it much easier.

Thorn went second and gave Click directions. Occasionally Loon could hear them from behind. —No, left, left! Left is to your left, right is to your right, straight ahead is straight ahead! Why can't you get that? Tell me what you call them and I'll say that instead! I'm tired of you getting it wrong!

—Roop, Click said, pointing right. —Roop roop, pointing left.

—So there you have it, Thorn said heavily. —If you can do that, why not call them right and left?

The silence from Click suggested he didn't have an answer for that.

—Mother Earth, Thorn finally said. —You're just trying to make me angry.

After that he hiked closer to Click, and with his spear tapped the old one on one shoulder or the other as he said, —Hey, hey, that way, while pointing with the spear. —Go that way, that's left, roop roop, left, and he would whistle a piercing whistle with an upward slide, like a hawk. Later, with a tap on the right shoulder, —Go right, right, roop, that's right, with a down-sliding whistle. All through that day Loon could hear Thorn badgering Click about this matter of directions. —Straight is just straight! Not right nor left, just straight ahead. That way!

Loon wanted to say, He knows the way better than you do! but he didn't have the strength to spare for speaking. He could only put his snowshoes in the holes and try to avoid the pain on the left. Click was probably taking the best way no matter how Thorn jayed at him.

Late in the afternoon, the valley they had been descending opened onto a broad plain, so big that its full extent was not visible in the falling snow. Thorn considered the white sky flocking down on them for a while, and then pointed Click in a certain direction, and off they went across the soft new snow. After a time they came to a flat stretch that was clearly a river. Like the big river back north, this one was about to break up, but under its new blanket of snow it was hard to say when or where it might happen. All the usual sounds were muffled. There were snow-capped plates of ice poking up in irregular lines, and black leads visible in long stretches of the far shore. From downstream, farther than they could see in the storm, came a low wet roar.

Then right before their eyes the new snow lying on the river straight out from them started trembling, and in a series of muffled cracks broke off and crashed downstream, riding a black spate of immense power. Down the river at the farthest bend they could see, crackling ice dams stacked up, building quickly into log jams of ice, then bursting away and rushing downstream.

Upstream from where they stood the ice on the river still held. The black river sheeted out from under it like a giant spring out of a white hillside, an amazing sight.

—Go! Thorn shouted at the other three. They could barely hear his voice. He pointed upstream and then took off, and they hurried after him up the bankside. They were too tired to hurry very fast, even Thorn, and soon Click took back the lead and stomped the snow down for them, and Thorn was right on his heels talking to him, and Elga not far behind. Loon did the best he could to keep right behind Elga, hoping that Thorn would not lead them across the river too close to the broken edge and its stupendous flow. He knew the faster he went the sooner they would be able to cross, and the better their chances would be that the ice would hold long enough for them to cross. And if Loon was close behind, Thorn might feel confident enough in their speed to go a little farther upstream before crossing. So Loon put his head down and hiked and poled along in the tracks of the others, ignoring the hot flare in his ankle, huffing and sweating, intent to keep right on Elga's heels. She was fast, and looked different in her newly sewn clothing—taller, rangier. Suddenly it came to him again that she was there, that this was his Elga right there in front of him, free of the ice men, on the run with him, fleeing captivity, running for home. Something in his heart flew at that realization, and he bared his teeth at his ankle and pounded along, taking care not to knock the front of his snowshoes into the busted rims of high soft snow separating one track from the next. Step high and clean, huff and puff, curse the pain. Feel the cold air go to his head, leaving him as sharp as if hunting, or terrified. He only looked at the snow under him, also the river beside them, still white and unmoving. Everything in that bubble of falling snow had become closer and sharper and brighter, all of it pulsing with his pulse, bright even in the dimness of a snowy day. Everything was lit from inside itself, and he was seeing the way hawks must see.

Thorn tapped Click and turned toward the river, and seeing it Loon began sucking air through his teeth with fear. He bent forward and redoubled his speed, wanting to be with the others whatever happened, even if it was wrong, even if it put more weight on the river ice and caused them to break through. Thorn looked back at him, as if aware of his fear, and pierced him with a glance.

I slipped up into him in that moment, and seized him as tightly as he was seizing his poles. Slow down. Remember what the northers taught you, out on the frozen great salt sea.

He watched Thorn and Click as they roamed up and down the bank, stabbing the snow-blanketed river ice. He realized that it was probable he knew more about ice now than they did. Downstream the roar of open water reverberated in the trees, pulsed up through their feet.

Loon saw a good patch against the bank, which looked like it extended most of the way across the river. He walked as if his legs were both all right. —Let me lead! he said as he passed Thorn and stomped down the snowy bank onto the river ice. —I've been doing this all winter.

He struck out over the ice, stabbing ahead with delicate taps, as if his walking poles were short unas. He shuffled along at a slow but steady speed, feeling the ice below him for any flex. His body was thrumming in a way it had once when he had been stung by several bees. The snow falling in the air was now very small, making almost a mist of floating little flakes, swirling as they were tossed on a slight breeze.

Out on the middle of the river they could hear the open water downstream better than ever. The ice under them was heaving a little under its snow blanket, and it groaned all around them, including upstream. Clearly it was feeling the break-up moving upstream toward it, and so it was flexing in place and crying out, whether in fear or desire Loon could not tell. He shuffled forward at the same deliberate speed. The other three were bunched right behind him, keeping a little less distance from each other than the northers would have in the same situation.

Downstream a gigantic crack and a number of low booms announced another break-off. Ice plates reared downstream, and the black flood was more visible than ever. The roar was like rolling thunder.

Loon shuffled along as fast as he could go. He had no awareness of Badleg; his whole body buzzed equally. He kept his eyes fixed on the ice they had yet to cross. They were getting closer to the other bank: no river is very wide if you run across it. The outside turn of a bend is where the ice is thinnest. And this time there were open leads blocking their way.

Loon veered to the left, upstream, and poked ahead to make sure the ice was solid under its blanket of snow. The pokes sounded some solid thunks, which seemed to indicate ice thick enough to hold him; he turned right and shuffled quickly over that section to the bank, and stomped up the snow there, establishing steps for the other three to step into. The other three followed him up very neatly, as if performing a big-step dance they had danced a thousand times before.

When Thorn joined them at the top of the bank, he tilted his head to the clouds and howled. The others joined in, they howled like wolves. In the roar of the breakup and the wind they could barely hear themselves.

I myself howled, and then slipped back into my place.

Now the burn of their crossing throbbed all through Loon, and he discovered to his surprise that Badleg was griping ferociously. His whole left leg was hot to the touch. He went to a fallen tree trunk, swiped the new snow off, and sat. He rested his sack on the front of his snowshoes, his elbows on the sack, his chin on his hands. He watched the great roaring spectacle of the river as the ice plates broke off and clunked downstream.

Elga sat beside him. Click crouched on a rock. Thorn took off his sack, put it down on the snow, and did a little dance in place, singing the break-up song again.

—Shut up or you'll make the ice stay! Loon exclaimed.

Thorn ignored him, if he heard. And as they were almost certainly going to stay sitting there until this part of the river broke up completely, it was only setting him up for an I-told-you-so. So Loon shut up and watched Thorn sing and howl. After it went on for a while, Loon dug around in his sack, and was shocked to find his food bags so small. Somehow he had thought there was another full bag in there, and there wasn't.

—How are we for food? he asked.

But at that moment the river ice straight out from them heaved up and broke, then floated away around the bend, white rafts smashing together. The noise was incredible. The rushing black water now visible under them was shocking to see in a world so white and still.

Now they could hear each other if they shouted, but there was nothing to say, so they sat there speechlessly watching the spectacle. Ice broke off and floated by, raft after raft of it. Upstream the black water poured out from under a jagged white line that moved farther and farther away. The whole valley boomed with the noise of it.

Upstream, at the bend where they could see no farther, a shallows had been revealed, studded with rocks that nobbled the water and caused gnashes of white to bubble the black sheen. The rushing clatter and tumble of water in a rapids came back to them, a sound they hadn't heard all winter. Ice chunks kept sweeping by. After a time the river was all black, from the bend upstream to the bend downstream.

Thorn finished his break-up song. —No one's going to be crossing this river for a good long time, he said. —So let's make a fire!

They moved a little up and away from the bank, and found a flat spot in the middle of a small grove of bush pines and birch. By now the storm had covered everything with snow, so they could do nothing but stomp down a space in the snow with their snowshoes, and move some stones from a nearby boulder pile, the heaviest they could carry, to make a rough fire platform and some seating for themselves. They were going to have to bed down on snow; but with a fire, and their caribou hides, that wouldn't be too bad.

The work of making camp took them the rest of that day, and by the time they were done, Loon was a one-legged man. Thorn had brought an ember from their last night's fire with him in his belt flap, and with that and some duff and fat-soaked twigs and artful breathing, he got the fire restarted, after which he was very pleased with himself. In the cloudy dusk they settled in around their fire, their nook of trees again reinforced by Elga into walls of brush and snow. And between them they had gathered a tall stack of firewood.

It should have been a good moment. No one would be able to cross the river behind them, not for a fortnight for sure, and maybe not until late in the summer. So they had escaped the ice men, barring a twist of fate in which the northers took a completely different route to this same spot. That was so unlikely that it was not worth worrying about. So it was quite an accomplishment, outrunning such determined hunters. They should have been proud. And their fire was bright in the gloom.

But they had so little food. And it was still snowing.

They took account of what they had. Thorn had a nearly full bag of nuts, and he counted out a few for each of them, and passed around his water bag. They ate slowly as they dried themselves by the fire. They were quite wet, so that took a while. Loon had not even completed drying his things when he began falling asleep beyond any ability to fight it off. He gave up and lay on the snow just outside their fire ring, curled to stay as wrapped in his hide as he could. He was just barely aware that Elga was doing the same next to him.

Through the night he slept hard, only waking when cold air

poured in some gap in his wrap and chilled part of him. He would shift, pull the hide closer, check the fire, throw a branch on if one was needed, then tuck his chin on his chest and fall asleep again. It kept snowing through the night, so it never got too cold.

In the morning they woke and stirred as soon as it was light. It was still snowing, and had become windier again. Even in the dim light it was obvious to Loon how gaunt his companions had become, and he supposed he looked the same; he could feel hunger pinching the inside of his backbone, making him weak and light-headed.

They sat up, added branches to the fire, drank water, regarded their remaining food, placed on a cleared stone next to the fire for their inspection. There wasn't much. Nuts, dried meat, honey seed-cake. Thorn heaved a heavy sigh as he regarded it, and took out his sharpest blade and began to cut very thin strips from the edge of his butt patch, lengths like the cords he had used to sew Elga's clothes. Leather and fur: not an appetizing meal. But he handed strings to each of them, and started chewing one of his own. One nut, a bite of dried meat, a piece of leather and fur. Biting off the leather was hard. One chewed the leather for a long time before swallowing it.

The snow continued to fall, hissing into the fire. The renewed wind called up the choruses of trees on the slopes around them. It was not a good day to travel. Possibly they could dig up some roots to eat, if they spent the day foraging under the blanket of new snow. And they had a good bed of embers here. So it seemed like they should hunker down and wait another day, and Loon watched Thorn apprehensively as Thorn went out to take a look. But the moment he left their little knot of trees, three enormous claps of thunder broke, booming from ridge to ridge overhead, as if some river above the clouds were experiencing its own great break-up.

Thorn still had the spirit to smile a little as he ducked back into their camp. —I guess we're supposed to stay here today. Let's gather more wood, and see if we can find anything to eat.

Sixth month after a bad spring: one of the worst times for foraging. A time of starvation and drowning in snowmelt. Well, that meant they might be able to scratch up some dead little creatures. It was easier to face that kind of foraging than another day of walking.

So they spent the day making short excursions out into the storm, bringing back more firewood after scratching around with sticks looking for things to eat. They kept the fire big. At one point in the afternoon, feeling weak with hunger, plopping down by the fire to recover from a bout of light-headedness, Loon again said to Thorn,

—Do you know where we are?

—Yes, Thorn said shortly.

But he couldn't know, as far as Loon could see. Not that Loon doubted that Thorn's knowledge exceeded his own in many things. And maybe here too. But maybe all he meant to say now was that if given a chance, he would be able to find out where they were. Loon saw by his look not to inquire further. They weren't going anywhere that day, and even the next day was now questionable; all this new snow dumping down, being blown into drifts, would make the flats difficult and the slopes dangerous. And Loon was discovering he could barely walk. He could not put any weight on Badleg, he felt weak with pain when he tried. Thorn shook his head when he saw that, out near their boulder pile, and waved Loon back to the fire. Nothing to be done now but eat some more leather and wait it out. Find their way when they could move again.

That night was long. The hungrier you are, the colder you get: they proved this old saying again. They had to eat fire, as it was said; it was all they had. Only the fire kept them going that long night.

The next day it snowed harder than ever. There was no question of walking in it.

Late in the day, as the dark got darker, Elga went out and found a little meadow under its snow blanket, and came back with her sack stuffed with meadow onions she had dug up with a stick. They went back out with her and got more.

Roasting them on the fire made them taste bigger. They were not much in their stomachs, but something to join the leather strings. They ate some portion of the green stalks topping the root bulbs as well, and at one point, chewing on roasted greens, Thorn eyed Elga and said, —I never really wanted to live the swan wife story, but here I am. And only as the old helper at that.

Elga pursed her lips and shook her head. —I'd fly away if I could, she said.

Thorn barked his short laugh, not unlike a snort from one of the unspeakable ones, trundling through the forest. He held out one of the meadow onions at her.

—Have some more goose food and maybe you will.

Again the night was long. At one point Loon woke from a dream in which his father was warning him against crossing the ice on a river. He had been telling his father that it was all right, that they had already made it across. But now apparently they were supposed to be crossing the other way. It was going to be hard, he said to his father anxiously, with the ice gone.

The fire was almost out. Just a flicker inside the bed of embers, a pink glimmer all crusted with gray, going black and hissing where snowflakes fell on it. He placed three branches on the bed and fell back asleep before they had even caught fire.

In the morning Thorn woke them, kneeling on the snow behind Loon and Elga. His lips were pursed and he looked like a big lizard. —Click is dead.

—What? Loon cried. —How? Why?

He had not meant to say why, and the word hung there in the air like a hummingbird standing on its own flight. It could have been awkward, but Thorn was busy in his own thoughts, and did not appear to have heard him.

—I don't know, he said at last, —he might have choked on something. Or been hungrier than we thought. Anyway he's dead. Nothing to be done.

Loon and Elga found themselves sitting up. It was still snowing. Elga had a fist to her mouth, and was looking across the fire at the hide-covered lump that had been Click. His body lay there in its furs, motionless. Loon saw that it was true: there was no mistaking a dead body. So much went away.

Thorn stood, took one of his deep heavy breaths: in, out. —I'm going to move him away from the fire.

He stomped unsteadily around the fire to Click, crouched and stared at the old one's face, which was turned away from Loon and Elga, as if Click did not want them to see him dead. Thorn reached down and pulled the man's bearskin blanket up over his head. It already wrapped the rest of him; now he was no more than a man-sized lump in a bearskin hide. Thorn grabbed him by the part of the bearskin wrapped around his feet and hauled him away, following the path in the snow they had stomped while passing in and out of their tuck. Snow fell in tumbling flurries, and the hillside pines sang their airy windy song.

When Thorn had pulled Click's body out of sight, on the other side of some trees, Loon and Elga could hear him singing one of his shaman songs, one of the ones he sang to help dying people into the next world:

Now you are going into the sky
Be at peace we will remember you

Then for a while there was silence, punctuated by some grunting and thumps. When Thorn returned to the fire he had Click's coat bunched in his hand. He sat down heavily on his rock by the fire, got one of his blades out of his pack. Without a word he began to cut Click's coat up into lengths of leather.

After a long time he suggested that the other two go out and gather firewood. Elga got up and left the tuck, avoiding the way that would lead past Click. Loon stood and hopped around. Badleg would not move at all, and his whole left side ached, also his chest and shoulders. It was clear by the parts of him that were sore that he had made extreme efforts to walk on his poles. He went to the closest trees and knocked around, looking for dead wood under the drifts. Snow flocked down.

That night was windy. They kept the fire big, and slept hungry.

The next day was stormy again. They lay wrapped in their furs, staring into the fire. From time to time one of them would get up and venture out to relieve themselves, or to collect more wood. They had a bed of embers now that would burn damp or green wood, so it was not hard to supply the fire. But it was hard to get around in the deepening snow, hard to think about anything but their hunger, eating them from inside. It was hard to believe it was the sixth month. Although sixth-month storms were known to be bad.

That night was windy again. They kept the fire big, and slept hungrier than ever. And hungry means cold.

In the gray morning light Thorn built up the fire to a roar, then stood facing east, his arms raised and outstretched. He sang a song with words Loon didn't know, words so strange that maybe they were just sounds.

When he was done he turned to face Loon and Elga and put his hands on his hips. They looked up at him from their wraps.

—We need to eat, he told them. —We can find our way home when this storm is over and the snow settles, but we have to have food, or we can't do it.

He stared down at them.

Elga said, —So we have to eat Click.

Thorn nodded deeply. He looked at her in a way he had never looked at Loon.

—Yes, he said. —Exactly. Click has been dead two days. He's frozen. So I am going to go cut a few steaks out of him, and we will then cook and eat them. It will be tough old meat, but it's all we've got. I'm sorry to do it, but Click will understand. I've just finished talking to him about it, and his spirit is well clear of his body by now, out in the stars. He said he is happy to still be of service. He said thank you. Just like he always did.

Loon glanced at Elga; he could feel all of a sudden that his mouth was hanging open. She returned his gaze, swallowed. Loon closed his mouth, swallowed too. He was salivating. He had to pee, and his mouth was running at the thought of cooked meat. —I have to pee, he said.

—Go that way, Thorn said, and pointed away from Click. —Then leave me alone. And he tromped through the new snow toward where he had stashed Click's body, blade in hand.

Loon got up and went out the other way to pee. The air was frigid. He could feel the hunger in him. The worst of it was not the weakness in the muscles, but the light-headedness. The world around him was depthless, washed out. Trees on the higher slopes bounced in the wind, he couldn't look at them, he had to turn his head or he would lose his balance. He couldn't tell how far away things were. This was the real danger that hunger brought, that and the sheer lack of strength.

Back at the fire he found Elga sitting up, wrapped in her hide and tending the fire. New branches were bursting into flame. She looked up at him and they shared a glance, and Loon could see what she was thinking: nothing to be done. They would back each other in the time to come, tell the same story. Nothing to be done. Now it was time to live.

He sat down beside her in a little collapse, and they wrapped both their hides over their shoulders, over their heads. They huddled together like kits when the vixen is gone.

Thorn came back with his leather patch wrapped around a mass he held before him with both hands. He sat by the fire and took up a slender old branch, stripped of its bark, and broke off its end. He pulled open his wrap and took a chunk of meat from it, about the size of his fist; rump, by the look of it. Still frozen. He had to poke a hole in it with his blade to get the sharp end of the branch to stick into it. When it was securely stuck on the branch, he held it out into the fire. First right in the flames, to sear the outside; then beside the flames, to thaw it; then above the flames, to cook it. It sizzled a little when fat and blood dripped from it into the fire, but hearing that, Thorn pulled it back and let it steam in the air. A few ticks of snow fell down from the trees over them, pushed by the wind. He tested the meat with his lips, exposed a fang tooth like a cat and bit into it; chewed off a piece, examined the meat where the bite was: pink. It was done. He chewed and swallowed the piece. —Ah, he said. —Thank you.

He handed the cooked piece, branch and all, to Elga, who thanked him and bit into it matter-of-factly, as she would any other cut. Loon's mouth was flooded with saliva, and he was glad when she handed him the stick and gave him a bite. The meat tasted a bit like bear meat. Very tough. It was as if Click's whole body had been made of heart muscle. Briefly Loon's face spasmed and he cried, but Elga and Thorn ignored that.

Thorn cooked a second chunk, and as they ate that, he cooked a somewhat smaller third cut, possibly the back or front of a thigh. They passed the stick around and ate in silence. When they were done, Thorn passed around his water bag. He watched the sky for a while; the clouds were still low, scudding quickly east, but they were breaking up too, into dark gray masses separated by bright white filaments, like seed threads. —Lie with that good food in you, let it spread out in you, he said. —You know how it is, after a while your stomach is so empty it forgets how to eat. We shouldn't go anywhere today anyway, the snow will be too soft. After a while we'll eat again, and then tomorrow we'll go.

And it was true, what he had said about food on an empty stomach; for a time Loon felt sick and hard-bellied. It was easiest just to lie there and watch the fire, clutching Elga by the arm. After a while he felt better: warmer, stronger, clearer in his sight. Later he had to go out in the snow and shit, and back by the fire again, warming back up, he felt better than ever.

All day the three of them lay there, soaking in the fire's radiance and warming from the inside as the meat from Click gave them strength. Each went out into the gray windy day from time to time to relieve themselves, or just stomp the feeling back into their feet. Loon was worried to find that Badleg no longer had any feeling in the foot. It didn't seem frostbitten, but it was largely numb. It was better than pain, but he didn't see how he could walk.

Next morning dawned clear and cold, and after one last big build-up of the fire, and another small meal of Click's cooked flesh, his calves, they stood and gathered their things together, packed their sacks. Quickly they were ready to leave.

Thorn stopped them. —We're taking Click with us, he said. —We're going to need him.

He held up a rope that he had made out of Click's coat. He had knotted all the strips he had cut into a line. It was longer than Loon would have thought the coat could stretch, and looked strong. Thorn went out to where he had left Click, and came back hauling the body feet first, wrapped in its bearskin along on the ground, the hide tied at each end by lengths of leather, so that it made a kind of sled which could be pulled over the snow. The rope was long enough for Thorn to be able to wrap it around his middle twice in a quick harness, and return it to the bundle to tie off on the foot tie. He pulled the bundle out of their grove and onto open snow, then came back for his snowshoes and sack. He strapped on his snowshoes while in the sled harness.

They began walking. The snow was not yet completely settled down, but the snowshoes were once again a big help, holding them ankle deep on snow their boots would have plunged deep into.

But on the first downhill, Loon fell to his left and could not get back up. Badleg wouldn't bend at ankle or knee, and he couldn't feel its foot. He cried out and struggled, got up to his knees, straightened the snowshoes, used his arms and the walking poles to stand, then at the next step fell left again. He stared up at the others helplessly.

—I told you we would need Click, Thorn said grimly. —Loon. Crawl over here and sit on top of the sled. Lie on your side on it. It won't make any difference to Click. And we have to move.

—I'll pull it, Elga said. —You find the way, she told Thorn. —I'll pull them.

—All right, Thorn said. —That's good. As they got the rope arranged into a harness around Elga's chest, he added to Loon, —I like your wife.

Briefly they all laughed.

It was like lying on a fallen log. They all had done that at one time or another in the forest, lying down for a nap on the flattest surface around. The bearskin wrapping Click covered him completely, and Thorn had it well tied at toe and head. And Click was frozen hard. With her snowshoes on, and two walking branches to propel her, Elga hauled the sled over the snow without many problems. When the snow softened later in the day it would get more difficult. But under the layer of new snow the old snow was rock hard, so Loon and Click would only sink in so far and then stop. And in a day or two the new stuff would get harder too. And Elga was strong.

When they went downhill, she had to let the sled slide down before her, and had to be careful not to be pulled off her feet when it got steep. Loon could help at these moments by putting Goodleg and one of his poles into the snow to slow them so they did not pull her down. Lying on his side he could look right at Elga's face on these downhills. On the steeper slopes the creases between her eyebrows formed a deep wedge on her forehead. Her eyes were sunk deep in her head, her top ribs stuck out; the pads of fat behind her eyes and around her ribs were gone.

Once or twice Thorn led them on traverses down slopes, and she tried to follow, but the sled was always hanging straight downslope from her, so she had to stomp her snowshoes down several times, balancing just so, then stride down and stomp the next step down, leaning back fast if the snow gave way. Loon was frequently astonished by the fluid balance and power of her moves; he did not think he could do what she was doing, even if his leg were fine. Suddenly he saw that she was an ice woman, had grown up in snow. His wife came from a different world, just as Thorn had suggested by the fire with his talk about the swan wife story. She stood there huffing and puffing in the difficult moments, face red, eyes squinted to slits, but her moves were sure. And she kept on making them.

Thorn too saw the difficulty the sled gave her on traverses, and he began to range ahead, glissading down slopes first to get a look around points of stone, then gesturing up to her to follow, or trudging painfully back up to them to continue in a different direction.

The valley they were in trended south, and it became clear that Thorn wanted to head east. At midday he stopped for a rest, and while Loon and Elga sat on a log by the sled, he stuck a stick in a flat spot in the snow, and broke other sticks to measure how long the stick's shadow was at midday. It was the middle of the sixth month; Loon wasn't exactly sure which day, the moon had been so long hidden by the storm. But Thorn knew. And he also knew, as he explained to them while he broke sticks into different lengths, how long the shadow of a stick would be relative to its height, at midsummer noon in their home camp. Which meant he might be able to see whether they were north or south of their camp, by how much longer or shorter the shadow was than it would be at home. At home the shadow was one-sixth the length of the stick.

Here, about the same. And because the shadow was close to the same length, he decided, after a close inspection, accompanied by a great deal of muttering, that all they had to do was head east and they would reach home. Because he was quite sure they were west of their camp.

—We're lucky I know that, he added, —because there's no way of telling whether you are east or west of a place, only north or south. Old Pika taught me the trick, and he said his raven taught it to him, and that he was the first human to know it. He was always saying that, but I never heard any other shaman talk about this trick, at the eight eight or anywhere else.

—If we were east of camp we would be in the big mountains, Elga pointed out.

—True.

So. They were to head east when possible. But the valleys in this region were trending south. So it was hard.

Eventually they climbed over into a narrow but smoothed-floored valley that curved east, and Thorn led them up its floor, somewhat away from the creekbed, on the hardest snow he could find. On they went for the whole of that afternoon. When the sun was low behind them, such that their shadows stretched away in front of them far up the valley, Thorn stopped by a copse of trees where a little snowed-over tributary met the valley's creek. There was an open lead in the snow where the two creeks met, and this water gurgled happily at them, almost the only sound in the landscape aside from their breathing.

It was windless at last. Clouds were visible over the horizon to the south. It was going to be cold that night, and Thorn stomped down an area for their fire ring. He had carried another ember in a mass of pine needles, tucked in a burl in his belt; with it he coaxed more of his duff supply into flame. It was very well done, but he did not bother to congratulate himself this time. He pulled Click away from the fire so that he would stay frozen. Loon hopped around on Goodleg and his poles and collected firewood. In this task especially they missed Click's help, as he could break off branches none of them could. It was almost dark before they had a sufficient supply for the night.

Once again Thorn squeaked off over the hardening snow, blade in hand. The sky in the west was a rich pure blue, cut off sharply by the hilly black horizon. The lightest part of the blue lay right on the black of the hills, and pulsed and crackled redly in Loon's eyes. If he opened his mouth he could hear his heart tocking at the back of his throat. He was hungry again.

Thorn came back as he had the night before, his leather patch wrapped around a lump which he carried farther out from his body than was normal. He flame-seared and then roasted the chunks. Once again Loon's mouth ran with saliva, and he hadn't even been walking that day. Elga's eyes were fixed on the meat such that the whites of her eyes were visible all the way round.

They ate in silence, then wrapped themselves up by the fire and built it up to burn a big bed of embers. They went out under the starry sky to relieve themselves one last time, and Thorn moved Click back in a bit closer to the fire, so that night scavengers would keep their distance. One didn't have to be very far from the fire to be in freezing air; it was going to be another cold night, maybe the coldest of their trek so far. The end of a storm is its coldest part.

They bundled tightly into their furs and lay around the fire so close that the smell of singeing fur filled their nostrils from time to time. After midnight it got so cold that without discussing it they pressed together like horses in a storm, with Elga between the two men at first, but then as the night crept on at the slow pace of the stars' creep, the one farthest from the fire moved inside the one closest to it, and pressed back against them. The coldest part of the three of them was thus pressed into the warmest, and the person newly on the outside huddled against the back of the one in the middle. Round and round, fist after fist, like kits in a litter. Finally the moon set, breath by breath, the only time when you could easily see the sky rolling. After that there were only a couple of fists of the night left to endure.

In the first graying of the eastern sky Loon woke to find himself next to the embers, pressed back into Thorn. Some movement across the fire caused him to lift his head. It was Click. He was standing on his knees, because of course Thorn had removed and cooked his shanks. On Click's face there was an expression Loon couldn't quite understand, some odd mix of pride and longing, disappointment and grief. Loon shaped his lips to say roop, but he didn't want to speak, for fear of waking Thorn and Elga. He realized that he was still asleep too, that he was dreaming. He mouthed the shapes of the words, and spoke them in the dream: —Thank you; and put his head back down and closed his eyes, thinking, Now Click's spirit will keep watch over us for the rest of the night. Although only a spirit would be out on such a cold night, so nothing would challenge him.

The next three days were hard. It warmed up a little. Their sled got shorter. Loon got up and walked as much as he could, but each time he did he was forced to get back on the sled long before he wanted to. Elga and Thorn now took turns pulling it. Elga was still losing weight: her breasts were almost completely flat, her eyes sunken deep in her skull, her top ribs sticking far out. It was easy to see the shape of her skull. Thorn, always skin and bones, had turned into a snake's head, earless, lipless, fleshless. He spoke very little, especially for him, and was always anxious to get up on ridges that might give him a view to the east, walking ahead of the other two frequently. They followed his tracks and found him up on the ridges, gazing east with hand over eyes, searching for a sign, fretting. No one mentioned that they were lost. Every afternoon they stopped and made a fire, successfully using an ember from the night before, and every evening in the blue dusk they ate cooked meat, including kidneys, liver, and the heart itself, tougher even than the tough old muscles they had started with. At night they lay bundled together by the fire. Only one night was close to as cold as the last night of the storm had been, and the morning after that one, Thorn went out and came back with a double handful of starlings, holding them by their feet; he had found them under a knot of black spruce trees, where they had frozen in the night and fallen off their perches. Roasted, they made for a welcome change.

They also found more meadow onions in meadows they passed. Eating those made them feel bloated and gassy, but they did it anyway. The new snow melted off quickly, and every day the old snow melted a little more, and now during the afternoons, sheets of black water rushed over more and more black ground. Summer was finally arriving. Now they had to search for snowy stretches to make it easier to pull the sled. As the last old snow melted, the remaining suncups got bigger and bigger, and these were almost as hard for sled pulling as bare ground. Loon walked for longer and longer stretches, using his sticks in place of Badleg, but Thorn was impatient, and sometimes would demand that Loon get back on the sled and be pulled. Elga only pursed her lips and pulled the sled, with or without Loon on it. Sometimes Thorn took a turn, but he was getting too light to hold the sled on the downhills, and was forced to give it back over to Elga whenever their way went down.

Then an afternoon came when Elga fell on the snow, and was very slow to get back up. Loon got off the sled, so much shorter and lumpier now, and hopped over to her, feeling terrible. He saw all of a sudden that she was emaciated, sunburned, almost too weak to get back up. She had walked herself into the ground without saying a word about it.

—No! Loon said, when she finally stood and tugged on the sled lines. —Now it's my turn.

He took the harness off her and put it around his waist. Between his walking poles and his legs he had become a four-legged creature, in form not unlike a hyena, high-shouldered and ugly. But still he could hop along, hauling Badleg and making it help whenever he could manage it. Elga limped behind him in the shallow trench over the snow that the sled made.

By now none of them were walking very well, but they were moving at about the same pace as each other. They stumped along wordlessly, and made camp earlier each day, and hunted for bulbs as well as firewood, and at night slept on dry ground, or dry stone slabs, warm in the fire's heat.

Finally a day came when they all were failing. On that day it was Badleg who saw them through, having the only muscles among them not completely tapped out. As Loon walked it was now Badleg who gave the most push, painful though it was. So sometimes Loon hauled the sled by itself, sometimes with Thorn on it, once even with Elga, who wept with frustration to have to lie down and be pulled. But Loon insisted. Badleg was fresh compared to them, and Loon quickly learned to contain the pain to a little stab of agony that burned at a single point in every step, a pain to be ignored as an unwelcome guest, an intruder, someone to thrust past unacknowledged time after time, like a hyena or a pike. Step after step this attitude worked, almost. His third wind, or some wind beyond the third wind, had come into him, and he gritted his teeth and felt the strength, still there in the parts of Badleg that didn't hurt. Even Goodleg was not as strong as Badleg now.

I am the third wind
I come to you
When you have nothing left

When you can't go on
But you go on anyway
In that moment of extremity

That afternoon they ascended a forested snowy slope to a bare ridge running southwest to northeast, resting every three or four steps. On the ridge Thorn shaded his eyes with a hand, staring east.

Suddenly he said, —Here now, what's that?

He pointed. —See that peak just over the horizon there, over those trees? That's Ice Cap South. Puy Mir.

—Are you sure? Loon couldn't help saying.

Thorn kept staring. Then he looked at Elga and Loon and smiled. It was like seeing a snake smile, unexpected and repellent, but a smile nevertheless.

—I'm sure.

The idea that they knew where they were did a lot to restore their spirits, of course. But their problems were by no means over, because Ice Cap South was well to the west of their camp, and all the rivers and even the creeks were now broken up and running high. No more crossing ice, which was a relief given the break-up they had seen; but they were too weak to cross streams at any ford higher than their ankles. Camp lay to the east of them, but the ravines here ran northeast to southwest, so they often had to walk across the grain of the land, and cross creek after creek. Usually the best way over these little creeks was a tree that had fallen across them. As he didn't trust Badleg's balance, Loon found these logs about as frightening as any ford. On every crossing he sat down and scooted himself across the fallen trees, or crawled, even if they were logs so thick that ordinarily he could have crossed them standing on his hands. Meanwhile Elga and Thorn, who had recovered a little, had to cross while grabbing the two ends of Click and lifting his body, like a fur-wrapped log, over and between branches sticking up. Loon could do nothing to help them with this.

Now also, as the days were warming to well above freezing, from about midday to just after sunset, poor Click was thawing a little in the afternoons, then refreezing at night. His meat was therefore going off. Thorn spent a final session with him, one night after they chewed on some of his ribs, and came back to the fire with three last bags of meat that he thrust into a snowbank near them.

—You can walk all the time now? he said to Loon.

—Yes, Loon said, hoping it was true.

—Good. Tomorrow we'll leave him. We can come back later and give his body a proper burial.

He took Click's leggings from one of the bags and put them on the fire to burn, chanting the good-bye farewell to Click's spirit:

Now you are gone, we loved you
Now you are gone, we thank you
Now you rest in the sky above
And we will always remember you

After another cold night bundled together by the fire, a night unvisited by Click, they woke to a cold north wind. This was very unfortunate; wind was by a long way the worst of their foes; snow would have been better, even rain. Their luck seemed to have left them entirely, perhaps because of their treatment of Click, but anyway: bad.

When they were as bundled up as they could get, they went together to the remains of Click's body, hauled it to an area of south-facing rocks, and laid it out for the birds. Already black buzzards scrapped around overhead in the gale. Thorn sang the funeral song and made a promise to Click to return and collect what bones might remain, for proper disposal when the time was right.

Then they took off on their own.

Now Loon walked as much as he could on his poles, but of course Badleg had to do its part, there was no way around it. Whenever they were on remnants of snow in the afternoon, it still helped to be on their snowshoes, and that involved Badleg no matter what. Loon just had to stride over that little click of agony. It was an almost audible click. Indeed in the mornings, when he was stiff and it was quiet, he could actually hear the click as he felt the pain jolt up him. It was very like one of Click's little click words, and so it began to seem to Loon that Click had taken over from Badleg, and from Crouch, and had now settled in their place. Click had moved into him to protest the bad treatment he had received from his comrades after his death, or perhaps to help him along. Step by step Click clicked in him.

Thorn kept a steady slow pace, although whenever he approached a ridge that looked like it was going to give him a view east, he hurried up it with a speed that suggested to Loon that the old man still had a little reserve of strength. Elga was slower, and Loon could see that she was wearing down. She had eaten all she could of her own fat, and was now as thin as she could get. But she was stubborn too. He knew that now full well, and could see it clearly in the set of her shoulders, and the deep wedge between her eyebrows, and the look in her eye. She was not going to stop now that they were so close.

So really it came down to a matter of isolating Click to his single objection, the same stab over and over again, and then getting along without any more hurt than that. Over wet ground, over rocks, over big suncups when they could not be avoided; they were getting really bad, whether hard in the mornings or soft in the afternoons. Up ravines and over passes, sometimes following animal trails, with some human trail signs too. Keeping a general aim east. From every high point they stared east hungrily, and Thorn would point at something he recognized, and on they would go, down again toward the next creek crossing, the next up, the next pass.

That night by the fire they ate the last of Click's flesh, and Thorn built the fire larger even than usual and warmed his hands at the flames, dancing just a little in place. —Tomorrow we'll be there, he said.

—Really? Loon and Elga said together. They looked at each other, sharing their surprise.

—Tomorrow or the day after, if we're slow tomorrow. But it doesn't matter. We're going to make it. Thank you Click, thank you Click, thank you thank you thank you.

The next day they woke and drank water, sat by the fire warming up, went out to perform their ablutions. Stood stiffly and shuffled off again. As that day wore on, and they came to what Thorn said was a tributary of West of Northerly Creek, Elga tied her snowshoes on and led the way down a valley of softening suncups, stomping down a path for Loon to follow; and Thorn too followed. Now, at the very end, Thorn was finally slowing down, taking each step as if it were a complete effort, as if he were utterly tapped out, with no second wind or third wind, or any wind at all; just one step at a time, each a full effort. So he was like Loon in that regard, and Loon wondered if Thorn had hurt himself, or had just run out of wind. He only shook his head when Loon asked about it, and stepped on in the same gait.

—Remember! Loon said, mimicking Thorn's teaching voice, —in a journey of twentytwenty days you can still trip on the last step!

Thorn just shook his head. He was too tired to object. But he had always said that a little irritation could jolt one's spirit in a good way. So Loon kept it up. How often he had heard this one. —Oh, yes, he repeated in Thorn's tones, —in a journey of twentytwenty years, you can still fuck up on the very last step! So don't! He almost laughed, he had heard this one so often.

The first feature of the landscape that Loon recognized on his own was the giant boulder that lay in the middle of West of Northerly Creek, straddling most of the streambed. He stared at it, feeling stunned. A little seed of relief was sprouting in him, right behind his belly button. He had often visited this boulder with Hawk and Moss, when wandering up this canyon; the charcoal drawing he had made of a cave bear was still there, on the big white side of the rock that fell straight into the water. He had had to climb the boulder from the other side, then hang down from its top and draw while hanging upside down. Hawk and Moss had laughed themselves silly. But there the bear shambled with its sloping forehead, eyeing any viewers on the bank as if considering whether to attack them. Excellent work for someone hanging upside down, and Loon found he was weeping to see it, not for the drawing, or even for home, but just at the idea that he could soon stop walking on Badleg. Only a certain finite number of steps now. They were less than a half day from home.

Although it took them longer than that. Still, in the last good light, late that afternoon, when everything was lit yellow from the side, the sky overhead darkening, the world big with the approach of night, they stumbled up after their long shadows to West Pass and looked down on the headwall meadow. It was empty. But then around a tree strolled Heather.

She stopped short as she saw them. For a moment she was frozen with surprise. Then she turned her head over her shoulder, and said, —Child, your parents are here. Even the unspeakable one is here.

Then she sat down abruptly on a log and stared at them as they approached. —I thought you were gone, she exclaimed, and put her face in her hands.

Their child stared curiously at Elga, who dropped her poles and caught him up, then lifted him into the air. He stared down at her, suspended between fright and some huge surprise. Loon joined them, and the two of them held the child between them as he began to sob and struggle to get away.

Heather wiped her face and watched this from her log. —You are one lucky boy, she said to the child.

She stood up and hugged Elga and then Loon, and then even Thorn.

—What about Click? she asked.

Thorn shook his head. —He died. I'll tell you about it later.

Heather regarded him. Finally she said, —You're uglier than ever, I see.

—You stole my beauty long ago, Thorn replied, turning away from her. —Here, take our sacks. Take Loon's sack. His leg is bad again.

—He can thank his shaman's wander for that.

—Woman! Thorn said. —Shut up. Please. Shut up now, and help us get down to camp. We're tired.

ALL THE WORLDS MEET

The Wolves' camp under its little abri, overlooking Loop Meadow, Loop Hill, the Stone Bison, the river in its gorge. Midsummer sunset slanting in from the gorge to the west, cutting through the smoke from their fire. Home home home home home.

Heather walked them in, carrying all their things, and by the time they limped down the last part of the river path into camp it was after sunset, early dusk, and the firelight caught every face, they were all masks of themselves, expressing joy at the travelers' unexpected return: Hawk and Moss shouting in his face, seizing him up in fierce hugs, everyone reaching in to touch them all, to be sure they were real, it was such a surprise. Even Sage gave him a kiss. It reminded Loon of the night he had come in from his wander, but this time launched above the sky, to a dream place more real than real. Or else this time it was the real real, as undeniable as pain, flush in his face.

They stayed up for a time talking and sipping duck soup, until exhaustion felled the travelers and they were carried to bed. All night in his dream, all Loon saw was the firelit faces, laughing, masklike. His pack.

Next morning he woke late and staggered like a wooden man to the east end of camp. The Stone Bison still arched over the river, morning light filled the gorge, the camp basked in the sun, the air was full of summer smells and the cluck of the river, the twitter of the birds. Every tree was a beehive. The sky was blue, and it seemed impossible they had been freezing in the wind and snow just a few days before. The sixth month could be like that. And home stayed home whether you were there or not. Loon kept looking around, he sat down and touched the ground, tasted some dust. It was hard to believe. The feeling in him was like some spring bud that he could look at and know it would grow into something big.

*   *   *

Folded back into the life of their pack, Loon and Elga and Thorn rested and ate, then rested some more. Their child clung to Elga, and would not let her out of his sight. In the evenings he sat between Elga and Loon, or on one of their laps, a little fist clutching each of them by their clothing. Seeing it Heather would shake her head and say, —You are a lucky boy. I thought you were an orphan.

Everyone wanted to hear Thorn tell stories around the fire again, and he did, croaking away as he stared into the fire, or up at the stars. Sometimes after he told one, someone would ask for the story of his rescue of Loon and Elga. But Thorn would shake his head.

—I can't tell it yet. It's not ready to tell.

People knew that the old one had died during the rescue, of course, and so they left Thorn alone, to tell it in his own time. Aside from that, he seemed willing to tell any of the old stories, starting with how wolverine pulled summer out of winter, which now as he told it seemed to resemble what he had just accomplished, in pulling Loon and Elga out of the icy north and bringing them back to their sunny abri, so that he told it with palpable satisfaction.

Indeed every story he told he seemed to be enjoying more than before. Then in the mornings he would sit by Loon and require Loon to tell the stories on his own, nodding and teaching him hooks to remember it. These lessons were not like they had been before, when Thorn's words had gone in one flicked ear and out the other. Now Loon watched Thorn's face as the old shaman talked, and found he could hold more in mind afterward, and repeat the story in much the same way, sometimes by seeing a memory of Thorn saying it, with all his little squints and scowls and crooked little smiles, and most of all, tones of voice. They had to be remembered as songs with tunes, that was the trick. And Loon carved some sticks with sequences of Thorn's tells too, to help him later.

Also the rules for remembering were clearer to him now, more helpful: the rule of threes, the up-to-down and down-to-up, the helpers and their chores, and so on. It was still hard for him, and even when he succeeded, a fortnight later he would too often find that it had all gone again. And because he now wanted to please Thorn, the losses were more frustrating than ever. His heart would sink a little as he realized that now that he was back, and saved, he was going to have to learn these stories, even if he never got good at them. Not until now had he ever believed he would have to do the things a man had to do.

But mostly, he was just happy. He watched Elga eating like a mink, filling out right before his eyes, and he could hardly believe she was there among them. It felt like a dream, and he was afraid sometimes that one day he would wake with the sunlight turning the gorge mist yellow and find that he had woken up in a different world where it hadn't happened. That they had gotten her back was perpetually amazing to him; he would never get over it, he would always be a little stunned. He wanted nothing ever to happen again.

Heather was clearly pleased they were back. —It was dull without old unspeakable spouting all his carbunculosities. The men in this pack are mostly fools, and the women are in a little showdown right now, so there was no one left to talk to. And a pack needs its shaman, I guess, even if they're a little snake of a shaman.

She regarded Loon closely. —I'm glad to see you too, Loon. But listen to me: you need to take care of that bad ankle, or you'll be lame for life. You're still a young man, just a little more than a boy. You don't want to be lame for twenty years. You need both legs to get by in this world!

—I know it, Loon said fretfully. —Believe me, I know.

—So why are you still walking around on it then?

Loon was surprised. —Because I need to be helping! I can't just sit around and be fed like a baby. Even if I can't hunt, I can at least get firewood.

She was shaking her head as he said this. —We were doing fine before you got back. We don't need you. Listen! If you don't sit down for a moon and rest that leg, you'll never be able to hunt again. And we need your hunting, and we can do without you for a while around camp. Everyone will understand. Even Ibex will understand.

And if he doesn't, I'll make him. This last in a dark tone that made Loon shiver a little.

She put that darkness into a look and pinned him with it. —So will you do what I say or not?

—I'll try.

After that Loon sat around camp, even during the day when everyone was out and about. He helped look after Lucky and the other kids, and knapped blades from cores, and cured hides, and cut and sewed new jackets and leggings for Elga. His sewing was serviceable, but several of the women made clothes so much finer than his that he gave up and turned to carving figures out of sticks, and grinding earthblood to powder, and reciting some of the stories he was learning. No matter what he did, Heather didn't want him standing up. On many days, and every night, she heated water in buckets by putting fire stones in the water, then poured the hot water into bladders and draped them over the ankle of Badleg. She also tried a few of her poultices, although when she inspected his leg after these applications, she shook her head dubiously. Clearly she thought the hot water bladders were helping the most, and they felt good to Loon too. After the heating was done, she would hold his foot and ankle and press gently on the skin over the swollen top of the ankle, testing where it hurt, or trying to rub some healing into it.

—You should do this too, she told him. —You can feel it better. Sometimes if a ligament or sinew breaks, they just won't heal. But other times they will. A lot more of these tears and breaks heal than you might expect. So you have to assume the best, and act like it's going to work out. You can get over this. At the very least, you should be able to get around without pain.

—That would be good.

It was true that it didn't hurt as much as it had on their trek. But certain accidental movements, or slips of balance, still caused the little snick of agony to shoot up his leg. Heather could see that, and she also saw that he wasn't going to be able to keep sitting around for too much longer. Soon it would be a month of it; soon they would be preparing to head north; he would have to get up and give it a try. So one morning she told him she was going to make a healing shoe for him.

—What do you mean?

—Let me show you.

She sat him down in the sun with a supply of sticks, antlers, mammoth tusk pieces, sinews, leather strips, and cedar bark cord, and they took all morning to make a wooden frame somewhat like a boot, with leather straps, so that Heather could bind it to his foot, ankle, and calf. With the frame strapped to his foot and lower leg, all the way up to his knee, he could only walk by swinging the whole thing ahead and landing each step on the bottom of it. This made for quite a limp, but no matter how he stepped, no matter what he did, the left foot and ankle were held in just one position. That would give the break time to heal, Heather said. And it was true that when he wore it he never felt the click, even when walking.

So he could help collect firewood, and do other slow tasks around camp. As the days of the seventh month began, and he continued to use the wooden boot, and apply hot water bladders to the ankle by night, he felt less pain from the area, and could see there was less swelling. He was slow, he moved ugly, as Hawk put it, but a day finally came when he could dispense with the boot, go barefoot, and not feel any pain in the ankle when he walked around. There was stiffness there, and weakness when compared to Goodleg, but no pain. This was astonishing to Loon; he had not expected it, had not dared to hope. Heather had cured him!

She shook her head when he said this to her. —No no. Your body healed itself. But I know what you're trying to say. When you're hurt, it's very difficult to believe your body can heal itself. Mostly it seems to go the other way. We fall apart and die, that's how it goes. But sometimes healing happens. I've seen it too often to doubt it, I've even felt it in myself once or twice. No, healing is real. But why does it come into us some times and not others?

She shook her head darkly. —No one knows. Really we know nothing. We only know the shit that Raven dumps on our heads, we only know what comes out of the world's asshole onto us. But what that world is up to up there, why we get the particular shit we get, no one knows.

They were sitting against the cliff wall in the sun, with the smell of thyme and gray stone and the river percolating in the warming air. Loon rotated his ankle slowly and carefully, and couldn't help grinning.

—Pretty good shit this morning, he pointed out, sniffing the air and looking around.

She glared at him, still wanting to indulge her bad mood. Finally she changed the subject. She had a list of forest plants she wanted him to go out and find and bring back to her. He could take it slow, and she suggested he take the wooden boot along with him, in case he ever felt like he needed it. —The last thing you want is to injure yourself again just as you're getting well.

It was mostly women's work, but boys or old men or shamans did it too, especially in this month. Quite a few of the girls worked for Heather and thus learned what she knew about plants and healing and midwifery, without her making any special thing about it. Loon wished Thorn would be that way about the shaman stuff. But the women did things differently. Many of them often went out trapping by day. These women would disappear up and down the riverside to set underwater snares to drown muskrats. Some of them threw spears too at the small animals in the gorge, killed some sisters to pass the time during their monthlies, when not a few of them were surly. Yes, the women were all hunters too in their way, whether they went out or not. Some of the ones who stayed in camp were the scariest of all. They worked as a gang within the pack, they stared at you. They judged you. They would slit your throat if that's what it took to get what they wanted. Even Elga, with all her warmth, and the way she loved him, the way she took him in her, the way she had pulled him back home through the snow, even Elga had a look in her that was more cave bear than elg. She was not to be crossed, now less than ever. Which was fine, because Loon only wanted what she wanted. And anyway her cave bear look was mostly directed at Thunder and Bluejay, and Sage.

Best stay out of that. So he crossed the Stone Bison and wandered the thick forests on the north-facing slopes on the other side of the Urde-cha, looking for hellebore and nightshade and mint and mushrooms and truffles, and finding them under beds of ferns, or around the little springs that gurgled out of the holed cliffs on that broken shady wall of the gorge, often where the cliffs met the forest tilt sloping down to the floor of the gorge. Places that were always in the shade nurtured plants that grew nowhere else. Rocks in permanent shade were covered with mosses and lichens, and footed with ferns and sprawling nets of shrubs. Cool wet green smells were spiced by little flowers, and by the dry scent of thyme wafting in from sunnier air. Robins pecked around on the forest floor near him. They were known to be calm and wise birds, who would hang around people who didn't bother them. Loon felt blessed by their presence. Out across the gorge, pine needles on the sunny side were flashing in the wind.

Loon walked painlessly, always testing the miracle, finding it again sound, then plopping onto his knees at a likely bed of ferns, and knocking around under it hunting for nightshade. From time to time he stood and looked down at the river sliding through its little gorge, and their camp across the river. It was nice how most of the best overhangs in this gorge were under walls on the north side, thus facing southward to the sun. The river had wanted people to be comfortable in its bed, and had arranged things accordingly. Over here on the shady side an overhang would be wasted, and a few were, being the wettest places of all. But they were good for certain shady plants.

He stood up, crushed the leaves and new buds of blossoms of mint under his nose, felt the scent cut into his head. Down there in camp, he could see Elga and Lucky sitting by the fire, Elga punching leather with a bone awl, Lucky playing with what looked like the little wooden owls Loon had carved for him.

It was hard to believe he wasn't dreaming. But here he stood, upright and pain-free, in the cool of an ordinary morning. Really it was the things that had happened during his time away that were now dreams, even though they still seemed to threaten him. Real in their time, terrifying and hopeless in their time, they were now gone. They could not happen other than they had, they could not hurt him any more than they had. He did not have to fear them anymore. He had woken up from them, to this dream that was not a dream. Again he had stepped into the next world over from the one he had been in. All the worlds meet. Time to feel that and be happy.

Thorn, however, was not happy. Loon was at first surprised at this. But then he began to understand: Thorn would never be happy. It wasn't his way. Maybe all old people were like that. But no, Windy had been as happy as anyone, till right near her end. It was just Thorn. Had he always been that way? Loon couldn't remember.

One night they were sitting around the fire, eating salmon steaks and a seed mash Thunder had cooked on a hot rock. Thorn was standing, drinking from a ladle, and Loon was sitting by the fire, massaging his left foot and feeling the new hard little lumps in there, so solid and painless. He looked up because Thorn had started, and saw that Thorn was staring over Loon's head, across the fire at something, his face a wooden mask of itself, flickering in the light. No one else was acting any differently, they chattered to each other about this or that: only Thorn had frozen. Suddenly Loon realized that Thorn was staring at Click's ghost. That was what his mask of a face said.

Loon felt his stomach shrink and the hair on his forearms rise. He did not dare turn around and see the ghost himself, he was much too scared for that; Click could be there half-eaten, bleeding, red eyes ravenous for revenge, teeth all fangs. Not for anything could he turn and look.

Thorn remained transfixed. The moment hung suspended: people talked in the orange flicker. Loon became curious despite himself. He wanted to see without looking, know without seeing. Holding his breath, asshole painfully tight, he turned his head and looked down at the fire; then, eyes straining far to the right in their sockets, he glanced over the flames in the direction Thorn was staring.

It was Click all right. He was standing at the edge of the firelight, in the dark between two trees, so that the firelight flickered him in and out of existence. But most certainly it was Click. His pale face appeared frozen, his hair and beard and brows frosted, but his eyes were alive, and they were fixed on Thorn. His expression was reproachful. All the parts of him they had eaten appeared to still be there under his bearskin cloak.

Then his frozen gaze shifted from Thorn to Loon, and Loon quickly whipped his head back around, completely unnerved. His face was tingling. Thorn glanced down at Loon, then back at Click. It was clear from his expression that he was still seeing him. Loon hunched over, head down, helpless to do anything but peer fearfully up at Thorn.

Thorn took his flute from his belt, very slowly, and played a tune that reminded Loon of the one called Fools the Wolves. Then it took a turn, and he recognized it as a version of Click's triple walking whistle, turned somehow into a lament. One two three, one two three. All the time he played this, Thorn stared across the fire at Click. Finally he finished, nodded, kissed the flute, put it away. Then he turned and walked off toward his bed.

After that, Click's ghost starting hanging around camp. At night by the fire Loon often realized that Thorn was seeing Click there at the back of the firelight, like a hyena at the edge of a kill site. Thorn played his flute when it happened, but to Loon it didn't look like that was enough. Maybe when they gave Click's bones a proper burial, his spirit would be satisfied and go away. Loon put his hopes in that.

Thorn passed the days wearing a little scowl of endurance. More than ever he looked like a black snake. Sometimes Loon could distract him with a carved knot or antler, or an etching on a slate, or an animal painted on a slab of wood. Loon also told many of Thorn's favorite stories, including the one about the man who married a swan woman and ruined his life, ending up a seagull. That one caused Thorn to smile a gloomy little smile when Loon finished.

—Well said, youth. That's your story all right. And you're getting better at telling it too. Much better than that time at the corroboree. There's some real heart in your ending now. You know how it feels, eh? But don't forget the part about the old man who helps him.

The summer month was nearing full moon. At some point it had been established that they were decided not to go to the eight eight this year. Lots of reasons were given all around, but the main one seemed to be Schist's desire to avoid an immediate confrontation with the northers. He suggested they go as far as Cedar Salmon River, fish the salmon run, and spend the following fortnight hunting in the canyons west of the ice caps, forgoing the caribou steppe to go after horses and musk oxen and sheep and bears, and all the other creatures of the west. It had been such a stormy spring and summer, possibly the caribou wouldn't be coming anyway. Storm years had been known to do that before.

Of course some of them thought this change was a mistake, and no one liked missing the eight eight, except perhaps for Loon. So it was another thing not going well for Schist. He was losing the ability to make the pack feel whole. Ibex was always berating Hawk and Moss for one thing or other, and Hawk did not hesitate to mouth back at Ibex, always eyeing Schist as he did so. Youth will have its way. Thorn, the oldest of them all, except for Heather, was supposed to be the one who could reconcile all disputes, being their shaman. But he remained distracted, and offered no opinion about the pack's summer, but only played his flute for longer and longer parts of the day.

So they stayed in camp that summer, and some of them went to Cedar Salmon River for the fall run, and some went out to hunt the herds of horses that came through the gorge, driving them up kolby canyons from which they could not escape. Those who stayed in camp trapped deer. They had to gather enough food to get through the winter, and also have enough to give back to the Raven pack what they had given them in the hunger spring, plus a little more as thanks. It was quite a task, given the loss of the caribou harvest, and it was interesting as the fall months passed to find that they could do it; all but the return to the Ravens, anyway.

—We may have to wait on that a year, Schist admitted. —Or see what happens in the spring, and decide then.

—We'll have to make a compensation to the northers, too, Thorn warned him. —When we go to the eight eight next year. Even if it was their fault. The corroborators will make the judgment, and it could be against us. So we need to be ready for that too. But that shouldn't be food, it has to be something else.

Loon had an idea about that. —We took some of their snowshoes when we escaped, and broke the rest. So we could give the snowshoes back, but better.

—Better?

—I can make snowshoes better than theirs, and we could give them those.

Thorn nodded thoughtfully. —That's the kind of thing the corroborators like. We'll tell them that we forgive the northers for stealing Elga, so they have to forgive us for whatever we did to them when we got you two out of there. We'll give back the snowshoes we took, but they'll be even better. Then let bygones be bygones, or else we'll fight them to the death. And the corroborators don't like fighting at the eight eight.

Schist said, —It sounds good. No one wants the ice men thinking they can push around the corroboree. So it might work. And we need to go back.

*   *   *

After that, as part of his fall foraging, Loon kept an eye out for wood to use in making snowshoes. They had stolen four pair, so he intended to make that many, ignoring the memory of the many more he had broken. The ones he made were going to be better than the jende's snowshoes. He had thought about this sometimes while tromping over the snow by the great salt sea, hauling the jende's sleds. They had to make their snowshoes out of the gnarled little spruce trees that filled the nearby ravines, and with occasional pieces of driftwood they collected from the shore. Little trees made for little lengths of wood, and so their snowshoes were strapped-together things. Down here under the sun, the trees were so much more big and various that there were all kinds of tough woods that could be used.

And Loon now had an image in his eye, which he painted on a flat rock. He was quite sure that the most important thing for a snowshoe was that the foot be held steady, while the frame was still free to rotate up and down over the ball of the foot. The jende had solved the problem of these contrary requirements by strapping their tall boots onto mammoth tusk crossbars that crossed the snowshoe just behind the toe hole, so that the toe of the boot could angle through the snowshoe into the snow when you went uphill, and the snowshoe would stay flat when you took a stride on flat ground. Their crossbar tie worked well enough on flat snow, and when going straight up or down a slope, but on any kind of a traverse the boot would twist and slide, and a great effort had to be made to place the foot as flatly as possible on the snowshoe, and the snowshoe also as flat as could be on the snow. On traverses this couldn't really work, so one was always slipping, and it was easy to tear straps, or break the bar under the foot away from the rounded frame. A broken snowshoe makes a bad day, as the saying went; and yet it happened pretty often.

The way to secure the foot on the snowshoe, Loon had decided, was to lash a wooden boot sole to a tough crossbar stick across the back of the toe hole, with a wrap made of bear leather sewed to this boot sole, so that the whole thing was a permanent part of the snowshoe. One would then place one's boot on the wooden sole and tie the wrap over it. One's foot would be stabilized on the wooden sole, which would make traverses very much easier. With a strong frame made of a single curve of ash wood, and wide cross straps of leather, or spruce roots, tied to the frame, the result would be very strong. He could consult with Heather and Sage about the best knots to use. Also, antler tips lashed or glued to the front end of the wooden soles would give them more grab going uphill, which would be a great thing, and they would be almost retracted when the sole was flat to the shoe, which it would be during a downhill glissade.

He could see it so well, he easily drew it: the best snowshoes ever. The northers simply didn't have the ash trees to make them, even if they did suddenly think up Loon's design, which he doubted they would, having not done it before. They lived on a coastal plain, while Loon was a hill person; maybe that explained it and maybe it didn't, but when the time came and the northers tried Loon's snowshoes, they would see they were better, and never make them the old way again. Maybe. It was worth a try.

So all that fall and winter, while Thorn was struggling with Click's ghost, and the rest of them were packing on their winter's fat by eating and sleeping as much as possible, Loon spent a lot of his time in camp working on snowshoes. Quite a few of the pack got interested in what he was doing, because whenever the snow was soft they themselves went out on snowshoes that they had never taken much trouble to make. But there were a lot of storms that winter, and better snowshoes would be a good thing, all agreed.

Thorn was interested but dubious. —You need to make sure they have some give. If they're too rigid they'll break under a strain, and then you've got no snowshoe at all. Better to give a little over and over than give it all at once.

Loon nodded. It was true that his design would only work if the foot bar was very strong and well attached to the frame, and the wooden sole well attached to the foot bar. These were the parts that would be tested the most, time after time in the ordinary course of walking, and with extra force during traverses and step-throughs and glissades. So he did a little jumping up and down on them while they were suspended between rocks, to see what they could handle. They performed pretty well. Some he found difficult to break no matter how hard he tried. That was really pleasing.

Heather took an interest in these tests, because she liked tests. She came over and watched Loon closely, and even made some jumps herself. —Try making them a few different ways, she said, —and see how they do before you make any more. Different shapes for the shoe, different attachments and bindings. I wonder, could you reinforce where the foot bar fits into the frame? Make frame sockets out of tusk or antler?

Loon tried various things. There was a lot of time that winter around the fire, during the long nights and the stormy days, so much time that it was hard to sleep through all of it. Elga was sewing new clothes for him and Lucky, and all in all, there was little he was needed for once night fell. So he worked on the shoes. Eventually Thorn came to agree that the wider variety of trees in their region, especially ash, and the sheer number and size of trees, should allow for the making of snowshoes superior to the northers', and any design improvements would be good too. Being better would make them an excellent compensation, because they would compensate while also being a little put-down. There was no doubt they were going to be locking horns with the northers at the eight eight one way or another, so a little poke in the eye was always a good thing. You had to front up to such crass barbarians, he said, especially if you happened to have scalded some of them for their badness. —But they can't be so stiff they break, he said more than once. —You can always deal with a little slip and slide on a traverse, but a break can be a really bad thing.

—I know, Loon said, and was about to explain yet again how much flex there was in ash wood, and how the foot bars were to be seated in mammoth tusk sockets, when he saw that Thorn was staring white-eyed across the fire again. The hair on Loon's arms prickled, and Badleg started humming inside his ankle. Slowly Thorn pulled his flute from his belt, and again breathed through it the low tune of his apology. He had recently begun adding to it some birdlike notes that sounded like Click's roop roop. As he played this song he continued to look across the fire, eyes still round, pleading with Click's ghost to understand, to forgive.

During this particular visitation Heather was sitting by the fire, using its light to see dried branches of various herbs, plucking off their leaves and seeds and making careful piles on little patches of qiviut cloth, made from the underfur of the musk ox. She continued to do this without indicating in any way that she saw what was happening to Thorn.

It was only when she and Loon were alone the next morning, by the purling and chuckling ford of Upper Creek, that she said to Loon,

—Is it Click that Thorn thinks he's seeing?

Loon didn't want to talk about it, but he could not help but nod, almost in the same way Click would have.

She stared at him as he looked at the ground. —What happened to Click? How did he die?

Again Loon didn't want to speak, but the words came out of his mouth anyway, like rocks he was spitting. —We woke up one morning and he was dead.

He told Heather about how they then took his frozen body along to use as a sled, a sled that they ate as they went, because without it they would have died. He told her how Badleg had forced him first to ride on Click's back for a day, then to sit on Click's frozen body and be pulled by Elga, while Thorn found the way. How Click's ghost might have moved into Badleg during that time, because Click's legs were among the first parts of him they had eaten.

Heather listened in silence, only nodding occasionally to show Loon that she heard him and understood. She sniffed from time to time.

When he was done she heaved a sigh.

—You need to collect Click's bones and give him a proper burial. The ravens have cleaned them by now.

—We know. But until then...

She shrugged. —It's going to be a long winter. It may be he will never leave this, no matter how long he lives. You never know how he'll respond to things. He's a hard man to guess.

—That's true, Loon said.

Come second month of winter, he had the best pair of snowshoes he could make. When he was satisfied with them, or had defeated his dissatisfactions as much as he was able, he made another pair just like it. He invited Thorn to take a walk with him, and one morning they strapped the two pairs on and went downstream, as was proper for a first walk in a new pair of snowshoes. Thorn swerved left and right like a cliff swallow, traversing down the slopes to the river, cutting up and over the knob leading to Next Loop Down, and glissading down the steep slope on its western side. When he came to the confluence of the river and Upper Creek, he stopped over the lead. Black water slid smoothly by just beyond his snowshoes. He threw back his parka hood, and his earless balding head looked like a big black snake rearing up from a rock to look around. Liplessly he smiled at Loon. —They're good. If Schist can keep from messing things up at the eight eight, we should be fine.

—You can help him, Loon suggested.

Thorn gave him a sharp look, but did not disagree.

One sunset soon after that Loon was on the ridge between Lower and Upper Valleys, and up the ridge beside the ridge trail he saw Click coming down. He leaped back in fear, then looked closer and saw that it was a different old one, a real one and not a ghost. Then he was afraid in a different way, and as he hurried down the ridge trail toward camp he pondered whether it would have been worse or better if it had been Click's ghost. Possibly better. He could feel Click's back, carrying him through the night he couldn't walk;

he could see Click's snowshoe tracks, veering away to improve on Thorn's routes. A spasm of grief cause him to groan like a loon in the night.

Full winter, but the days getting longer; storms; sitting around the fire, making things and telling stories. Making love with Elga in the night when everyone else was asleep, doing it silently among the rest, feeling themselves melt together into one silently spurting and clutching beast with two backs, nearly motionless under their blankets, a way of doing it that made it strangely intense, a fusing of two into one, a secret love blossoming like a red prong out of the snow. The snow, the iced-over river. Black leads that they didn't have to go anywhere near. Elga wedge-browed at something she didn't like that Thunder or Bluejay had done, hard-eyed and silent as she thought what to do about it. Starry taking care of all the new kids. Lucky babbling, learning to talk a little, learning to walk. Making them laugh. Hawk with Ducky. Despite all the talk, the women had recently arranged several in-pack marriages. Apparently, they were told now, this was not unusual.

Eating what Schist pulled out of his holes, watching his face to see how they were doing.

Remembering the previous winter, and feeling luckier than Lucky.

In the spring when the snow had melted off the south-facing slopes, and black water was opening on the sunnier ponds, Thorn and Loon went back to the tree west of Northerly Valley where they had left Click's body to the ravens. Thorn never said a word about why they were going there, and Loon didn't either. There was no need to point out something so obvious: Click's ghost led them every step of the way, slipping through the trees ahead, occasionally looking back at them as if to make sure they were following. Thorn resolutely ignored these sightings, and Loon felt a warm humming in Badleg that made him nervous, as if the pain would come back if he did not behave well. If it had not been for Thorn's presence he most certainly would have turned tail and run back to camp like a rabbit, keeping his eyes on the ground the whole way.

They got to the tree, which Thorn located without a problem. There was Click's exposed ribcage and skull, with the other bones scattered around, moved by the little scavengers of that spring. A number of his bones were obviously missing, but then again they had not given the complete body to the ravens anyway.

Silently Thorn and Loon gathered the bones. Almost all of them were picked clean. Thorn stacked them carefully against each other, like sticks of firewood arranged for easiest carrying. Loon carried the skull inside the ribcage, at Thorn's request. Before putting the skull and jawbone in the ribcage, Loon touched the skull to Badleg, and whispered inside himself, Thank you Click. If you want to help me, stay in me here. If not, go to your place in the sky, and leave Thorn alone.

They carried the bones down to the narrow pond that was the highest one in the canyon they were in. On the deepest part of the shore, Thorn took Click's skull and jawbone out of his ribcage. He sang the spirit-freeing song:

When we die
We fly into the sky
And everything begins again

Loon looked at Click's thick bony brow, his bulky forehead, his skull so long, his big worn chompers. His teeth still looked just as they had in life when they had been revealed from inside his lips in a fear grin, or a shy smile. Seeing that gave Loon another stab of grief, a hot rush in his eyes and throat. The skull was both Click and not Click. A body was just clothing; Click was his spirit, as was made clear by his ghost, still out there in the forest with them. Although now he was concealed, which was a great relief, even though they could feel that he was nearby.

Thorn sang with his eyes closed, then opened them. He looked around, and it was clear he saw nothing but the ice-edged pond, the trees, the tight valley walls, the sky. Loon saw a weight lift off Thorn's shoulders at that moment.

Loon took in a deep breath, let it out. He realized, by the bee-like humming that had now started in his leg, that Click's spirit was inside him, occupying the numb spot in his ankle. Again he decided that Badleg's new name would be Click. Badleg was gone. Loon would carry Click along inside him and hope that Click would be his friend, even though Loon had been forced to eat some of him. That seemed like a lot to ask. But Click had been willing to help them. Ever since Heather had tended him back to life, he had been willing to serve. So, possibly that would continue. Loon would find out later.

For now there was just Loon and Thorn, alone in the forest. Carefully they set the bones in an open patch of black water and watched them sink into the pond, one by one, while they chanted together the good-bye:

We who loved you in the time you lived
Who cared for you as you cared for us
We lay you to rest now   to sleep in Mother Earth
So your spirit can live on in peace
Free of this world   in dreams above the sky
We will always remember you

In the seventh month of that year, with Elga pregnant again, they left for their summer trek, past the Ice Caps and then north to the steppes. The walking was so unlike their forced march home of the year before that their escape seemed more than ever a dream. Or else this now was the dream; to Loon it often felt like one. The skies were clear, the air warm; the salmon run at Cedar Salmon River gave them more than they could eat. When they had smoked a load of fish they walked on, hauling the travois only a fist or two at a time. Short hikes, long rests, with every valley, every ford, pass, rest stop, and camp familiar to them. On the steppe they followed the trails along the curving streams north to their caribou ravine, and though there were not as many caribou this year as two years before, they still managed to direct a line of the beasts into their chute with its little cliff, and the resulting glut of meat kept them busy both day and night.

One night before going to sleep Elga and Loon went down to the river to wash off, and they heard two loons downstream. Loon looned his loon cry, and the loons looned back, and then Elga tried it, and the loons hesitated, and then answered her too. They held each other and laughed aloud to be so blessed. There's nothing like a loon's cry.

Then it was new moon of the eighth month, and they were off to the festival. Everyone in the pack began to act a little jumpy, but none of them could possibly have been as nervous as Loon, who could not bring himself to leave Elga's side for even a moment. She was about halfway through her pregnancy.

So they came into the festival valley in a completely different mood than in summers past, clumped tightly together, with the men at the fore and all the kids tucked in among the women, who were dressed to kill, their hair braided and tied up in a way they usually would be only for the eighth night dance. The men's spears were prominent in a way they wouldn't normally be at festival. Schist and Ibex and Thorn took the lead, with Hawk and Moss and Nevermind and

Spearthrower flanking them, and even as they proceeded to their usual campsite they called out to the corroborators that they had arrived and needed a judgment.

And it was true they did, for the northers were already there, at the northern end of the meadow in their usual spot, if they came at all, and their men had spotted the Wolves and were even now crossing the camp, spears in hand. This made it clear to the corroborators that their presence was required, and they too converged at speed from wherever they had been. All this hurrying and shouting drew everyone else at the festival too, of course.

The ice men were roaring, —There they are! Thieves, murderers! We want justice! We're going to kill them if we don't get it!

But Schist was good at projecting an immovable resolve, and he stood at the point of the Wolf men holding his spear in both hands across his chest. All the Wolf men stood the same, spears up and ready. Loon's heart was thumping hard in his throat. He stood right next to Elga.

The big men among the corroborators bulled to the center of the growing crowd, and one of them shouted for order. Festival protocol demanded compliance to this command; any fighting now would cause the fighters to be beaten ferociously and then kicked out of the festival, and perhaps not allowed to come back. Most of the corroborators were from the packs who lived closest to the festival grounds, and they wouldn't abide any challenges to their rule; if they sensed that their right to rule was being questioned they would swell up like toads and mass together like lions at a kill, their eyes fixed and round. They were like that now, bristling, ready to leap and pummel. Seeing them like that made it clear that the northers and Wolves were by no means the most dangerous men there, even if they were the angriest. And some of this anger was a pretense, it had to be; the crimes causing the anger had happened many months before.

The corroborators' spokesman threw up his hand. The crowd went silent.

—Speak, he said heavily, glaring at the northers in a way that made it clear he meant, Speak and speak only.

One of the jende from one of the other houses spoke for them, a man Loon had worked for a few times in the ravines, and at the sound of this man's voice Loon's stomach shrank to the size of a nut.

Some of the corroborators knew the jende tongue, and one of those gave a short version of the norther's statement in the southern tongue most of the people there spoke. It was as expected: Loon's pack had stolen one of their women three summers before, and the following summer they had taken her back, and prevented Loon from stealing her again. Then Loon's people had invaded their camp and with Loon's help burned down a house and kidnapped her again. The attack had hurt a bunch of people, a woman and child had died by scalding, and one of their biggest houses had been destroyed.

—The woman in question came to us on her own three summers ago, Schist declared as soon as the translator had finished. —She was never a part of these ice men's pack. She doesn't even speak their tongue. She came from the east, and joined us at this festival of her own free will. You all saw it. She married into us and we took her in. Then the ice men stole her. Then we got her back. We did what had to be done. It's too bad some of their people got hurt, but we didn't start it.

Lots of shouting from the jende men followed this statement, and Schist's fierce retorts cut right through them. Louder and louder insults led to the shaking of spears, and at that the corroborators swelled even bigger, and hefted their thick sticks over their heads, ready to strike. Again their spokesman raised his hand, in a fist this time, and the noise wavered and then died down.

Suddenly Elga stood forward between Thorn and Schist, with Lucky in her arms. Hastily Loon stepped up behind her.

—I came from the east, she declared loudly,

From a pack on the other side of the mountains east of here.
Most of my people were killed in a spring flood,
And the rest of us went to find our brothers
Who had married to the west of us, among the Horse pack.
They took us in, and they came here to this festival.

These ice men heard what had happened to us, and
    captured me.
I got away from them after a time
And came back here and joined this Wolf pack.
The women of Wolf pack took me in,
And I married this man Loon, and had his child.
Then the next summer the ice men stole me again.
I was a captive of theirs and they treated me badly.
They keep captive wolves to do their hunting,
And maybe that's what gave them the idea to do the same
    with people,
Because they have captives they don't treat like real people.
But I say, anyone who keeps captives,
THEY are the ones who are not real people.
I'll never go back to them. I'd kill myself
If you made me. It's too bad some of them got hurt
When I was rescued by my husband and my pack,
But it's their fault. They started it
And so now   THEY DESERVE NOTHING AT ALL.

She said these last words in a voice so choked and furious that
everyone jumped back a little. Loon and the rest of the Wolves were
amazed, their eyes wide, mouths agape; they had never heard their
Elga say even half as much as this, and never in such a strangled
angry voice. But now was the time. Elga who always slipped aside;
this time she had gone straight at it. Now she stared around at the
crowd, and they could not take their eyes from her. She had won
the day.

The ice men had their answers for her, of course. They contested
what she had said, and insisted that people had not just been hurt,
that a child had died by scalding, a woman too later on. And a house
had been torched, and things stolen, and so on. Even without the
translator it was clear what they were saying. It was beginning to
seem like the two languages being spoken shared more words than
anyone had realized until now.

Schist didn't concede any of their points in any way, but only began to grate out more insults. Then Ibex joined him in that. This began to enrage some of the ice men, and the toad-swollen corroborators turned toward Schist and Ibex; they didn't like it either. The young Wolf men were not shouting with Schist and Ibex, they were letting their leaders stand to the fore, and this was encouraging more abuse from the ice men, while also making Schist more vehement.

Thorn finally cut in front of Schist and Elga and raised his hand, which held one of Loon's new pair of snowshoes, tied together with red cords. When silence fell, Thorn said,

I took back our people from these kidnappers.
I went in like an otter into a beaver's den
And wreaked some havoc so we could make our escape.
The man they took is my apprentice,
A young shaman in the making, pretty good as a painter.
His wife came to us from somewhere else,
Maybe even from these ice men,
I don't know and it doesn't matter.
She's part of our pack now, she chose us herself
And our women took her in.
So what we did has been right all along.
But listen, for the sake of the eight eight,
We're willing to make some compensation
For any damage we did when we rescued her.
We took four pairs of snowshoes with us,
And now we're willing to give them back,
To make up for whatever their losses happened to be.
And these new snowshoes are better than theirs,
They're the best snowshoes ever made.
These ice men couldn't make snowshoes this good
Even if they knew how to do it,
Because they don't have the right kind of trees in their
     frozen-butt land.
So they should be happy and the whole matter over,

Over for good and no more claims,
No more sniveling like babies that don't get their way,
No! No! No! (shouted loudly) We make good any bad we do,
Like any pack that knows how to get along,
And then it's simply over, that's all.

The last part of Thorn's speaking was aimed mainly at the corroborators, who liked being appealed to. They liked it also when Thorn gave them the four pairs of snowshoes to pass along to the northers. Loon and the other Wolves passed them forward, each pair tied together bottom to bottom by red leather cords. Loon found himself holding his breath, as if in the crucial moment of a hunt. He forced himself to breathe.

The corroborators, and the crowd too, were pleased that Thorn and his pack had thought to bring compensation. The ice men were of course still very unhappy, but they were also eyeing the new snowshoes that the corroborators held in the air, interested despite themselves. Their men conferred briefly; it looked like their headman was urging his hotheads to be satisfied. And indeed, when they were done they spoke in low tones to the corroborators' translators, and those men nodded and spoke briefly among themselves. Their spokesman leaned into the discussion, and after listening for a time nodded with a satisfied expression. He and his helpers took up the four pair of snowshoes and walked with them held overhead to the northers, and gave them to four of the norther men with a ceremonial flourish. Then the spokesman for the corroborators held both his hands overhead, palms out, as he rotated in place and blessed the crowd.

—This matter is settled, he announced loudly. —No more fighting over this, be warned! It's exile for good to anyone who disturbs the peace about this any more.

—And Elga is ours, Heather added loudly from the center of the Wolves.

—Yes, the festival spokesman said, looking pointedly at the ice men. —The woman Elga belongs to the Wolf pack. Know that, all of you!

Briefly the crowd cheered or howled, then dispersed. Twenty-twenty people at least were standing there in the broad meadow, and now they all wanted to trade and dance. It felt good to think they could douse such a fire with words alone. Everyone knew that when packs fought people got hurt, even killed, after which it could go on for years. It was not that uncommon. But not this time. The dispute would give them something to talk about for a while, which was another pleasure, but mostly it was time to forget it and start dancing.

So then the eight eight went on as it always did. The Wolf pack stuck together more than usual, and Loon never left Elga, who never left their camp, so that it was a subdued festival for them. Everyone avoided the jende, and the northers stayed away from the Wolf camp. No one got in any fights. Even the young men who wanted to fight didn't want to fight there. In the end the jende left two mornings later, without either apologizing or accepting apologies.

So all was well. But Heather scowled when Loon said that to her in the camp, when only she could hear.

—We're just lucky your shaman was there, she said, —because bad as he is, he's not as stupid as Schist.

—What?

—It was Schist's task to make peace, and instead he was throwing fat on the fire. Thorn had to step in and save him. Schist has gone foolish trying to match Thunder and Bluejay, and it's dangerous to have a fool as your headman. He was never that good, and Ibex is worse. And now Hawk is making him so nervous that he's worse than ever.

—Hawk?

Heather stared at Loon. —There is a curse on this pack, she muttered to her right hand as she turned away. —All its men are stupid. All but the unspeakable one, and he's unspeakable.

—I don't know what you mean, Loon said.

—I know.

Elga laughed at Loon's stickiness during the rest of the festival, so like Lucky's all the time, and she looped a long knitted horsehair scarf around all three of their necks to mark their bond. They walked around always together. Part of Loon was giddy with relief, while another part of him was still twisted to a little ball of apprehension, and the two feelings mixing together made him unsteady, a little sick-drunk, even though he drank none of the mash. The gorgeous attire of all the people passing their camp was more than his eye could take in, and everything blurred as if beyond the rising heat of a fire, or in the side vision of a dream. At the big bonfire on the eighth night, he watched the bursts of colored fire that spilled out of the firemasters' sachets, and looked around at the dancers, and the stars overhead, and it seemed to him that everything was made of banners of colored fire, shimmering in their burn from one moment to the next. He held the scarf running from his neck to Elga's, felt her tugging him here and there like a child, realized the tug itself meant he was not dreaming, because it was all too much right there tugging at his neck, too real to deny.

On the morning of the last day, he and Elga and Lucky went to the broad sandy bank of the meadow's river, where there was a group of men in the sun busy at work on their bird's eye views. As always it was mostly an old man's game, and the more they had wandered in their lives the better they were at it, and the more interested. It was a traveler's game. Now a lot of old men, and a few old women, maybe two score in all, were strolling about watching those who were actively making views.

The makers crouched and tiptoed about on the edges of their patches, stretching far out to smooth and shape the sand to what they thought some part of the world would look like from the sky, if shrunk to the size of their patch. The areas they portrayed were sometimes big, extending from the festival grounds and the caribou steppe to the mountains to the south, and the great salt sea to the west. Others portrayed smaller areas. There were distinct styles, which Loon thought were somewhat like the way wall paintings were either three-liners or fully detailed: some views were made simply of wet sand molded into the shapes of the land by hand and stick, so that one saw the stripped flesh of the land, so to speak; others used moss for meadows, twigs for trees, pebbles shoved into the sand to look like the gleam of water seen from on high, even some little toy animals and shelters and people, taken from kids' camp games. Someone had even packed down snow to represent the ice caps on the central highlands, and in one old woman's view, even the great ice wall of the north, here ankle high.

It was funny to see these little worlds as if one were an eagle at the highest point of its gyre, and some of the decorated views were quite beautiful. But what the makers mostly discussed was how accurate they were. Long sticks were used to point out features; traveling stories were related, with lots of argument about what a day's walk meant in terms of a stretch of land. This last argument was impossible to resolve, both in principle and in relation to the shrinking they had done to reduce a big part of the earth to three strides on a side; but it obviously gave many of them immense pleasure to discuss it at length, with sand hills and canyons to point to: —I was in this valley you mark as shallow, but it's deeper than that, I passed through it twelfth month and the sun never came over the southern ridge, so you need to have it deeper. —Maybe so, here I'll scoop it down a bit.

And so on. At the end of the session they would all declare their favorites, and a best of day would be declared, and the winner given a bucket of mash and a chance to brag for a fist or two, and then they would all stand around the edges of the view, observers and makers both, and leap out onto the little worlds and tromple them to a chaos of torn sand, worse than the mud at a caribou ford. Gods destroying worlds: and while it lasted it was the best dance of all, they shouted and laughed as they leaped and kicked, it felt glorious.

Still, Loon only really began to relax when the festival was over and they had dragged their dried meat and new goods back home to their abri over Loop Valley.

In autumn we eat till the birds go away,
And dance in the light of the moon.

    Loon began to feel like his life was real. Ever since his wander, it had not felt real; it had felt as if in some instant of the wandering days he had wandered into a different world and never come back out. Wandered into a dream and not woken up. That happened to people; some of Thorn's stories told of it happening, and Loon fully believed it, because it had happened to him before, as a child, when his mother died. And then again during his wander.

    And now, yet again. He had walked into a different dream, stepped through the place where all the worlds meet, into the next world over. In this one the clench slowly left his belly, and he could laugh without a catch in his throat. Elga sat there by the fire, big among the other women, fattening up on the autumn's bounty, growing big around the new child inside her, soon to be born; still not much of a talker, and eyes hard as pebbles, always watching; but always there, too, listening to the other women and nodding patiently, asking questions that kept them going. The questions made her sound skeptical, but Loon noticed that her eyes would be on Lucky, or the skyline, as she talked with the other women, and with a simple —But why? she could have the other woman talking for most of the next fist, while Elga continued to eye something else beyond their talk. She could do several things at once. She was harder than before, no doubt about it. But she still had a warm spot for Loon, he could see that in the way she looked at him, feel it in her hands and the way she kissed him at night. She seemed to give him the thanks for her rescue, although Loon didn't think he deserved it, as he had had to be rescued himself; and in the end it was Elga who had hauled him home.

    But it was true that Elga was thankful to Thorn too, as she made clear often, bringing the old sorcerer things by the fire, or down by the river, or at his bed: ladles of soup, needles, birdskins, buckets of water, morsels from the kill. Loon did the same when it occurred to him, and he saw how much Thorn liked Elga's thanks, much more than Loon's, which he accepted as only what was due. Loon ignored that, which seemed proper to him anyway. Thorn had come and rescued them, and now Loon was going to be the pack's next shaman, it looked like, so he needed Thorn to teach him things. It was exactly the reverse of how he had felt after his wander, which again made him feel like he had fallen into a different world. As for Thorn with Elga, no doubt it felt good to Thorn when she was nice to him, considering the treatment he always got from Heather, her constant needling. Very different to have a woman be sweet and kind, and a young strong woman at that, fat with child.

Also: Elga never thought about what had happened to Click. She did not see Click's ghost, or if she saw it, pretended to perfection that she didn't. She refused even to see how the haunting had affected Thorn, or Loon too for that matter. She never mentioned the past at all. Thorn liked that in her.

Because for Thorn the past was still alive. Loon could see it. There was a dream world Thorn could stumble into, even while fully awake. Although it was true that since they had buried Click's bones in the lake, Click's spirit had stopped hanging around at the edges of the firelight. He was not inside Badleg either, as Loon could tell because he walked around painlessly, and without the sound of humming bees from inside him. The lack of pain there remained new enough to Loon that he remembered to know it was a miracle. It seemed to him a clear sign that the burial had been good, and Click's spirit content. And it looked like Thorn was seeing signs of this too, although he was still wary at the end of most nights; he kept his gaze on the fire itself, and did not look sideways or out into the night. And so there were no more moments when his fireside face would turn to a wooden mask as he looked out at the flickering trees at the edge of the light.

But then one day Hawk brought back an antler fragment he found in Quick Pass, and gave it to Loon while Thorn was there. The moment he saw it Loon snatched it up and tried to keep Thorn from seeing it; unfortunately the snatching motion drew Thorn's eye, and before Loon had it hidden in his fist Thorn too had seen: it looked just like Click's body after they had eaten the legs, the same truncated thighs at one end and long head at the other, all rough but obvious. And Thorn recognized it. His mouth tightened hard at the corners. Click's spirit had said hello to him.

Loon took the antler fragment away, and refused to see the little incisions that one could have made to clarify the neck and crotch, which would have made it a toy in just the shape of Click's body. Instead he cut away with his burin until the fragment was splittable, and then split it and turned the lengths into needles for Elga and Heather and Sage. So much for that.

Although it could also be said that now Click's spirit was always there among them, and getting all sewn up in the seams of their clothes, and occasionally even sticking them in the thumbs. Loon realized he should have just lost the fragment in the forest, or cast it with the appropriate song into the pond with Click's bones. He still didn't have enough practice dealing with ghosts to understand how subtle they could be.

Thorn did, having spent many years in concourse with them; and the look on his face as Loon had hurried away with the antler piece had said that there was no way to avoid a spirit, if they wanted to visit you. One could do one's best to assuage it, but in the end the spirit did what it wanted.

So Thorn kept his head down, and was as peaceable as he had ever been. He tended the sick with a particular regard, formal and distant, but intent and meticulous. Scared of Fire started vomiting, and Thorn listened to his breathing, then conferred with Heather before devising his healing ceremony; and when consulting her, he treated Heather with the same regard he gave to Scared. All of his ceremonies he performed with particular care. He did the monthly counts with perfect etchings on his yearstick. He made his old jokes. He ran the kids through their songs and riddles in the mornings.

All this unthorny behavior, as if with Elga there about to give birth, and Lucky underfoot, he could be content despite all his thinking. And yet one night when the fire had died down and he was approaching his bed, he stifled a cry and stepped back. Loon saw

this from his own bed and exclaimed, —What? before he could stop
himself.

Thorn didn't answer. He was standing back, hands out, staring
at his empty bed. Loon tried to look sidelong, not wanting to see.
Thorn's bed appeared empty to him. But not to Thorn. Loon flexed
Badleg a little, felt nothing there. Click was not in him.

Loon didn't know what to do. He had never heard any stories
about such a situation, and it wasn't clear to him what Thorn might
want him to do. Well, Thorn would want him to stay out of it. Possibly there was something Thorn could say now to Click, something
he could do . . .

And yet he seemed at a loss. His lips were flopping like a fish out
of water, mouthing words soundlessly, just like fish did. Loon had
never seen him so taken aback.

Finally Thorn pulled himself together, drew himself up, sighed
heavily. He flicked the back of his hand, the way he would at kids
who had gotten in his way. —What? he complained in a low voice.
—What am I supposed to do? Just tell me and I'll do it.

Then he stood there for a long time. Finally he went back down
to the fire. Loon fell asleep before he returned, having never seen
Click or felt a twinge.

That winter people began to say that Thorn had lost his luck. They
didn't know about Click, they didn't see Click around the camp,
but still they saw something in Thorn, and said what they said. Not
when he could hear them, of course, although sometimes he heard it
anyway. If he did he only turned his head away, sometimes nodding
to himself. The hunters often talked about losing their luck, that
was the only way one could deal with it; you had to face up to Narsook, and if it happened to you, let your friends know about it, and
let them take the lead for a while to help you, and then something
might happen and your luck would come back to you.

But for shamans it was different. They ventured into realms far
beyond luck, into dreams, into the sky, into animals and Mother
Earth. They entered spirits, and spirits entered them. Clearly they

needed their luck to do that, or something like luck; and if their luck was gone, not only would their shaman's work get harder, but the whole pack might suffer. So no one liked to see it, and after a while, anyone who talked about it was told to shut up.

On a cold winter's night, a new person was born into Wolf pack. A woman, salmon clan. The men sat around the fire smoking from Thorn's pipe. Thorn sang a long version of the swan wife story, laughing cheerfully at his own jokes, and cuffing Loon more affectionately than ever before.

Loon spent a lot of time with Elga and Lucky and the new babe, and in helping Thorn do things. When he wasn't busy, he carved figures out of antlers and little sticks of mammoth ivory they had gotten at the festival. Some were toys for their new baby. Elga was happy to see them, but she was tired with the new baby, and distracted with the things going on among the women.

—Is everything all right? Loon would ask when he saw her face.

—No, she would say. —But it's the women's affair, nothing you can do anything about. Thunder and Bluejay are beginning to notice that no one likes them anymore. Actually no one ever liked them, but they think it's changed to that, and that the change is my fault. Which it is, too. So, it's too late for them now, but they're just realizing that and are mad about it, and making things worse to make them better. Which never works. But we have to get through that one way or another. Don't you worry about it. Someday you and your friends may have to get involved in a solution. But right now you just take care of Thorn.

—I will.

Before giving the little carved figures to the baby to play with, he took them to Thorn and asked for his comments on them. Same with his cliff paintings in Upper Valley, and his charcoal boulders on the river, which he asked Thorn to visit and look at. Thorn would join him in a walk to the river, then when they were there Loon would walk over the river's ice and go to work. Curve after curve, animal after animal.

Thorn would sit by a little fire he would light, interested in Loon's work. When they returned to camp after these days, he often took out a big smooth slate and a stick of earthblood mixed with beeswax, and gave them to Loon and then called out animals and postures for Loon to three-line:

—Hyena looking over its shoulder at you.

—Ibex horns, seen from behind.

—Ibex horns seen from straight on.

—Bull elg, wasted after the rut.

—Baby rhino stuck in the mud.

—Female lion on the hunt. Oh, that's very nice. That's the exact look in her eye there, with just a dot and a tear line.

—Stallion throwing his head up to threaten a rival near his wives. Ah, well done. You are getting very good at horses.

Loon didn't know what to make of these unthorny comments, but just wiped the slate clean and waited for the next prompt. —Horses are beautiful, he said.

—Yes.

Both of them only looked on when Hawk and Moss went at it with Schist and Ibex. This could be regarded as an aspect of Thorn losing his luck, in that if they had a shaman feared by all, then they might have behaved better in front of him. But probably it would have happened no matter what, because Schist kept making decisions about food that no women but Thunder and Bluejay and Chamois liked, from the winter stores to that night's meal. And also because Hawk and his friends were now bringing home most of the winter meat. And really because the two of them had never liked each other, not since when Schist had been Hawk's babysitter, Heather said.

So they knapped away at each other, bang, bang, bang, and sparks would fly. Schist would be sitting by the fire sniffing his mash, and Hawk would come into camp all bloody with a saiga rear over his neck and the hooves hanging down his chest before him. The mass over his shoulders gave him a bison look, and as he passed between Schist and the fire he dipped his head toward Schist, as if to a female being told to submit. Schist saw it and surged to his feet, which meant he almost got a hoof in the eye, and he swept the hoof aside, but this brought the other hoof into the side of his face, even though Hawk was stepping back as it happened, and could pretend it was an accident and laugh. Schist fumed while Hawk hefted the rump and legs off his head and held them out as if to protect himself. Schist cursed him, red-faced, and Hawk waggled the saiga hooves at him, another bull command to bison women. —Out of my way, old man. I was just trying to get by the fire to the cutting stone, don't know why you jumped up at me like that!

To which Schist could only scowl and stomp off to the wood pile.

Endless number of incidents like that. It got tedious. Their jokes were too pointed. There were two score nine of them in the pack now, and three of the married women were pregnant. In a lot of ways things were good. They had not starved last spring very much, and it was looking like they were going to be all right for the coming spring. Seemed like that could last for year after year; so why the tension? Was it just something about the men who took charge, the ones who wanted to be headman? The young one going after the old one, the old one fighting back? They saw that a lot out in the herds. But did the pack really need a headman? A lot of packs seemed to work fine without them; the men did what needed doing, the women made the family and clan decisions without fuss in a continuous flow of talk, and things went fine. It would be good to be in a pack like that. Loon had cause to wonder whether Hawk would like it too. But he thought Moss would. And Hawk disposed, but Moss proposed. This was something Loon knew without Heather's help, that he had seen his whole life, since they were all little boys together.

Once Loon was down by Ordech-Meets-Urdecha, and he came on two rhinos having a fight in a snowy meadow. He stepped back behind a tree and sat to look around it and see them. The wool on the two low round creatures was thick and long, black on top, crusted with snow on their undersides. They were funny-looking animals, like the unspeakables of the forest but with their horns proud and dangerous-looking, like prongs on their nose turned into spears. These were their weapons; they seldom bit each other, but instead swung their heads sideways together in great clacking collisions that sometimes caused them to stagger back and the skin around the base of their horns to bleed. A quick sideways thrust could cut a throat or put out an eye, so it could go from a dominance fight to a deadly quarrel at any instant, and almost every bull rhino was scarred around his head.

Now these two faced off, snorting and panting. They had been at it a while and both were bloody, the snow under them splotched with red. Their little eyes bulged as they glared at each other and waited for an opening: they wouldn't have seen Loon even if he had danced right between them.

They slapped horns together in the usual way, with a kind of dance timing that reminded Loon how much the two fighters had to be in agreement to fight. The clacks sounded like when big solid barkless branches were knocked together, but more hollow.

Then one dipped his head left, and when the other swung to meet it, ducked his horn under and jerked it straight up. The other one saw this and leaped back to avoid the upward thrust, and immediately the first one charged, slapping left and right with furious speed, battering horn against head in a rapid sequence of smacks. The retreating one turned while roaring, very agile on its hooves, and ran hard away. The winner could have followed and horned him in the rump if he had wanted to, but he stood foursquare on the bloody snow and lifted his nose, sniffing disdainfully and then opening his little mouth to emit a short low roar.

Loon went out on a winter hunt with Hawk and Moss and Nevermind and Spearthrower. Thorn came along too; now that he had recovered his strength, he could keep up with the young men in all but their fastest sprints.

Up Lower's Upper, onto the broad moor to the north. Ah the huge pleasure of walking hard with his friends, uphill and down, pushing the pace, out on a dawn patrol. Left leg stiff, and with a little numbness inside, suggesting things Loon shouldn't try, reminding him always to rely on Goodleg to take the load when there were any questions: but no pain. Ah the glory of the dawn hunt!

They were going to go west on the plateau, along its edge to the head of Northerly canyon, and then creep down the headwall to the meadow below the cleft between the Ice Tits, where a herd of bison appeared to be wintering. If they got to the Giants' Knapsite before the bison passed by, they might be able to spear some from their usual blind. They had not been there since the previous fall.

It was a crisp late winter dawn, the air in the valley hazy. Fire-starter was plunging into the western skyline, dimming as the sky went gray and then pale blue. The rabbit in the moon was stirring her red paint to throw at the dawn. The meadow at the head of Northerly canyon was empty except for a handful of snow hares, nearly invisible in their white coats, looking nervously around, nostrils pulsing. They were very hard to kill with a throwing spear, which did not keep the men from trying a throw from above, everyone at once, a rain of long flexing spears lancing down onto the meadow, and by chance one of them pinned a running hare right to the grass. It was dead by the time they got down to retrieve it, and it turned out to be Loon's spear. —Thank you! Loon exclaimed to the hare with a brief kiss to its forehead. He bagged it and looped the bag over his belt at his back, and the hare joined him for the rest of the day, which would make him fast. It would also add to their scent, but they were already completely obvious to the animals with a nose anyway, so it didn't matter. They would cook the hare if they stayed out that night.

Down the winding route they had established in Northerly's highest part. Through a notch between rocks taller than they were, down to the Giants' Knapsite, to wait in the blind and see which way the wind blew.

The Knapsite was a tumble of big flinty boulders, mostly free of smaller rocks. The exposed cliff above them was spalling onto the slope below it, and the slope was at an angle that sorted the rocks by size, with the biggest falling the farthest, as usual. Some house-sized boulders had rolled far enough out to pinch a meadow that curved around them and extended both upstream and down.

There was a flat spot incised into the top of one of these boulders, as if the giants had wanted men to hide there. They hauled themselves up a number of knobs that allowed one to climb the boulder's uphill side. The incised platform was big enough to hold all of them easily, and its lookout spot gave a view of the head of the curving meadow. The valley walls were steep, and lightly forested with brush pines. The wind was flowing downstream in typical morning style, so if any animals came downvalley they would not smell the men or the dead hare. It was warm for a winter day, though cold in the shade. The sound of the creek making its slow turn under the ice came mostly from the lead at the outlet, clucking away.

Hawk took the lookout first, and soon hissed, and the men fell completely silent as they flowed to positions beside him, hoping to see for themselves.

The bison were there. A little pack of them, hairy-headed and ragged after the winter. Nine women bison followed the chief bull, the women in better proportion than the men because they did not have such massive heads. Beautiful creatures, as always, their close tan fur only a little darker than lions' fur, their hairy heads the brown nearest black; all moving slowly together, chewing their cuds, the sunlight diving right into their bodies, so that they glowed with their weight, floated on the snow of the meadow like visitors from a denser world. Dream creatures, walking through the waking world.

Three of them had birds standing on their rumps, the birds patiently poking around in the beasts' fur in search of the fly grubs growing in there. The grubs were a delicacy, as the men well knew. Loon's mouth was running a little with saliva anyway, just seeing the beasts.

But the bison appeared to realize the men were there. All their tails were raised, and several were shitting or pouring out thick streams of urine, the clear yellow arcs steaming in the morning light. The majestic beasts did not have great eyesight or hearing, but their noses were good. And often if humans were close enough to see them, they just seemed to know it. Bison were hard to hunt for that reason.

Now again it was happening. They hugged the far side of the meadow from the boulders. But even over there, they were within reach of the spears. It was just about as far as they could throw them with spear throwers, so far that it would be a matter of luck to hit anything in particular.

Thorn whispered, —Shall we try?

Hawk nodded. As quietly as possible they placed the cupped ends of their javelins on the knobs on the end of their spear throwers. It took some silent maneuvering to get themselves lined up so that they weren't in each other's way.

—Don't hit anyone with your spear thrower, Thorn whispered as he always did, and they all checked their throwing space and nodded to each other: they would not hit each other, nor the boulder they were on. Ready to throw. They shifted back and forth on their feet like cats getting ready to leap, feeling in themselves how their throws should go. Then Hawk whispered, —Everyone aim for the bull in front. Ready—set—now! And they all threw at once, silently.

Most of the bison bolted as the javelins flashed through the air toward them, but two spears thwacked into the big bull, and the men cried —Yes! Or —Ha! or —Thank you! as they saw it.

—Oh I norbled my throw, Nevermind lamented, —I wristed it again.

Thorn, however, was holding his lower back with his right hand. —That hurt, he said, looking puzzled. —I must have thrown it too hard, maybe, and pulled a muscle.

—Sorry to hear, the others said.

Most of the bison were now at the lead in the meadow outlet, stamping about uneasily, looking back at the chief bull. He had his head down, and was stepping forward hesitantly, as if trying to figure out what he could do. Blood began to pour from his mouth, and some of the men said, —Yes! because one or both of the javelins must have slipped between ribs and punctured a lung. That meant the end of the chief bull. The men slapped each other on the shoulders, watching closely.

They still had their short spears left, and it was a simple task to get off the back of their boulder and stalk the mortally wounded beast, dispatch it with a charge and several thrusts to the gut and in the ribs. One of those thrusts was a heart stab, and the big beast went to its foreknees with a groan, then collapsed onto its side and died.

After that they had a hard day's work of it, getting the skin off it and breaking up the body into quarters, boning the rear legs and getting it all ready to carry home. Thorn got a fire going, and they ate the usual kill site lunch of liver and kidneys, and changed around the tasks as they got tired, while always keeping guard against lions and hyenas. A little cloud of ravens gyred over them, so they wouldn't be alone for long. It was important to get the bison chopped up as fast as was convenient. But they were in a good mood too. All but Thorn, who stayed silent.

—Are you all right? Loon asked him.

—I don't know. I must have pulled something.

Thorn was looking for Click but not seeing him. Loon considered taking another antler fragment and carving an image of Click and putting it gently down in the water of the pond where they had buried him. Then again, if he did that he might disturb one of Click's bones and distress the old one. The thought of seeing Click's skull with its familiar teeth in the water looking up at him was also bad. But to keep Click away somehow...surely there was something he could do. If this, if that: it was a little eddy of ifs that he could circle in too many times, always thrust out by that last bad image of Click's skull in the water looking up at him. Leave that spot, go somewhere else!

So it was better to keep a little distance from Thorn.

They got through the winter without too much hunger in the spring. But sometime during that winter, Loon noticed that Thorn never threw things anymore, and that he avoided lifting his right arm above his shoulder. And he got gaunter than the rest of them in the hunger month. His was just an old black snakehead now, with lion fangs swinging from the few strands of hair left behind his ears and on his neck. He seemed to be peering out at them all through something that lay between him and the rest of them. He watched Elga and the new baby, and Lucky by the fire, with a most curious expression.

One afternoon just before sunset Pippiloette came by with Quartz, the shaman of the Lion pack to the east. They hallooed into camp with gifts for all, Quartz singing a song and the women all clustering around Pippi as always, but Pippi went through them right to Loon and hugged him, held him and looked at him, saying —I'm really glad to see you here, I'm sorry about that night you got taken, I heard those northers grabbing you and I rolled into a tuck before they saw me, and after that there was nothing I could do, except follow you a while and then go tell Thorn what happened, which I did, as I'm sure he told you.

—Yes, Loon said. —It's all right. I figured that was what happened. Pippi nodded. —And all's well that ends well.

—We made it back, Loon said, feeling a little uneasy, as if it might not be true.

That night by the fire Pippi told them the story of his travels, and Quartz told the story of the bison man in the cave, one of Thorn's favorites. After that he and Thorn retired to the edge of the firelight with a bucket of mash and talked together long into the night. Loon joined them for part of this, and while he was there Thorn and Quartz discussed whose turn it was to paint the caves. The Lions were to have the spring, the Wolves the autumn. This meant the Wolves would have to deal with the problem of the cave bears coming back to sleep for the winter.

—I'll get them to leave you a cleaned bit of wall to work on, Quartz promised.

—That's good, Thorn said.

It occurred to Loon that Thorn was probably going to have to paint with his left hand, unless he made a stool to stand on.

—What will you paint? Quartz asked Thorn.

—I'm thinking about horses, Thorn said. —How about you?

—We're talking about doing some ibex and mammoths. Quartz looked at Loon and said politely, —And what about you? If Thorn lets you do anything?

—I saw two bull rhinos fighting, Loon said. —I'd like to try that.

Then one night Thorn froze once more as he approached his bed nook.

—Not you again, he muttered, followed by something else Loon couldn't make out. After a while standing there, Thorn raised up his hands and entered his little nest. He sat down hard on his bed. —Let me be, he said in a low voice that Loon could just hear. —What else could I have done, you tell me that. You see what came of it. That's all I have to give you. Look at them and leave me alone.

But Click must not have been convinced. Thorn saw him often now, usually at night when he went to bed.

And something kept hurting him in the ribs. Just talking sometimes he would wince, or when walking come to a sudden halt, sometimes with a hiss. Once in the forest, when he thought he was alone, Loon saw him stop and sit down.

He even went to Heather about it. Loon was there helping her, and when Thorn saw he was there he frowned, and then sat down and asked Heather to take a look at him. Heather had him take off his cloak, and touched him all over his torso with her fingertips. Then she put her ear to his back and chest and mouth, smelled his breath and skin, felt his pulse. She made him move his arms around, and noted when he winced. She saw what Loon had seen, that his right arm could not go over his head.

When she was done, she crabbed over to her herb shelf and nosed around among the little bags lined up on it. —I don't know, she said without looking at Thorn.

Only Loon was there with them, and with a brief glance at him, Thorn said, —Come on, tell me. Tell me what you don't know.

She snorted. —I don't know anything. Just as you have always told me.

—Well, it's true, isn't it?

—Yes. So, here. She gave him a bag. —It will dull the pain. And smoke your pipe.

—But if it's my lung?

—A little smoke won't matter.

Thorn gulped, then glowered at her; he didn't like what she was suggesting, he didn't want her telling him that. His lip curled in an ugly little snarl, and she stared back at him flint-eyed. Loon saw that the two of them were not going to be getting along any better now that Thorn was sick.

After that Thorn ignored Heather and everyone else, and got on with his days as usual, often going out to scavenge firewood, or gather shaman herbs and mushrooms. He started the day by smoking his pipe. Around the fire he watched Elga and Lucky and the baby. By the way his eyes stayed fixed on things and did not look around, Loon concluded that he was seeing Click follow him around through the course of his day. After this went on for a while, something in the way Thorn wouldn't look to his right revealed both that Click's ghost was sitting there beside him, and that he did not mind it as much as he had before. He forbore to look that way not because he was afraid, but as a kind of courtesy.

He started calling their new baby the finch, because she was alert and her movements were fast and jerky. He would sit around and watch the baby and Lucky while Elga and Loon went off to do things. And when the suncupped snow left the earth, he went off on his scavenging forays in a better mood. —Things happen, he said to Loon once when they were standing by the river watching it purl through a sunset. —There's not a thing you can do about it.

Then one morning putting wood on the fire he crouched to the ground with a muffled cry, curled around his right side. He crawled to Heather's nest, refusing help from Loon and groaning from time to time. Loon could only walk beside him, shocked and frightened.

When Thorn got to Heather's he stared up at her. —It hurts, he hissed.

—Lie down, Heather said. She helped him onto her bed. —Get yourself comfortable.

—I can't get comfortable!

—As comfortable as you can.

She was digging around in her bags. She gave him some of a root to chew, and rubbed some mistletoe berry paste into his gums. She sent Loon to get Thorn's pipe and shaman herbs. When Loon came back with them, she dug through Thorn's stuff as if it were hers, and had him eat some of his own dried mushrooms.

—Now's the time to be a shaman if ever you're going to be, she said.

Thorn did not reply. He smoked his pipe when Heather loaded and lit it for him with a splinter brought from the fire. —Why this sudden thing? he asked her when he had exhaled a long plume.

—It cracked a rib.

He stayed on her bed that night. They brought him seedcakes and bits of cooked meat, but he shook his head at them and wouldn't open his mouth even to speak, until the food was taken away. After these attempts to feed him he would sip water from a ladle, and look at Heather.

—Why should I? he said to her.

Heather didn't answer. She arranged for his furs to be brought over to her bed, and put them against a log so that Thorn could sit up. She knew before he said it that this would be a less painful position for him. She set a bucket of water by his side, with a ladle in it, and sat beside him when he tossed and turned.

—I could try to drain it, she said to him after inspecting his right side.

—Could you? Thorn's red-rimmed eyes gleamed with sudden hope.

—We can always try. It might hurt to puncture it.

—It can't hurt more than it does.

She sniffed at that, but the next morning she took him down to the riverside with Loon. She had him lie down on his left side, on the leather side of a big bearskin, right on the bank where he could put his feet and hands in the cold water of a long black lead.

—Chill yourself as much as you can, she instructed him.

He put his feet and hands in the black water. Heather washed the skin over the bump under the bottom of his ribcage, and then with one swift motion stuck him there with an awl. He hissed and trembled in the effort to stay still. She pulled out the awl, wiped the blood away with a leather patch, and stuck a long elderberry tube, like her blowdart tube but longer and narrower, into the wound she had made. Thorn was sucking air in through his teeth. Heather instructed him to move onto his belly so that the tube was pointed slightly down from the wound. He shifted and rolled onto his chest and belly, pulling his feet and hands out of the water. Blood began to run from the tube. Heather said to him, —Stick your head in the water and keep it in there as long as you can hold your breath.

He took a breath, held it, and ducked his head into the water. Heather crouched down over him and sucked hard on the end of the tube. She spat out a mouthful of Thorn's blood, then sucked again and spat out some whitish pus, not much of it. Thorn yanked his head out of the river and blew a quick few breaths and ducked in again. Heather sucked again on the tube, cheeks folding far into her toothless face. She spat out a little bit more pus, but not much was coming. She tapped the tube in a bit farther, which caused bubbles to burst the surface of water around Thorn's head. He hauled himself out yelping.

—Once more! Heather said sharply. —It's working now.

He ducked his head under again and she tried several more hard sucks, but got very little out.

Finally he pulled out of the water, gasping, and she pulled the tube from his side and pressed some dried moss against the puncture wound. Thorn crawled up the bank and sat, then dried his head with a clean leather patch. Heather washed her mouth out several times with river water.

—Any luck? Thorn asked.

—Not much, she said, looking downstream. —It's not like pus. It's more solid.

—Could you cut it out?

She looked at him, eyes round. —It's inside your ribs.

Thorn stared at her for a long time. —Fuck, he said. For a little while he breathed hard, looking down the river. Heather put her hand to his knee, and he looked back at her. For a long time they looked at each other.

—All right, Thorn said.

A fter that he stayed in Heather's bed.

Most of the pack's people stayed away from camp more than they might have otherwise. Loon passed his days with Elga and the kids, down by the river. Some days he went to see Thorn in the afternoons when Heather was out gathering. But Thorn did not want to talk.

One day Hawk and Moss were going out on a hunt, and Loon decided to go with them.

It was a cool morning, and his two friends fell into their hunting lope almost as soon as they got out of camp. Loon found he had no problem keeping up with them; he could run on his left leg in a way he hadn't since his wander, poling over that foot as if he were still wearing his wooden boot, in some kind of leaping limp. In most ways he felt stronger and faster than he ever had, and the stiff leg was like a stout walking pole, powerfully deployed. He crashed through brakes and danced over talus and scree with a speed he had never felt in him before, and when he saw how it was he took the lead from his friends and ran off with it.

He saw as he passed them how he was the third friend to them, the walking pole for their two legs. But they knew him well, and he knew them. They were grinning now to watch him fly, surprised but pleased to be huffing to keep up with him; they followed him gladly over Quick Pass and down into the meadow in Lower's Upper. On the last slope they shushed each other and began to run silently, which took the utmost finesse in one's footwork, also a complete control of one's breathing, which had to be open-mouthed and silent. After a bit of silent running it was as if their bodies were catching fire.

And running so, they came on a little herd of chamois, drinking at the meadow stream, and on sight they instantly threw their javelins, which had been nocked in their spear throwers ready to fly. The spears flew flexing through the air, and all three hit the same chamois. She was dead by the time they got to her. They howled and thanked her and set to cutting her to pieces, and Loon was as neat as

Heather with his blade, as sure as Thorn. They did the work with a clean swift rigor.

On the way home they tired, struggled, got their second wind. Humped the meat over Quick Pass and down Upper Valley back to camp, bowed over but in a steady triumph. They scarcely spoke as they returned; they hardly spoke all day.

As they approached camp Loon said, —Remember how we used to do this? Remember how I used to be the fastest, how I used to be the best hunter among us?

—Seems like you still are, Moss said. —That was quite a hunt.

—No, Loon said. —That was just today. You're the hunters now. But listen. Elga's been telling me how things are going among the women, and between Thunder and Bluejay and Schist and Ibex. It's getting bad, she says. She doesn't like it, and she doesn't think it's going to get better. So I've been thinking we should move west and start our own pack. Maybe you've already been thinking about that.

Hawk and Moss shared a look. —Tell us, Hawk said.

—There's too many of us now. So many that Schist and Ibex can't keep the pack fed through the spring. And they don't like you.

—They don't like you either, Moss pointed out.

—True, but I'm going with you. And I'll get Heather to come with us. Then beyond that, just our families.

—That will gut this pack, Moss said.

—I'm not so sure, Loon said. —Schist and Ibex will do all right with a smaller pack, just their kin and the others closest to them. They'll have that many fewer to feed, and they get along. The only thing I worry about is what they'll think of us taking Heather.

Hawk and Moss stared at him. Hawk said, —Loon, you're the only person in this whole pack who isn't scared shitless of Heather.

Moss and Hawk laughed at Loon's surprise. They were sure they could take Heather without objections, despite her obvious usefulness. Apparently it came with too much scorn, too much weirdness. Loon was relieved to hear they thought so, because he wanted his Heather.

Moss pointed out that packs did this all the time, that it didn't have to be a formal split or an angry thing, but just a matter of building a subsidiary abri upriver a ways, to reduce the crowding at the main site. If Schist and Ibex ever needed any more muscle, the younger crowd could come on down and help.

Hawk was nodding at this. Loon saw again that Moss proposed and Hawk disposed.

—But what about if they want Loon? Hawk said.

Loon would be shaman of both packs, like Quartz with the three Lion packs, or any number of the shamans at the corroboree. This Moss said while looking at Loon to see if it were true.

Loon nodded. —I want to do that, he said, —because I want to keep painting in the cave.

They were coming into camp, so Moss said, —Let's talk about it again later. There's no reason to hurry with this. Although we need to do it before we start gathering food for winter, maybe.

—Later, Hawk said.

Thorn lay sprawled over Heather's furs, leaning back against the big log wedged into the hillside. A lot of the time he slept.

Once Loon and Elga helped him stand and shuffle out onto the hillside to shit, but it hurt him to do it, and when they were getting him back to camp he said, —That's the last time I'll ever take a shit. I'll miss that.

He was mostly silent after that. When he spoke it was to himself, muttering away in a rumble no one could follow. Loon gave him water from a wooden cup, using an elderberry stick made into a drinking straw. Sometimes his cracked lips clamped down so hard on the straw that Loon could not pry it out of his mouth. Heather didn't want him drinking too much at a time, so he had to put the right dose of water in the cup, because there was no way to keep Thorn from draining it once he got going. But this thirst struck Loon as a good sign. When Thorn was asleep, Loon sometimes looked at his desiccated face, and saw his eyes were sinking back into his skull as the fat pads behind the eyes got eaten away by whatever had him. His nose was bending down like an eagle's beak, and his fingers and toes curled in as he rested. Drying out. Being eaten from the inside, by himself as well as the other thing. Living off himself for the final stretch. —Wait, I see something, he whispered once to Loon. —The river is tearing away things about me.

—An island, Loon said quickly.

—Yes. With a little snake's smile. He watched Loon's face for a while, then said, —Did something chase you, when you were out on your wander? You would never tell me. But I've been meaning to say, I think Quartz puts on his lion head and goes out at night, to put a scare in the other shamans' apprentices. He was Pika's apprentice too, the oldest one, and it made him mean. So, if some kind of thing came after you, it could have been him.

—Ah, Loon said.

Later Thorn shook off one of Heather's attempts to help him. —I've been the healer many times, he said. —I know when it won't work. You can't fool me.

Once he saw Heather's face above him, and complained to her,
—I don't like having it happen now. I'm only two twenties old.

—What do you mean only? Heather said.

—Ha! Thorn's laugh was painful to him now. —Easy for you to
say. What are you, four twenties? Five?

She shook her head. —Lots of twenties. But they're all gone now.

—Ha, Thorn said again, and lapsed back into his silence.

Much of the time he slept. Heather dosed him with teas she had made
for sleeping. Days passed, and Thorn never ate. Loon became more
and more amazed by how long it went on. It was like a bear's hibernation. There was an endurance in it that Loon could scarcely watch.

I am the third wind
I come to you
When you have nothing left
When you can't go on
But you go on anyway
That moment of extremity
Is what brings the third wind

When Thorn woke and looked around to see what was happening, Loon would feel himself go calm. The old man's gaze on him
made him feel alert and distant, it drove him into his proper place. I
helped him with that.

Thorn sometimes asked him to recite one or another of the stories he had tried to teach him. Loon did the best he could, without
worrying about any details he might forget. That lack of concern
made it a lot easier than it had been when he was a child. Just get to
the point, say what was important, say what happened in the way he
remembered Thorn saying it. He told the story of the bison man and
the wife he took from the salmon clan; Thorn had the bison for his
animal, and wore Pika's tattered old bison head during the ceremonies, and now as Loon told the old story he wondered how much it
had to do with Pika, and with Heather, and with Thorn.

—No, no, Thorn interrupted at one point in Loon's telling.
—Don't forget to tell about the woman running away with a bison, before the man turns into one himself. If they don't know that, they won't be able to figure out why he does it.

After that Thorn stopped him once or twice to tell the story himself for a while, in a hoarse voice, short-breathed.

Sometimes he asked Loon to start and then seemed to fall asleep, but frowned if Loon stopped.

Once when Loon had stopped in the middle like this, Thorn clutched his hand hard.

—You're what I had to carry it along. Do you understand? You're what I had to work with.

—I know.

—So you have to remember.

One morning at dawn Thorn woke after a hard night, in which he had never once settled comfortably. He looked around at the camp, the hills, then at Loon.

—I'm getting weaker. I can feel it.

That day he rested more easily. He drank as much water as Loon would give him. That afternoon he looked at Loon and said,

—You have to remember the story of the ten-year winter. Also the story of Corban getting blown all the way across the great salt sea and then walking back home over the ice to the north. Also Pippi's story of the man who walked east to find the end of the world. Those are the ones I liked best. Then also, how summer was pulled out of the other world into this world. And the swan wife, that's one you can really tell. And the bison man.

He studied Loon's face.

—I'll be sorry not to see what happens next, he said. —I wish I could stick around a few more years.

—Yes, Loon said.

—You have to remember. Take care of the kids. They're the ones who matter. You have to teach them everything I've taught you, and everything you've learned on your own. It will only go well if we keep passing it all along. There are no secrets, there is no mystery.

We make all that up. In fact it's all right there in front of us. You have to have enough food to get through the winter and spring. That's what it all comes down to. You have to live in a way that will gather enough food each fall to get through winter. And you, you have to live your life, youth. You can help Heather. Be sure to do that. The old witch will need it. She's getting on herself. She won't like it, but she'll need help. You'll have to see that without her asking.

—I'll try.

—Good. Listen to me now. Bad things don't just grow on one path, they're everywhere. So don't blame yourself when those things happen. Don't let yesterday take up much of today. You've always been good at that. Just keep telling the stories around the fire. That's what needs to be carried on.

Then he couldn't get comfortable; he writhed on the bed, sweated and gasped. Heather made him drink more tea, and chew a paste under his tongue. After that he was less conscious, though his body still arched and twisted in its hunt for a better position.

A couple of days later he came to and lay there calmly.

—Weaker still, he said. —I can feel it.

—Do you want some water?

—Not now.

The morning passed; no clouds, little wind. Birdsong filling the forest, the chatter of a squirrel telling someone off.

—I wanted everything, Thorn said. —I wanted everything.

—I know you did.

—I worry what's to become of you all. What's going to happen when Heather dies? There's none of you old enough to know everything you need to know. You'll be limping along like it's the dream time again. It's fragile what we know. It's gone every time we forget. Then someone has to learn it all over again. I don't know how you'll do it. I mean, I wanted to know everything. I remembered every single word I ever heard, every single moment of my life, right up to a few years ago. I talked to every person in this whole part of the world, and remembered everything they said. What's going to become of all that?

He stared for a long time at Loon.

Finally he said, —It's going to be lost, that's what.

—We'll do what we can, Loon said. —No one can be you.

They sat there. Thorn's breath was shallow and fast, and he started to sweat and squirm again. Heather showed up and Loon was glad to see her.

A long time went by, two days or three: Loon lost track. It was all the same moment, over and over. Thorn's breath got shallow, he panted and gasped. Heather wetted his lips with a wet cloth, pulled it away before he bit it. One time this seemed to rouse him, and he struggled harder, he writhed under their hands. He croaked out some words they couldn't understand, his tongue big and dry in his mouth, his throat parched. With a twist of the head he cried out indistinctly, —Oh Heather, I don't know if I can do this!

—What did he say? Heather asked Loon.

—I don't know, Loon lied.

He moved around to the other side of the bed from Heather to keep her from seeing his face. He held Thorn's right hand, and Heather picked up and held his left hand. His body lay more comfortably there between them. From time to time Heather continued to drip water from the wet cloth into his mouth, just a drop or two at a time. Thorn did not respond to this in any way. He was no longer there with them.

Only once more did he regain awareness. Heather was away doing something. He opened his eyes a little, but could not focus them. He clutched Loon's hands, and Loon said, —I'm here. Heather will be right back. She's here too.

Thorn nodded. He closed his eyes. —Wait, he whispered. —I see something. Then he squeezed Loon's hand, and went back to sleep.

Heather returned and took up her seat. They sat there holding Thorn's hands. For a long time they sat there while Thorn breathed. His breathing slowed, it got harsh in his throat. His eyes were closed, and sunken very far into his head. His mouth was a lipless hole, jaw and cheeks stubbled white with beard hairs, nose a beaky blade. The old black snake, more reptilian than ever. Asleep and more than asleep. As they held his hands it seemed to Loon that Thorn's spirit was near them, but not in the body they held. Maybe looking down on them, as the body kept breathing its last breaths.

—Go get some more water, Heather told Loon.

—But...

—Go.

Loon took up a bucket and rushed down to the river, at first hurrying to return, then glad to get away.

He stood in the shallows filling the bucket, looking around at the yellow air of an ordinary sunset, thinking, Someday I will not be here for this. That was the truth, he could feel it.

He didn't want to go back up. He lingered by the sunset river. But then he thought he heard something, and he turned and hurried back up to Heather's nest.

When he got near he could hear from the center of camp the harsh rattling in-breath of Thorn, like the crackle a raven sometimes makes. Then there was silence and he ran hard to Heather's spot. Heather was sitting there, still holding Thorn's hand. She looked up at Loon briefly, a little reproachful for the length of his time away, but Loon got back in position on Thorn's other side and took up his right hand again, and Thorn pulled another great gasp of air into him, crackling in his throat again. Several moments had passed since his last breath, and Loon jumped when Thorn seized his hand as part of this effort to breathe. Thorn was still alive, somehow, although shrunken into himself completely, and looking just as he would when he was a corpse only. But then with another startling effort he breathed again. The death rattle; then another; and in between he lay there motionlessly, and Heather and Loon sat across him holding his hands and watching him, not looking at each other except once, when Loon said, —I wonder what he is thinking in there.

Heather shook her head. —He's not there.

—But he's still breathing.

—Yes, his body keeps trying.

It was true. Again and again he stopped, lay there; seemed dead; then jerked, sucked air into himself in a paroxysm of effort, gasping, crackling, rattling. The part of him still alive was making a huge effort. Then another stillness.

—Couldn't you give him something? Loon asked. —Help him out somehow?

She shook her head. —Let him go his own way.

Loon felt the stab of that, then went numb again. They sat there and waited. When Thorn breathed, they clenched his hands. They were both hunched over with the effort of listening to him.

As it went on, slowing down each time, the rattle becoming briefer, less violent, Loon began to feel calmer. Thorn was almost done now. His suffering was over. These last breaths seemed no longer sheer stubbornness and refusal to die, but a kind of farewell. So it seemed to Loon. Little Thorn jokes. Playing dead; then a little insuck, an attempt at the rattle. Ha, fooled you again. Then the long moment of nothingness.

—It's like he's fooling us, Loon complained.

—I know.

It went on. It kept happening.

After one of these little attempts at breath, Heather said to Thorn, —It's all right. We're here.

Then they waited. There came another little rasp. Then Thorn lay there still. They waited and waited for his next breath. There did not seem to be any hurry at that moment; they could wait him out. No rush to declare it over, and be proved wrong yet again. No rush to be right about it. They could sit with him in this in-between zone, on the pass between their valley and his.

Loon would never be able to say how long they waited like that. Thorn's eyes were half open, glazed and unseeing. Now he was clearly the dead body of a dead animal. As always, death was unmistakable. So much went away.

Heather stirred at last. She reached out and closed Thorn's eyelids, then put her ear to his chest and listened. She lay against him like that for a long time.

Finally she sat up and looked at Loon. —He's gone.

They held his hands for a while longer. There was no hurry now.

SHAMAN

Everyone in the pack took something of Thorn's to remember him by, but all the things that had come to him from Pika were given to Loon, meaning his flute and pipe, and fire kit, and painting kit, and the bison-headed cloak.

Loon played the flute when they put Thorn's body on the raven platform on top of Loop Hill. It seemed to him that the flute made the music, he only had to breathe through it and listen with the rest to whatever came out. That was quite a discovery. While he played he saw everyone's faces, and he was surprised to see how distraught the other members of the pack were. He had not realized what Thorn had meant to them; he had been too close to see. He himself felt nothing.

When they were done laying his body out on the platform, Loon stopped playing the flute and said,

We who loved you in the time you lived,
Who cared for you as you cared for us
Now lay you here and give your body to the sky
So your bones can rest peacefully in Mother Earth
And your spirit live on freed of this world,
Live on in the dream above the sky
And we will always remember you.

That night by the fire, Loon stood before all the rest of them wearing Thorn's bison head, and told them the story of the swan wife. Young man marries swan woman, goes to live with the swans, it doesn't work out, he ends up a seagull. One of Thorn's favorites, and all of them had heard him tell it many times. And then Loon and Elga and Thorn had lived it.

In the same way as the flute's tunes, the words just spilled out of him. Suddenly he knew to stop knowing it. It would come breath by breath, in an even in and out, and he only had to breathe out the part of the story that fit that breath. He added a couple of skipbacks to pick up dropped points that occurred to him, he foretold a few parts; that was just part of the game. Although this time he was telling the story as simply as he could.

All that day Heather stood at the edges of the group, facing away from the rest of them, not saying a word. When he was done with the story Loon helped her back to her bed, and she seemed light to him, and ancient.

She sat on her bed. Loon looked down at her and saw her desolation, which from his curious new distance, his bird's eye view of everything, which was maybe the shaman's view, surprised him a little. She and Thorn had always fought so. —I'm sorry, he said.

She did not look at him. —I don't know who I'll talk with now, she said.

He could not fall asleep that night, and under the waning moon he realized that he wanted to go in the cave by himself, to paint something new. In the autumn it would have been Thorn's turn to go in, and Loon knew Thorn had had big plans, though as usual he had not said much about them. But Loon didn't want to wait that long. He wanted to go in now.

Next day he said to Moss, —If I work fast, Thorn's spirit will still be around to help me paint. So I have to do it before the ravens are done with him.

Moss nodded. —Heather will help gather your supplies, and we'll hold things together out here while you're inside.

—Good man. He held Moss with his gaze. —It's our turn now.

—I know, Moss said.

They helped Heather pack a backsack with the painting gear and several bags of fat for the oil lamps, also some food and a water bag. Hawk and Moss walked with him up to the cliff and its narrow ramp to the cave entry. Pika's Cave, the biggest and most beautiful of them all, right over Loop Valley. The shaman's entry to Mother Earth, the kolby of the world.

At the entry they stopped and hefted the full sack onto his back. Moss took an ember from his belt and puffed up a flame at the end of a wick, then got it arranged in a fat lamp, then lit the wick in another lamp. In the light of the afternoon it was difficult to see the lamp flames, hard to imagine they would be enough in the world below.

He sat and smoked Thorn's pipe with Hawk and Moss, both of whom sucked down their burns eagerly. They continued to smoke while Loon ate some of Thorn's dried mushrooms and artemisia, then sang the cave hello.

Hawk and Moss were looking worried; they had only been in the cave's deepest depths twice, when they were kids trying to break the rules, and the second time they had almost gotten lost. They didn't think it was safe to be going in alone like this, and though they were forced by circumstances to do dangerous things all the time, maybe that made them even less inclined to take on any unnecessary dangerous things, and in cold blood.

But that was what shamans did. So they sat to each side of him and pressed into him shoulder to shoulder as he sang the cave hello, and they sang too when they knew the words. There was quite a bit of wonder on their faces as he hugged them good-bye and took off, into the big dark kolbos of the passage at the back of the day chamber of the cave, down into the dark.

As he walked into the passage it was broad at first and lit by daylight. Then came the turn into the dark, followed by a narrow passage. As he shuffled past that turn the shadows got blacker, and his lamps shed more and more light, until they were all he was seeing by, the two flames brilliant in his hands. As he walked the lit walls and black shadows shifted with him, flickering with the same flicker as the lamp flames, so that it was clear they all made one thing.

He stopped for a while to let his eyes adjust, as Thorn had taught him, and then continued forward with the short steps that were best in the cave, to be sure the floor had no unseen blocks or drops. It would be very bad to fall and knock out his lamps. Thorn had tried to teach him to spark a fire in the dark, using the sparks themselves to see the duff well enough to light it, and touch the wick to the burning duff, and breathe the wick back to flame; but it had proved to be very hard. Now Loon carried a live ember inside a burl in his belt, which would make it much easier to relight the lamps if he needed to. But it would be so much better not to need to. Better to treat the lamps as little sparks of his own spirit, so precious that he could be said to be carrying his life in his hands.

So it was a long slow walk to the far end of the pale-walled cave, through the various big chambers and the narrow passageways connecting them. Down here it was the cave's own air, always the same, cool but bracing, in wintertime warmer than the air outside. No sound from the cave mouth reached this far. The body of the earth lay over him completely. It was almost entirely silent, but that allowed him to hear little creaks and gurgles, always coming from the shadows outside the space jiggling in the light, and often seeming to rise from below. There was a musty smell, a cave bear smell, mixed with mud. A faint charcoal whiff. Big groups when they came back this far brought brush pine torches, and the pine's sappy blaze made the walls dance and leap. But that was light for seeing, not for painting.

Now the two lamp lights were pale and steady. They quivered in time with his steps. He was by himself, no one else here. Thorn's spirit did not seem to be present, nor Click's. If anything he felt the presence of Pika, whom he had never met. The madman who had started painting in this cave, the notorious bison man.

But even Pika was now absent. Loon could feel it: he was alone in there. Just him. He could recall quite a few times in his life when simply being alone like this in the dark would have been enough to terrify him. Often when alone, at night, he had sensed something out there, something unseen, maybe even invisible, that was at that moment tracking him with senses he did not have, following him by way of signs he could not hide, like his smell. More than once that apprehension had overwhelmed him with terror and caused him to run panicked like a rabbit through the moonlight for camp. Stricken with terror, bolting with terror, and all from being alone in the dark, when a feeling came over him!

Now all that was completely gone. He was empty. Being alone meant nothing to him. This was his place. He had been here before, he remembered it perfectly. It was just as before. Slowly he shuffled past the place where the roof of the cave had fallen down and now stood on the floor, a big mass of white and orange rock, which sparkled in the lamplight as he moved. Onward, past the big cats on the wall to the left. Then a left turn and on to the stone reeds that covered the floor here, so strange and beautiful. The stone reeds on the floor stood below stone reeds hanging from the roof, dripping; a few dripped even now. They were like the sand drip towers kids made on the riverbank. How many drips, with water so clear? How many years? Since the old time, the time when all the animals were people, and they walked in a dream together. Since the world was born out of its first egg.

He followed the path always taken through the reeds, doing his best to step in the same footprints. That was how it was done in here. And it was true that the floor of the cave was often coated with a slight mud that squished between the toes, and in places gave way to about the depth of one's foot. Stepping in old steps helped with that, although at the end of almost every spring the cave floor flooded, leaving a layer of new mud in their steps. Walking in the cave had its own sound because of this, a little squick, squick, squick that often echoed.

Go slowly. Move to the cave's speed. It burbled, it pulsed, it breathed, but all very slowly, so slowly one could only dance in time with it, as with a slow bass thump, hitting five or nine to its one. Breathe deep the black shadows. The darkness behind him was darker than the darkness before him. Someone had fingered an owl on the far face of the fallen roof pile; it watched you with its big eyes as you passed it. Follow the trail around the corner.

There hung the pendant of rock from the roof, the stone bull's pizzle, with its painting of the bison man about to mount the human woman, her legs and kolby drawn there under him, the biggest blackest kolby ever, like a little triangular door to another cave. Pika's work. The whole story of the bison man and his woman, right there on a pizzle like the one that had done the deed.

This room was where Loon intended to paint. To the left of the pizzle there was a section of curving wall that extended far higher than he could reach. Inspected from arm's length, it proved to be a somewhat uneven surface, bossed and spalled with bulges and cavities, and some small cracks; but on the whole it was a clean curve of stone, with lots of flat smooth surface.

He put down the lamps, took off his sack, unpacked it, picked out the caribou shinbone from the other things. He made one scrape with the shinbone at just above head height, revealing a lighter rock under the brown skin: the bare flesh of Mother Earth, very bright compared to the shadows in the corners around him.

This was the wall Thorn had said he was going to paint. For the first time Loon felt a little touch of Thorn behind his ear, and he heard the remembered sound of Thorn's voice, saying just his ordinary things. Come here, boy. The particular timbre of Thorn's voice suddenly pierced him, so buzzy and nasal compared to the clear tones he made when he played his flute. There was no other voice like it. Although it was true that no two voices were the same, so that meant nothing. But he would never hear that voice again. He would have to hold on to it.

Loon said to the cave, —Hello, Thorn. Before I start, I want to go look at your painting of the lions on the hunt. Come with me if you like.

He picked up one lamp and stepped down the twisted passage to the end chamber. Now that Thorn was dead, he would have to follow Loon around if he wanted to talk to him. So Loon was free to go where he wanted. Loon could feel that as he walked, could feel how it would irritate Thorn.

Now he stood in the farthest end of the cave, in front of the great lion chase he had watched Thorn paint so long ago. He saw again: it was by far the greatest painting in the cave, maybe the world. Maybe it would always be the greatest painting. The hungry look in the lions' eyes, the sharp wariness of the bison peering over their shoulders at the great cats; the way the animals moved when you moved the lamp next to the wall; the massed groups, hunters and hunted, both flowing across the wall from right to left, moving even as they were still, moving as you breathed, the lions diving in, the bison bursting out. All these aspects together made this wall more alive than any painting Loon had ever seen or imagined.

He sat there and looked at it, and remembered what he could of Thorn on the night he had painted it. The old man had been very calm and relaxed, almost friendly. No, friendly. He had smoked his pipe and played his flute. He had stopped to eat or take sips of water. He had put his head to the hole in the corner of the floor that breathed and sometimes gurgled, listening for what the cave could tell him. It had taken a long time to paint that wall, but he had never hurried.

The lions moved in place, and yet stayed where they were. The cave breathed in time with Loon's breaths. Deep below him it sounded like someone was talking. He saw that he wanted to do it like Thorn had done it. He would do what Thorn had done, every mood and move, make it happen again. That was what he would do; and that was what he would teach some boy to do. If you did it right, on it would go.

Loon put the lamp down, sat on his fur patch, took out Thorn's pipe. Used the lamp flame to light a splinter, squinted and lit the leaf in the pipe's bowl, breathed in some smoke, held it in his lungs. Exhaled.

The cave exhaled with him. He drank from his water bag. When he was finished looking at Thorn's lions, he got up, taking some care to be sure of his balance. A little dance in place. He picked up the lamp, walked back to the other lamp, in the big chamber with his empty wall. He set the second lamp down, had a look around. The bison man still humped the human woman, and he approached it to have a look at how it had been drawn. The black triangle of the woman's baginaren had been very carefully cleft at the bottom by a scratched white line. The door to the next world, clear as a cut on a finger. He had a burin in his pack to use as just such a line scraper. He had charcoal stumps, a bag of charcoal powder, a bowl for mixing, chamois leather patches, some brushes. Two bags of water. The wall scraper shinbone. He had to finish the scraping.

He moved the lamps around until the light on the wall was the way he wanted it. The two together set up crossed shadows, and he wished that he had a third lamp, or even more. Ah yes, he did; in the sack. He found the lamp stone with its indentation, set it up, filled the dip with lamp fat, placed one of the wicks in it, used another splinter to move flame to it. He sat by the lamp a while to make sure it was burning well. It flickered, then burned steadily, the flame still except right there at the wick it enfolded, where it crinkled off the black into existence.

The cave was murmuring a low song. There was a river running under the cave. Its sound seemed to indicate that its water moved slower than water on the surface of the earth.

He took up the shinbone in his right hand and finished scraping the wall clean of its brown nobbling. He saw that a cave bear had reached up and clawed the wall, as if trying to get through to something. The claw scratches were white, and under Loon's scraping the wall was almost tusk white. Like old yellowed tusk, or the belly of an ibex. Above the scraped section was an arch of stone, and the wall above that was reddish brown.

On the far left of his wall, around a slight curve that way, there was a low hole in the wall. The floor was wetter under the hole.

He took up a charcoal stump, and on the left side of the cleared section drew the backs of a rising line of bulls. That gave him his left border.

He stepped to the lower part of his cleared area and drew the two rhinos he had seen fighting by the creek. He wanted to show the way they had slapped their horns together, in those big horny thwacks that rang across the meadow. It must hurt when horn caught flesh. Both of the rhinos had been bleeding. He drew the lines of their horns right through each other: it was the only way to show it. Round curve of their low rumps, so massive and strong. They were so much faster than they looked. He could suggest that speed if the curves were right. And all the force of the fight was there in their faces and horns. He took his time, smudged with a leather cloth inside the lines of head and horn, to make them blacker. The one on the right had its right foreleg set, and was thrusting up and through the one on the left, catching it in the side of the head. Curve of the muscle swinging from the force of the blow. Scrape with a burin inside the right one's mouth, open as it grunted. The one on the left had been rocked back by the blow, rounded up by it. Draw the fore-feet rounded, show them almost hanging in air. Curves in the rock were shaped nicely to show the weight of the beast thrown back. Dot the eye just over the horn, looking shocked. Give him two front horns; this was a Thorn trick, to show movement. Knocked back by the blow, back into the cave wall itself.

When the rhinos were done he sat down for a while. He had a longer charcoal branch than usual, and as he sat there, he reached out and drew a little bison with it, a three-liner at first, but then he kept pointing the stick into the mass of winter hair between its horns. Just something to do while he rested and looked at the wall above. It was a great wall. It was breathing in and out with his breath, coming closer and then moving away.

The stumping was making things look good and black, so he added another bull to the stack of them on the left side of his wall, blacked it in completely. A little scraping with the burin could remove just enough of the blackened face to suggest an eye. Black eye of a black bull, and yet visible. Under the muzzle of this black beast he drew a horse with a big head, small body. That looked good, black stumped down its chest, legs just lined.

That left the biggest scraped space, to the right of the bulls and above the fighting rhinos. It was a good space, and he sat down next to his sack to look at it for a while.

He refilled his lamps with fat. He drank some water. He inspected his hands; his palms and fingers were black with charcoal. He held the right hand up before him, turned it palm side then backside. Bent little finger. It pulsed blackly, seemed to go away and come back. This living hand. He held it up against the wall, as if to blow an outline. From this distance it covered the space he had left to draw on.

He closed his eyes, watched colors flow and spark there on the inside of his eyelids. He saw that horse at sunset, rearing on the ridge across the valley. He recalled the way it had felt, there at the end of his wander when he was scraped raw, when the horse had seen him and then reared, and suddenly in the sunset light it had become clear that everything meant something he could not catch, something so big that it couldn't be said, couldn't be felt. Something big that they were all caught up in together. It had taken his breath away then, and it did again as he remembered it.

Make that horse. Stump it until it was the black inside black. Show the rearing up, that moment when the sight of it had transfixed Loon, standing there the next ridge over.

He stood and started painting again. Start from the top and work down. Make a sequence of heads that would show that rearing in the sunset, like what Thorn had done with the lions, but different. He used his hand to measure; there was room for four heads.

He started to draw the top head. First the forehead, as in a three-liner. Down the long nose to the nostril and the little curve of the mouth. Then pause. The second head would need to fill the space below. He took the stick and pressed hard against the wall, stumping the charcoal off as thickly as he could, carefully up down, up down.

The curve of the rearing mane, pressing lighter as he drew the back behind the mane. Good. Then the eye, looking across the valley at Loon. Not a friendly look. He stumped and smudged black all over the inside of the line, darking the forehead, the cheek.

He took up the burin then and scraped a little around the eye to make a white surround for it. He saw that he could scrape around the head too, whitening the wall to make the head stand out even more than it already did.

Slowly, carefully, he scraped tiny bits of rock away from the wall. It had to be a perfect line, making a perfect contrast of white and black. The head would seem to emerge from the wall, because indeed it did.

He went on scraping for so long that one of the lamps went out. He staggered back in the newly shaped shadows, and in his haste almost knocked one of the two remaining lit lamps over; lunging to right it, he also almost stepped on the third lamp. He could have knocked them all out right then and there.

He sat down for a while, frightened by his own clumsiness. The cave was rumbling a warning. He wished Thorn were there to talk to, and suddenly he realized that would never happen again. No more Thorn. It was impossible to believe. Not to have that face, that voice, those irritated and irritating thoughts. No one to talk to, as Heather had said. Dropped into the lonely world of the shaman, deep into dreams and visions, always alone, even when in the pack. He had wanted his wander to go on forever, and now it would.

I picked him up then. I carried him to the wall, I raised his hand, I drew the mane of the next horse.

Then, looking at it more closely, I realized that I had started the second horse too high, too close to the first one. Four heads as close as these two would be too close, leaving a gap at the bottom that would look bad. I had made a mistake. I didn't know how to fix it. In the depths of the cave, trying to help Loon past his bad moment, I had made a mistake. Startled, dismayed, not knowing what to do, I sank back into him and left him to it.

*   *   *

Loon stepped back and stared. He had drawn the mane of the second horse without thinking, and now he was appalled to see that it was too high. Thinking about Thorn had distracted him, and he had painted without looking. A huge mistake!

And no way to fix it. If he continued with this new head in this position, the four heads would be too close together: but the space wasn't big enough for five heads.

Startled still, sick with frustration, he stepped back again, careful this time not to go near the lamps. He sat down next to his sack and looked at the wall and thought it over. He recalled Thorn's bison in the farther chamber; one of them had seven legs to show it was running. He saw again against his eyelids the black horse on the ridge, rearing and throwing his head toward the sun. The way the light had caught on his stiff short black mane. The way black horses seemed to jump out of a landscape into the eye.

He stood again and went and touched the wall under the mane. He could leave that mane detached and on its own, and place the second head a bit farther down. It might look like there was an extra horse in between the two, as often happened when one looked across a herd. Or it might suggest the horse's rearing, like the seven legs of Thorn's bison. The world seen by lightning flash, as Loon often saw it, storm or not. Moments of being one after the next, snapping in the eye once and then forever.

The wall was cold under his fingertips. His feet were cold, and he flexed up and down on his toes and heels, trying to warm them. The wall pulsed out toward him, then sucked back away from him, trying to pull him off balance, cause him to fall into it and be captured. There were smaller horses in the valleys to the west, their women had no manes. He saw he could make a little joke; the four heads of the rearing horse would also be from four different horses. And the detached mane could also be smudged in a way that made it look like the top horse's cheek, while remaining the mane of the horse under it. Then a maneless horse, with little ears on top: a colt, or almost.

So in a single toss of the head the horse would age through its whole life, or rather become all the black horses Loon had ever seen. Well, the story it told was not his problem. He just needed to draw them, and after that they would tell their own story. He wouldn't be sure what he would get until he drew it.

The curves of the wall under his fingers showed him that the second head was looking less into the wall than the top one had been. Part of the toss of the head. Rearing away, defiant. The back line of the blackest bull, to the left of the horses, was a faint line between the two horses' faces, making a triangle. He took up the burin and scraped that triangle a little whiter, working as carefully as he could in the corners where the lines met. The rock-on-rock scrape rasped into the black shadows of the cave. A big black nostril. The sound of the stick against the wall was so much woodier than the burin.

Loon stood back to see how the second head looked. It seemed to be sniffing the drawing of a little old rhino, standing on end. His third horse would be sniffing this same rhino's rear. That would not make the horse happy, it would keep its mouth and nostrils shut to avoid the smell of that rhino's rear. Horses and rhinos definitely did not like each other. Really no animal was happy to be around a rhino. Only mammoths would even come near one. Mammoths did not care who they approached, although they did take care around rhinos. It was a standoff between them when they both wanted the same water. Once Loon had seen a rhino and mammoth stand watching each other across a creek for an entire fist of the day without moving, each not quite looking at the other, both seeing who would wait the longest. Loon had left before they decided it.

He made the third head a woman horse, with a very short mane, neat and demure. Coloration a lighter black, achieved by a close mottle of wall and charcoal, requiring a very light touch with the end of the branch, and some finger smudging, very light. The wall here was slightly chipped, which made it perfect for this effect; black on the high points, dimples white. Each horse was going to be a slightly different black.

The fourth head, at the bottom, he decided would be the blackest black of all, something to really draw the eye, to start the viewer at the beginning of the tossing of the head. One would look first at this bossy mass of black, then the eye would move up with the motion of the rearing. The heads would move and lie still both at once. The Thorn touch, yes, of course; Thorn would have liked this painting. So, one of the smaller kinds of horse to start things. A young stallion, black as the cave when the lamps went out, and whinnying. This noisy black creature would be the start of it all: a horse startled, his eye round, scraped white around it, a white tear streak under the eye, also scraped. Mouth open as it whinnied in protest at being seen, then reared and wheeled away, as it had done on the ridge, in that moment when some part of Loon had been born, his wander's great moment, when he had realized the world was stuffed with a meaning he couldn't express. Right here he would express what could not be expressed, for all to see.

He filled in the black. He scraped with the charcoal stick, fingered the soot into the rock. His fingers were pure black now too, and as he rubbed the charcoal in, there were times when he felt and saw his fingers go right into the rock, right into the horse's body. Bristles of the mane as stiff as lion whiskers, bunched and upright. Black the whole head, all except a little stretch where neck met chest, just to round the figure, give it the curve that the wall itself gave the horse, a little curve of a bump so that the horse's left leg stood out from the wall. This would be a great touch when he brought the pack in to see it, and moved the lamp to make shadows on the wall dance. He couldn't both move the lamp next to the wall and see its effect from the center of the cave, but he could tell it would be good, a real movement. And above it the horse would toss its head.

Now his hands plunged deep into the stone of the wall. He had to move them around slowly, as if in thick mud, to keep from breaking off his fingers. The wall was cold, his fingers were cold.

When he was done with that blacking, the blackest blacking he had ever done, it took him a while to pull his hands out of the wall. When he did, he stepped back to his sack to look at the wall.

It was good. The free-standing mane between the top two heads was still strange, but there was nothing he could do about it. It worked as the cheek of the top horse, or the top of a horse seen between the upper two, or the mane of the second horse, rising before its head did, leading the head. All of those, sure. Part of the movement. And the black of it was good. Loon loved the black of the lowest horse, whose whinny seemed to echo in the dark reaches of the cave, the black spaces that the lamps did not light.

He went back to the wall with the burin, and began to scrape the area around the lowest head, to make its outline that much sharper. The mouth inside the whinny had to be as white as the woman's kolby, there under the bison man looking across the chamber at him. Scrape it clean. Get it just right. The stone had such a texture here, granular but smooth; he could scrape it very clean, get a smooth white surface to delineate the black mass of the horse. Ah, watch out, a scrape too far down—pick up the charcoal stick, wet the finger, cover the scrape mark. The lower line of the jaw had just the jowl of that horse on the ridge, two little indentations marking it.

There was a burbling moan from below, and then a gust of wind, and all his lamps went out at once, leaving him in pure blackness, a black as black as if the lowest horse head had spilled out and poured over him and filled the whole cave.

This was bad. The blackness was absolute. He could make colors appear in his eyes by squeezing them shut, but there was no point to that. He had no sight. The world was black.

The cave moaned again. It chuckled at his capture. How did the cave bears guide themselves in here? How could they see in this?

They didn't. They smelled their way. And the chamber that contained their hibernation nests was much closer to the cave mouth. They just bumbled blindly in and smelled their way to the place where they always slept, and slept again, and woke and sniffed their way out.

For a moment he lost his line of thought, and a panic of sheer terror washed through him in a flood that left him hot and gasping. —No, he groaned, and heard a little ringing that might have been an echo or a response.

He stepped around carefully, trying to keep his face toward the wall, to keep a sense of where he was. Facing the wall, the way out was to his left. He got down on his knees and crawled, sweeping with his hand ahead of him to feel for the extinguished lamps, for his sack—for anything that might be his, and thus help him.

But when his hand hit one of the lamps, it was no good; the wick was cold, the lamp's little depression was out of fat oil. Possibly he had gotten so caught up in the four horses' heads that all the lamps had burned their fat and gone out together. Maybe there had been no gust of wind at all, no laugh from the thing under the floor. Although it was laughing now. Anyway it didn't matter. He had to find his sack.

Finally a sweep of his hand ran into it. Knowing its location allowed him to find his second lamp, and then the third. They were all out of fat, or so close that their wicks had gone out. He brought them back to his sack, missing it for a while and briefly panicking; but there it was at last, so that the terror of the dark subsided in him.

He sat on his fur patch and dug into his sack, feeling for the bag of fat grease. He found it, and that was good. In that bag was light and sight. Then he reached in the fold of his belt, and found the burl with the ember inside it, and when he felt the burl he took it up with desperate care, untied the cedar cap with trembling hands, and poked in gently with his finger, hoping to be burned: but it wasn't even warm. Just ashes. He had stayed too long.

He sat back and whimpered with fear. There in his sack were his bags of food, and the rest of his painting things. The bag of earth-blood powder, it felt like, ready to mix with his water to make red paint. But he was almost out of water. And nowhere in his sack did he feel the firestarter flints, or the little bag of duff and dried wood chips he needed to start a new fire.

He didn't know what could have happened to them. Terror struck him again, swept through him and took him off. He needed to ice over that torrent of fear and stand on it. Needed to be ice cold, and yet he was burning with fear.

After a time the terror let him go, it flung him to the floor crying. It occurred to him that he might have taken the firestarter kit out of the pack when he lit the third lamp. Although he had lit that lamp from the ones already lit, of course, using a splinter, so there would have been no reason to take out the flints and duff. But it could have happened. That had been nearby; he wasn't sure exactly where, because in the blackness he had carried all the lamps to this spot by the sack.

He crawled in the direction he thought the third lamp had been, felt the floor of the cave. Nothing. Then he lost the sack for a while, trying to return. When he relocated the sack he cried again, and after that he took the sack with him as he crawled around. He found some rocks on the floor, and some charcoal sticks tucked against one wall in a little hole. A jaw with teeth, giant in the dark, bigger than his head: a cave bear skull, it had to be, long and toothy, with the bump and rise in the forehead that marked it as a cave bear, although its sheer size was enough to tell.

Nothing. He had lamps, wicks, and oil, but no flints or duff. No way to make fire. He banged the rocks he had found against each other, and some brief sparks flew red across the blackness, like shooting stars, but nothing like what it would take to start duff burning; and besides, there was no duff.

He was stuck in the black of the cave. There was no way out, except to try to walk or crawl in the right direction.

By now he had no idea what direction was the right direction. He needed to find his wall again to get oriented, but standing up and walking around, hands stretched before him, he came to one wall, then another wall; he reached up and felt for scratches, smelled his fingers to see if they were perhaps smearing charcoal; but everywhere felt the same in the pure blackness, and his fingers always smelled like charcoal now, no matter what he touched.

Cold, tired, hungry, thirsty. Filled with fear, and then, as more time passed, with a rending grief. Oh that it should come to this! Thorn would be so mad at him if he turned up in the spirit realm so soon, having gotten lost in their own cave! It was almost funny to think of the look that would be on the old snake's face. But it wouldn't be funny if it happened. And what about Elga? She would be angry too, but so sad.

He crawled around on hands and knees until he felt something like a footprint. There were many bear prints in the hardened old mud of the floor, as they were deep enough to last through many a spring flood. They pointed in all directions. And he could feel by putting his own feet in them that they were far too large to be a person's footprint. When he found another one, he fitted his foot into it, and knew it was a person's footprint. Encouraging. But people had walked around. It didn't mean he had a clear direction.

If he went toward the end chamber, there would be a series of drops. While on the other hand, if he had to step up, and if he was lucky enough to encounter the stepping stone placed at the bottom of that one big step, he would know he was headed in the right direction, at least for as long as he could keep any particular direction steady.

So he filled his sack with his things and put it on his back, and tried to go uphill. If he ran into a wall, he tried to determine which way the floor was tilted, and continued as upward as he could.

He crawled on and on, using his hands to feel the floor ahead of him. He felt like he was holding a straight line as he went, but he wasn't sure. Thorn had once remarked that no one without light would ever be able to find his way out of a cave this big.

*   *   *

He lost his sense of time. He got colder. The cave's air seemed colder now, and down below the floor, something was laughing at him louder than ever.

At some point, it felt like many fists later, he stopped to eat the last of his food, and without wanting to, he drank the last of his water. Some parts of the cave's walls and floor were wet; he could lick the walls for moisture, perhaps. In him a despair was growing, a realization that dying in here was quite possible. He refused to accept that, even to think about it. It was impossible to come to grips with anyway. But the laughter from under the floor of the cave sounded like the thing that had chased him into the crack in the gorge cliff, on the last night of his wander. Quartz or not, that thing had known it almost had him. It had laughed at that knowledge then. And now it knew it was right.

He lay there and cried. The blackness itself was getting to be enough to suffocate him, to strangle him right there on the cold mud floor. Thorn was going to be so angry! Elga was going to be so sad!

He fell into sleep, or something like sleep.

Later, shivering with cold, he woke and pushed up onto his hands and knees and crawled forward. As he crawled Thorn said scornfully in his ear, Every time you run into a wall, turn to the left. Then, even if you have to circle the inside of the entire cave, you will eventually find the kolby and be born out of the earth. Isn't it obvious?

Loon crawled on, feeling dully that he had a plan he could pursue till death. Onward.

Then a hoot seemed to come from somewhere:

—Loon! Loon!

He shouted as loud as he could: —I'm here! Help! HELP!

Part of the black turned gray. There grew a lightness there, and he turned to face it, to suck it into himself like a great draft of life itself. Yes, that was light, just as distinct as sunlight, even though it was merely a pale black among darker blacks. The cave walls in that direction were shadows in blackness, and the cave itself therefore loomed around him again, visible as black on black.

He shouted again. He didn't recognize anything of what he saw, couldn't tell whether the grayblack shapes were distant or close, a day's walk or something he could reach out and touch; he tried touching what he saw, but nothing was touchable.

He sat there. The light seemed to dim, and in terror he cried out again, —Help! Help!

Once before he had called out in this same desperate way, when as a child he had plunged into the river and could not feel the bottom, and somehow had thrashed back up to the surface and shouted out HELP to anyone who might hear. Such a cry of fear! And that time his father had pulled him out.

The sounds in the cave began to say, —Loon! Loon!

Then the light grew, and suddenly he could make out the cave roof above him, folded and ribbed like a gut. He was going to be reborn out of Mother Earth's kolby; this was what the birth passage looked like from inside. His tongue had felt folds in Elga like what he saw now looking up.

Then he heard that one of the voices was Elga's. A prick of light stabbed him right in the eye; he threw up his hands to block it, crying out in shock and relief and joy as he clambered slowly to his feet. He stood there swaying unsteadily, staggering as he called out, —Elga! Elga! Elga!

The blazes of light came from torches. Their flames bobbed wildly, shadows flew all around him like flocks of giant birds, ah: he saw that the spirit ravens of this cave had been gathered over him, ready to pick his bones the moment he died. Now they flew blackly away, giving him back to the light. The torch flames were so bright and yellow he could see nothing else, it was as if fire alone approached him through the black air of the cave.

Then he saw the people carrying the flames. Elga and Heather and Hawk. Elga gave Hawk her torch to hold, and ran up and embraced him.

—You're so cold! she exclaimed.

—I'm fine, he said, and felt his face grinning as he wept. Now his teeth were chattering.

They told him Moss was back up the cave a ways, holding a torch for them. And from Moss's location they knew the way to the red chamber, and then the day chamber. Elga was wrapped around him, almost holding him up. He had been gone too long, they said, so they had come in. It had been four days.

—No, Loon said.

—Yes, Elga said. —Four days. So we came in.

—I'm glad you did, Loon said. —My lamps went out. I couldn't get them relit. It's been dark a long time.

—Where are we? she asked, looking around the part of the cave they were in. It had no animals on its walls, although in one area there seemed to be cross-hatchings that did not look like a cave bear's, they were so squared off.

—I don't know, Loon said. —I don't think I've ever been in this part. I don't recognize it. A quick violent shudder of cold and fear rattled him, and she held him closer.

—This is the way out. Toward Moss.

They had trailed a rope behind them from the last spot they could see Moss's torch; it lay there on the cave floor like a snake. Now they rolled it back up as they returned, and soon saw a glow in the passage ahead. As they came through it, Loon saw that they were actually returning to his chamber, with his new painting there on the wall to their right. He had gone down a passageway deeper into the cave, but in a different direction than Thorn's lion room. There was his painting right there, and he peered at it curiously, wondering what he had done.

The others were caught by it too, and stopped briefly to look. But Elga wanted them to leave as soon as possible. —We'll come back with the whole pack, she said. —First let's get you out of here.

Loon picked up the cave bear skull he had stumbled over in the blackness. Feeling it in his hand as he looked at it, he could see the blackness in how it had felt to him in the dark. Something had tried to eat him.

He put the skull on a block of stone that stood waist high in the middle of the room. He looked around at the chamber he had spent four days in, first painting, then in darkness. He could not tell which part had been longer. It had felt like four years, or four lives. When they came back in here, he would ask his pack to gather every cave bear skull they could find, and bring them in here to mark those four lost lives. Something had to say what had happened here.

Elga nudged him along. Past the owl on the rock, past the stone reed bed. Then there was Moss's light beyond, at the far end of the big empty chamber. Moss shouted loudly, excited to learn they had found Loon alive. He ran down the room, torch blazing, and seized Loon up in a great hug, swinging him around in the air. —Good man! You made it!

—I did.

—But you're so muddy!

—I crawled a lot, Loon admitted.

They stood there for a while chattering at him. He was shivering. There was a dim light in the far passageway that they all knew to be the light of day. That was a good light to see.

Suddenly Loon felt how tired he was. Now that they were almost out, he found he could hardly walk. He couldn't feel his feet. Moss and Elga walked at his sides, held his elbows and helped him over the lumpy mud of the old bear beds. They stopped and let him gingerly stomp the ground, trying to restore some feeling to his feet. His left leg was achy. He did a little circle dance to loosen it up.

He found himself facing a wall that had a big smooth expanse, there between the two doors to the room of the bear beds. There was a red paint mark on this wall, and suddenly Loon said, —Wait, I see something. I need to do one more thing.

They all disliked hearing this, and said so, but Loon cut through them.

—I have to do one more thing!

He stared at each of them in turn, and they quieted and let him be. The world waited for them, after all, just a few score steps toward the light, around the last corner. Given that, they could not deny him.

Loon took the bag of earthblood powder from his sack, got out a bowl, asked Elga for water. He mixed up the powder and her water into a bowl of red paint, thickened by spit he had to ask the others to provide; he was too dry-mouthed to spit.

When the paint was ready, he went to the wall and put his right hand carefully in the paint, so that only his palm was wet with it. Then he pressed the wet hand against the wall, pulled it away: a red palm print, almost square.

He did that over and over. He crouched to work low at first, then stretched up as far as he could. He placed his handprints so that they made the rough shape of a bison. A new kind of stump drawing, one might say. The more he pressed his hand against the wall, the angrier he got. He didn't know why, or at what. Somehow it had to do with Thorn, or with Thorn dying. We had a bad shaman, we had a good shaman; we had a shaman. And by this stump drawing of a bison, made with his own living hand in earth's own blood, he would stick Thorn's spirit to the wall. Let it reside forever in this cave that had almost killed Loon, while Loon would escape out into the world. Something to show what the bison man had been like, his greatness, his power. He pressed his hand into the paint and onto the wall: he wanted to show the sheer mass of him. His hand when he pressed went in the rock right to the elbow. All the worlds in this wall. He made the red marks until the paint was entirely gone. That was Thorn.

Then he was truly tired. He drank some of Elga's water, and as they walked up and out of the cave, he put his arms over Moss's and Elga's shoulders. His left leg was going numb. Trying to keep him in the cave forever. He ignored it and stumped on up into the day.

The cloudy daylight made him throw his arm across his eyes.

—Mama mia, you really are a mess, Elga observed. —You have mud all over you.

Moss said, —You look like you caught fire and then jumped into a mud pit to put the fire out.

—Yes, Loon said.

After a while his eyes adjusted, and he could stand to look at the world. Down below them spread Loop Meadow. Early summer and the Stone Bison straddling the river. All still there, calm in early morning light. It was cloudy, wind pouring over them. They carried him down to camp.

In camp they washed him off and set him in bed, and Elga took care of him for a day. His feet throbbed as they warmed up. He was thirsty, even though he had already drunk a lot. He was hungry too. And he wanted to see things.

After a day of rest, he went out for a walk.

Looking around their river valley, he saw it all very clearly. He only wanted Elga, he only wanted their days together. They would have a certain number of days, a certain number of years. But he was the shaman now too, no matter what he wanted. In that regard, he would never get out of the cave. And his wander would never end.

He went out with Hawk and Moss on the night of that full moon, sixth of the year, and they walked up to the gorge overlook, as they had so many times before. In the moonlight the air held its usual shimmery awe.

—We should go, Loon said. —Elga told me it's time. She knows just which ones will go where. Time to be our own pack, and live here at the overlook. You two will guide us, and I'll be your shaman.

His friends nodded, looking a little uneasy. This was just Loon here, after all. They knew he didn't have any magic powers. At least he hadn't in his childhood. Loon saw what they were thinking, and he said,

—I don't know how I'll be as a shaman. I'll find out when I try it. You both know me. You've known me since before we even had names. I can't travel in my dreams, or above the sky. There aren't any spirits that talk to me or through me. I can't sing the songs. I can't help people who are sick. But I'll tell you this,

and he raised his right forefinger before them and seized them with his eyes:

—I can paint that fucking cave.

Moss and Hawk nodded. —We know, Hawk said. —We saw.

No one else could paint the way he did, Moss told him. The cave was certainly his to take care of. It had been passed along to him from Thorn and Pika, along with the other shaman things. As for the packs, Wolf pack new and old, they could all visit in there together during the ten ten festival, sing the songs and look at the animals in the torchlight, the way they always had. Those were big nights, remembered for years. Those nights would help keep the two packs one, and the nearby packs friendly as before. The Lion pack would surely support them. Loon could definitely lead them through all that. And Thorn's flute would play the old tunes through Loon. Hawk and Moss could see that in him already; they had heard it; they were sure of it. Maybe there was other shaman's magic that could be learned later, that the old shamans passed on one to the next. He would find out at the corroborees. Heather could help him too. A way of seeing, a way of being. Cast yourself out into the spaces you breathe, watch what happens.

—All right? said Moss, looking at Hawk.

—All right, Hawk said.

So late the next day Loon went looking for Schist. He found him down by the river. It was the sixth day of the sixth month. The half moon hung overhead in a twilight sky, which on this evening was a rich mineral blue, arcing east to the coming night, roofing the world with its gorgeous span.

—I'm the shaman now, he said to Schist. —Thorn taught me how, and I spoke with him in a dream when I was in the cave. He told me I'm ready. We'll go into the cave soon, and you'll all see what we've done there.

Schist nodded, watching him closely. —All right. That's good. We need a shaman.

Loon said, —But look, some of us are going to move upstream to the abri at the Northerly overlook. The pack is getting too large to make it in one camp. You and Hawk keep fighting, and we all see it, and it could get ugly. It's already a little ugly. But if one of you beats the other up, it will be even worse. And it's like that among the women too. They are split worse than anyone. So I'm going to move Hawk and Ducky and Moss and Heather and Nevermind and Rose and all their kids down to the new abri. We'll be close enough to stay together and work together. We'll all be the Wolf pack still. I'll still be your shaman too, and I'll take care of the cave. Heather will still be your herb woman. We'll keep doing our ceremonies together, like we do now with the Lion and Raven packs. It will mean you can get what you need to live here. You'll have your kids you're bringing up, the pack to handle. You can't do that with Hawk on you all the time. You'll be better off without that. This is how we'll do it. The Northerly overlook is a good campsite, we should have put a claim on it a long time ago, made it a Wolf place. Now we'll do that, and on we'll go.

All the time he was saying this Schist was glaring at him, jaw muscles bunching and unbunching like a hyena chewing on bones. Loon never flinched, but spoke as peaceably as he could. He felt peaceful. After what had happened in the cave, this kind of thing was really nothing. He could see it all as plain as Schist's bulging face:

things that happened in the light of day, on the surface of Mother Earth, these were very clear and simple things. In this moment he felt like he might stay calm forever.

When he finished, Schist did not at first reply. He stared at Loon's face as if trying to recognize him, as if he had lost his Loon and was trying to find him in this new person. As he failed at that, he realized he had a different Loon to deal with. Becoming a shaman changed you, of course. Shamans got strange, went crazy. Loon could see all this in Schist's face. He almost grinned, almost made a shaman's story face, even a woodsman's crazy face. A wooden mask with a look to chill.

But he didn't want to distract Schist, who was now thinking over what this new Loon had said to him. He was a quick thinker, this was why he was the Wolf pack's headman. He had made a lot of decisions and judgments over the years, and they had not been hungry for most of the winters he had led them, and people had gotten along. It was an achievement. Thorn had respected him.

Now at last he looked away and said, —I'll have to talk to Thunder about it.

He glared quickly at Loon, as if Loon might scoff at this, or point out that this was precisely Schist's problem.

But Loon knew better. He merely said, —I've already talked it over with Elga, and she's the one who told me to do this. The women run every pack. We aren't any different in that.

Schist nodded, his glance surprised and grateful.

Seeing that, Loon added, —Elga said you should get Starry in charge of things as soon as you can.

—Starry is nine years old, Schist said.

—Elga said that doesn't matter. She said some people are just born ready.

Schist nodded slowly. —All right. You all moving up there could be good. It will make it possible for us to take in the people from Mammoth pack who were asking about joining us. That would be good. But if we do that, we won't be able to help you if you get in trouble. I mean, we won't be able to take you back in.

—That's all right, Loon said.

At the summer solstice ceremony he stood to sing the solstice song, feeling still very calm. Both parts of the pack had regathered for the occasion. Everyone could see and feel the change in him. Even Sage, who had stayed with Schist's group, now looked kindly on him. He stood before them in Thorn's bison headpiece, and the loon cloak Elga had sewn for him, and raised Thorn's last yearstick to the midday sun, and sang.

That night, after the eating and drinking, but before the dance, he led them all in a torch procession up to the cave. On the ramp they passed all the paintings and engravings on the cliff, all the lines and dots Pika had painted there, sparking a welcome to the world inside the cave. They went in together, in a line, and left a series of lamps on the floor to light their way. Loon told them the story of his visit. He showed them Thorn's great lion hunt, and it almost shook him to see it again; he felt Thorn so strongly he almost wept, but then the shaman's calm came back over him in a blink, and he took them all to see his new wall of bison and horses. They sat on the chamber floor where he had groped and crawled in the blackness, and he moved the torches around so that they could see the animals move and flow in the flickering light. He told them to watch the horse rear its head, and moved the torch to help them see it, and some of them gasped. He took out Thorn's flute and led them through the end of the solstice song:

Thanks be to summer come again
Please give us this winter enough to eat
We rejoice in the glory of this day

He instructed them to take lamps and go off and look around the nearby chambers of the cave, and bring back any cave bear skulls they might encounter. They enjoyed this hunt, which lasted half a fist or so, and when they reconvened in the horse chamber, they had seven skulls. They laid the skulls with ceremonial care on the ground around the block where Loon had placed the one that he had found in the blackness. Then he led them singing back out of the cave, the ones at the end of the line picking up their lamps as they went: out of the cave, down the ramp to their midnight fire, which they built up and danced around through to the dawn which came so quickly. Summer was here again. Soon they would trek north to the caribou and the eight eight, the two packs one again for a time.

I am the third wind
I come to you
When you have nothing left
When you can't go on
But you go on anyway
In that moment of extremity
The third wind appears
And so it is I come to you now
To tell you this story

In the hour before that early dawn, Loon left the dancing and went back to their new camp up at the overlook, and lay down on the bed he shared with Elga and Lucky and the finch. He felt all of a sudden as tired as when he had first emerged from the cave.

He looked down from their ledge over the river, seeing the entry to the gorge, the Stone Bison, the ridges behind. Dawn's light leaked into the world. He sat there on his bed and watched the day begin. The sky shifted from gray to blue, like a jay's back when the jay hops around.

Then he was standing on the back of the Stone Bison, the river flowing under him, and Thorn standing there beside him. The iced-over river was soon to break up, and it rumbled and cracked from time to time.

—I thought you would stay in the cave, Loon said.

Thorn shook his black snake's head. —You can't get away from me that easily.

Loon sighed. It was obviously true. —I'm sorry about what happened to Click.

—Don't you worry about Click, Thorn said. —Click is my spirit to bear. I'll find him and keep him away from you. You don't have to worry about him. It's me you have to worry about.

—I can see that.

Thorn nodded. —Me, you're not going to be able to get away from. I live inside you now.

—You should feel free to go, Loon suggested. —You did what you had to do. Now you can go be the base of the Firestarter, the star in the middle, where the stick meets the base.

—I don't think so. I'm going to stay here and haunt you.

Loon sighed again. All those red handprints sticking him to the wall of the cave, but Thorn didn't care. Loon said, —I wish you wouldn't, but I can't stop you. You'll do what you want. Whatever you do, I'll do what I want too. You're going to have to follow me around. You'll be like Heather's cat. You'll be just another camp robber hanging around.

Thorn nodded. —That's fine, so long as you remember. Remember the old ways, and all the old stories. Remember the animals, your brothers and sisters. Remember to take your place and play your part. Remember me and what I taught you. Remember!

Then he stepped to the side of the Stone Bison and dove off and flew away, down the gorge, holding his arms out like an eagle. The sight of his flight was so startling it woke Loon up.

He looked around at the morning. People were lying on their beds, asleep after the big night of dancing. Elga was down at the riverbank, talking to some of the other women. Lucky was at Loon's feet, sitting on the head of their bearskin, talking to himself. The finch was beside him, wriggling in her basket and babbling. Heather was just above the camp on her new shelf, digging around in her bags and buckets.

All right, Loon said in himself to Thorn. If that's the way you're going to be, I can take it.

Something the baby girl did met with Lucky's disapproval, and Lucky shook her basket. —No! No!

—Hey, Loon said. —Leave your sister alone.

—She was eating her gloves!

—That's all right. Let her. Here, tell me the season song again.

Lucky stood up and sang:

In autumn we eat till the birds go away
And dance in the light of the moon
In winter we sleep and wait for spring
And look for the turn of the stars
In spring we starve till the birds come back
And pray for the heat of the sun
In summer we dance at the festivals
And lay our bones in the ground

—No no! Loon said. —And lie in twos on the ground! Remember!
And he reached out and flicked the boy on the ear.

Acknowledgments

My thanks for help on this novel to:

Djina Ariel, Mario Biagioli, Terry Bisson, Simon Bisson, Jim Bunting and Briganne Carter, Darryl DeVinney, Glenn Farris, Karen Fowler, Cecelia Holland, Tim Holman, Joe Holtz, Kimon Keramidas, James Leach, Lisa Nowell, Paul Park, Shauna Roberts, Carter Scholz, Gary Snyder, Mary and Andy Stewart, Pascal Thomas, and Jan Zwicky.

extras

orbit

meet the author

KIM STANLEY ROBINSON is a *New York Times* bestseller and winner of the Hugo, Nebula, and *Locus* awards. He is the author of more than twenty books, including the best-selling Mars trilogy and the critically acclaimed *Forty Signs of Rain, Fifty Degrees Below, Sixty Days and Counting, The Years of Rice and Salt, Antarctica, Galileo,* and *2312.* In 2008, he was named a Hero of the Environment by *Time* magazine, and he works with the Sierra Nevada Research Institute. He lives in Davis, California.

If you enjoyed
SHAMAN,
look out for

2312

by Kim Stanley Robinson

The year is 2312. Scientific and technological advances have opened gateways to an extraordinary future. Earth is no longer humanity's only home; new habitats have been created throughout the solar system on moons, planets, and in between. But in this year, 2312, a sequence of events will force humanity to confront its past, its present, and its future.

The first event takes place on Mercury, on the city of Terminator, itself a miracle of engineering on an unprecedented scale. It is an unexpected death, but one that might have been foreseen. For Swan Er Hong, it is an event that will change her life. Swan was once a woman who designed worlds. Now she will be led into a plot to destroy them.

Prologue

The sun is always just about to rise. Mercury rotates so slowly that you can walk fast enough over its rocky surface to stay ahead of the dawn; and so many people do. Many have made this a way of life. They walk roughly westward, staying always ahead of the stupendous day. Some of them hurry from location to location, pausing to look in cracks they earlier inoculated with bioleaching metallophytes, quickly scraping free any accumulated residues of gold or tungsten or uranium. But most of them are out there to catch glimpses of the sun.

Mercury's ancient face is so battered and irregular that the planet's terminator, the zone of the breaking dawn, is a broad chiaroscuro of black and white—charcoal hollows pricked here and there by brilliant white high points, which grow and grow until all the land is as bright as molten glass, and the long day begun. This mixed zone of sun and shadow is often as much as thirty kilometers wide, even though on a level plain the horizon is only a few kilometers off. But so little of Mercury is level. All the old bangs are still there, and some long cliffs from when the planet first cooled and shrank. In a landscape so rumpled the light can suddenly jump the eastern horizon and leap west to strike some distant prominence. Everyone walking the land has to attend to this possibility, know when and where the longest sunreaches occur—and where they can run for shade if they happen to be caught out.

Or if they stay on purpose. Because many of them pause in their walkabouts on certain cliffs and crater rims, at places marked by stupas, cairns, petroglyphs, inuksuit, mirrors, walls, goldsworthies. The sunwalkers stand by these, facing east, waiting.

The horizon they watch is black space over black rock. The superthin neon- argon atmosphere, created by sunlight smashing rock, holds only the faintest predawn glow. But the sunwalkers know the time, so they wait and watch—until—

a flick of orange fire dolphins over the horizon

and their blood leaps inside them. More brief banners follow, flicking up, arcing in loops, breaking off and floating free in the sky. Star oh star, about to break on them! Already their faceplates have darkened and polarized to protect their eyes.

The orange banners diverge left and right from the point of first appearance, as if a fire set just over the horizon is spreading north and south. Then a paring of the photosphere, the actual surface of the sun, blinks and stays, spills slowly to the sides. Depending on the filters deployed in one's faceplate, the star's actual surface can appear as anything from a blue maelstrom to an orange pulsing mass to a simple white circle. The spill to left and right keeps spreading, farther than seems possible, until it is very obvious one stands on a pebble next to a star.

Time to turn and run! But by the time some of the sunwalkers manage to jerk themselves free, they are stunned—trip and fall—get up and dash west, in a panic like no other.

Before that—one last look at sunrise on Mercury. In the ultraviolet it's a perpetual blue snarl of hot and hotter. With the disk of the photosphere blacked out, the fantastic dance of the corona becomes clearer, all the magnetized arcs and short circuits, the masses of burning hydrogen pitched out at the night. Alternatively you can block the corona, and look only at the sun's photosphere, and even magnify your view of it, until the burning tops of the convection cells are revealed in their squiggling thousands, each a thunderhead of fire burning furiously, all together torching five million tons of hydrogen a second—at which rate the star will burn another four billion years. All these long spicules of flame dance in circular patterns around the little black circles that are the sunspots—shifting whirlpools in the storms of burning. Masses of spicules flow together like kelp beds threshed by a tide. There are nonbiological explanations for all this convoluted motion—different gases moving at different speeds, magnetic fields fluxing constantly, shaping the endless whirlpools of fire—all mere physics, nothing more—but in fact it looks *alive*, more alive than many a living thing. Looking at it in the apocalypse of the Mercurial dawn, it's impossible to believe it's *not* alive. It roars in your ears, it *speaks* to you.

Most of the sunwalkers over time try all the various viewing filters, and then make choices to suit themselves. Particular filters or sequences of filters become forms of worship, rituals either personal or shared. It's very easy to get lost in these rituals; as the sunwalkers stand on their points and watch, it's not uncommon for devotees to become entranced by something in the sight, some pattern never seen before, something in the pulse and flow that snags the mind; suddenly the sizzle of the fiery cilia becomes audible, a turbulent roaring—that's your own blood, rushing through your ears, but in those moments it sounds just like the sun burning. And so people stay too long. Some have their retinas burned; some are blinded; others are killed outright, betrayed by an overwhelmed spacesuit. Some are cooked in groups of a dozen or more.

Do you imagine they must have been fools? Do you think you would never make such a mistake? Don't you be so sure. Really you have no idea. It's like nothing you've ever seen. You may think you are inured, that nothing outside the mind can really interest you anymore, as sophisticated and knowledgeable as you are. But you would be wrong. You are a creature of the sun. The beauty and terror of it seen from so close can empty any mind, thrust anyone into a trance. It's like seeing the face of God, some people say, and it is true that the sun powers all living creatures in the solar system, and in that sense *is* our god. The sight of it can strike thought clean out of your head. People seek it out precisely for that.

So there is reason to worry about Swan Er Hong, a person more inclined than most to try things just to see. She often goes sunwalking, and when she does she skirts the edge of safety, and sometimes stays too long in the light. The immense Jacob's ladders, the granulated pulsing, the spicules flowing...she has fallen in love with the sun. She worships it; she keeps a shrine to Sol Invictus in her room, performs the *pratahsamdhya* ceremony, the salute to the sun, every morning when she wakes in town. Much of her landscape and performance art is devoted to it, and these days she spends most of her time making goldsworthies and abramovics on the land and her body. So the sun is part of her art.

Now it is her solace too, for she is out there grieving. Now, if one were standing on the promenade topping the city Terminator's great Dawn Wall, one would spot her there to the south, out near the horizon. She needs to hurry. The city is gliding on its tracks across the bottom of a giant dimple between Hesiod and Kurasawa, and a flood of sunlight will soon pour far to the west. Swan needs to get into town before that happens, yet she still stands there. From the top of the Dawn Wall she looks like a silver toy. Her spacesuit has a big round clear helmet. Her boots look big, and are black with dust. A little booted silver ant, standing there grieving when she should be hustling back to the boarding platform west of town. The other sunwalkers out there are already hustling back to town. Some pull little carts or wheeled travois, hauling their supplies or even their sleeping companions. They've timed their returns closely, as the city is very predictable. It cannot deviate from its schedule; the heat of coming day expands the tracks, and the city's undercarriage is tightly sleeved over them; so sunlight drives the city west.

The returning sunwalkers crowd onto the loading platform as the city nears it. Some have been out for weeks, or even the months it would take to make a full circumambulation. When the city slides by, its lock doors will open and they will step right in.

That is soon to occur, and Swan should be there too. Yet still she stands on her promontory. More than once she has required retinal repair, and often she has been forced to run like a rabbit or die. Now it will have to happen again. She is directly south of the city, and fully lit by horizontal rays, like a silver flaw in one's vision. One can't help shouting at such rashness, useless though it is. Swan, you fool! Alex is dead—nothing to be done about it! Run for your life!

And then she does. Life over death—the urge to live—she turns and flies. Mercury's gravity, almost exactly the same as Mars's, is often called the perfect g for speed, because people who are used to it can careen across the land in giant leaps, flailing their arms for balance as they bound along. In just that way Swan leaps and flails—once catches a boot and falls flat on her face—jumps up and leaps forward again. She needs to get to the platform while the city is still next to it; the next platform is ten kilometers farther west.

She reaches the platform stairs, grabs the rail and vaults up, leaps from the far edge of the platform, forward into the lock as it is halfway closed.